The Last Secret of the Ark

James Becker is an author of conspiracy, espionage and action thrillers. He spent over twenty years in the Royal Navy's Fleet Air Arm. Involved in covert operations in many of the world's hotspots, he brings a high level of detail and authenticity to his work. He also writes action-adventure novels under the name James Barrington and military history under the name Peter Smith in the UK.

Also by James Becker

The Titanic Secret
The Ripper Secret
The Dante Conspiracy
The Templar Heresy
Cold Kill
Trade Off

The Hounds of God

The Lost Treasure of the Templars
The Templar Archive
The Templar Brotherhood

THE LAST SECRET OF THE ARK

JAMES BECKER

CANELO

First published in the the United Kingdom in 2020 by Canelo

This edition published in the United Kingdom in 2020 by Canelo

Canelo Digital Publishing Limited
31 Helen Road
Oxford OX2 0DF
United Kingdom

A CIP catalogue record for this book is available from the British Library.

Print ISBN 978 1 80032 027 7
Ebook ISBN 978 1 78863 904 0

Printed and bound in Great Britain by Clays Ltd, Elcograf S.p.A.

Prologue

Jerusalem

587 BC

Their instructions were clear and unambiguous, and from the moment the Babylonian soldiers surged through the splintered remains of the doors of the Temple, they ignored them. The red mist had descended on them and the shouted orders from the officers behind them didn't even register. The pent-up frustration engendered by the eighteen-month siege had culminated in a slaughter that had seen some streets in Jerusalem running almost ankle-deep in blood. Despite their orders, the priests would not be spared.

They had barricaded the building in a futile last-ditch effort to keep out the invaders, but once the city walls had been breached, it was only a matter of time – just a few hours – before the attackers fought their way to the top of the Temple Mount, the final stronghold and highest point of Jerusalem.

As the tall gilded doors crashed open, the baying mob of Babylonian troops, their sword blades slick and crimson with the blood of countless fallen Jews, poured inside. The priests were unarmed, and there was nowhere for them to run. Their end was swift and brutal. The first soldiers through the doors swung their swords in devastating arcs, severing limbs and opening gaping wounds. The Temple rang with the exultant yells of the Babylonians and the screams of the wounded and dying.

As well as about a dozen priests, some twenty Jewish civilians, mainly women and children, had taken refuge in the building, huddled in a group at the far end. As the head of the last remaining priest tumbled to the ground and his body collapsed, the soldiers turned their attention to the terrified survivors. The Babylonians had appetites and needs that had been heightened by the battle they had fought, and the bodies of the women – and those of the children as well – had uses, and possibly even cash values later. Those they segregated, roughly tying their wrists and ankles. There were also three male civilians, all old men. The soldiers forced them to their knees before brutally decapitating them.

Jerusalem had fallen to the Babylonians, and not for the first time.

A decade earlier, Nebuchadnezzar II had captured the city and installed Zedekiah from the House of David as the vassal king, a puppet ruler. But Zedekiah had rebelled, prompting the inevitable and brutal Babylonian response. As the siege had approached its end, he had fled the doomed city with a group of his followers, but his escape would be only a temporary reprieve. He would be captured on the plains of Jericho to the east of the city and transported to Babylon. There he would be forced to watch his sons being executed before he himself was blinded. He would be held prisoner, sightless and in chains, for the rest of his days as punishment for his perceived treachery.

The end of the siege was not the end for Jerusalem. Immediately afterwards, Nebuzaradan, the captain of Nebuchadnezzar's bodyguard, was ordered to flatten the city. His men plundered the place, razing the buildings to the ground and destroying what was left of the Temple of Solomon. Those Jewish nobles who had survived were taken in shackles to Babylon, and virtually the entire surviving population was dispersed, with only what amounted to a skeleton staff of farm workers, principally husbandmen and vine dressers, being allowed to remain to manage and maintain the land and crops.

Yet although the horde of Babylonians seized whatever they could carry as the spoils of war, the most precious object held within the walls of the Temple of Solomon eluded them. It would have been kept inside the *Kodesh Hakodashim*, the Holy of Holies, the dwelling place of the holy spirit or *shekhinah*, but when the Babylonians smashed their way inside the sacred building, the relic was not there. And there was nobody left alive who could tell them where it was.

The crucial secret knowledge of the object's location was lost to the world through the thrusts and swings of Babylonian swords as the soldiers slaughtered the priests of the Temple. Searches were fruitless, because the invaders had no idea where the object was, or even whether it had been in the city when it fell. There were hiding places without number inside and beyond Jerusalem's city walls.

The relic remained lost, though remembered and revered and prayed for by the Jewish nation.

As it still is today.

Chapter 1

Axum, Tigray, Ethiopia

Eight months ago

'I'm not entirely sure this is a good idea,' Chris Bronson said, as he and his former wife Angela Lewis walked side by side along a dusty street in Axum in the northern part of Ethiopia. It was early evening, the sun was sinking towards the western horizon in what promised to be another spectacular display of primary colours, and they were heading for their hotel and an early dinner. 'I know the locals we've met have been perfectly friendly, but that might change if they knew you were here to investigate and possibly disprove one of the most important traditions they have.'

'That's a fair point,' Angela conceded, 'so how about we don't tell them? We won't be able to get inside the building, so all we can do is examine the claim as best we can and reach a conclusion. And that will be *our* conclusion, not to be published or shared with anyone, least of all the Christians of Ethiopia.'

'You mean you won't use the device?'

She looked at him as if he were mad.

'Of course I'll use it, as long as we get the opportunity. Why else do you think I asked you to buy the bloody thing?'

'I'm still a little hazy on why you think this really might be the last resting place of the Ark of the Covenant. Or why you're so interested in finding it.'

'Actually,' Angela replied, 'I don't think that what the Ethiopians call the *Tabota Seyen* – the Ark of Zion – *is* here.

They've got something, but I don't think it's that. And I would have thought that the reason for my interest was quite obvious. The Ark is far and away the most important and significant of all the ancient relics that have vanished from the pages of history. It's the only one allegedly created on the specific instructions of God, and if the Bible is to be believed, it was a weapon of devastating power. Searching for the Ark has been one of my personal quests for a long time, and a lot of people have taken the Ethiopian claim seriously. I think they're wrong, but I needed to investigate it. And for a few years I've had a feeling that things were changing slightly, and that there was at least a chance that the relic would be revealed. Back in June 2009, the Patriarch of the Orthodox Church here said he was going to show the Ark to the world, though he changed his mind the next day. And a couple of years later, the roof of the chapel started leaking and there was speculation that the relic would have to be removed from the building and would then be visible. But that came to nothing as well. So it's a kind of Mohammed and the mountain situation. If they won't bring out the Ark and prove that they have it, then I want to somehow see the relic so that I can be sure that they haven't.'

'So why does anybody think it *is* here?'

Reaching their hotel, they walked out of the noise and dust and clamour of the street into the relative cool of the lobby and through into the restaurant. Most of the people they'd talked to in Ethiopia spoke at least some English, the language being taught in schools there alongside Amharic, the country's official language, and the waiter was no exception. Bronson ordered a couple of Cokes, and they sat down at a corner table in the almost empty dining room.

'That's a fair question,' Angela replied. 'The trick is separating the legends from the facts, and there are precious few of those. We have to go back to the time of King Solomon, the man with the wisdom—'

'And the mines and the gold,' Bronson interrupted.

'That's one of the first anomalies. Some historians don't believe Solomon was a real character, but let's assume he did exist and did rule Israel. You mentioned King Solomon's mines, so let me ask you this. Where were these mines, and what did he dig out of the ground?'

'I assume they were gold mines, and because he ruled Israel, they were probably somewhere near Jerusalem.'

'Well, at least you're consistent,' Angela said, 'even if you're consistently wrong. Solomon did have mines, but for copper, not gold, and the latest research puts them in the Timna Valley at the southern tip of Israel, roughly two hundred miles from Jerusalem. Remnants of organic material found in the remains of the smelting camps were radiocarbon-dated. The result was a surprise. It had been assumed that the copper industry in that area was part of the New Kingdom dynasties of Egypt, dating from the thirteenth century BC, but the remains were tenth century BC, the time of King Solomon.'

'If he existed,' Bronson said.

'Quite.'

The waiter crossed over to their table, put down a couple of menus and their drinks and walked away. Bronson took a swig of his Coke and looked across the table at Angela, his ex-wife and still his best friend.

'Let me ask you a question,' he said. 'I'm consistently wrong, you just said. You must have heard the conundrum about a tree falling in the forest. If there's nobody there to hear it, does it still make a noise? Well, here's a variant on that. If a man goes into a forest and makes a definitive statement and there's no woman close enough to hear what he says, is he still wrong?'

Angela grinned at him. 'Probably,' she said. 'Actually, you weren't wrong about Solomon's wealth. According to several accounts, he had massive amounts of gold, but there were no gold mines anywhere in his realm, so the assumption is that his wealth probably came from trading outside Israel. There's evidence that he controlled trade routes in the eastern Mediterranean, and that Israel supplied grain to the Phoenicians in return for gold from Orphir. That place hasn't been definitively identified, but it was probably part of the Tigray region at the northern tip of Ethiopia, more or less where we are now.

'And then we meet another player. In Solomon's time, this area was allegedly controlled by the Queen of Sheba, Queen Makeda. Again, many modern scholars claim that she was entirely fictional. Those that do accept her historical reality believe her territory was actually located east of the Red Sea, in what is now Yemen, and that Sheba was the southern Arabian territory of Saba, near Yemen's capital city, Sana'a.

'Wherever she came from, the Old Testament – the second Book of Chronicles – claims she visited Jerusalem to consult Solomon and as a gift took him five tons of gold from her mines, a generous present. She was supposed to be beautiful, and they had a relationship that produced a son, Menelik. His Arabic name was Ibn Al-Hakim, which means "son of the wise", appropriate if Solomon was his father. His birth united the two kingdoms and he inaugurated the Solomonic dynasty in Ethiopia. Tigray, by the way, is still a good source of gold. You can find it just by washing sediment taken from the banks of the river.

'Another part of the story is that Solomon built the First Temple on the Temple Mount. It was decorated with copper and gold and was designed to house the Ark of the Covenant in the Holy of Holies. That was the temple destroyed by the Babylonians in 587 BC, and at that point the Ark vanished from the historical record. There are no claims that it was seized by the Babylonians, and the Bible never mentions it again.'

They'd both been glancing at the dinner menus while Angela had been talking, and when the waiter appeared, they ordered their meals.

'There's a wrinkle in this,' Angela said as he walked away. 'According to Ethiopian legends and a holy book called the *Kebra Nagast*, which means "the glory of kings", when Menelik came of age, he visited Solomon. They apparently got on well, and Solomon asked his son to stay and become his heir and rule Israel, but Menelik refused. He wanted to become his mother's heir and returned to Ethiopia.

'According to one legend, when he got back, he discovered the Ark among his possessions. It had been accidentally taken from Jerusalem by members of his entourage. The alternative explanation in the *Kebra Nagast* is that it was a deliberate theft. Menelik had allegedly had a replica Ark built, which he then swapped for the original. And there's a third *alternative* alternative story in which he was given a replica of the Ark by Solomon but found out during his return journey that they'd left the replica in Jerusalem and had possession of the original. That's three different explanations for the same event, none of which exactly cover Menelik or anyone else in glory. Oh yes, and yet another version that states he was given the Ark by Solomon himself.'

'So that's why the Ethiopians believe the Ark is somewhere here,' Bronson said.

'Yes, but relying on the *Kebra Nagast* as a source is problematic. The book dates from the thirteenth century, when there were two dynasties competing for power in Ethiopia. One was the Zagwe dynasty, who stated that their lineage went back to Moses, while the Axumites claimed that their descent from Solomon was confirmed by the presence of the Ark of the Covenant in Ethiopia and by the *Kebra Nagast*. This book was supposed to have been a fourth-century Coptic manuscript that was translated into Arabic by Ethiopian clerics in about 1225. Now, bearing in mind how strongly the text supported the Axumite claim, it's possible these clerics actually wrote it as a piece of political propaganda and that there was no original Coptic text.

'But even if you believe that the *Kebra Nagast* is accurate, there are numerous holes in whichever version of the story you accept, one of which is glaringly obvious. The Ark of the Covenant was the most sacred religious relic the Israelites possessed. It was kept in its own special room in the Temple, the *Kodesh Hakodashim*, the Holy of Holies, a secure room that could only be entered by one man, the High Priest of the Temple, and only on one day of the year, Yom Kippur, the Day of Atonement. The reason why the Wailing Wall in Jerusalem is still so important to the Jewish faith is because that's the closest any Jew can get to where the First Temple once stood and where the Ark was kept. It's just possible that Solomon permitted Menelik to look into the room while he was in Jerusalem, but the Temple priests would never have allowed any more contact than that. Not even Solomon had the right to enter the Holy of Holies.'

Angela broke off as their starters arrived. Ethiopian cuisine featured a lot of vegan and vegetable dishes, usually highly spiced. Angela had selected a local dish called *ful medames*, fava beans served with hard-boiled eggs and *injera*, a sourdough flatbread, while Bronson had more cautiously chosen a small dish of pasta and beef. Angela would normally have started with a salad, but whenever she travelled outside Europe, she avoided anything that had been washed rather than cooked. There were no pharaohs in Ethiopia and never had been, but that didn't mean the pharaoh's revenge wasn't waiting in the wings to pay her a visit.

'Don't forget,' she went on, 'that the Ark had been designed by God for the Israelites and was of overwhelming importance to them. It was also very dangerous. There are stories in the Old Testament of people being killed instantly if they touched it, sometimes if they even looked at it, which is why it was always covered when the Israelites were wandering about the desert, and then held in the Holy of Holies in the Temple. The idea that Menelik's people could have knocked up a convincing replica and then just strolled into the Temple to swap them over makes no sense at all. They simply couldn't have done it. So the story's badly flawed for that reason alone.

'And then there's what apparently happened after that. The Ethiopians believe that after the Ark had been removed from

Jerusalem, it was transported via Egypt to Ethiopia, to the island of Tana Kirkos in Lake Tana, where it stayed for four hundred years. Today that island is home to about thirty men, all of them priests or monks. Women haven't been allowed there for centuries in case the mere sight of them inflames unwanted passions in the younger monks. There's no electricity or telephone, and virtually no contact with the modern world. There's a small monastery, a church and a few houses.

'According to some of the monks there who have talked to Westerners trying to trace the history of the Ark, it was kept outside in the open, placed on a specific flat rock that still bears faint marks where its feet would have been positioned. That makes no sense either. The Ark was basically a wooden box, and it would already have been old by this time. The Bible, as usual, is noticeably vague about dates and facts, but from the time of its construction to its placement in the First Temple couldn't have been less than about a century and was probably a lot longer than that. If it had been left out and exposed to the elements on that island, I doubt it would have lasted four months, never mind four hundred years. And the Ark was never, ever supposed to rest on the ground. Even when it was in the tabernacle, it was always on some kind of a stand.

'Quite probably something *was* placed on that island, but I don't think it was the Ark. Next to this rock is a green-painted metal shed with a corrugated-iron roof, and inside are shaped stones used for the sacrifice of sheep and goats, animal sacrifice being a feature of the early Judaean religion. That does suggest a link between Ethiopia and Judaea. For years there was an oppressed minority people here called the *Falashas*, black Jews. They practised the earliest and oldest Jewish traditions, including animal sacrifice, for centuries after the mainstream Jewish religion had abandoned them. Most of them left Ethiopia in the 1970s.'

'Okay,' Bronson said, finishing his pasta. 'I can't pick holes in what you're telling me because I know almost nothing about it, and you always do your research. So you've traced the Ark, or more likely something completely different, to this island in the lake. Where's it supposed to have gone from there?'

Angela mopped up the last mouthful of *ful medames*.

'It was moved to Axum, not far from where we're sitting now. The official resting place of the Ark of the Covenant is the Cathedral of Our Lady Mary of Zion. It's visited by thousands of people every year, drawn here by the story. In fact, there are two cathedrals and the Ark isn't actually in either of them. It's allegedly kept in a separate building known as the Chapel of the Tablet in the cathedral grounds. It's occupied by a single man, a guardian monk, chosen by divine prophecy. Once selected, he stays in the chapel for the rest of his life. He's not allowed to see the Ark, only to guard it and pray to it.'

'And that's the building you're interested in,' Bronson said.

'Yes, because if the Ark really is here, despite all the evidence against it, that's where it'll be. In fact,' she added, 'there are lots of Arks here. The Ethiopians refer to them as *tabots* in the local language, though the word means the tablets, the Ten Commandments, not the Ark itself. And that extends to the name of the chapel. It's called the Chapel of the Tablet, not the Chapel of the Ark, which is a bit of an anomaly. Every Ethiopian Orthodox church worldwide has a replica of the Ark and the tablets in its own *mak'da* or holy of holies, where only the most senior priests can enter. If it hasn't got one, then it can't be classed as a church, so they do take this idea very seriously.'

'Could we get to see one of these replicas?' Bronson asked.

'Possibly, but it wouldn't do us any good, because they aren't really replicas in the sense that you or I understand the word. They aren't copies of the original in shape, size or material and don't even resemble each other. They're just wooden boxes of various sizes holding stone copies of the Ten Commandments, and their function is purely symbolic. But even these replicas are believed to have huge power.

'Every year on the nineteenth of January there's a celebration called *Timkat*, meaning the Feast of the Epiphany, when every church in the country brings out its own *tabot* to parade it through the streets. I've read one account of the *Timkat* here in Axum that was filmed by a Westerner outside the church. Normally a priest carries the replica Ark on his head, with a cloth covering it. The person watching saw one side of a red wooden box decorated with three large metal protrusions incorporating a starburst design, and four smaller ones. He estimated it was about two and a half feet long and roughly a foot high, which means it was much smaller than the genuine Ark. Other replicas seen in public look like flat boxes only a few inches high, so there's no commonality in their design. They're just symbols, nothing more.'

Bronson nodded as the waiter approached with their main courses, both of them opting for pasta.

'I like pasta,' he said defensively as Angela looked at his plate with a slightly raised eyebrow, 'and so do the locals round here. It's a legacy of the Italian occupation during the last war. So the short summary is that we're just wasting our time here. Is there any chance at all that the Ark really is here in Axum?'

'Not in my opinion. Even if Menelik's people did manage to steal it, and against the odds it survived the journey here from Israel and its time on the island, it still might not be here. It could have left the country later. The Knights Templar visited Ethiopia in the thirteenth century, and if they had found the real Ark here, I've no doubt they would have taken it away with them, by force if necessary. But I still think it's very unlikely it was here in the first place. And there's one other piece of evidence that's particularly significant.

'A man named Edward Ullendorff served here as a British army officer during the Second World War. When he was interviewed in 1992, he said he had been inside the church here in Axum in 1941 and had been able to examine the alleged Ark for himself. I remember his description of it. He said: "They have a wooden box, but it's empty. Middle- to late-medieval construction, when these were fabricated ad hoc." The real point is that he wasn't just some soldier giving an uninformed opinion about a box he'd seen. Ullendorff knew a lot about this country – he ended up as a professor of Ethiopian studies at the University of London, so by any standards he was an expert witness. As far as I know, he's the only non-Ethiopian ever to have seen the alleged Ark here, so his opinion is a clincher as far as I'm concerned.

'The counter-argument is that because the Ark and the tablets have supposedly been guarded in the same way almost since the days of Menelik, no visitors could possibly have seen the genuine article. If they had seen anything like an Ark, it must have been a fake. But I still think what Ullendorff said is probably correct.'

'So I was right about something,' Bronson said. 'We're just wasting our time here.'

'Probably, yes.'

'But you still want to check out the chapel?'

'Yes. That's why we're here. Let's try tomorrow morning, when it's warm but not too hot. The guardian's job is to guard the Ark, obviously, but he's also required to pray beside it, surrounded by burning incense and worshipping God. But he doesn't stay in the chapel all the time. He wanders about within the metal fence surrounding the building, and sometimes talks to people, especially priests or monks, as long as they speak Oromo or Amharic. We'd get nowhere with him using English, but we don't want to talk to him. We just want him outside the chapel and ideally distracted by a visitor. If we wait until the afternoon, it'll be too hot and he'll probably stay in the chapel because it'll be cooler inside. Is the device ready?'

'I've checked it, and I've made the modifications I told you about to increase its endurance. That makes it a bit unstable but nothing I can't handle, so as far as I can see we're ready to go.'

'Good. Let's watch the sunset from our balcony. And tomorrow afternoon I thought we might just do the tourist bit and take a taxi ride down to Lalibela.'

'What's there?' Bronson asked.

'You'll see tomorrow, but I guarantee you'll be impressed, even amazed. It's one of the must-see places in the world. Think Petra in Jordan, only downwards not sideways.'

And with that somewhat enigmatic statement, Angela stood up and led the way out of the dining room.

Chapter 2

They were up, breakfasted and walking along the cobbled pavement of the street outside the hotel by 9 a.m. Angela was carrying a large bag made of colourful woven material that she'd bought locally, and Bronson was carrying nothing at all.

When they reached the cathedral, they found several people around the building and in the grounds. Most were locals, judging by their dress and skin colour, but there were also clumps of tourists, some in organised tour groups and others couples or families having a look around.

They walked around the old Cathedral of Our Lady Mary of Zion, which looked more like a fortress than a place of worship, with solid stone walls pierced by very few openings and crenellated around the top. Dating originally from the fourth century AD, it had been destroyed and rebuilt over the years, and last rebuilt and enlarged in the seventeenth century. It was unusual in that only men were permitted to enter it, probably because in the tenth century the building was destroyed by the forces of Queen Gudit. The only woman permitted inside was Mary, the saint to whom the building was dedicated, and she was a permanent resident.

Almost next to it was the new Cathedral of Our Lady Mary of Zion, a much more modern building begun in the 1950s by the Ethiopian emperor Haile Selassie. This one was open to both sexes. It was a circular domed structure with an impressive and restful interior.

Nestling between the two was the Chapel of the Tablet, a small, brownish single-storey stone building marked by blue-painted decoration within the windows, blue fence posts, a crucifix above the door and another adorning the dome in the centre of the roof.

Angela looked around as they approached. There were a couple of locals standing right beside the steel perimeter fence, perhaps hoping to exchange a few words with the guardian monk. He was obviously inside, the door of the chapel shut.

They were in no hurry and picked a spot to sit some distance from the boundary fence, because women were not permitted to get close to the chapel. From that location they had a good view of the door of the building, and also the benefit of a tree to provide a measure of shade.

'This is almost ideal,' Angela said, lowering herself to the ground and opening her voluminous bag to take out a thick novel. She passed the bag over to Bronson and adjusted her wide straw hat to shade her face from the sun. She was wearing a pair of large sunglasses that rendered her eyes invisible to anyone looking at her, which was convenient because she wasn't reading the book she was holding but watching the door of the chapel.

Bronson was also wearing sunglasses and a hat, as was every other tourist, male or female, in the vicinity, but he didn't have a book to read. Or even to pretend to read. Instead, he reached into the bag Angela had handed him, took out a small cardboard box with a brightly coloured lid and opened it up.

Inside were a few sheets of paper covered in printing, diagrams and pictures, and underneath those were two objects. The first was what looked like a small computer game controller, including a clamp that was obviously designed to hold a smartphone. He took his mobile out of his pocket and fitted it in place. The previous evening at the hotel he'd synched the components together and tested everything.

He removed the other object from the box, a tiny plastic mechanism that he had purchased – on Angela's detailed instructions – for this single purpose. It was an Eachine E10W mini quadcopter, a so-called nano-drone, fitted with a tiny high-definition two-megapixel camera capable of taking both video and still images. Two versions of this nano-drone existed, the other model being the E10C, which was slightly cheaper but lacked the FPV – first-person view – facility that was essential for what Bronson intended to do. This allowed him to see the view through the drone's camera on his linked mobile phone screen. He would be able to tell exactly where the device was pointing, just as if he were actually on board the drone.

Fitted with four rotors, the E10W was a mere six centimetres – just over two and a quarter inches – in diameter and was not in exactly the same state as it had been when Bronson had first opened the box. On a flying object of that size, weight was critical, so he'd identified the lightest battery he could find with the same or better power output than the one fitted inside the drone, then attached it to the underside of the quadcopter and wired it into the device.

The first test flight hadn't gone well, but after a certain amount of fiddling about, he'd sorted out the weight distribution and got the quadcopter into a controllable state. More importantly, he'd doubled its total endurance from about five or six minutes to roughly eleven minutes, a very significant increase. And he knew he'd probably need every extra second he could manage. He'd spent hours learning its characteristics and how to pilot it, concentrating on navigating it in confined spaces.

The E10W came with LED lights to identify it in poor light conditions. The one thing Bronson definitely didn't want was bright lights flashing on it: the whole point was for it to be as undetectable as possible. So he'd removed both the LED lights and the associated wiring. Tiny, lightweight components, but on something weighing only fifteen grams, even the smallest fraction of a gram was significant.

As standard, the drone had a white underside, white rotor blades and metallic blue paint on its upper surface. Bronson had applied the thinnest possible coat of blue paint to the underside and the blades. The device was so small that its rotors would be inaudible more than a few feet away, and the new paint meant that it should also be invisible from below against the almost constant solid blue sky over Ethiopia.

The onboard camera was supposed to take a memory card, but Bronson hadn't fitted one to save a little bit more weight. His smartphone would record whatever the camera saw as well as letting him navigate the drone.

He'd fully charged all the batteries overnight, including the two on the drone, and he made a final check that the tiny machine was ready to fly. When he was happy with it, he put the controller and the drone back in Angela's bag. Now all they could do was wait.

The door of the Chapel of the Tablet remained firmly closed until just after 10.30, by which time Angela had stopped pretending to read and was already well into the third chapter of her book, and Bronson had begun dozing off in the warm still air.

The door suddenly swung wide open with a creak and a groan from the hinges, and the guardian monk, a tall and somewhat gaunt figure wearing a saffron-yellow robe, sandals and a dark-coloured turban appeared in the opening and stared out for a few moments, blinking in the harsh sunlight. Then he stepped back inside, leaving the door wide open.

'You know he has to be a virgin, don't you?' Bronson asked as the tall figure disappeared. 'I read about it on the Internet. And that when he knows he's near death he has to discuss the matter of his successor with senior priests and then nominate the chosen monk, who also has to be a virgin. I'm not quite sure how can you tell that, for a man.'

'Personally I'm more interested in how often he washes and who does his laundry,' Angela replied. 'A single man, living on his own, who can't leave the premises? The mind boggles. Still, at least we know he's now up and about.'

About ten minutes later, the guardian reappeared and walked out into the small area enclosed by the boundary fence around the chapel. He appeared to be in no hurry, which was unsurprising, as by definition he had almost nothing to do apart from praying beside the Ark, and all day to do it.

'God, he must be bored,' Angela said, watching him slowly walk over to where a man who looked like a local was standing, leaning on the boundary fence. 'He probably looks forward to a chat because otherwise his life would be like solitary confinement.'

The two men appeared to exchange greetings and then began a conversation together.

'Should you do it now, maybe?' Angela asked.

'Not yet,' Bronson replied. 'They're standing between us and the open door and there's still a chance they might hear or see it. I'd rather he was further away and ideally down the side of the chapel somewhere. I'll wait. We've got plenty of time.'

Without making it obvious, they watched as the guardian talked to his visitor, the conversation apparently friendly and at times animated.

'Perhaps he's catching up on all the latest gossip,' Angela suggested. 'The other man isn't a monk as far as I can tell. He's not wearing a yellow robe, just the loose white clothes that most men wear here, so they're probably not in a deep religious discussion.'

Whatever they had been talking about, after about a quarter of an hour they separated, the visitor walking away from the chapel while the guardian slowly retraced his steps and vanished through the doorway.

'Coffee break? An early lunch? Another prayer session with the Ark, or just a visit to whatever kind of lavatory I hope he's got inside?'

'No idea,' Bronson responded, still watching the open door.

It might have been the last option Angela had suggested, because less than five minutes later the guardian was back, again walking slowly around the enclosed ground within the perimeter fence. There was another man, this one probably a monk because of the yellow robe he was wearing, standing beside the boundary fence over to the right-hand side of the chapel, and the guardian made his way over to him.

'We'll give them a few minutes,' Bronson said, reaching into the bag to pick up the controller and the nano-drone. 'Just in case that bloke's only come to deliver a short message or give him something.'

But it was soon clear that it was going to be a longer conversation. There was nobody between Bronson and the perimeter fence in front of him, and the grounds around the two cathedrals were largely empty. He doubted they would have a better opportunity.

He stood up and tried to look as if he was watching something on the screen of his mobile, his hand concealing as much of the drone controller as possible. He held the nano-drone in his other hand. It was so small it was completely invisible.

He wandered towards the fence, not directly, but as if he was heading towards the new cathedral, which took him away from the guardian and the other man but kept him close to the chapel. When he reached the corner, he opened his left hand and activated the controller. With a faint buzzing sound, the nano-drone lifted straight up off his palm and climbed to about twenty feet above the ground.

The limiting factor was battery power, and Bronson knew it. He took a quick glance around but nobody seemed to be paying him the slightest attention. He looked down at the screen of his smartphone, which was displaying a very clear image of the front of the chapel. He adjusted the controls. He was using the wireless controller rather than his phone because that was easier and gave him better range, and he'd selected the slower of the two speed options because that made the device easier to control. The open doorway seemed to accelerate towards him as the nano-drone approached it at a slight angle. He straightened it up just before it moved from the sunlight into the darkness beyond the doorway, and flew it straight into the chapel.

He hadn't known what to expect. The word 'chapel' suggested an open space, but the interior was more like that of a dwelling house. There were windows all round, so although it had looked dark from the outside, it was actually quite light in there. He brought the drone to a hover. The camera showed that it was in a hallway with two open doors on each side. He turned the drone to the right and steered it through the first doorway. That was a storeroom, probably for food judging by the look of the boxes and packets he could see. He reversed course back into the hall and steered the drone down the corridor towards the next doorway, but then changed his mind and again brought it to a hover. The image through the camera was very clear, and he thought he could detect something like smoke in the air. He rotated the drone through a complete circle, searching for the source. It seemed to be coming from the far end of the hallway, and he could only assume – and hope – that what he was seeing was incense and not, say, smoke from the guardian's burning lunch.

'Chris!'

Angela's voice was sharp and clear, and he looked up from the screen of his smartphone to see that the guardian monk had finished his conversation at the fence and was making his way slowly back in the direction of the chapel door.

He'd hoped to have several minutes to explore, but now he had only a few seconds.

He steered the drone through another doorway. He saw a simple, basic room equipped with a single bed, the sheets and pillows neatly stacked on it ready for it to be made later, a crucifix on the wall above the head of the bed and a small wardrobe at the other end of the room. It all looked clean and strictly functional.

He quickly reversed direction, and as he did so, he saw a wisp of smoke coming from a half-closed door at the far end of the hall.

He glanced sideways. The guardian was only a few yards from the door. At that moment, Angela trotted forward and called out to him. The monk stopped and turned to look at her. She was holding her phone in front of her, very obviously wanting to take a picture of the guardian, and calling out to him in English, which she knew he probably wouldn't understand, to ask if she was allowed to do so.

Bronson knew he had maybe twenty seconds left. He steered the nano-drone through the gap and into the room where the smoke tendrils were coming from.

He found himself – albeit only virtually – in a very different place. The light level was much lower because heavy curtains had been pulled across the tall windows, and he could see burning incense sticks positioned around the perimeter and beside what looked like an altar at the far end of the room. He flew the drone directly towards it, brought it to a hover a few feet away and made sure that his smartphone was recording what he was seeing.

In the semi-darkness, it was difficult to estimate dimensions, but there was a kind of low plinth that he guessed was about six feet long, four feet wide and perhaps a foot high positioned centrally at that end of the room. On it was an oblong shape. He couldn't tell what it was because it was covered in a heavy, rich-looking material that appeared in the half-light to be a deep red in colour but shot through with threads of gold. It was obviously the focus of the room, in fact of the whole building, but what he couldn't tell was whether or not he was looking at the Ark of the Covenant.

What he needed was a measure of some sort, something he and Angela could use to estimate its actual size. He turned the drone on its own axis in the room, looking for something, anything, with dimensions he could use.

He glanced again at the guardian, who was standing in the same spot, looking angrily at Angela and scolding her in what was probably high-speed and irritated Amharic for being too close to the chapel, for daring to address him and, quite probably, for being a woman. Then he turned away from her and began walking steadily towards the half-dozen wide stone steps that led up to the door of the Chapel of the Tablet.

Bronson dipped the nano-drone and rotated it to see the floor of the room. There was a rectangular carpet directly in front of the shrouded object, which was presumably where the guardian spent most of his time when he was in the building, on his knees and praying. Other than that, the room was devoid of furnishings.

He looked back at the alleged Ark and moved the drone closer, focusing not on the wrapped rectangular object but on the incense sticks smouldering in front of it and on both sides. Each stick was in a separate small brass or bronze holder. That might be all he needed.

He looked towards the guardian. He'd almost reached the top of the flight of wide steps directly in front of the chapel door. Even at the slow pace he was moving, he'd be walking into the building in less than ten seconds.

Chapter 3

Bronson steered the nano-drone out of the room and back into the hallway, turning it towards the open door, keeping it about ten feet above the floor. The hallway had a high ceiling and the door itself was probably ten or eleven feet in height. As the guardian monk stepped in through the doorway, he flew the drone through the open space directly above his head and out of the building. The man looked up, a puzzled expression on his face – he had obviously heard the buzzing of the rotors – then ducked down, perhaps thinking that it was an insect, and turned his head to follow the sound.

The moment the drone cleared the doorway, Bronson climbed it to about thirty feet, where it would be completely inaudible to anyone on the ground and invisible against the blue of the sky, and steered it away from the chapel towards the spot where he and Angela had been sitting earlier.

The guardian had turned around in the doorway and was looking up into the sky. After a few seconds he seemed to give a slight shrug, then turned away and stepped back into the chapel.

Bronson made his way back towards Angela, shutting down the drone as he did so.

'Did you get it?' she asked eagerly.

'I think so, yes,' he replied quietly. 'We'll talk later when we can watch the footage. Now I think we need to make ourselves scarce before the guardian starts to wonder if that really was a sodding great wasp or something else that passed him in the doorway.'

He put the controller and the drone back into Angela's bag and they made their way towards the new cathedral and then out into the street beyond. On their way back to the hotel, Bronson managed to lose the quadcopter, the control unit and the box in separate piles of rubbish, and then for safety he sent copies of the footage he'd captured to his and Angela's email addresses from his phone.

He didn't think they were under any suspicion, because the actions of the guardian monk suggested that he thought he'd been passed by an unusually large insect that he hadn't seen clearly and couldn't identify. But it was important to behave normally, so he and Angela walked back to the hotel after their morning's 'sightseeing', sat in the bar for a few minutes having a drink and then went into the dining room for lunch. Only after they'd finished and had their coffee did they head upstairs to their room.

Bronson connected his smartphone to Angela's laptop and they sat side by side on the bed to watch what he'd recorded.

'That's really not a bad picture,' she said as the video began playing, showing the view as the drone accelerated towards the chapel.

They watched in silence as the drone's camera showed the interiors of two of the rooms and then headed towards the third door.

'This is the one,' Bronson said.

The difference in ambient light was immediately obvious, but the pictures from the camera were still clear enough.

'That's the relic,' Angela said as the drone came to a hover near the shrouded shape on the plinth. 'We need scale, something to measure it.'

'I know. The only other thing in there, apart from that prayer mat, are these incense sticks and the brass holders.' He pointed at the laptop's screen, where the incense and holders appeared in sharp focus. 'We've seen pots like these in some of the shops here, and we know how long most incense sticks are, so maybe that will be enough.'

‘Maybe.’ Angela sounded doubtful. ‘But the one thing that’s really obvious to me is the shape. That looks like a fairly heavy material covering it, but if that is the Ark, then where’s the lid? What we’re seeing looks more like a regular box, but the lid should have the two raised figures of the cherubim on it. And that hasn’t. You can see that even with the cloth over it. And they wouldn’t separate the Ark and the lid. It comes as a piece.’

‘Look, let’s try measuring it, just to be sure.’

Bronson ran the video backwards and then stopped it when he reached a particular image. He pointed at the screen.

‘That brass incense holder beside the box is probably no more than four inches tall, but let’s say three to give a margin of error. It won’t be what you might call high-tech, but it will give us an estimate of the size of the box.’

He took a piece of paper and a pencil, held the paper against the image of the incense holder on the screen and made two faint pencil marks to indicate its height.

‘Right,’ he said, resting the paper on a magazine and using the pencil to thicken the two marks. He reached over to Angela’s laptop bag, took out a plastic six-inch ruler and proceeded to produce a very simple scale on the paper, marking it every three-inch equivalent, four for a foot and so on. In less than a minute he had the equivalent of six feet marked out on the edge of the paper.

‘Can you just remind me what the dimensions of the Ark were supposed to be,’ he said.

‘Burned into my brain,’ Angela replied. ‘It was fifty-two inches long, thirty-one inches high and the same wide.’

‘Right.’

Bronson held the edge of the paper against the frozen image on the screen, measuring its length. He jotted a figure down and turned the paper through ninety degrees to estimate the height of the object.

‘You’re sure those figures are accurate?’ he asked.

'As accurate as anything else in the Bible, yes. The dimensions come from the Book of Exodus and are given in cubits, obviously, along with very detailed instructions on how the Ark is to be made. In fact, the same dimensions are given twice in Exodus.'

'Then that isn't the Ark of the Covenant. We've probably underestimated the size of that incense holder, but if it was three inches in height, the length of the object, including the cloth that's covering it, is no more than forty-three inches. Take away the cloth and you could probably knock at least a couple of inches off that because of the folds in the material, so we're looking at something about forty inches long. That's a foot too short for it to be the Ark. And the height's wrong as well. That works out at no more than two feet.'

'I knew it,' Angela said, a note of triumph in her voice.

Bronson ran the video forward a few frames, then backwards until he found a good shot of the top of the shrouded object and froze the image again.

'This won't be as accurate because the drone has moved,' he said, using his paper measure again, 'but the depth is wrong as well. I reckon that's about eighteen inches, and it should be almost double that.'

'The other thing you can see in this shot,' Angela said, 'is that the aspect ratio is wrong. The Ark was supposed to be two and a half cubits long, one and a half cubits high – thirty-one inches – and the same wide, which is a square cross-section. Without doing any measuring at all, you can see that this box is taller than it's deep. The cross-section is oblong, not square. It's not the Ark.'

Bronson scrunched up the sheet of paper and lobbed it into the waste basket on the other side of the bedroom.

'Good. I'm glad that's out of the way. Can we go home now?'

'Tomorrow,' Angela said. 'This afternoon we're going to do the tourist bit and visit Lalibela. We've flown halfway across the world, so let's do some sightseeing.'

Tens of thousands of pilgrims visit Lalibela every year. What draws them is a collection of monolithic churches constructed in an entirely unique way. At the ancient site of Petra in Jordan the ancient Nabataean people carved tombs and dwellings out of the rock cliffs, producing spectacular buildings as fine as anything found in ancient Greece or Rome, each one an architectural wonder in its own right.

The ancient Ethiopians obviously decided to substantially increase the degree of difficulty in constructing their places of worship. Instead of building churches out of rocks or stones, or even hacking them out of cliff faces like the Nabataeans, they decided to construct their churches starting at the top. They carved them out of the bedrock, working vertically downwards. And as the buildings dated from about the twelfth century, their only tools would have been hammers and chisels.

Each church is set within an open shaft carved straight down into the rock to form what is effectively an underground cathedral, a type of church found nowhere else in the world. It would be remarkable enough if they had constructed one such place of worship, but there are eleven of them, linked by tunnels and passages. The complex is named after the Ethiopian king Lalibela, and it's been theorised that he was trying to replicate Jerusalem, albeit in a rather unusual way.

'This is a weird, weird place,' Bronson said as he looked across at a square opening in the rock in which sat Biete Giyorgis, the Church of St George, the flat top of the cruciform monolith marked by three crosses, nestling one inside the other and carved into the solid rock. And it wasn't just a roughly cut lump of stone. The church gave every impression of having been constructed from below in the traditional manner, with decorations on the walls, carved windows and impressive doorways, the whole standing on a shaped plinth. But it hadn't been.

'You got that right,' Angela said. 'Let's explore.'

They wandered through the complex, down stone staircases and along narrow passageways, marvelling at the skill of the masons who'd done the work.

'These may be churches,' Bronson remarked. 'Well, they *are* churches, but they could also be fortresses. They'd be really easy for just a small group of people to defend because the passages are so narrow and they're the only way in.'

The interiors were amazing, not least because of some of the curious carvings.

'That's the Star of David,' Angela said, 'but inside it there's another symbol that we've met before.'

Bronson looked where she was pointing and nodded. 'A cross *pattée*. The unmistakable symbol of the Knights Templar. In fact, I've seen Templar crosses and symbols all over this place.'

'They were here in the thirteenth century,' she reminded him.

They left after about an hour and climbed into the waiting taxi to return to Axum and their hotel.

'So now what?' Bronson asked when they were once again having a drink in the bar. 'What's your next step?'

'That's the problem,' Angela replied. 'I know where the Ark isn't, so I'd like to find out where it is. My best guess is that the Temple priests hid it somewhere in Jerusalem – most probably down in the tunnels that honeycomb the Temple Mount – before the Babylonians overran the city in 587 BC, and it wasn't recovered because the only people who'd known where it was were killed at the end of the siege. It might still be there, but I doubt it because of the nine years or so that the Knights Templar spent exploring and excavating the Temple Mount, and what happened when they finished. I believe they found it, used it to blackmail the pope and then hid it somewhere else. And then it again vanished from the historical record.'

'So it's a dead end, then?'

'Maybe,' Angela replied, 'or maybe not. Sometimes things that are lost suddenly get found again. Maybe a clue will surface somewhere. Or maybe not. I don't know. I hope that one day something will just turn up. And when it does, I'll be right on it, digging away.'

'And you know I'll follow you on the trail,' Bronson said. 'Just like I always do.'

Chapter 4

Rue des Remparts, Limoux, Languedoc, southern France

Ten days ago

'*Pour la dernière fois, où sont les fichiers? Les archives?*'

The speaker, a heavily built man wearing a dark suit and a five o'clock shadow so pronounced that it made the lower part of his craggy face appear almost black, looked and sounded irritated, an impression that was entirely accurate. He was also losing patience with the slim, balding, bespectacled clerk sitting in the upright chair in front of him.

The clerk was named René Maréchal – not that Luca Rossi had bothered asking his name – and he'd been lashed to the chair with plastic cable ties by the man who had accompanied Rossi when he'd kicked in the locked side door of the notary's office half an hour earlier. Or rather, the former notary's office, as the business had closed about three weeks ago and Maréchal, the longest-serving member of the firm, had been told to catalogue and properly dispose of the files – the *fichiers* and *archives* – and process any outstanding paperwork.

Maréchal was obviously terrified of both Rossi and the black automatic pistol pointing directly at his stomach. Any person who uses a tool on a regular basis develops a familiarity with it that is readily apparent to an observer, and Rossi handled his pistol with the same sort of casual confidence that a carpenter would exhibit for a hammer or a saw. He looked like a man who could and would use the weapon without the slightest hesitation.

Maréchal shook his head, despair clouding his features. 'I've told you already. I have no idea where those records are,' he said in French. 'You've made me check the file room and they're not in there. I don't even remember seeing them when the office was open.'

'Then think harder.' Rossi's French was quite fluent, but his accent betrayed the fact that it was not his first language. 'They were here, we already know that, and now they're not. So where are they? Who took them? Where did they go?'

'How do you know they were here?' Maréchal asked, professional curiosity temporarily overcoming his fear. 'This was a private office, a long-established notarial firm, so how could you know what documents we held? And why do you want papers that date from over two centuries ago? What's the point? Who are you people?'

Rossi didn't bother to answer, just repeated his own question. 'Where are the records?'

Maréchal shook his head again.

Rossi nodded at the other man. Roberto Lombardi was almost Rossi's twin, heavily built with black hair and a dark complexion, and his job was not to ask questions but to do what he was told to do when he was told to do it. He was standing beside the clerk's chair and watching both Rossi and the captive. When Rossi nodded and lowered the muzzle of his Walther, Lombardi stepped in front of Maréchal, paused for a couple of seconds so the clerk would know what was coming next, then drove his right fist straight into the man's midriff before resuming his previous position. Maréchal bent forward as far as his bonds would allow as the air was forced out of his lungs and he gasped for breath. It wasn't a hard blow, because the man looked as if he was well over seventy years old and it was essential that he provided the information they sought. They couldn't kill him. Or not yet, anyway.

Rossi waited until the clerk's breathing had almost returned to normal before he spoke again.

'Now that I have your full attention, let's try one more time. Where are the records?'

Still struggling for breath, Maréchal replied, his voice cracking, 'But I don't know. If I did, I promise I would tell you.'

Rossi gestured again, but before his enforcer could deliver another blow, Maréchal cried out.

'Wait, wait. Tell me the name again.'

Rossi – who like Lombardi was wearing latex gloves to avoid leaving fingerprints in the office – pulled a slip of paper from his jacket pocket and read the name printed on it.

French pronunciation is precise, as any English tourist who has ever asked for a Coca-Cola in a French bar without placing the stress on the first syllable of 'Coca' can testify. Saying the product name the way the rest of the world pronounces it will normally produce a puzzled frown and a Gallic shrug but no drink. Rossi's first language was Italian, and Maréchal clearly didn't recognise the French name he'd spoken.

'I don't know it,' he said. But as Lombardi stepped forward again, he called out, 'Don't say the name again. Let me read it.'

'Show him,' Rossi ordered, holding out the paper.

The enforcer took it from him and held it in front of the clerk's face.

Maréchal read the printed name and nodded, his relief evident in his expression.

'Now I know who you mean. I do know about this estate and the Hautpoul papers,' he said, pronouncing the name in an entirely different way to Rossi. 'I think you're Italian, and your French…'

'So where are they? The records?'

'I need to check my ledger. It's the green book on that desk over there.' Maréchal nodded his head towards the volume he wanted.

The enforcer picked it up and held it in front of him.

'You'll have to open it for me,' Maréchal said, stating the obvious. 'Towards the front of the book.'

Lombardi opened the ledger at the first page, where details of the oldest documents were listed, and then began displaying the pages one at a time to the clerk.

'Stop,' Maréchal said. 'That's it.'

'Tell me,' Rossi ordered.

Maréchal read the entry on the page, then looked at the man holding the pistol.

'The records aren't here,' he said, something like relief in his voice. 'The archive was sent to Paris, apparently for research.'

'What? Why?'

'I have no idea. I presume the decision was taken by the notary before he retired.'

'Where did it go to in Paris?'

Maréchal peered again at the entry. 'As it was for research purposes, presumably to a library or university, but that's just a guess. The destination address hasn't been filled in. The entry just says "To Paris" and gives the name of a courier. I have no idea where it actually went.'

Rossi strode across the room, grabbed the ledger and looked at the entry himself. The name of the archive was clear, as was the date, almost two weeks earlier. But at least he now had a lead that he could follow. He took out his mobile phone and snapped a photograph of the page, which he could send to his masters to show them what he had discovered. That just left the clerk to deal with, and in that respect his orders were quite clear.

Rossi was a well-paid and dedicated contractor employed on a casual but frequent basis by the *Congregatio pro Doctrina Fidei*, or Congregation for the Doctrine of the Faith – the CDF. This wasn't so much a successor organisation to the Supreme Sacred Congregation of the Roman and Universal Inquisition as exactly the same organisation wearing a new suit of clothes, or at least with a new name. It was formed in 1542 and was the oldest of the present nine congregations of the Roman Curia, the administrative entities that effectively ran the Catholic Church.

Just like the original Inquisition, which began its bloody and brutal work in France during the twelfth century, the *CDF* was charged with spreading Christian doctrine – something that was arguably harmless – and more importantly defending the Church and its traditions against heresy. Heresy in this context meant anything the Vatican didn't agree with, a task that historically had proved to be the exact opposite of harmless, as the countless millions of 'heretics' executed by the Church over more than half a millennium in the most brutal and painful manner possible, all in the name of a loving God, could have testified.

Despite being an important part of the Vatican's machinery, the CDF was based not in the smallest state in the world, but in the Palace of the Holy Office, just beyond the walls of the Vatican. Rossi had never visited this building, all contacts with his paymasters taking place in anonymous and neutral locations, but his instructions allowed no room for manoeuvre. In those matters in which he was told to involve himself, no trace of his participation or that of the CDF was permitted, nor any evidence of what a particular operation had been intended to achieve. And above all, no loose ends were allowed.

Which was unfortunate for René Maréchal, because in that place and at that moment it was difficult to describe him as anything else. He'd correctly guessed Rossi's nationality, and he now knew exactly which archive the Italian was looking for. Those two facts alone meant that the clerk was expendable. With immediate effect.

For a couple of seconds Rossi toyed with the idea of shooting him, but the Rue des Remparts in Limoux was a fairly busy street and the sound of an unsilenced gunshot would certainly not pass unnoticed. So that left something quick and quiet, and sometimes the old methods were the best. Then he noticed something about the chair the clerk was sitting in.

'*Garrotta*,' he said simply, pointing.

The silent enforcer followed his gaze and nodded. The upright chair had a high back, and in the top centre of it was a decorative hole, positioned almost directly behind the clerk's head. Lombardi picked up a length of thin rope, perhaps used for tying heavy parcels, and clicked open a switchblade to cut about a metre from it. He tied the ends together, passed the loop through the hole and dropped it over Maréchal's head.

The clerk obviously realised what was happening and began struggling frantically, desperately trying to break the cable ties. As he opened his mouth to scream or shout, the enforcer stuffed a rag into his mouth as a makeshift gag and tied it around his head, silencing him.

Then he picked up a short length of wood from the cluttered floor, inserted it into the other end of the loop and began rotating it, twisting the rope and increasing the pressure on the clerk's somewhat scrawny neck.

It was all over in about three minutes. The garrotte bit deeply into Maréchal's neck, cutting off the arterial blood supply to his brain and constricting his windpipe, stopping his breathing. His face flushed deep red, his eyes behind his glasses seemed almost to pop out of their sockets, and his tongue protruded from his mouth with a ghastly rattle.

It wasn't a pretty death, but then very few deaths were.

Rossi checked that the clerk was definitely dead, then glanced around the office and nodded his satisfaction.

'Pick up that ledger. We'll take that as well. Now let's get out of here. We can be in Paris by tomorrow morning.'

Chapter 5

Paris, France

As in every other Western European nation, courier services are common in France, providing an essential service to individuals and organisations that need, for whatever reason, to send a package direct to an addressee and track its progress for the entire journey. DHL and UPS are the big names, the international couriers, but there are dozens, probably hundreds, of others, some working locally to cover a particular city or district while others are national, operating over much of the country.

The company selected by the notary in Limoux was a firm with a national presence. Rossi had learned this from the ledger, but not the destination address. With hindsight he knew he should have searched the office until he'd found the consignment note or whatever the courier firm called their transit documentation, but he had no idea where to look for it, and the thought hadn't crossed his mind until after Lombardi had garrotted the clerk. But he had got a company name and he thought that would be enough.

It was late morning the following day when the two men checked into a mid-priced hotel in the Rugis district to the south of the centre of Paris, near Orly airport, an area that saw hundreds of arrivals and departures every day and where they would not stand out. They'd been driving all night, taking turns at the wheel and stopping only for fuel, snacks and coffee, and both men were exhausted. Rossi booked two adjoining rooms, told Lombardi to get some sleep, and then immediately went to bed himself, setting his mobile phone alarm for three in the afternoon. He was snoring within minutes.

Getting specific information out of a commercial organisation was usually only a matter of finding someone to ask. And it wasn't as if what he wanted to know was exactly a secret. He didn't expect it would be very difficult.

That afternoon, with both men showered and shaved and looking as much like businessmen as possible, Lombardi followed the directions supplied by the car's built-in satnav to the nearest office of the courier company, then stopped the vehicle on the street while Rossi went inside.

He'd decided the easiest and probably quickest option was to claim there'd been an administrative cock-up, that the Limoux notary's staff had failed to record the destination of the documents, and he was there to try to sort it out. That had the benefit of being true – to a degree – and he had the original ledger with him as confirmation.

'It's just to complete our records, you understand,' he explained to the counter clerk, showing her the incomplete ledger entry. 'As a law firm, we are required to provide proof of the disposal of all documents in our charge.'

'They've already been delivered,' she said, looking at the screen of her computer, 'so we can't give them to you.'

Though that was of course precisely what Rossi was hoping to achieve, he shook his head firmly.

'Of course. This is purely administrative. I just need to know where they were sent, nothing else.'

The clerk nodded and again checked the screen of the computer in front of her. 'That's no problem. The delivery address was the Bibliothèque Serpente in the Rue Serpente here in Paris. They were signed for on arrival by a Monsieur Lefèvre, initials R. C. That's all I have.'

When he heard the word *bibliothèque*, Rossi's spirits lifted. Almost by definition, libraries usually allowed free and unrestricted access, at least to members. Maybe he would have to register to join, or produce some sort of authority, but actually getting inside the building should be fairly easy.

'Do you have the full address?' he asked. 'Just so I can complete our records.'

'I'll print you a copy of the delivery note,' she replied, and moments later the laser printer beside her spat out a single sheet of paper that she handed him.

Rossi read the address as he walked out of the office towards the waiting car, and immediately realised that getting inside might not be quite as easy as filling out an application for a library card.

The Bibliothèque Serpente was a part of the Maison de la Recherche, one of the research departments of the Sorbonne. Rossi guessed that the chances of a casual browser being able to just wander into that particular library in search of the Hautpoul family papers were probably fairly slim. It wouldn't be like borrowing a book. He would need academic credentials of some kind to get inside and find what he needed.

But his employer had access to the halls of academe in numerous countries, so providing him with suitably convincing forged credentials would probably just be a matter of time. Even as Lombardi steered the car away from the kerb, Rossi was already writing an SMS to alert his contact at the CDF to what he had discovered and what he would need. The mobile number he sent the message to wasn't registered to anyone. It was a burner phone obtained for this one operation and would be destroyed once it was over.

-

Three days later, Luca Rossi visited a post office in Paris and collected papers that identified him as Angelo Romano, a professor of post-medieval European history at the Università di Bologna. Using his new documentation, he had little difficulty in getting inside the Bibliothèque Serpente, being welcomed as a visiting academic. The following day he was able to access the documents he needed to see and began talking about them to members of the staff and faculty who worked there.

The day after that, he left the library and walked out into the Rue Danton – despite its address of 28 Rue Serpente, about half of the imposing building that was the Maison de la Recherche was actually located in the Rue Danton at the intersection of four streets – clutching a document folder containing copies of all the papers the notary had sent, the principal part of his mission accomplished.

In his hotel room that afternoon, he used a portable scanner to copy each of the papers, or at least those that were clearly of interest; most of the documents were old land deeds, property transfers, mortgages and the like, and of no consequence to anyone except the participants involved. But just in case he'd missed something, he would send the entire copied archive by courier to Rome before he left Paris.

He then attached the scans to several emails because of the amount of data involved and sent them to a temporary email address used by his contact at the CDF.

He followed those with another message to deliver the inevitable bad news.

The orders he had been given were to find and recover – or at least to copy – the documents, which he had done. He had also been ordered to destroy them if their recovery was not an option, but the security precautions at the Bibliothèque Serpente meant that that would have been impossible. At least it would have been impossible if he wanted to walk out of the building without a police escort and wearing handcuffs, and spending a few years in a French jail charged with vandalism or arson wasn't something Rossi was prepared to contemplate. The CDF employed him on a contract basis, but they certainly didn't own him.

What he had managed to do was remove two of the loose pages from the Hautpoul papers when he'd been inspecting the documents. Both were hand-written, one clearly encrypted and the other written in what looked like Occitan, though what had attracted Rossi's attention was the date at the top of the page. These he had secreted inside his jacket when he was sure nobody else in the reading room was paying him any attention.

Even if it could have been achieved, there was a reason why destroying the documents would have been pointless. In fact, there were two reasons.

First, while every book received by the Bibliothèque Serpente was simply listed in the library's computer database, documents of the sort that comprised the Hautpoul archive were scanned and stored in a named folder on the computer and on numerous backup locations to create multiple permanent records. So destroying the papers would achieve nothing, as the data was securely stored on several different hard drives that Rossi couldn't even identify, far less access. In fact, it would make the situation worse, because people would then start studying the scans of the papers to work out why somebody had wanted the originals destroyed.

The second reason was that it was already too late. One of the researchers Rossi had talked to in the building was an Englishman named George Anderson, on secondment there from the British Museum in London. He'd looked at the papers as soon as they had been scanned and had been quite happy to talk to the visiting Italian professor about them.

'Not a lot in them,' he'd said over coffee when Rossi had successfully steered the conversation in the direction he wanted it to go, 'unless you have a burning desire to study the histories of a handful of obscure French noble families, mainly the Aniort, Blanchefort, Hautpoul and Voisin dynasties. They were all interconnected to a certain extent, mainly because they all lived in the same area for centuries, had dealings with each other and were linked through a few dynastic marriages, but I can think of much more fertile and rewarding ground to study.

'There was one point of interest, though,' Anderson had added. 'Some of the later documents in the bundle were typewritten, but most of the early stuff was done by hand, and one of the papers was not only hand-written but also encrypted, so that would offer a bit of a challenge.'

'I think I noticed that one,' Rossi said, without a trace of nervousness despite the knowledge that that particular page was even then hidden in his inside jacket pocket. 'Is anyone here – anyone at the Sorbonne, I mean – investigating it?'

'Not as far as I know. We've all got more pressing stuff to get through than something like that. And just because somebody went to the bother of devising a code to conceal something doesn't mean it was anything important. It could be something as mundane as a traditional family recipe they didn't want anybody else to have, or perhaps an explanation of something potentially embarrassing, like why one child in a family had blonde hair and blue eyes but all the other kids had black hair and brown eyes. All families have secrets, you know.'

'So that'll be a secret that stays secret?' Rossi suggested.

'Oh, I don't know about that. As I said, we've all got scheduled work to do here, but I have a colleague back in London who's always been fascinated by this kind of thing, so I've sent scans of the relevant documents over to the British Museum.'

'Who's your colleague?' Rossi asked. 'Just in case something interesting crops up.'

The English academic wrote down a name and the department at the British Museum where his colleague worked, and gave it to Rossi.

The name meant nothing to him, but he included it and details of the relevant department as part of his follow-up email to the CDF, with the obvious conclusion that there might now be multiple copies of the papers in existence if the researcher in London had decided to duplicate them while they were being worked on.

Rossi was unfamiliar with the English idiom, but this was definitely a case where it was far too late to close the stable door. That particular horse had already bolted.

Chapter 6

Languedoc, France

Present day

'Do you feel anything?'

Chris Bronson glanced at his former wife.

'I can feel lots of things,' he replied, waving his arm in an expansive manner to encompass the hills and valleys and fields that surrounded them, 'but mainly right now I can feel the wind in my face and a growing need for food and drink. I thought this was supposed to be a holiday, but all we've done today is clamber over rocks and climb hills.'

'It is a holiday,' Angela Lewis replied, 'but it's also kind of work, I suppose.'

'I knew it. So what are we looking for this time?'

'Nobody knows.'

'That should give us a head start, then. Why did you ask what I was feeling?'

Angela almost replicated his gesture to indicate the terrain on which they were standing.

'Some people claim that if you go to certain places where a huge loss of life has occurred, there can be a sensation in the surroundings that tells you something dreadful happened. Places like Culloden or Auschwitz or Treblinka. I just wondered if you felt anything like that in this place.'

Bronson looked around. Under a clear blue sky dotted with intermittent small white clouds, the land rose and fell in an irregular but pleasing manner, broken up here and there by steeper slopes that rose to craggy heights extending above the treeline. Behind them, one of these high points dominated the landscape. A mountainous peak, technically a volcanic pog, climbed above the trees and was itself topped with a ruined castle. They were surrounded by grass and trees, serenaded by birdsong and warmed by the sun. To him, the scene looked like the kind of raw material a landscape artist would revel in discovering and then translating into an image on canvas. But what he didn't get was any indication of some past tragedy.

'I don't feel anything like that,' he said. 'So what happened here?'

'Of course,' Angela said after a few seconds, 'we might not be in exactly the right place. That's something else nobody knows.' She pointed at the volcanic pog and the ruin that capped it. 'But you do know something about that, even if you don't recognise it. That's the castle of Montségur, or rather it isn't the castle of Montségur if you're talking about the Cathars.'

That apparently confused sentence made perfect sense to Bronson. He did know something – in fact he knew quite a lot – about the Cathars and Montségur, and he and Angela had discussed it before. And then he knew what had prompted her earlier question.

'That's Montségur?' he replied. 'I've never seen it in the flesh before. It looks different in photographs because they're usually taken closer to the ruins, or from the air. So you think we might be standing where they built the stockade or whatever the correct term is for a mass execution pyre?'

'This place is called the *Prat dels Cremats* in Occitan, or the *Champ des Brûlés* in French, which both mean "field of the burned". This might be the right place because it's fairly flat. But that's not where the Cathar monument is.' She pointed up the slope. 'That's further up the hill.'

They continued along the path until they reached a rough stone platform built on two levels, on which had been erected a solid stone stele, the sides tapering inwards from the base and ending in a circular shape at the top. There were symbols carved in the stone circle at the top and an inscription on the body of the monument. Bronson leaned forward for a closer look.

'It reads: "*Als catars als martirs del pur amor crestian 16 mars 1244*." That looks to me like Catalan,' he said.

'You're nearly right,' Angela replied. 'It's actually *lenga d'òc*, or Occitan, which was spoken in this area in the Middle Ages. But Occitan and Catalan are quite similar. It translates as "To the Cathars, the martyrs of pure Christian love", which is a pretty accurate summary of what happened here.'

'If it's as old as it looks, it's lasted well.'

'Not as well as you might think,' Angela told him. 'It might appear almost medieval because of the carvings and the language used, but this stone was only erected in 1960. But I don't believe this is where the executions would have taken place. I think they chose this spot for the memorial because it's right by the path that leads to Montségur and reminds people on their way to visit the castle about what happened here eight hundred-odd years ago.'

'I see what you mean. There's quite a slope where we're standing, and they would have needed level ground to burn the heretics. Do we know exactly how the executions were carried out?'

They continued striding along the path that led towards the ruined castle, frequently losing sight of their objective as they entered the woods.

'There are a few near-contemporary accounts,' Angela replied, 'but they're all a bit short on detail. Bearing in mind the number of Cathars executed, certainly more than two hundred and five and maybe as many as two hundred and forty, it would have been too time-consuming to prepare an individual stake for each victim, and until the Cathars came down from the castle, the Crusaders wouldn't have known how many heretics they were going to have to kill. What the accounts say is that they constructed a kind of wooden stockade and filled it with branches and kindling and maybe oil or some other accelerant, then closed the gates with the Cathars inside and fired it. Nobody knows for sure. But there is one point upon which all the accounts are in agreement.'

'That all the Cathars went willingly to their deaths?' Bronson suggested.

'Exactly. Death by being burnt alive must be one of the most painful ways to go, and we know from accounts of other executions that most victims had to be dragged to the stake and then chained to it, because rope would burn away too quickly. This method of execution was enshrined in the law of most countries in Europe as a punishment for heretics, and in the eyes of the Catholic Church the Cathars were perhaps the ultimate heretics. There were refinements that could increase their suffering or relieve it. In Britain it was common for the victim to be strangled at the stake before the fire was lit, but to compound the agony he could be doused in oil or made to wear a garment infused with sulphur. Even the type of wood used had an effect. Dry wood literally roasted the victims, while if the fire was made from damp wood the smoke would asphyxiate them. According to one account it had rained and snowed at Montségur the day before the executions, so it was probably the smoke that killed the Cathars.

'According to the accounts, they weren't forced into the stockade but walked there as a group singing hymns, as if they were entering a church rather than heading to an execution pyre. And why they did that is one of the great unanswered questions about the Cathars.'

'We do know they placed their faith in their souls and were unconcerned about what happened to their bodies.'

'That's a good way of putting it,' Angela agreed, 'and you're right. But walking into a fire is a somewhat extreme way of releasing your soul. And it's worth remembering that not a single Cathar actually had to die on 16 March 1244. On the first day of that month, when it was clear that the nine-month siege was effectively over and that Montségur would fall, a truce was negotiated with the besieging Catholic troops. All of them – the mercenary soldiers of the castle garrison, the non-Cathar servants and, most surprisingly, the Cathars themselves – would be allowed to walk out with their weapons and possessions at the end of the fifteen-day truce. The only stipulation was that the Cathars were to renounce their heretical beliefs in front of the Inquisitors waiting for them. Bearing in mind the utter brutality of the Church's two Albigensian Crusades, which had resulted in the deaths of perhaps one million Cathars in the Languedoc region of France over the previous thirty-five years, it was an astonishingly lenient offer. And the most bizarre aspect was that the Cathars rejected it.'

The climb was getting steadily steeper, some sections of it formed from rough steps supported by wooden planks. They stopped beside a small wooden structure on the right-hand side of the track to pay their admission fee to a bored-looking man sitting inside it, then continued onwards, moving more slowly as the slope increased.

'I've never understood that,' Bronson admitted.

'You're not the only one. And even more bizarre is what happened on 13 March, the spring equinox, which we know was important in Cathar beliefs. On that day, twenty-six soldiers and other non-Cathars in Montségur asked to be given the *consolamentum perfecti*, the sacrament Cathars took when they became *perfecti* or perfects. Doing that guaranteed they would die in the flames.'

Angela paused to catch her breath as the grey stone walls of the castle loomed above them, the structure looking almost as if it had grown out of the rock beneath it rather than having been constructed by man.

'And that,' Bronson said, also stopping for a brief respite, 'brings us to the last two or three or four mysteries of the Cathars of Montségur.'

'How many?' Angela asked.

'It all depends on how you count them. There's the reason why the truce was agreed so easily, why it was long enough to include the spring equinox and why the terms were so lenient. That's three separate but related questions right there. Then there's the story about the handful of Cathar *perfecti* who allegedly slipped out of the castle using ropes, probably down the steep northern flank of the mountain, carrying the treasure of the Cathar movement. Most accounts state that these men made their escape after the spring equinox celebrations had taken place and after the truce had been negotiated, which again doesn't make sense. The Crusaders had already agreed to let all the inhabitants of Montségur leave with their possessions, so why didn't they just wait until the siege ended and walk away with whatever they had? And then, finally, there's what happened when the Crusaders gained possession of the castle. Why did they then tear it to pieces? Obviously they were looking for something, but as far as I know, nobody has any idea what it was. Or if they found it.'

'I'm surprised you know all that,' she said as they stepped into the open ground bounded by the castle walls.

'I like mysteries,' Bronson said. 'Not least because it's part of my day job, being a copper.'

'And you're right. There are a lot of unanswered questions associated with this place. Some of the points you raised might be linked, like the lenient terms of the surrender, the escape of the small group of Cathars and the dismantling of the castle. If the leaders of the Crusaders believed the Cathars possessed something of huge value, they may have agreed to let them walk free on the assumption that when the siege ended they could simply seize it from them or recover it from the castle. That would explain why they tore the place to pieces when they couldn't find it because the Cathars who'd escaped had taken it with them.'

Bronson nodded. 'I know. I think most researchers have concluded that the treasure was either books or manuscripts sacred to the Cathars, or material wealth like gold and silver. One of the suggestions is that because the spring equinox was important to the movement, there would have been ceremonies performed on that day that might have used a particular relic or manuscript. That might also explain why the twenty-six non-Cathars decided to become *perfecti*. Perhaps the Cathars owned some religious relic that was so powerful they were prepared to embrace that religion in the certain knowledge that it was right and the massed Catholic forces outside the walls were wrong, even though they knew that to do so was also to embrace a certain and excruciatingly painful death. Realistically, only something like that could have persuaded so many of them to walk down the mountain and into the flames of the execution pyre.

'And I've read something about the wealth of the order as well. Although the Cathars took a vow of poverty and lived simple lives – many of them worked as itinerant manual labourers – the order as a whole was notably wealthy by the end of the twelfth century. Many of the *perfecti* were rich men who had donated property to the movement, and the ordinary members of the church, the *credentes*, frequently left what they owned to the order on their deaths. These assets were used by the Cathar movement to help people in need in the Languedoc. The Cathars of Montségur were almost the last of the line, so it would be reasonable to assume that most of their remaining wealth was in the castle with them. But the big problem, as I see it, is that however many *perfecti* managed to escape from the fortress, they couldn't have carried everything of value.'

'That's the crux of the question,' Angela agreed. 'Abseiling down from the top of this mountain means they could only have been carrying something reasonably small, or at least fairly light in weight. An object or objects of huge importance to them, rather than heavy boxes full of gold and silver.'

'So what were they carrying?'

'As I said before, I don't know. Nobody knows.'

Angela looked around the old walls of the fortress and shivered slightly.

'You cold?' Bronson asked.

'No,' she replied. 'I just had one of those moments where the age of a place gets to you. This site has been occupied for a long time. Roman currency and other stuff has been found here, so the legions probably built a fort on the mountain, and the name itself is derived from Latin. The Romans called it *mons securus*, meaning "the safe hill", and that became the two words *mont ségur* in Occitan, and then just Montségur. No trace of what the Romans built here remains.

'What we're standing in is referred to as Montségur III. The first castle constructed here in recorded history was Montségur I, and all we know about it is that by the end of the twelfth century it was in ruins. It was rebuilt early in the thirteenth century by Raymond de Perella, one of the lords of Montségur, a title he shared with his cousin Pierre-Roger de Mirepoix. That was Montségur II, and by 1233 it had become the *domicilium et caput* – the seat and head – of the Cathar religion. And we know what happened to it, of course. At the end of the siege, the royal troops dismantled it completely, but over the next three hundred years or so, it was rebuilt into what we're now standing in: a typical post-medieval French fortress.'

'It is kind of creepy up here,' Bronson said, 'even in the bright sunlight. You could believe almost anything might happen in a place like this, and the height of the pog makes it pretty much impregnable unless you could starve out the defenders. I can see why the Cathars chose to make this place their base.'

'Yes,' Angela replied, 'and it makes sense that whatever religious assets or treasures the order had accumulated would have been kept here, where they would be safe.'

Bronson looked quizzically at her. 'Right,' he said, 'so we're standing on the foundations of a Cathar castle inside the ruins of a later fortress talking about a treasure that may or may not have existed and that may or may not have been secreted here and that may or may not have been smuggled out of this place eight hundred years ago and that may or may not have been taken to an unknown destination that may or may not be in a different country and then hidden so well that nobody's ever discovered it. If you *are* hoping to find it, I'd say the trail – assuming there actually is one – has probably gone quite cold.'

'That doesn't sound very positive,' Angela responded, 'except in a very negative way.'

'Well, I assume that because of where we're standing, what you're looking for has something to do with the Cathars. And I know you well enough to also assume that we aren't ambling round the Languedoc just to enjoy the occasional bowl of cassoulet and take in the impressive views. We didn't visit this part of France and stumble on Montségur by accident. You have a reason for us being here, so why don't you tell me what you've found. Let me in on the secret.'

'It's not really a secret,' Angela replied, 'more a matter of identifying the dots and then trying to join them up. So let me just ask if you know anything about some of those dots.'

Bronson looked at her expectantly as she paused for a moment. 'Go on,' he said.

'It's more a kind of cluster of dots, I suppose, or rather several clusters of clusters, but let me try you with these. Do you know what links a plague of haemorrhoids, Auch Cathedral, the Knights Templar, this castle and the inheritance of Élisabeth d'Hautpoul?'

Chapter 7

Monteverde district, Rome, Italy

'How did this happen? And more importantly, what the hell are we going to do about it?'

The other two men seated at the small circular table outside the cafe bar near the crossroads of the Viale del Quattro Venti with the Via Francesco Bolognesi didn't respond immediately but stared at the man who had spoken, their eyes invisible behind the large-framed sunglasses they were all wearing. Strictly speaking, their eye-wear was unnecessary for their visual comfort, because the street was lined with apartment buildings and dotted with established trees that shaded them from the heat and glare of the sun. But they were wearing them because it would make their identification more difficult should anyone take an interest in them. They looked almost like clones, each having a typical Mediterranean complexion with black hair and tanned skin, and they were even dressed alike, wearing very dark and clearly expensive suits.

In the Via del Condotti or the Via dei Fori Imperiali or in a cafe in one of the numerous *piazzas* that characterised the centre of Rome they would have appeared quite at home, but in the grittier, more commercial and residential surroundings of Monteverde they looked out of place. The district was about a mile south of Vatican City and east of the Parco di Villa Pamphili, a crescent-shaped green space that encompassed the Lago de Belvedere, which was in truth more of a pond than a lake, despite its name.

Monteverde was not a part of Rome on any tourist itinerary, and nor was it an area that any of the men were familiar with. And that, really, was the point. This meeting, like any other meeting they would have in the future, would take place on neutral ground, in a part of Rome that none of them knew and where, more importantly, nobody would know them.

The cafe was tiny, with just two small round tables outside on the pavement, and again their choice of venue had been deliberate. If anyone had been sitting at the second table, they would have suspended their discussion and talked about mundane daily matters until that person had finished their drink and walked away. The cafe door was shut and they knew that what they said would be inaudible inside the building, and they stopped talking every time a pedestrian passed close to their table. As a final precaution, all three men were fluent in English and that was the language they were speaking, just in case anyone did manage to overhear them. Many Italians in Rome knew a few words of English, but it was not a language most of them spoke fluently.

In Rome, just as in Florence or Venice, the price of a cup of coffee depends on where you are and whether you're sitting or standing. If you're sitting at an outside table in a cafe with a front-line view of an important attraction, the price of an *espresso* can reach double figures, but if you're prepared to stand at the bar in a back-street establishment the same drink will only cost a euro or two. It all depends on whether you're there for the drink or the view. The three men in Monteverde weren't there for either, but as a bonus the *cappuccinos* served by the cafe were good and reasonably priced.

The silence that followed the two questions was somewhat strained. The man who'd posed them was the youngest of the three and in the view of his companions inclined to be somewhat blunt. On the other hand, if the operation turned to worms, he would most likely be the one directly in the firing line, and so a little bluntness wasn't entirely inappropriate.

The man who was clearly the most senior, or at least the eldest, of the three leaned forward and rested his elbows on the metal table, the other men unconsciously following suit.

'You're quite right, Marco,' he said quietly. 'Those are both completely valid questions, and I will try to give you definitive answers. But I think,' he went on, glancing at each of his companions, 'knowing what we do, we would all agree that if we don't take action of some sort, the potential consequences for the Church would be calamitous. If what we fear actually occurred, if this object were to be recovered and that fact made public, even without the disaster that would befall Jerusalem, I can see the Vatican ceasing to exist in a matter of months and the Catholic Church having no relevance anywhere in the world in less than a decade. And you don't need me to tell you that that would be a disaster, not just for those of us holding positions in the Mother Church, but also for more than one billion Catholics around the world who rely on our guidance, support and moral and religious authority. Without the eminence of the pope, the world would be facing a religious divide that could easily degenerate into open warfare on a scale that has not been seen since the days of the Crusades. And the biggest difference between the medieval period and now is that the death toll would be much, much higher because of the vastly superior weapons that nations possess today. By any standards it would be a catastrophe.'

The man paused, lifted his cup to his lips and took a sip of his third *cappuccino*. Behind his sunglasses and wearing his suit, he looked like a successful businessman, but if he had been wearing his normal working dress, the black and scarlet robes of a senior cardinal, he would have been immediately recognisable to almost anyone in the cafe or on the street. Like many people who normally wore a uniform, Cardinal Julius Caravaggio was acutely aware that it was the clothes that people saw first, identifying the rank or status of a person before they looked at the face to identify who was inside the outfit. Despite having been one of the most high-profile figures in the hierarchy of the Vatican for over a decade, Caravaggio had never been recognised while out on the streets of Rome wearing civilian clothes.

'To answer your questions,' he continued, 'you already know the nature of the object we are seeking.' Despite speaking what was to most Italians an incomprehensible foreign language and knowing they could not be overheard, none of the men would use the real name of the relic in their conversation, just in case. 'The Church has been looking for this relic for nearly two millennia, and as far as I can see, we are no closer to finding it now than when the search started.'

'From what I know of this matter,' Marco Ferrara said, 'it seems quite possible that the object may have been destroyed centuries before the Church began looking for it. In fact, before our religion even existed.'

Caravaggio nodded. 'You may well be right, but this is too important for us to take the risk.'

'So what changed? Why the sudden urgency?'

The cardinal glanced round as he considered his reply, and what he said wasn't what Ferrara had been expecting.

'Let me just say that the secrets of the confessional are not always as secret as most people would like to believe. In exceptional circumstances a Catholic priest may learn something so important and significant to the Church that he feels obliged to both record it and report it.'

Caravaggio noted the expression on Ferrara's face. 'Trust me, this is relevant,' he said. 'One such event occurred in a small French village in 1870, though it was a further two decades before the report reached the Vatican. That was because the priest decided to retain the information he had been given until the confessor had died. That was probably a mistake, certainly from our point of view, but at the same time a difficult decision to challenge. And, of course, we knew nothing about it until it was too late to question the confessor. It was not the first indication we had received, but it was an important pointer to where the search for the object could begin.'

That was news to Ferrara, and it showed.

'So why didn't the Church investigate it back then? Wouldn't that have made more sense?'

'We did try, but all we had to go on was the report from the priest, which was lacking in detail, and a suggested location of the records the man had been referring to. Those records, we understood, related to the location of the relic. And we discovered almost immediately that they were locked away and inaccessible to us. In the circumstances, the Church decided not to pursue the matter. To have done so would have created speculation about our motives, and that was the last thing we wanted.'

'The English have an expression about sleeping dogs,' the other man at the table said. He was calling himself Francesco, but that was not his given name.

'Exactly,' Caravaggio agreed.

'So what has happened now to alarm the higher echelons of the Church?' Ferrara asked, almost repeating his earlier question. 'Obviously something has changed.'

'Something has definitely changed. The Church has identified a variety of relics, papers and the like around the world that could, in the wrong hands, cause damage, in some cases even irreparable harm, to us and the religion we serve. In most cases, these potentially dangerous relics are held in religious institutions, museums and galleries and cause us little concern. But others lie completely outside our control, and those we watch as best we can. The papers I'm referring to are one of these uncontrolled threats, for want of a better expression.

'For well over two hundred years they had remained securely locked away in a notary's office in a small town in southern France, out of our reach but also out of the reach of everybody else. About two weeks ago, we discovered that the notary had retired and the office had been shut down. Our informant had no idea whether the relevant documents, which would have had no obvious significance today, were still held in the office or had been disposed of.' Caravaggio paused, his irritation clearly showing. 'Our informant had no way of investigating the matter further,' he went on, 'so we decided to send in a team. You know Luca Rossi, I believe?'

Ferrara nodded. 'I know him,' he agreed. 'He's undeniably efficient. I presume he recovered what you were seeking?'

'Not exactly, or not completely, and it was a bit messy. Because he didn't know exactly what he was looking for, or rather exactly where he should be looking for it, Rossi decided to wait until one of the notary's clerks was in the building. And since this mission was much too important to be compromised in any way, it was necessary for him to sanitise the scene.'

The cardinal's circumlocution was transparent, and Ferrara made the obvious deduction.

'You mean he killed the clerk?'

Caravaggio looked faintly shocked, but Ferrara guessed this was more likely to be because of his plain speaking than because of the act that had been carried out in the cardinal's name by the Italian enforcer.

'He really had no other option. Anyway, he discovered that the relevant papers hadn't been shredded or burnt, which was good news, but instead boxed up and sent to Paris by courier. He quickly established their destination in the city, but trying to gain access to them – they had been sent to a library at the Sorbonne – took longer. When he managed to get inside the building, posing as an Italian professor' – Ferrara had difficulty suppressing a smile at that, because he found it impossible to envisage Luca Rossi passing as an academic in any circumstances – 'what he found wasn't good news, and there was worse to follow. He couldn't steal or destroy the papers because of the security systems, and in any case they had already been scanned and copied onto the library's computer system. That was bad enough, but he also discovered that copies of the documents had been sent from Paris to London and had been given to somebody we have had dealings with in the past.'

Caravaggio looked keenly at Ferrara. 'Tell me, have you ever had contact with a person we usually refer to as David?'

Chapter 8

Languedoc, France

'You won't be entirely surprised to hear,' Bronson replied as they walked outside the walls of the castle to begin the descent back to the road, 'that I have no idea what you're talking about. I obviously know who the Knights Templar were. We've had dealings with them before, or rather with what they left behind, and we both know about their legacy and the heresy they embraced. I know exactly what a haemorrhoid is, though not, I'm pleased to say, from personal experience. But what links all that lot is a mystery to me. I'm sure you'll be happy to enlighten me.'

Angela nodded. 'I'll do my best,' she said, 'but this is very much a work in progress, and there are gaps that need filling in.'

'I'm all ears.'

'My work at the British Museum mainly involves ceramics, as you know, but I've got interests in other fields, so occasionally some object from a completely different discipline is sent to me.'

'You mean somebody gave you something you couldn't resist investigating?' Bronson asked. 'Is that it?'

'More or less, yes. In this case it was a collection of old French legal documents. We work closely with the Sorbonne in Paris, and in particular with what's known as the Maison de la Recherche. That's the part of the Sorbonne that studies history and geography and includes the Serpente Library. The library received a job lot of documents, none of which seemed particularly interesting or of historical importance, but one of my colleagues working at the Sorbonne spotted a few old French family names and a couple of locations in this part of the country – Montségur itself, and Rennes-le-Château – and sent me copies of the relevant documents. He thought I might like to see them because of our previous exploits and my interest in the Templars. And at one time the Templars were very big in this part of France.'

'You mentioned family names. What were they?'

'They probably won't mean anything to you. The two he mentioned were Aniort and Blanchefort.'

'You're half right,' Bronson said. 'I've never heard the name Aniort before, but a man named Bertrand de Blanchefort became the Grand Master of the Templars in the middle of the twelfth century, and he spent some time in this part of France.'

'Right. Now, the documents I was sent date from long after the time of the Templars and the Cathars. The earliest one was a kind of compendium that listed properties and assets alongside a somewhat rambling history of two local noble families, the Voisins and the Hautpouls. Neither was a name I knew, and both had links to the Aniorts, another family I'd never heard of. One obvious anomaly was a statement dated 1870 by a local notary explaining why he wouldn't surrender the Hautpoul family deeds that his firm had held ever since the eighteenth century, when Élisabeth d'Hautpoul had delivered them, despite the fact that the man making the request for the papers was the then head of the family, Pierre d'Hautpoul.'

'Good heavens. A lawyer not doing what his client wants him to do? How unusual is that?' Bronson asked, a grin on his face. 'I mean, whatever next? What was his excuse?'

'That's one of the peculiarities,' Angela replied. 'He said that to release the documents would be to create a serious act of folly – I'm paraphrasing, but that was the gist of it – which is unhelpfully non-specific. But there may actually have been some grounds for his decision, because of something Élisabeth d'Hautpoul claimed. To understand why this is significant, we need to go back to the purging of the Knights Templar in 1307. The Voisin family was closely associated with the Templars in southern France, and after Philip the Fair ordered the mass arrests of the knights, the Voisins did what they could to help them. According to some accounts, they assisted numerous members of the order to escape to Spain.

'Then in 1422 the Voisin and Hautpoul families were linked when Pierre-Raymond d'Hautpoul married Marcafava de Voisin. The Hautpouls were known as the Kings of the Black Mountain, but they'd fallen on hard times. In fact, they'd brought the hard times on themselves because they'd sided with the Cathars during the Albigensian Crusades, which was a dangerous thing to do, and the French king had reacted in the way you'd expect, confiscating Hautpoul properties and assets. Three centuries later, in 1732, there was another important marriage when François d'Hautpoul wed Marie de Négri d'Ablès. She was the last surviving member and the sole heiress of the Aniort family. Her dowry included all the remaining assets of the Aniorts. That's almost the end of the genealogy, which is dull but important. The couple produced three children, all daughters, and one of these was Mary-Anne Élisabeth d'Hautpoul.'

'The woman who gave the family documents to the notary,' Bronson put in, as much to prove he was paying attention as for any other reason.

The path was quite narrow in places and they paused to allow a small gaggle of tourists, some with cameras around their necks but most clutching smartphones, to continue walking up the slope. Bronson watched as the last of them disappeared from view among the trees, and noticed something that he'd almost been expecting to see.

'Correct,' Angela said, picking up the story again as they walked on. 'Élisabeth never married and there was something of a family dispute between her and her sisters about the Aniort inheritance. She was the keeper of the family files and refused to hand over any of them to her siblings. She said she believed it would be dangerous if she did that, but she didn't explain why. But she did make a slightly curious suggestion, proposing that the documents should be decoded and examined to confirm which were family records and which were not. The fairly obvious conclusion is that along with the usual property deeds and stuff there were documents that had nothing to do with the family, and by implication some of these were written in or contained a form of code.'

They'd covered about half the distance down the path from the castle, and Bronson was beginning to feel in more urgent need of liquid refreshment. And food as well.

'I'm sure this is all jolly interesting,' he said, 'and I presume you're now approaching the nub of the story, the bit that's dragged us across the Channel and down here to the northern slopes of the Pyrenees, but could I suggest we walk back to the *chambre d'hôte*, pick up the car and then find somewhere to have lunch.'

'That was my plan as well, actually,' Angela replied. 'There are restaurants in Montségur village and there's a small museum that's worth a visit. Anyway, the nub, as you put it, of this matter is the link between the Cathars, the fall of Montségur, and the Aniort family. As we know, a truce was negotiated between the defenders of the fortress and the besieging Catholic forces. The two principal negotiators on the Cathar side were the cousins Pierre-Roger de Mirepoix and Raymond de Perella. I mentioned them before. They were both lords of Montségur and Raymond de Perella had rebuilt the castle the Cathars were occupying. The negotiations were supervised and safeguarded by Raymond d'Aniort. He was then the lord of both Rennes-le-Château and Rennes-les-Bains, and one thing we know for certain about him and his three brothers is that they were implacably opposed to Simon de Montfort, the military leader of the king's forces besieging the castle. All of which raises a couple of obvious questions.'

'Yes. Why were the two noblemen who effectively owned the castle of Montségur representing the Cathars? They were the landlords, if you like, speaking for their heretical tenants, which is unusual in a situation like this. And why was a man whose sympathies obviously lay with the Cathars supervising negotiations between them and the besieging army?'

'Exactly. There are another couple of peculiarities about the Aniorts. Because of their alignment with the Cathar heretics, the Aniort brothers were excommunicated by the Church and, like the Hautpouls, their estates were confiscated. That's what you'd expect to happen, but their excommunications were lifted shortly after they'd been applied, and most of their properties were restored to them. Perhaps stranger still is that Raymond d'Aniort attended the royal court, where he was treated with respect and even deferred to by the king. This makes no sense in any context bar one. Raymond had allied himself with the Cathar heretics, which meant he had rebelled against the king, and he was arguably a heretic himself, a crime punishable by death in those days. About the only explanation that makes sense is that Raymond or the Aniort family had some power, or at least a measure of control, over the king. That could mean that they possessed something so powerful or significant that its very existence frightened both the king and his court.'

'We've encountered something like this before,' Bronson said, 'but a lot earlier. As far as I know, nobody has ever come up with an explanation for Pope Innocent II issuing the papal bull *Omne datum optimum*, which exempted the new Knights Templar order from all taxation and obedience to local laws. The most likely reason is that the Templars had found something in their excavations under the Temple Mount that was so threatening to the Church or the papacy that the pope had to do what they wanted. Maybe the Aniorts had something like that hidden away.'

'Maybe they did,' Angela agreed, 'and maybe it was even the same something. Back to Montségur and the Cathars, and the escape of the four *perfecti* who were supposedly carrying the treasure of the order. That's the number given to the inquisitors by some of the surviving heretics under interrogation. A contemporary report states that once the *perfecti* had made their escape and had safely reached level ground, a man called Escot de Belcaire lit a signal fire on the top of a nearby hill called Bidorta, and that the purpose of the fire was to let the besieged Cathars know that the operation had been completed.'

'And that's significant because...?'

'Because Escot de Belcaire was a special personal envoy of Raymond d'Aniort, so the Aniorts were not only protecting the interests and ensuring the safety of the Cathars during the negotiations, but were also actively working with the besieged garrison of Montségur.'

'I follow all that,' Bronson said, 'but there are a couple of questions that I think need answering. First, fascinating though all this medieval history is, I still have no real idea what we're doing here. And second, I was wondering if you've acquired a new boyfriend, because there's a young man about a hundred yards behind us right now, following us down the slope, who also followed us up to the castle from the car park. Don't turn round. Just take my word for it.'

'Rubbish,' Angela scoffed, glancing behind her despite what Bronson had said. 'He's just another tourist. This bit of France is a popular destination and Montségur is one of the main attractions.'

'Maybe. He was also sitting at an outside table at the cafe when we had lunch yesterday and eating at a corner table in the same dining room as us when we visited a different restaurant last night. So if he is just a tourist, it seems odd that his tastes match ours so closely.'

'This may be a tourist area,' Angela pointed out, 'but there aren't that many hotels and restaurants nearby. There aren't even many houses. That's one reason why we're staying in a local *chambre d'hôte* rather than some glittering five-star establishment stuffed full of receptionists and chefs. That may be why he's dogging our footsteps – if you're right about that – rather than spying on us or whatever you think he's doing.'

'Perhaps.' Bronson sounded unconvinced. 'But if we find him sitting at the next table when we have lunch, I'm going to assume it's enemy action. And I might have to do something about it.'

Chapter 9

Monteverde district, Rome, Italy

'David?' Marco Ferrara asked, looking at Julius Caravaggio. 'I don't think I've heard that name, or at least not in this context.'

'That's good,' the cardinal said. 'It's a random code name.'

'David' was not any part of the real name of the person to whom he was referring, and the use of the alias was to provide a layer – actually two layers – of obfuscation. The cardinal glanced round, reached into his jacket pocket and pulled out a small memory stick, which he passed to Ferrara.

'This contains what you need to know about David, as well as the other information we have obtained about this matter, including scans of the data that Luca Rossi recovered.'

'I understand that, but I still don't know why this person is important to us.'

It was Francesco who replied. 'David is important because copies of the documents we were hoping to recover from that notary's office in France have ended up on his desk. And that's definitely a problem, because of who he is and what he does.'

Cardinal Caravaggio leaned forward again and slightly lowered his voice.

'David is a professional in one of the archaeological disciplines,' he said, 'but more importantly he has a peculiar knack for finding lost relics that we would much rather stayed lost. He has no love for the Church and on several occasions has managed to thwart our efforts to perform certain operations. It is vital that this does not happen in this matter. As Rossi discovered, an English academic at the Sorbonne sent copies of these papers to him. I've discussed David's character with people in the Church who have dealt with him in the past, and we were certain that as soon as he'd looked at the papers he would take the next step. We were right. He immediately started to search for the object that we seek. Under no circumstances is he to be allowed to find it.'

'Obviously we have experts working on the data right now at the Palace of the Holy Office,' Francesco said, 'but we cannot guarantee that we can decipher the documents and work out where the trail leads before David does. That's why you're here, Marco. You're our insurance policy, a way of achieving the result we need.'

'And our goal is…?'

'To recover the object itself,' Francesco said, 'or obtain definitive and unambiguous proof that it has been destroyed. Either outcome would be sufficient for our needs.'

'I understand,' Ferrara said. 'So I presume you want me to follow David, and if he manages to locate the object you want me to take it from him?'

'That is precisely what we want.'

'I will follow your directions, of course, Your Em—' Ferrara broke off before finishing the formal address. 'I apologise,' he added quickly, glancing around to make sure nobody could have overheard what he'd said. 'I presume he is already under surveillance?'

'Of course, but with a small team and from a distance, just to monitor where he is and what he's doing.'

'I cannot do this by myself,' Ferrara said. 'Even watching one target all the time will require several people, so I assume I can recruit whatever additional men I need?'

'This will be your operation,' Caravaggio told him, which Ferrara immediately recognised as a subtle passing of the buck, 'so that will be your choice. Now, unless there's anything else, I think we've finished here. Visit my office first thing this afternoon and I will give you enough cash to begin the operation, as well as an unlimited credit card. And remember, this is an enormously sensitive matter for the Church, so there is to be nothing in writing. Don't retain receipts or any other form of paperwork and don't print any of the information you'll find on the memory stick. Make your progress reports to me, or to Francesco if I am unavailable. You can call us on the mobile numbers you'll find listed on the memory stick. The SIM cards in both those phones are unregistered and have been loaded with pre-paid credit, and I have a similar phone in my office for you.'

Ferrara nodded. It was exactly what he had expected once the scope of his mission became clear. So that really only left one thing to clarify.

'And David?' The question was obvious to him, and possibly the answer as well.

'His assistance will no longer be required,' Cardinal Caravaggio replied, the tone of his voice bleak and the unstated implication perfectly clear.

Ferrara nodded again.

Caravaggio glanced at both men and nodded as well. Then the three of them stood up and walked away from the cafe to make their way back to the Vatican by three different and well-separated routes.

Chapter 10

Jerusalem, Israel

Every intelligence service keeps an eye, or rather lots of pairs of eyes, on the activities of a target nation, organisation or individual. The methods used can include recruiting informers, covert and overt physical surveillance, and electronic surveillance, using signals intelligence or SIGINT. This originally meant listening in to enemy radio broadcasts but now has a much wider remit and concentrates on the busiest communication methods: telephone calls, emails, websites and social media posts.

An important technique employs trip wires of various sorts, ranging from detecting when a particular person visits a premises under surveillance or meets another suspect individual, to setting software alarms on the Internet to produce an alert when a specific website is visited, allowing the intelligence service to identify where the visitor is located through their IP – Internet Protocol – address.

Of course, it's not just intelligence services that do this. At opposite ends of the spectrum, manufacturing companies keep watch on their competitors and on the marketplace to keep aware of new trends and developments, and terrorist groups watch other terrorist groups and the forces of law and order to ensure their operations are successful.

The disparate collection of zealots who called themselves Zeru did not consider their group to be a terrorist organisation, though their avowed aim would have been described by most people as a terrorist act, though welcomed by many others. Zeru was a shortened form of Zerubbabel, an Old Testament figure named in the book of Zechariah, whose single most important accomplishment exactly mirrored Zeru's aims. Zeru was not an active organisation in the general sense of the word, because its members were waiting for one single event to take place. In their eyes this event would be a legitimate signal for them to fulfil their stated objective, an objective that they knew would certainly embroil the Middle East and potentially much of the rest of the world in a bitter religious conflict. But that did not concern the men – and they were all men – from Zeru to even the smallest degree. They believed the event they awaited would be an entirely unmistakable message from God, and therefore whatever blood was spilled or lives were lost, it would all be God's will.

They had no idea when this event was likely to occur, but they'd done extensive research, tracing a tortuous path through the centuries, picking up a clue here and a hint there to produce a timeline that provided possible answers to some of their questions. What it didn't do was supply the final piece of information they needed, because at some indeterminate date in the medieval period, the trail went cold. But what the men from Zeru *had* been able to establish was that if the clue still existed and was recorded anywhere, it would probably be found somewhere in the Languedoc region of southern France. And that was enough.

They'd done what an intelligence service faced with that kind of problem would probably have done. Not knowing exactly where to look, they'd set trip wires across the region in every place and using every medium they could access, covering local newspapers, radio stations and television programmes that dealt with the subject in even a peripheral sense. They didn't expect these sources to yield positive results, but they were still worth checking. They had concentrated most of their effort on the Internet, focusing on blogs run by people in the region, reasoning that these were likely to be the most productive since they had to fill the computer screens of their electronic visitors with fresh material on a daily or weekly basis. A small team of Zeru members monitored all the sites of interest from their base in Jerusalem, while newspapers, free papers, news sheets and the like were obtained by a couple of local sympathisers and any relevant material was scanned and emailed to Jerusalem to be scrutinised.

In the event, this allocation of their priorities turned out to be correct. One website, mainly used by its blogging owner as a public display for photographs he'd taken of local attractions plus snippets of interesting news from the region, reported a seemingly senseless crime.

An office in Limoux belonging to a former notary, a man who'd retired prematurely due to ill health, had been broken into late one afternoon. Nobody had seen anyone, but because of what the *gendarmes* found when they entered the building after being called by a resident who'd spotted the splintered door, the assumption was that at least two people had been involved in the crime.

The body of a man named René Maréchal, a clerk who'd worked for the notary for some two decades, had been found inside the office. His death had been termed *une exécution* by an unidentified police source, though the method of his killing had not been made public. There appeared to be no obvious motive for the break-in: there were four reasonably expensive computers in the office, plus scanners, printers, a high-speed router and even two mobile phones, and they had all been left untouched.

So robbery clearly hadn't been the reason for the crime, but Maréchal had been deliberately killed, hence the conclusion by the *gendarmes*. Local enquiries revealed no apparent reason why he had been murdered. He owed no significant sums of money to anyone, he had no connections to organised crime, or indeed to any form of crime, and had no known criminal associates. In fact, he was almost a cipher because so few people in Limoux, either near the office or in the vicinity of Maréchal's home on the outskirts of the town, appeared to know him well.

The one thing missing from the office was the document ledger that one of the other retired members of the notary's staff claimed should have been there. But stealing a book that served no purpose other than to record the arrival and disposition of legal papers and other documents handled by the notary made no sense. As the former member of staff had explained to the local newspaper, the information recorded in the handwritten ledger was duplicated on the local area network, the office computer system. The notary had been old-fashioned, however, and insisted on a paper record too, because he fundamentally distrusted computers.

According to information the blogger had obtained, the *gendarmes* had summoned an IT specialist, who had sat in front of one of the office computers and read every single entry in the file containing the ledger's data. The process took almost a whole day, and at the end of it he'd found nothing significant. Certainly nothing that appeared to provide even the smallest possible sliver of a motive for murder.

So it didn't look as if the ledger had been taken because of a piece of information it contained. And nor, the former clerk maintained, was the book itself of any value. Almost identical ledgers were readily available from most commercial stationers.

The *gendarmes* had apparently given a collective Gallic shrug, mentally marked the case as unsolved and pencilled it in as a cold case until such time as some villain turned up at a *gendarmerie* and admitted that he'd done it. Nobody seemed to think that was a very likely outcome.

The office, the blogger stated, remained a crime scene pending a full forensic examination. The broken door had been fixed and bright yellow tape was secured across the door and windows bearing the legend *BARRAGE DE POLICE – NE PAS TRAVERSER* in heavy black lettering. He included a couple of pictures of the office and the tape in his blog.

And that was all the Zeru people needed. It was in about the right location, and it was exactly the kind of anomalous event they had been looking for.

Chapter 11

Languedoc, France

'So now you think he was just a tourist?' Angela asked.

Contrary to Bronson's expectation, the youngish-looking man who had followed them all the way up to Montségur, and then all the way down, had disappeared from view when they had returned to the *chambre d'hôte* to retrieve the hire car, and he had not been in evidence when they visited one of the restaurants in the village below the castle for dinner.

'I don't know. Maybe. Or perhaps he was watching us from a distance and just followed us to the restaurant and then back to the *chambre d'hôte* but kept out of sight. Maybe he's somewhere behind us now. There are about half a dozen cars following us, quite well spread out. Or maybe he's not. I don't know,' Bronson said again. 'But I do have the distinct feeling that we're being watched, and not just by the idiot driver behind us.'

He glanced thoughtfully at the Peugeot's interior mirror. The closest car following them was, as was usual in France in Bronson's experience, holding position about three feet behind the rear bumper of his hire car, apparently desperate to overtake on the narrow twisting road, but the driver looked very clearly female. Either that or he was a small, slim male undergoing a serious gender identity crisis, if the cascade of blonde curls outlining a tanned face dominated by bright red lips was any indication. But his or her irritation was also obvious.

'I do know that he's not right behind us,' Bronson said, 'unless he's lost a lot of height and weight and changed his sex.

And taken an angry pill. But we've no idea who we should be looking for, because mounting surveillance isn't something that can be done by just one person. You need a team of something like six people as a minimum, typically two in a car, one on a motorbike and three on foot to cover all the possibilities. Plus you need another team the same size, with different vehicles, to take over from the first team at some point, and maybe a third team as well. There might be half a dozen people in the cars behind us, all part of the same surveillance team.'

'So you don't know?'

'That *is* what I said,' Bronson replied, 'but the real question is *why* anyone would want to tail us. You still haven't really explained why what we're doing over here would attract attention.'

'Ah,' Angela said. 'There could be some competition, shall we say.'

'By all means say that. Ideally you can then tell me precisely what you mean and what you think is going on. And the other thing you could do is explain where we're supposed to be going right now, because all you've told me is to drive to Toulouse, which is what I'm doing.'

'OK,' Angela said. 'Well, the first thing is that we're not actually going *to* Toulouse. We're going *through* Toulouse, or rather around it on the local ring road, the *périphérique*, and then continuing out to the west.'

'Let me guess,' Bronson said. 'We're heading for Auch. That's west of Toulouse and you mentioned the cathedral there.'

'Exactly. I also mentioned several other things, including a plague of haemorrhoids, and they're connected – indirectly, I'll admit – to Auch Cathedral. The reason we're in France is because of those documents I received from the Sorbonne. I can't read one of them at all, and I'll tell you about that later. But I recognised that another of them was written in Occitan, and I had it translated for me. One of the great things about working in the British Museum is the number of experts we have in all sorts of disciplines, including linguistics. Anyway, in that document, which was probably part of a medieval journal, there was a reference to the greatest of all the lost treasures of antiquity. In Occitan it was called the *Arc de l'Alianca*, and the French refer to it as the *Arche de l'Alliance*.'

'The Ark of the Covenant?' Bronson replied. 'Do you know, I kind of guessed it was something like that, after our brief visit to Axum last year when we didn't find it where the entire population of Ethiopia believes it has been kept for centuries. You *are* serious about this?'

'I'm perfectly serious. The document stated that the Ark was the Cathar treasure the four *perfecti* smuggled out of Montségur just before the end of the siege. And that makes some sense out of what happened on the mountain. The non-Cathars voluntarily took the *consolamentum perfecti*, knowing that they would die in the flames a few days later. That means they must have been given an utterly convincing religious reason to do so. And the sight of the Ark of the Covenant might have been enough.

'Think about it. It was a holy relic that had been created in accordance with the word of God one and a half millennia before Christianity had even been invented. It had been constructed to God's own specifications to hold the decalogue, the stone tablets listing the Ten Commandments, which were God's instructions to humanity. It was also supposed to be a device for talking to God and for God to make his own voice heard. I'd say that was a pretty impressive religious relic, wouldn't you? Something with infinitely more authority than some local priest standing in a pulpit and spouting the usual platitudes.'

Bronson glanced at her. 'Do you believe all that stuff? Moses climbing up Mount Sinai to collect the Commandments and then constructing the Ark to carry the tablets? And God addressing the faithful from the gold lid of a wooden box?'

Angela grinned at him. 'What you and I believe or don't believe is irrelevant. It's what the Cathars believed that matters.

And just as a point of order, according to the Hebrew Bible it wasn't Moses who constructed the Ark but a man named Bezalel, assisted by another chap called Oholiab and a team of craftsmen, all working under Moses's direction and to God's design. But to answer your question, no, I don't believe any of it, from the existence of God downwards. I'm a scientist and I'm rational, and there's no room for any kind of supreme being in my universe. You can trace the origins of the Ten Commandments right back into Hittite and Mesopotamian customs and laws. They were nothing more than rules of conduct that most civilised people would accept as being a fairly normal and moral way to live.

'But to go back to the Cathars. They were gnostics, and they didn't want, need or accept the hierarchy of the Church. They believed that if you wanted to pray to God, that was what you did: you knelt down and prayed to God. There was no need for a priest or a church, and certainly not some old man elected by a bunch of other old men and sitting on a throne in the Vatican, a long, long way from the country where the Christian religion began. The Ark was supposed to allow God to communicate with you and the other way round, so as far as the Cathars were concerned, it was the ultimate confirmation of their belief system. It was so much more than a wooden box covered in gold. It was an object that negated the entire apparatus and hierarchy and endemic corruption of the Catholic Church by its very existence. At that time and in that religious climate, I can absolutely see how it would have inspired utter devotion and persuaded people to convert to the religious order that possessed it, irrespective of the consequences.'

'I get all that,' Bronson said, still keeping a wary eye on the woman in the car behind him and wondering on which blind bend she'd next try and overtake, 'but you still haven't told me why we're here. There are enough written references to the Ark of the Covenant throughout history to suggest it was a real object, and I can believe that it was the treasure that the Cathars smuggled out of Montségur in 1244, but so what? How do you know if it still exists? It was basically only a wooden box. And if it is still in one piece, do you know where it is now, or how to find it?'

Angela smiled at him. 'Not exactly,' she said, 'but one of the documents that Élisabeth d'Hautpoul refused to hand over to her siblings and entrusted to her local notary is both handwritten and encoded. That almost certainly means it's not a family document, because there would be no point in enciphering something like that. More interestingly, the text has a title, of a sort: the three letters A, D and A, each followed by a full stop, which suggests they might be abbreviations. One of the other papers refers to the A. D. A. *quête* or quest, and to the *piste d'indice*, which I'm sure you know is nothing to do with skiing.'

'It's not,' Bronson confirmed. 'It means something like a trail of clues, that kind of thing, which would link up with the idea of a quest, I suppose.'

'And there's something else,' Angela added. 'At the bottom of the page of encrypted text is a rough sketch showing an oblong shape like a box.'

'Which could be anything,' Bronson pointed out. 'Not necessarily the Ark.'

'You're right, except for one other detail. This box – assuming that's what it represents – has a lid. All the descriptions of the Ark state that the lid was gold, probably solid gold – unlike the box itself, which was made of acacia wood and then covered with gold plating – and was decorated with two cherubim. The lid was known as the *kapporet*, which is usually translated as "mercy seat". There are no more detailed descriptions than this, so it's not clear if the two cherubim were depicted as standing or kneeling, which would be more respectful.'

'Remind me,' Bronson interrupted. 'What's a cherubim?'

'It's not an "it" but a "they", to be pedantic,' Angela replied. 'The singular form is "cherub", and according to biblical sources like the Book of Ezekiel, they're tetramorphs, meaning they incorporate four different elements or characteristics. Traditionally they were shown with four faces, those of a lion, an ox, an eagle and a man, representing, respectively, wild animals, domestic animals, birds and the human race, and they also had two pairs of wings and, usually, cloven hooves like a bull. They were really important entities. In both Abrahamic and Islamic literature, they're angels of the highest rank, the closest to God. That's presumably why they were chosen to ornament the cover of the Ark, so that God would appear or speak with a cherub on either side of him.'

'I thought a cherub was supposed to be a plump naked boy with wings,' Bronson said. 'Not these four-faced characters ambling about on bull's legs.'

Angela grinned. 'Another example of the way things change. In ancient classical art, there was a being called a *putto*, a naked winged male child, which represented some aspects of the profane. In the Baroque period, the *putto* changed and became a kind of representative of the omnipresent God, a symbol meaning that God was there even if you couldn't see him. And later in Western Christianity this figure became known as a cherub. God was rarely depicted, but the angels who served him were, so cherubim became quite common in Western religious art, with a completely different meaning to their original function.'

'You were talking about the drawing?' Bronson reminded her. 'The lid?'

'Oh, yes. So the lid of the Ark, the *kapporet*, had two cherubim on it. Most depictions of the Ark show them facing each other and kneeling, their wings extended forwards, almost meeting. If you saw the Indiana Jones film, the way the Ark is shown in that is the most common representation. Those with standing cherubim are rarer. Anyway, the sketch that I've got shows the oblong that could be a box with two lumps on the lid that look like this.'

Angela clenched her fists, pressed her hands together at the knuckles, then raised and crooked her thumbs to point at each other. It was surprisingly graphic, and Bronson knew immediately what she meant.

'I get it. Two cherubim kneeling down, facing each other, with their wings outstretched. But is that what it really shows, or are you seeing more than is there?'

She nodded. 'It's not a big drawing and it's not that clear, but that's what it looks like to me. And there's also the A. D. A. title and the encrypted text.'

'So,' Bronson said, 'what are we doing in this part of France? Do you think the Ark is hidden somewhere here?'

'No. I think it *was* here, but it's long gone now.'

The road straightened for a few dozen yards and the angry-looking woman in the Renault behind them swept past with a roar of her engine and a blast from her horn, presumably intended to let Bronson know that he was driving much too slowly, even though he was cruising along at pretty much the legal limit.

'I'd forgotten that speed limits over here were more of a target than a restriction,' he said, as another French-plated car moved into position a few feet behind them and again far too close for comfort. Or safety. 'So this is the start of the hunt?'

Angela shook her head. 'Yes and no, really. Yes, it's the start of our search but not where the Ark started its journey. I think it travelled a long way to get here, and then continued its journey to somewhere else, somewhere very different. But I wanted to see Montségur and I wanted you to see it as well. And I needed to explain what information I had so you could decide if we were just wasting our time even starting the search.'

'You could have told me all this earlier,' Bronson complained.

'I wasn't sure you'd believe me without getting a feel for the place.'

'I'm not sure I believe you now, but I'm prepared to give it a go. You've obviously got some idea about where we should be looking. What does the encrypted document say?'

'I've no idea. I haven't managed to crack the coding yet. I thought you could give me a hand.'

Bronson was silent for a few seconds, mulling over what Angela had just said.

'So all you've actually got is an idea, a small, indistinct sketch of something that might be the Ark and a sheet of paper covered in writing that you can't read.'

'Yes,' she replied, nodding happily. 'But everybody has to start somewhere.'

'Quite,' Bronson replied.

Chapter 12

The same day they received the information about the Limoux notary, a three-man team from Zeru flew direct from Jerusalem's Ben Gurion Airport to Blagnac at Toulouse, arriving just before half past ten in the evening. They picked up a pre-booked hire car and reached Limoux at around one in the morning.

They parked their hired Renault about a hundred yards from the office on the Rue des Remparts and made their way on foot to the building, all of them pulling on latex gloves as they walked. One of the three was an expert locksmith, but in the event his services were barely needed. The lock securing the side door of the office was a standard Yale type, which surrendered in less than ten seconds to a slim torsion wrench and a snap gun, a device designed to nudge the pins out of the keyway.

'You could have done this yourselves,' Aaron Chason said quietly as the door swung open and they dodged below the police tape and stepped inside. He was a short, dark man with a heavy black beard atop a stocky body that looked as if it would develop a hunch in a few years. 'All you needed to get inside was ten seconds with a credit card.'

'Enough. We didn't know what we were facing. You were our insurance policy.'

The speaker was the leader of the group, Josef Gellerman. Tall, slim and clean-shaven, with light brown hair and blue eyes, he looked anything but Israeli; more Scandinavian than anything else. It was a useful natural camouflage.

'Watch the road outside while we work,' he ordered, gently pushing the door closed until the lock clicked shut.

Chason nodded and moved over to the window that offered the best view both ways along the Rue des Remparts.

The third member of the group, Lemuel Dayan, using a small pocket torch with the lens taped to reduce the amount of light it emitted, had already sat down in front of one of the office computers and switched it on. Now he waited for the operating system to load.

'Is there a password?' Gellerman asked.

'Probably,' Dayan replied. Like Chason, he was a short, compact man with a dark Mediterranean complexion and a beard. The pair could almost have been related, except that Dayan favoured more casual clothes than Chason's trademark black suits. 'But it's worth trying this first. The clerk might have removed the password to let the police inspect the computer. If this is the one they used, I mean.'

The password prompt appeared a few seconds later.

'He didn't, but no problem,' Dayan said and powered the system down.

He took a USB thumb drive from his pocket and inserted it into the system unit, then switched on the computer again. As soon as the screen came alive, he began repeatedly pressing the F12 key to enter the boot menu. When it appeared, he changed the boot sequence so that the USB drive would be accessed first, then pressed the enter key. While he waited for the program on the thumb drive to load, he took a slim but high-capacity external hard disk from his pocket and connected it to another USB socket.

'I'm in,' he said moments later. 'Will the file be called "*Registre*" or something else?'

Gellerman thought for a moment. 'Probably, or perhaps "*Le Grand Livre*".'

Dayan scanned the directory structure, finding both Word and Excel files named '*Registre*'. He opened them so they could check the contents, and then started copying them to his external drive.

'How long?' Gellerman asked, looking at the screen.

'Five minutes, maybe. They're big files.'

'While it's running, take a look around the hard disk and see if there's anything else that might help us.'

Minutes later, the copying process was complete. The three men slipped out of the office, got back in their hire car and drove out of Limoux, heading towards Toulouse. But their destination wasn't the airport.

They didn't know if they'd been under surveillance during their journey, but their passport details and tickets were now on record with the French authorities, and if they flew back to Jerusalem less than twenty-four hours after arriving in France, that was certain to raise official eyebrows at the very least. So Gellerman had a different plan.

Just before four in the morning, the men rented three rooms at a hotel near L'Union, to the north of Toulouse. It was a fairly new automated budget establishment, part of a chain, that offered free parking and access to the building at any time using a credit card. They separated at the door, found their rooms, washed and climbed into bed.

They planned to fly out two days later, and spend the intervening time in France using Dayan's laptop to analyse the data they'd copied, trying to identify whatever it was that the killers of René Maréchal had been looking for. When they found it, Josef Gellerman hoped their next flight out of Blagnac airport would not be back to Israel but to somewhere closer to their final objective.

The trail they were following was faint and cold, but it was a long way from being dead.

Chapter 13

Auch, Gascony, France

'The satnav says the cathedral is to the east,' Bronson pointed out, 'so are you sure you want me to go straight on?'

'Yes,' Angela said crisply. 'We need a place to stay, and there's a halfway decent hotel near the Place de la Libération in front of us. Find somewhere to park, then we'll get a room and visit the cathedral.'

Not for the first time, Bronson got the impression that he was just a passenger or perhaps an employee on one of his former wife's adventures. At least on this occasion he was in a civilised part of the world. The last time they had been involved in a quest together they had started by being chased across the deserts of Iraq by lorryloads of heavily armed terrorists, and ended up in an obscure Templar church facing even more armed men.

The hotel didn't have a dedicated car park, but there were several spaces in the Rue d'Etigny, which ran right past it, and within half an hour they had booked in, taken their bags up to a double room on the first floor and were back outside walking past a row of neatly trimmed trees towards the Cathedral of Sainte-Marie. The branches had been cut into squared-off oblong shapes to provide shade in the summer and made an interesting backdrop to the outside tables at a restaurant fronting the Place de la Libération. The cathedral, a huge building with twin towers facing the Place de la République, dominated the view as they approached.

The ornate front of the building consisted of a portico formed by three stone arches, each guarded by a set of double metal gates surmounted by a gold-coloured scrollwork frame. The central frame was the largest of the three, the decoration terminating in a cross of Lorraine on top of a crown, and with a form of heraldic symbol in an oval shield below that.

As they approached the entrance, Bronson stopped and pointed up at the scrollwork.

'I recognise the cross of Lorraine, obviously,' he said. 'That was the symbol of the Free French in the Second World War. But what's the device in the shield mean?'

'Not a clue,' Angela replied. 'Maybe it's the coat of arms of Auch, or even something to do with d'Artagnan. They're big on him down here; there's a statue of him a few streets away. But the crown might be a clue. There are a dozen or so different styles of French crown, ranging from a baron up to the *dauphin*, the heir apparent, and the king. None of them have much relevance today, for obvious reasons, but that crown looks to me like that of a *duc*, a duke, so perhaps the coat of arms is for some local nobleman.'

The two metal gates in front of them were standing open, as was the door of the cathedral beyond. They stepped inside the building, the almost refrigerator chill of the interior a welcome shock after the heat in the street outside. They waited a few moments until their eyes had adjusted to the relative gloom, and then Angela confidently led the way.

'This is what I wanted you to see,' she said, and stopped in front of an impressive bas-relief image.

The gold-coloured carving was an impressive work of art, though not historically accurate. Almost every text that described the Ark of the Covenant emphasised the fact that it always had to be shielded from view. Whenever it was being moved, it was completely shrouded in a cloth so that nobody, not even the priests carrying it, could see it. This was, at least according to some texts, because the Ark had such enormous power that anyone who looked at it could be struck dead by the sight. But the bas-relief in the Cathedral of Sainte-Marie showed the Ark being carried by four priests with the relic in full view.

'Forget the fact that it should be shrouded,' Angela said, pointing. 'What you're looking at is the classical representation of the lid, the two cherubim facing each other and kneeling with their wings extended forwards. And the Ark itself, the box, is really quite plain and simple. No fancy scrollwork or carvings, just the metal loops either side for the poles to go through.'

Bronson stared at the carving for a few seconds, then started to smile.

'What?' Angela demanded.

'Have you looked closely at the priest on the right?' he asked. 'Give him a pair of cowboy boots, take away the monk's habit and stick a sequinned jacket on him, and he could pass for Elvis Presley's double. He's even got the same haircut.'

Angela peered at the priest Bronson was staring at, and almost reluctantly nodded. The carved image did look incredibly familiar, and the hairstyle – somewhat unruly, worn long at the back and with a quiff at the front – appeared to be anything but ancient. 'Okay. I see what you mean. Especially about the hair. And he's definitely got Presley's nose and chin.' She laughed shortly. 'But I didn't bring you here so you could mock a monk, or even a carving of a monk.'

'I wasn't mocking,' Bronson protested, 'and I like Elvis's music. So are we here just so I can see what the Ark of the Covenant looked like?'

'Yes, and to show you how it would normally be carried by four people using wooden poles thrust through the loops on the sides of the box. It's not very big but it would have been heavy if the stone tablets were inside, and very heavy if the lid really was solid gold. And to go back to the legends surrounding Montségur, it would have been possible for four men to abseil down the mountain carrying something that size, which gives credence to the story.'

Bronson looked at the bas-relief carving again and nodded.

'We already knew the measurements of the box,' he said, 'but seeing it like this does make it seem more tangible. It gives us a better idea of what we're looking for, so all we need now is a clue to where it might be.'

'Exactly. So let's walk back to the hotel and crack the coding on that encrypted text. If you think your caffeine level has dropped a bit low, we can stop at the cafe in the square to get you a top-up.'

'It's a deal,' Bronson replied, and led the way to the door of the cathedral.

Chapter 14

Paris, France

Modern data systems, directories, encyclopaedias and the like can provide instant answers to almost every question, thanks to the magic of the Internet. These days you can find out nearly everything you need sitting in a cafe and using a smartphone.

Josef Gellerman had studied the list of entries in the register Dayan had downloaded from the hard drive of the Limoux notary's computer. Most of the data could be dismissed without even a second look, and they were in any case concentrating on the older papers.

In the end, they had about sixty sets of documents that looked promising, and Lemuel Dayan took up residence with his laptop in a cyber-cafe near the hotel they'd booked and started researching. Both he and Gellerman were good at spotting links and making connections, and by the end of the first day they'd eliminated all but eight of the names. By noon on the second day the only name left was Hautpoul, because by then Dayan had traced that family's connections back through the Aniorts and Blancheforts and all the way to the Voisins, and had established their links to the Cathars of Montségur.

'It must be the Hautpoul papers,' he had said.

Gellerman had nodded, looking over his shoulder at the screen of the laptop.

'So where are they now?' he'd asked.

'That's the tricky bit. The register isn't complete. It just states they were sent to Paris by courier for research, and that probably means they ended up in a library somewhere, a place where academics would have the opportunity to study them. Either that or a university or college, but I think a library's more likely. And I've already checked. There are fifty-seven libraries in Paris, which isn't good news.'

To Dayan's surprise, Gellerman hadn't seemed disturbed by this fact.

'That's less of a problem than you might think,' he'd replied. 'Go through the list and eliminate the obvious non-starters – libraries that concentrate on music or some other discipline – and get me the email addresses of the rest. I'll talk to one of my contacts in Tel Aviv and ask him to help us out here.'

Getting the result hadn't taken anything like as long as they had expected. By the time Dayan had produced a list of the libraries, Gellerman's contact had provided him with an email address belonging to an Israeli academic. He was a man sympathetic to the cause Zeru espoused and would forward whatever responses he received to Dayan's email account.

It hadn't been difficult for Gellerman to compose a suitable message. The information they needed was neither sensitive nor confidential, so he represented himself as an Israeli historian researching aspects of life in southern France in the medieval and post-medieval periods and searching for any sources relating to the Voisin, Aniort, Blanchefort and especially Hautpoul families. The fifth reply he was sent was from the Bibliothèque Serpente. The responder stated that they had general information about the first three names and limited numbers of documents, but that they had recently been sent a fairly complete archive of documents relating to the Hautpoul family.

Eight hours later, the three members of the Zeru team were in Paris, and had booked rooms in a hotel to the west of the city centre in the Saint-Cloud district. The following morning, Gellerman took the Métro and walked into the Serpente library.

He found somebody who knew about the emailed request from the Israeli academic and minutes later was sitting at a wide table in a reading room with the documents spread out in front of him. But it was soon clear that the information he had been expecting to find wasn't there. He was looking at the kind of typical documents any large family would accumulate over the years, a mixture of deeds, grants, mortgages, wills and transfers. That was all.

'Anything of interest?' an obviously English voice asked from behind him, and Gellerman turned around in his chair to look at him.

'Not much,' he replied in the same language. 'I was hoping for something more than deeds and conveyances. Most of this part of the Hautpoul family history I already knew from other sources.'

'My name's George Anderson,' the Englishman said, extending his hand. 'I'm just visiting from London for a few months.'

'Israel Mahler,' Gellerman said smoothly, the name of one of several aliases in his portfolio of disguises. 'From Tel Aviv University.'

'Funnily enough, you're the second visitor in the last few days who's been interested in the Hautpouls. I didn't think that particular family would have attracted so much interest, and the papers are really pretty dull. Apart from the encrypted page, that is.'

'Encrypted page,' Gellerman echoed. 'What encrypted page?'

'Didn't you find it?' Anderson asked, starting to root through the documents on the table.

A couple of minutes later, he stood back, a puzzled expression on his face.

'How odd. I don't think anyone else here is looking at it, because we keep all the pages in the folio together.' He stared at the papers in front of him for a few seconds. 'I don't like to cast aspersions,' he said, 'but it looks as if the previous viewer of this material may have borrowed that document, which he certainly shouldn't have done.'

'Who was he?' Gellerman asked.

'A visiting professor from Italy, from the Università di Bologna, if I remember correctly, but I can't recall his name.'

'Don't you make copies of all the documents you receive?' Gellerman asked.

Anderson looked at him and made an instant decision.

'Yes, that is the library's policy,' he admitted, 'but there's always a queue of documents waiting to be put through the scanner, and these papers are so new we haven't done it yet. What a pity. Do you think that page might have been important to your research?'

'I have no idea,' Gellerman said tightly, 'because I didn't get to see it.'

–

A few minutes after Israel Mahler had left the library empty-handed, George Anderson sat down at one of the terminals and spent a few minutes doing some research of his own, research that was nothing to do with his work at the Sorbonne.

Then he used his own laptop to compose an email, marked it high importance, and sent it.

Chapter 15

Auch, Gascony, France

In the hotel room, Angela produced the copy of the page of encrypted text that she'd been sent by George Anderson and handed it to Bronson.

It was exactly as she'd described, written in what looked like an educated hand with the 'A. D. A.' heading at the top of the page. The text consisted of about forty lines of apparently random characters printed without any breaks or punctuation marks, and at the bottom was a small rough sketch showing what looked like a box with a lid.

'You're right,' Bronson agreed. 'This does look like the Ark of the Covenant, and it's difficult to think of any other object it could be intended to represent. So how far have you got with deciphering the text? What have you tried?'

'I did some research and started with single substitution ciphers, Caesar and Atbash, just replacing one letter of the alphabet with another. That method of encryption always produces gibberish, which is what the text on that page looks like, so I thought it was a good place to begin.'

'Virtually all encryption methods produce gibberish,' Bronson pointed out, 'but I take your point.'

'The other thing about single substitution ciphers is that because each plaintext letter is always replaced by the same ciphertext letter, you can run frequency analysis on the text. In the English language the six commonest letters, in order, are E T A O I N, but as everything else George sent me was in

French, and the origin of the documents was France, I assumed the encrypted text was also written in French, or just maybe in Occitan.'

'Can't fault that logic,' Bronson said.

'Thank you. So in French, and ignoring accented characters, the six commonest letters are E A S T I R, a completely different sequence to English. I assumed that whatever letter appeared most often would be the ciphertext for E, the second commonest would represent A, and so on for the rest of the alphabet. Well, it wasn't. Doing the substitution – which took hours, by the way – just turned that piece of gibberish' – she pointed at the sheet Bronson was holding – 'into a different kind of gibberish.'

'So it's not a single substitution cipher if you're right and the plaintext is French. What else did you try?'

'I did the same check with Latin, but that didn't look any better. That's as far as I got. I stopped working on it, gave you a call and here we are. Over to you.'

Bronson shook his head. 'Cryptography really isn't my strong suit. I've done a bit of research, but I'm not an expert.'

'Nor,' Angela pointed out, 'was the person who produced that page of encrypted text. Or at least I don't think he was.'

'Looks can be deceiving,' Bronson said, 'and some of those early ciphers are virtually unbreakable even today because you need to know the keywords used to encrypt them. Polyalphabetic substitution ciphers can prove very difficult to crack.'

'I thought frequency analysis would crack a substitution cipher?'

'It can, but the crucial word in that sentence is the one you didn't include: single. So if it was a basic Caesar cipher with the ciphertext shifted three places to the right, for example, the plaintext letter B would be replaced by the ciphertext letter E, and so on. But with a polyalphabetic substitution cipher, multiple ciphertexts would be used, so a different letter would be generated each time. And the longer the keyword, the more alphabets would be used to encrypt the text.'

'Like a Vigenère cipher, you mean?'

'You *have* done your research. But if we're looking at a Vigenère cipher here, I have no idea how we'd crack it. It's way beyond my level of competence.'

'Such as it is,' Angela suggested.

'Yes. Such as it is,' Bronson agreed. 'Thank you for that.'

'No trouble. So what do we do? Give up and forget about it?'

'I didn't say that. I was just pointing out the reality of the situation as I see it.'

'We don't know when this was encrypted,' Angela said, 'but we do know that it was one of the documents Élisabeth d'Hautpoul entrusted to her notary. She was born in the mid eighteenth century and lived in the family home, Hautpoul Castle at Rennes-le-Château, until 1816, when she sold it. She died four years later. We don't know when she handed over the family papers, but it was probably late in the eighteenth century or early in the nineteenth, and the notary made his statement about not surrendering the documents in 1870. I don't think she was the author of this, because she suggested getting the papers deciphered, so presumably it was created by somebody else decades or centuries earlier.'

'I see where you're going with that,' Bronson said. 'If the document related to the Ark of the Covenant, then most likely the text would have been written at about the same time as Montségur fell. In that case, the text probably dates from the mid to late thirteenth century, and that was about three centuries before the Vigenère cipher was developed. So if that dating is right, whatever encryption method was used couldn't have been polyalphabetic substitution, because the technique didn't exist at that time.'

'That was what I thought. There are a lot of assumptions in that argument, but it does make sense based on what we know of the timeline. I think we can discount the Vigenère cipher. This has to be something a lot simpler than that. The other complication is that we don't know the language of the plaintext. There are three possibilities. It could be Latin, probably the medieval variant, because that was the commonest written language in Europe at that time; Middle French, which was beginning to be spoken in the country; or *lenga d'òc*, Occitan, the language of the region.'

Bronson nodded. 'So now all we need to do is work out how the encryption was done, decrypt it and then translate the plaintext into a language we both understand. It sounds easy,' he added, 'if you say it quickly.'

Chapter 16

Rome, Italy

Marco Ferrara had never been particularly good at following detailed orders. At achieving whatever task he was given, yes, but not at being micro-managed and told what he could and could not do. He preferred the broad sweep of a plain and simple command, ideally a one-liner. And, frankly, some of what Cardinal Julius Caravaggio had quite explicitly told him to do, or not to do, really didn't make sense.

For example, the prohibition against printing any of the data on the thumb drive. Ferrara would agree that printing some of the information would be an extremely bad idea if that printed matter then got into the hands of the media or somebody hostile to the Catholic Church. But if he decided to print some of the Hautpoul documents to study in private, that would make no difference at all. After all, any academic walking into the Bibliothèque Serpente in Paris would be able to read any of the papers. And Ferrara had a shredder to dispose of the evidence afterwards.

So that was what he did.

He didn't print everything, because even a cursory inspection of the scanned papers on the screen of his laptop showed him very clearly that much of the material was utterly irrelevant to his task. When he had studied all the documents that did seem relevant, he was left with only a handful of papers; and of those, only two seemed significant.

The first was what appeared to be a page torn from a diary or journal describing an event that had occurred shortly before the siege of Montségur ended. That was accompanied by a translation, presumably produced by a linguist at the *Congregatio pro Doctrina Fidei*, that showed Cardinal Caravaggio had been right.

What the author of the document stated was that the *Arche de l'Alliance*, the fabled Ark of the Covenant, *had* been in the possession of the Cathars during the siege of Montségur. It had been removed from the fortress under the cover of night by four of the *perfecti* just before the siege and the truce ended. But it didn't explain where the Ark had been taken after that, except to a place of safety. The text referred to a document described as *velat* in Occitan – a word that had been translated as 'coded' or 'veiled' – and stated that the place of safety, and the subsequent route taken by the Ark, was described in that document.

And that document, Ferrara had no doubt, was the handwritten sheet that had also been copied and stored on the thumb drive, a sheet containing a solid block of encrypted text. He had many skills, but cryptography wasn't one of them, so he folded the two sheets of paper – the encrypted text and the translation of the Occitan journal page – into small oblongs that he tucked away in his wallet, and shredded everything else he'd printed.

He glanced at his watch and grabbed his carry-on bag. It was nearly thirteen hundred kilometres by road from Rome to Toulouse. That meant a full twelve hours' driving at least, which luckily was *autostrade* in Italy and *autoroutes* once across the French border for almost the entire journey. Ferrara had no option but to travel by car because of what he was carrying in his bag. Trying to get even a largely plastic pistol like a Glock 17 onto an aircraft would hardly be possible, and the two boxes of ammunition he was carrying would show up on an X-ray screen like the testicles of a canine. The car was his only viable option.

The delay in joining the hunt didn't really matter. Luca Rossi was already on the spot, directing a small team of undercover surveillance people tasked with keeping 'David' in view at all times.

The real identity of 'David' had been a surprise to Ferrara. He'd been mentally anticipating an interfering English academic, a man with a talent for sticking his nose in where it wasn't wanted, and when he'd opened the file labelled 'David.docx', he at first assumed it was a mistake and an incorrect picture had been included.

But when he read the brief biography of the target, he remembered a couple of stories he'd heard about an individual whose interference had embarrassed the Church in the past, and something of what he recalled fell into place. He also realised why Caravaggio – if he had been the person responsible – had chosen the name David.

Assumptions were always dangerous, and Ferrara had made one when Caravaggio had been talking to him at the cafe in the back streets of Rome, an assumption that had fuelled his mental image of the person he'd been told to follow, rob and ultimately kill.

Any name conveyed more than just a label, a basic identity. Being told about a female called Sabrina or Roxanne produced an entirely different mental image to that of a woman named Agnes or Ethel, just as a man named David would appear very different to a male called Spike in the imagination of most people. David had sounded like the name of a scientist or academic, but irrespective of the image Ferrara had conjured up, he had had no doubt that he would be dealing with a man.

But the David.docx file showed the degree of obfuscation Caravaggio or somebody else within the offices of the CDF had applied to this particular person, because not only was 'David' not the sort of man Ferrara had imagined, he wasn't even a man at all.

He was actually a woman, a woman with blonde hair, blue eyes and an arresting curve to her lips that made it look – at least in the photograph – as if she was on the verge of a smile. The only thing Ferrara had guessed right was that she was an academic. Her name was Angela Lewis, and her beauty was undeniable and obvious. He would have no problem carrying out Caravaggio's instructions and murdering her – his first allegiance was and always had been to the Mother Church – but nobody had told him to do it quickly. He saw no particularly good reason why he couldn't find somewhere quiet and really take his time. The end result would be the same, but it would just be a kind of personal bonus.

There was a smile on his face as he stowed his carry-on bag in the boot of his two-year-old Alfa Romeo MiTo and slid into the driver's seat. He programmed the satnav, started the engine and pulled away from the kerb outside his apartment building in the Primavalle district of Rome, then began tracking west to pick up the A90 Circonvallazione Occidentale at the junction in Montespaccato.

As he increased his speed, he was already planning which service areas he'd use to stop for fuel and coffee, and where he'd be able to find a hotel, because he would have to sleep, at least for a few hours, en route.

Chapter 17

Auch, Gascony, France

It was a fine, warm evening, so rather than eat in the hotel, Bronson and Angela walked to the restaurant in the Place de la Libération and took a table outside. They finished their meal with coffee and sat for a few minutes enjoying the balmy evening air and watching handfuls of tourists and groups of locals walking the streets. Bronson checked for anyone paying them an unusual amount of attention, but saw nobody suspicious.

Back at the hotel, Angela opened her laptop on the desk in their room and woke it up. As soon as she'd entered her PIN, she checked her email account, deleting a couple of obviously very sincere and completely honest requests for her help in transferring tens of millions of dollars out of Nigeria and into her own bank account on the sole condition that she give the money to a charity of her choice; and also a personalised offer to extend the length of her penis.

'I mean,' she muttered in irritation as she pressed the delete key, 'my email address starts with Angela dot Lewis, and how many people called Angela have todgers, as you persist in calling them?'

'There are some websites I've seen where almost all the alleged women are embarrassingly well equipped,' Bronson said, 'but I suspect that's a bit of a niche market.'

'I don't want to know what you do in your spare time,' she said, 'and I especially don't if it's that kind of thing.'

He shook his head. 'Not guilty. It was part of an investigation into organised prostitution in Kent. We had to look at some very unusual images.'

'I'll bet you enjoyed that. In fact, if you… Oh.' She broke off in mid sentence. 'I don't like the sound of this.'

'What?'

'It's an email from George Anderson. You know, the chap working at the Sorbonne. Since the Hautpoul documents arrived at the Bibliothèque Serpente, two researchers have turned up there asking to look at those papers.'

'So what? Academics do research all the time. It's more or less a job description for most of them.'

'That's not the point. The first was a visiting Italian professor from the Università di Bologna named Angelo Romano, and the second was an Israeli historian called Israel Mahler, from Tel Aviv University.'

'That's probably a bit unusual. Why would the history of an obscure French family attract the attention of an Italian academic? And for an Israeli to be interested is even more unlikely.'

'That's still not the point. Because of something that happened, George decided to do a bit of checking. It turns out that the Università di Bologna have nobody on their staff called Angelo Romano and never have had, and you won't be surprised to hear that Tel Aviv University denied all knowledge of Israel Mahler. I told you there might be a bit of competition over this, and that more or less proves it.'

'You said something happened,' Bronson said. 'What was it?'

'The man calling himself Romano was given access to the papers in a reading room and later walked out of the library with copies of all of them. Nothing unusual about that. But when this Mahler bloke turned up to do the same thing, George discovered that the sheet of encrypted text and the journal entry written in Occitan had disappeared. The obvious deduction is that Romano removed them. After all, it's easy to extract two sheets of paper from a large pile of documents and then hide them.'

'But surely the library would have copied papers they received, so I assume the Israeli was given copies of the copies, if you see what I mean?'

'Oddly enough, no, because George got suspicious of Mahler and told him the staff were busy and hadn't got around to doing that. So the Israeli – if he was an Israeli – had to leave empty-handed.'

'That's something, I suppose,' Bronson said. 'But how the hell did anyone find out about this, and that the Hautpoul papers were at the Sorbonne? I'm amazed that two different people knew about it. Something must have happened that we don't know about.'

Angela shook her head. 'I've no idea, but I don't like it.'

'Nor do I. I didn't really take you seriously when you talked about there being competition, but I do now. I suggest you thank George and ask that he checks out any other wandering non-academics before they get inside the building. And you know what this means?'

'Yes. We have to get that bloody page of text decrypted as quickly as we can, otherwise when we get to wherever the Ark is hidden, we might find somebody's beaten us to it and the cupboard is bare.'

'Exactly. So let's get on with it.'

Chapter 18

Paris, France

To say Josef Gellerman was irritated by his failure to obtain a copy of the encrypted document – which he was certain was the key to the recovery of the relic – barely even hinted at his anger. Based on what Anderson, the English academic, had told him, he was certain that the Italian professor was bogus and that he had abstracted both the encrypted paper and a sheet from a journal written in Occitan. Anderson had discovered the second document was also missing when he'd inspected the folio of papers while Gellerman was still in the building. The fact that he couldn't remember the man's name was irrelevant. There would be no way of finding the Italian because he would have been using an alias.

Gellerman was used to playing catch-up, and he'd known from the start that he and his two companions were well behind the curve. By the time they'd heard about the break-in at the notary's office in Limoux, the crime had already been a week old. That delay would have allowed the bogus professor – who had almost certainly been responsible for the robbery and the murder of the clerk – plenty of time to get to Paris, visit the Bibliothèque Serpente and see the Hautpoul papers.

Gellerman was used to thinking laterally, approaching problems in a non-linear way, and there were two things he could do to try to resolve the situation. First, there was one possible method he could use to try to identify the Italian professor, and second, he'd had further thoughts about what Anderson had told him, and there was something he could do about that, too.

Lemuel Dayan spoke workable though not fluent French, and among the half-dozen or so identification documents the man always carried with him, Gellerman knew there was one that would fit the bill nicely. While Dayan followed his instructions tomorrow, Gellerman would spend a short time back at the Bibliothèque Serpente, following a slightly different line of enquiry.

Chapter 19

Legino, Savona, Italy

Marco Ferrara had got as far as Savona, roughly sixty kilometres beyond Genoa, before calling it a day and pulling off the E80 *autostrada* about an hour after the sun had sunk below the horizon in front of him.

Rather than take pot luck, he'd booked a hotel room a couple of hours previously, when he'd stopped for a coffee and a snack. He'd chosen his destination mainly because it was less than two kilometres from the nearest *autostrada* junction. It was a modern, square, white hotel located almost on the beach, with gardens that went right down to the sand, but Ferrara wasn't there to laze in the sun.

He'd had a drink in the bar and eaten a small plate of *spaghetti marinara* before returning to his room overlooking the Mediterranean and going to bed. He had wanted a decent sleep because of the long drive he would have the following day.

He was awoken the next morning not by the alarm clock on his mobile, which he'd set the previous night, but by a text message on his burner phone.

Like many people woken unexpectedly in a strange place, for a few moments he didn't know where he was or what had disturbed his slumber.

The first thing he did was check the time on his smartphone: 06:18. He knew the message would be important, because the only people who had the burner's number were Julius Caravaggio and Francesco.

He took a swig of water from the bottle he'd put beside the bed, rubbed his eyes and then opened the message. It was from Caravaggio.

> Urgent. Expedite. You have competition. Precaution: action David immediately. Follow trail yourself. Report soonest.

He read it twice before it really sank in, then he lay back on the bed and stared at the ceiling. It wouldn't change what he would do that day – he still had to get to Auch, where Rossi's people were watching 'David' – but it would certainly affect what he would do when he reached his destination.

Chapter 20

Auch, Gascony, France

Bronson and Angela had got precisely nowhere in trying to crack the cipher the previous evening. When it was quite obvious that that was the case, they'd given up, gone down to the hotel bar for a couple of nightcaps and then retired, slightly early, to bed.

In the morning, they got up about an hour earlier than usual and sat down to a typical French continental breakfast in the hotel dining room.

'More coffee?' Bronson asked, picking up the metal jug that he'd just used to top up his own cup.

'Full to the brim, please,' Angela replied, buttering a final slice of *baguette* and adding a spoonful of raspberry jam. 'The caffeine might jog my brain into some kind of useful activity.'

'That'd be a bonus. And there's one small *pain au raisin* left if you want it.'

'No. You eat it, then we must get back upstairs. We've got work to do.'

Back in their room. Angela sat at the desk and opened her laptop while Bronson lay full-length on the bed. He claimed that lying flat helped him think, which Angela didn't entirely believe, but in reality there was nowhere else in the room for him to sit. Or lie.

'So how far have we got?' he asked.

'Roughly or exactly?'

'Either or both.'

‘Nowhere,’ she replied. ‘Nada. Zilch. We’ve made no progress whatsoever.’

‘One of the problems is that we still don’t know when the document was written,’ Bronson said. ‘There are no clues on it, but I still think it was probably composed in the thirteenth century, round about the time the siege of Montségur ended.’

‘That’s my guess as well, and if that dating is right, it’s most likely that the plaintext will have been written in Occitan rather than Latin or French. And that,’ Angela went on, ‘leads to another rather more complicated complication. I didn’t know until I started doing research that there’s no standard Occitan language in written form. There are different versions based on various dialects, so when we do crack the cipher it might still take a while to work out what the Occitan text means. And because today it’s a very minor and virtually dead language, there isn’t an online translator we can use.’

‘I have seen a few online Occitan dictionaries,’ Bronson said, ‘so they should give us an idea of what individual words mean, and we could probably feed phrases into Google Translate and tell the program they’re Catalan. That might work. You’ve told me the two languages are pretty similar. If we get really stuck, I suppose we could bung the Occitan over to one of your linguist chaps at the museum and ask him to translate it for us. But the first thing we should do is find out the letter frequencies in Catalan.’

‘Give me a minute,’ Angela said, ‘and I’ll check it out.’

She opened up a search engine, typed a few words and then studied the results the program displayed.

‘It’s not as clear-cut as I was hoping. According to this website, the commonest six letters in Catalan, in order, are E A S R L T. The letters E and A both occur about thirteen per cent of the time, with E being slightly more common. The letter S is found much less frequently, only about eight per cent, and then R, L and T are all around the six per cent mark, as are the next dozen or so letters. So if we assume a single transposition cipher was used and we do a frequency analysis based on this information, the two commonest letters found would probably represent E and A, but with no way of telling which is which. I don't think that'll get us very much further, but we can try it if you want.'

'We might as well, I suppose. I'll note the letter frequencies if you read through the text.'

Bronson took a sheet of paper and a pencil and wrote out the letters of the alphabet in a column down the left-hand side. As Angela read out each letter of the ciphertext, he placed a vertical stroke against that letter, with a diagonal line through each group of four occurrences to make it easier to count the total.

'You were right,' he said when they'd finished. 'There are some letters that don't appear at all, and a handful that occur with roughly the same frequency. But what I don't see are any letters that are so common they could represent E or A, or even S.' He walked over to Angela and handed her the sheet. 'Maybe you can see something I can't.'

Angela scanned what he'd written and shook her head.

'No, nothing jumps out at me. The other problem is that the ciphertext is a very small sample. Frequency analysis works best with large blocks of text. So what do we do next?'

'I don't like making assumptions,' Bronson replied, 'but sometimes you really do have no other choice. So let's assume that this text was encrypted around the mid thirteenth century, and that it was done by someone in the Languedoc area of France. That implies that the language used was Occitan because that's what they were speaking at that time in that part of the country. I think we can also assume that whoever encrypted the text was either a Cathar or somebody very closely associated with them. If we take those as givens, and as we're probably not dealing with a simple Atbash or Caesar cipher but something more complex, maybe this document was encrypted using keywords or a key phrase, and employed something like a very basic double substitution system.'

'You need to explain that.'

'Okay. What I'm wondering is whether the person who did this used a kind of variant of the Atbash system. With Atbash you write out the alphabet, and then underneath it you write out the alphabet again, but backwards. so that Z is below A, or perhaps forwards but shifted a number of spaces to the left or right. Or backwards and shifted. Those are the only possible variants. But it would have been obvious to anybody using Atbash, even then, that each plaintext letter was always going to be represented by the same letter in the ciphertext, no matter whether they used the alphabet or some phrase. So maybe they thought of a wrinkle, a way to make it more difficult to crack.'

'Like what?'

'Well, something like having two ciphertexts underneath the alphabet, or one above and one below, so that they had two letter choices for each plaintext letter by alternating the use of the ciphertexts. Then frequency analysis wouldn't work, and you'd need to know both ciphertexts to decode it.'

Angela thought about that for a few seconds, then shook her head.

'Let's take a couple of steps back,' she said. 'That page of text was encoded for a reason, obviously. Now, if it was a secret that the writer didn't want to ever be revealed, then the obvious thing he could have done was nothing. No paper, no encryption, and the secret would be safe forever. But he didn't do that. Therefore, thinking about it logically, his intention must have been to encrypt it in a way that would allow it to be deciphered at some future date.'

'That makes sense. So he must have assumed that whoever wanted to decipher it would have known how to do it, and that could mean something like using a phrase or piece of text that every Cathar would know, for example.'

'Exactly. Either that or he would have left some clue on the page itself to suggest what the ciphertext should be. It had to either be common knowledge amongst the Cathars or a clue to the decryption process had to be provided.'

They both stared at the copied sheets of paper in front of them, seeking inspiration.

'Right,' Bronson said. 'I don't see anything on the sheet that could be a clue. The only odd feature, apart from the fact that we can't read it, is that a couple of the lines of text have been underlined, and I can't see how that is in any way significant. Maybe those two sentences are particularly important, but we won't know why until we've deciphered it.'

Angela looked puzzled.

'I've looked at a *lot* of medieval manuscripts,' she said, 'and I can't recall ever seeing one where two whole lines of the text was underlined like this. Underlining has been used for thousands of years to link words together or add emphasis. But this looks different. Maybe they're dividers.'

Bronson shrugged. 'Perhaps. But we won't know until we've cracked the encryption. Let's look at phrases or sentences important to the Cathars. Do you know if they had prayers or rituals that every Cathar would know but a non-Cathar wouldn't?'

'I'll check,' Angela replied, and started another Internet search. 'Okay,' she said after a few moments, 'the first thing is that the word "Cathar" was derogatory, meant to be a kind of insult. They called themselves *bons hommes* – "good men", meaning good Christians – but that's too short to use as part of the ciphertext key.'

'We need something a lot longer,' Bronson said. 'What about a prayer? If you ask a Christian – or even an atheist or agnostic – to recite a prayer, the one they all know because it's drummed into them at school is the Lord's Prayer. Did the Cathars have something similar?'

'Hang on a minute. Right, there's one authentic Cathar liturgy that's survived the years. There are two versions of it, one written in Latin and the other in Occitan. The Latin version is called the Cathar Ritual and the Occitan one is the Lyon Ritual. I don't know why it has two names because the text is the same. Only the languages used are different.'

'Yes, but a liturgy is a church service, isn't it, with a priest saying something and the congregation responding, and they probably had lots of them. Was that their most important liturgy, or was it the only one that's survived? If it was one of dozens, it wouldn't be important enough to use a line from it as an encryption key.'

'Pass. I've no idea how important it was, and that's a good point. Let me find out if they had a special prayer.'

She changed the search terms slightly and accessed a different website. She read what the site told her and then started to laugh.

'What?'

'You know what you were saying about everybody knowing the Lord's Prayer? Well, the Cathars had a prayer called the *Pater Noster*, and it's the same prayer, except that it's in Latin. In fact, according to this site it's probably the oldest prayer in existence and was allegedly created by Jesus. Some of the phrases in it are found in Jewish prayers, and the earliest versions were written in Greek.'

'Not Hebrew?'

'Oddly enough, no. In the first century the lingua franca of most of the Roman Empire was Koine – that means "common" – Greek, so virtually all Christian writings of the period were in that language. Some scholars believe parts of the New Testament were originally written in Hebrew or Aramaic and then translated into Greek, but there isn't any evidence for that. According to this site, it's more likely that translations went the other way, from Greek into Aramaic. But the Old Testament was different. That was written in Hebrew, and we know that because some very early versions were discovered back in 1947 among the Dead Sea Scrolls.'

She connected her portable inkjet printer, fed a sheet of paper into it and printed what she'd found. Then she passed the sheet to Bronson, who read aloud from it, stumbling over some of the Latin words.

Pater noster qui es in cælis, sanctificetur nomen tuum; adveniat regnum tuum.
Fiat voluntas tua sicut in cælo et in terra.
Panem nostrum supersubstancialem da nobis hodie.
Et dimitte nobis debita nostra sicut et nos dimittimus debitoribus nostris.
Et ne nos inducas in temptationem sed libera nos a malo.
Quoniam tuum est regnum et virtus et gloria in secula.
Amen.

'You know,' he said, 'this might be it. That first line's got about sixty characters in it, so if the man who encrypted this wrote out the alphabet and then that first sentence on the two lines underneath, that would give him two ciphertext letters for each letter of the alphabet. It wouldn't really be a polyalphabetic cipher, just something a bit more secure than a single substitution version.'

Angela nodded. 'Let's give it a go.'

Chapter 21

Paris, France

The first thing Lemuel Dayan did that morning when he walked down the Rue Serpente and into the Rue Danton was to look up.

He had no interest in the architecture of the buildings that lined the streets, but he was looking for something that most of them didn't seem to possess – a security camera. Unlike London, where almost every street corner, house and shop was festooned with CCTV cameras of various sizes and types, in that particular area of Paris he initially saw none. Perhaps there was a local law that forbade the mounting of such devices on the façades for aesthetic reasons, though the way French architects were capable of designing and building hideously ugly structures that were entirely out of keeping with the surroundings made this seem unlikely. Or perhaps it was just a low-crime area.

He finally got lucky in a small shop on the corner of the Rue Mignon, almost opposite the Maison de la Recherche. There was a small black camera positioned inside the glass door of the shop, clearly intended to record anyone who approached the establishment, but from the angle of it Dayan thought it might cover some of the street outside and the intersection. And beyond that was the target building.

He stepped inside the shop, reached into his jacket pocket and extracted a light blue plastic card with the words 'INTERPOL IDENTIFICATION CARD' in the top left-hand corner above a colour photograph of his face, and with his personal details printed on the right. The genuine articles were machine-readable smart cards, but at a casual glance what Dayan had looked real enough, and because almost no civilian ever saw either a real Interpol card or a real Interpol officer, the chances of it being recognised as a fake were almost nil.

'I wonder if you could help me,' he began, replacing the card in his wallet after the middle-aged male shopkeeper had stared at it for a few seconds. 'We're running a surveillance operation in this area looking for a particular person. He might have walked down this street and he could have been detected by your camera.' He pointed back towards the door. 'Could I take a copy of your surveillance tape for one specific date?'

He took out a small notebook and read out the date on which Gellerman had told him the 'Italian professor' had visited the Bibliothèque Serpente. Fifteen minutes later, he walked out with a copy of that day's camera recordings stored on the external hard drive in his pocket.

He found two other shops with similar security arrangements in the surrounding streets. Both were further away from the library but both were situated on possible routes to and from the building, so it was worth copying the videos.

–

While Lemuel Dayan was looking for security cameras, Josef Gellerman had taken up temporary residence in a cafe at the end of the Rue Danton, where it merged into the Place Saint-Michel. He'd chosen a table that offered a clear, albeit distant view of the Maison de la Recherche, though the main door of the building was out of sight. If he'd guessed right, that shouldn't matter. He had ordered a *café au lait* and a small basket of pastries and settled down for what might be a long wait.

In fact, he'd only been there for about three quarters of an hour when he saw George Anderson step out of the building and start strolling towards him. He'd paid for his drink and food when it had been delivered, so he left a few coins as a tip, ate the last corner of a *croissant* and then left the cafe.

He intercepted the English academic before he reached his destination.

'Mr Anderson,' he said quietly, stepping in front of the man and forcing him to stop.

Anderson looked puzzled for a few moments, but then his expression changed and recognition dawned.

'Ah, it's Mr Mahler, isn't it?' he said.

'It is,' Gellerman responded, 'and I have a small problem that I know you can help me with.' He steered Anderson over to one side of the pavement, away from most of the pedestrians.

'Look, I'm just on my way out for lunch so this isn't a very convenient time,' Anderson said. 'Could you see me in the library this afternoon?'

Gellerman shook his head. 'I really am in a hurry and this won't take more than a few minutes. And I promise it will be worth your while to help me out.'

'Oh, very well,' the academic replied. 'What is it?'

'It's really about you. You see, when I asked you about the policy of the library on copying documents, I don't think you were truthful. I don't believe that an important library, part of the Sorbonne, would accept documents of potential historic importance and then just dump them in a reading room somewhere for anybody to paw through without first making copies. But that's what you told me had happened with the Hautpoul folio and that's why two important pieces of paper went missing from it. I think you were lying to me. I believe the library would have made copies of all those documents as soon as they arrived, and only after that had been done would anybody have been allowed to study them. To me, that would make more sense.'

Gellerman's gaze didn't waver from Anderson's face and the Englishman's change of expression was easy enough to read. But before he could respond, the Israeli ploughed on.

'I don't want to make this difficult,' he said, 'and if we both go back to the Bibliothèque Serpente right now and you obtain copies of those two missing documents for me, then I'll walk out of your life forever.'

'If you come back this afternoon—' the Englishman began.

'No, right now,' Gellerman interrupted. 'I said I would make it worth your while, so let me just explain what I meant. If you hand me those two copies within the next ten minutes, you can go off and enjoy your lunch at one of these cafes. If you don't agree to do this, I will break both of your arms right here and right now. Believe me when I say that I have done this kind of thing many, many times before and there would be nothing you could do to stop me. It would take me less than ten seconds. A very painful and life-changing ten seconds for you.'

The Israeli could see the blood draining from Anderson's face. The man was an elderly academic, and in all probability the last time he had engaged in any kind of physical conflict would have been almost a half-century earlier on the playing fields of whatever school he had attended back in England.

'I understand,' Gellerman went on in the same conversational tone, 'that the French medical system is very good, with competent and caring doctors and nurses, but you would have an extremely unpleasant few minutes waiting for an ambulance to arrive. Then you'd have to spend about a week in hospital having your arms sorted out, and after that there would be weeks of convalescence and physiotherapy, not to mention the very real possibility of suffering aches and pains for the rest of your life.

'And,' he added with a chuckle, 'once I'd left you lying here on the pavement screaming in agony with a crowd around you, I would just walk down the road to the library and ask one of the staff members there if they could get the copies for me. It's easier for me if you do it, but it's really up to you. Either delay your lunch for no more than a quarter of an hour or face the consequences of fucking me about.' His voice hardened on the last three words.

Anderson swallowed a couple of times and then nodded.

'I'll get you the copies,' he said, his voice croaking with stress. 'Will you wait here?'

'So you can arrange for a carload of *gendarmes* to take me away somewhere quiet for a bit of heavy-handed Q&A? I don't think so. We'll go to the library together, just in case you have a sudden change of heart.'

It actually took a little longer than ten minutes before Gellerman walked out of the Bibliothèque Serpente with half a dozen copies of each of the missing pages tucked into a large envelope.

George Anderson remained in the building. For some reason, he seemed to have lost his appetite.

–

The three Israelis assembled in Gellerman's hotel room to look at what he'd obtained.

'This shouldn't be difficult,' he said, pointing at the journal page. 'It's almost certainly written in Occitan, so it's just a matter of translating it. It'll take a while, but we can do it.' He gestured towards the encrypted text. 'That will be more difficult. None of us have much experience with ciphers, so I'll email a copy to Jerusalem to see if they can help.'

He turned to Dayan.

'You know the people we're probably up against, so scan whatever the cameras recorded and see if you can spot any unwelcome faces.'

'I'm already on it,' Dayan said, plugging the external hard disk into one of the USB ports on his laptop and opening File Explorer.

Aaron Chason was a locksmith and engineer, and had no particular abilities in either translating an almost dead language or decoding an encrypted text, so Gellerman sent him down to the hotel bar to buy soft drinks and sandwiches so they could eat and drink while they worked.

By the time he got back with their scratch lunch, Gellerman had already sent the email and Dayan had eliminated the images from one camera altogether because the angle was wrong. It didn't show the street outside the shop, only the area beside the door: ideal for the shop's owner but useless for him. He grabbed a sandwich and a can of cola and opened up the second database.

'This is more like it,' he said to the room in general. 'The angle's fine and I can see the front door of the library.'

It took Gellerman most of the rest of the afternoon to complete the translation of the Occitan text, and even then he wasn't sure about a couple of words. But before he'd finished, Dayan froze one particular image on the screen of his laptop and showed it to him.

It wasn't crystal clear, the camera's principal focus being a short distance away so that the faces of anyone close to the lens would be easily identifiable. The figure Dayan had spotted was crossing the road and was perhaps twenty feet away, but it was clear enough, at least to Gellerman. And in truth, it was more or less what he'd been expecting ever since he'd heard about the Italian professor visiting the Bibliothèque Serpente.

'Oh shit,' he muttered. 'That's Luca Rossi. You know what that means.'

'Yes,' Dayan replied. 'It means the bloody Inquisition has stuck its nose in where it's definitely not wanted. We'll have to move quickly.'

Chapter 22

Auch, Gascony, France

They tried every combination they could think of using the first line of the *Pater Noster* prayer as the encryption key phrase in a double substitution cipher, and it took them most of the day to get nowhere. No matter how they used the phrase, offset or not, forwards or backwards, all they did was, as Angela had earlier described it, turn one piece of gibberish into another piece of gibberish. None of the results produced anything recognisable, apart from the occasional two- or three-letter combination that formed an Occitan word, but they were clearly accidental. Jumble up any group of letters in any language often enough and inevitably *some* random words will form.

'This is like the infinite number of monkeys with an infinite number of typewriters eventually producing the complete works of Shakespeare,' Bronson muttered, putting down the sheet of paper he'd been working on and rubbing his eyes.

'I thought it was a bit too complicated for somebody in the medieval period to come up with, using a double ciphertext system,' Angela replied, 'but I didn't have any better ideas. And, for that matter, I still don't.'

Bronson climbed off the bed, plumped the pillows into a more supportive shape and lay down again. He'd been there for most of the day, apart from an hour when they'd left the hotel to walk to Place de la Libération for a lunch of filled *baguettes* and coffee.

'I think I'll just do a bit of research,' he said, 'and see if there's some other medieval encryption technique that I haven't heard of.'

'Do you want to use the computer?'

'No,' Bronson replied. 'Just my mobile.'

He woke up his smartphone, opened the browser and began searching the Internet.

'Now that's an idea,' he muttered a few minutes later, having visited over a dozen different websites.

'What?' Angela sounded fed up.

'I've found a site that discusses ancient methods of encryption – not just medieval, but going way back. According to this, the commonest method of encryption was Atbash, which is what we've been trying to do all bloody day, but there were more devious methods as well.

'One was a variant of what's now called steganography, writing a message in plaintext but hiding it completely from view. Today this is done by, for example, reducing the image of a document to the size of a single pixel and then inserting that pixel into a photograph, so that it's just one pixel amongst millions of others and virtually impossible to find unless you know its exact location. But the basic technique is old, and the site gives some examples.

'In the early days of writing, they used wax tablets, flat pieces of wood with a border around the edge that formed a perimeter, and the interior filled with wax. Somebody would write a message on the wax, and when the recipient had read it, he'd run the flat of a knife blade over the wax to erase the message and then write his reply. To send a secret message, they'd remove the wax and write a message on the wood itself, then replace the wax and write an innocuous message on that. When the tablet was delivered, the wax would be removed and the secret message revealed. It would have been a bit cumbersome and time-consuming, but it would have worked.'

'No wax tablets here, as far as I know,' Angela pointed out.

'I know. It was just an example. Another method, if the message was important but not urgent, was to shave a slave's head, tattoo the message on his scalp, wait for his hair to grow back and then send him off to whoever needed the information. There his head would be shaved again to reveal the message.'

'Again, no handy slaves about the place and—' Angela began, but Bronson silenced her with a gesture.

'Give me a chance here. The site also mentions another method that wasn't really encryption at all because it just used the plaintext but jumbled up so it couldn't be read. That could be what we're looking at here, and the clue is those two sentences that have been underlined.'

'What do you mean?'

'Have you ever heard of a *scytale*?'

Her blank expression provided the answer.

'Okay. According to this site, the word comes from the Greek *skutálē* or *skútalon*, meaning a cylinder or baton, and that's the key. It was used by the ancient Greeks, in particular by the Spartans, as a way of sending an urgent message in battle that couldn't be mistaken or misunderstood.'

'Okay, you've grabbed my attention. How did it work?'

'The man wanting to send a message would take his wooden baton and wind a very thin strip of parchment or cloth tightly around it so that it formed a continuous cylinder. He would write his message on that: one letter on each section of the parchment and in a straight line down the baton, then the second line under that, and so on. Once he'd finished, he would unwind the parchment, one side of which would be covered in letters in an apparently random order. The parchment would be taken to the recipient, who would have his own baton, exactly the same size as the one carried by the person sending the message. He would wind the parchment around it and read the message. And because it was plaintext, it would be obvious if the letters weren't lining up correctly, so the parchment could be adjusted until they did.'

'Right,' Angela said, 'I can see exactly how that would work, and if the messenger was intercepted, the message couldn't be read without the right diameter baton. That's why those two underlined sentences in this piece of text are important. The sentences themselves are irrelevant; it's the underlines that matter. They show the diameter of the baton needed to decrypt this. That is what you're saying, isn't it?'

Bronson nodded. 'Got it in one,' he agreed. 'The only weakness of the *scytale* system was that anybody intercepting the message would see what it was, and it could be cracked by trying rods of different sizes, by trial and error. But what I think the person who created this has done is write out the message using a *scytale*, and then copy the sequence of letters into a single block of text to disguise how he'd done it. We've been fiddling about with Atbash ciphers because he'd managed to steer us in completely the wrong direction.

'But we have these two lines,' Angela said, 'and by the magic of mathematics, and thanks to an ancient Greek named Archimedes, who calculated the value of pi, we can work out the circumference of the baton used in this case.'

She opened her handbag, took out a fabric tape measure and placed one end on the first horizontal line in the text. She read out the distance to the second line and Bronson jotted down the number.

'We don't have to be too accurate about this,' he said, 'because there are loads of fudge factors. The photocopy may be slightly distorted compared to the original, the man who drew the lines may not have had his pen completely vertical, and we don't know how wide the original strip of parchment was, which would affect it as well. So this is going to be a guesstimate.'

'Agreed,' Angela said. Using the calculator function on her smartphone, she multiplied the measurement by the numerical value of pi to work out the circumference of the original baton. 'Okay, because this is going to be approximate, I used the rough value of pi of 3.142. The diameter by measurement was just over one and a half inches, so we're working on a circumference of about four and three quarter inches.'

Bronson nodded, scribbled down some rough calculations and then looked over at her.

'We're obviously talking about handwriting, and I've assumed that there'll be roughly five to seven letters per inch. That means, with the diameter of the baton you've worked out, the second letter on the unwound scytale would be between twenty-four and thirty-three characters after the first. Roughly. About. More or less. Approximately. Give or take.'

'I get the picture. Let's split it. I'll do twenty-four to twenty-eight, and you do twenty-nine to thirty-three. Take the first half-dozen letters with those spacings and jot them down. We'll see if they form what looks like a possible word and take it from there.'

It didn't take long.

'Anything?' Angela asked.

Bronson shook his head. 'Nothing that makes immediate sense to me. Shall I read them out to you?'

'Good idea.'

He read out the first three sets of letters that he'd transcribed. Angela stopped him.

'Read me that third one again,' she said. 'And spell it out.'

'SANTDE,' he repeated. 'S A N T D E. It could be a word, I suppose.'

'You suppose correctly. This is at a spacing of thirty-one characters, right? Let me make a prediction. Go through the text again and see if the next character with that spacing is the letter U.'

Bronson ran the tip of his pencil along the line of text, counting as he went, and then stopped.

'You're right,' he said. 'It is. So is SANTDEU a word in Occitan?'

'Oddly enough,' Angela replied, 'it isn't. It's actually two words – SANT DEU – which in Occitan means "Holy God". I was expecting something like this, some reference to God at the start of the text, because that was really common in medieval documents.'

She looked across the room at him. 'Well, don't just lie there like a beached whale. Start transcribing. And I'll make you a deal. While you do the transcription, I'll go down to the bar and get us a couple of cups of coffee. When I get back, I'll do the translation, and when I've finished it, you can take me out somewhere halfway decent and buy me dinner.'

Chapter 23

South of Carcassonne, France

Marco Ferrara steered his MiTo off the A61 Autoroute des Deux Mers and into the Aire de Repos du Belvédère d'Auriac south of Carcassonne, which offered a good view of the Cité de Carcassonne, the old medieval fortress that lay at the heart of the city.

He had been on the road all day, and although the Alfa Romeo was comfortable enough, he really thought he needed to stretch his legs a bit and breathe something other than air-conditioned air. Plus, he needed to make a phone call.

In fact, he needed to make two calls.

He locked the car and walked briskly around the perimeter of the rest area, located on the northern side of the *autoroute*, relishing being able to move freely once again. He was about eighty kilometres east of Toulouse, a little under an hour's drive, and he still had to negotiate the busy *périphérique* that ringed the city to get to the west side, and then drive another sixty kilometres on normal roads. Overall, despite the optimistic estimate provided by the satnav, which invariably assumed that every traffic light would be green, that there would be no traffic and that the car would be able to travel at whatever the legal maximum speed was on any journey, he reckoned he would be lucky to reach Auch in less than two and a half hours.

That was the reason he needed to make one of the phone calls.

The other reason was that he'd been wondering all day about the change of plan he had been told to implement in the text message he'd received that morning. Something had obviously happened, and he needed to find out what, in case it was a development that could directly affect him.

He took a folded sheet of paper from his pocket on which he had written three mobile telephone numbers: another of Cardinal Caravaggio's rules that he had broken. The first number was Caravaggio's, the second was Francesco's and the third was Luca Rossi's. He dialled the first one and it was answered almost immediately.

'Yes? Are you there yet?'

'No. The journey is taking longer than I expected. I'm still on the road and I should reach the address in about two and a half hours.'

Although mobile phone calls were fairly secure, neither man would mention the other's name or anything in the conversation that could identify who they were, where they were or what they were doing. That was another of Julius Caravaggio's rules, but it was one that Ferrara agreed with. Because they were both using burner phones, the chance of any law enforcement agency being able to triangulate their locations was infinitesimally small. Before triangulation could be authorised, the mobile had to be identified as suspect for some believable and convincing reason, and that was difficult to do with a burner.

'I understand. What did you want? Why did you call?'

'I got your message this morning. Is there a problem?'

Caravaggio paused for a couple of seconds before he replied.

'There might be,' he said. 'Information obtained by a source has suggested you may meet some competition in addition to David.'

'Competition from where?' Ferrara asked, wondering both who it could be and how the cardinal would convey the information. 'Or from whom?'

'From the place at the end of the alphabet where the people live who want things to be the same now as they once were.'

That made perfect sense to Ferrara. The place at the end of the alphabet in that context could only be Zion, a slang term for

Jerusalem, and the other reference was obviously to the Zeru or Zerubbabel group, which had been a thorn in the side of the Catholic Church for years. They were based in Jerusalem.

'Understood. How did you find out?'

'We have eyes everywhere. Three of them flew to where you are, and then headed north on the trail we discussed previously. We believe they now have the same information as you.'

Caravaggio obviously meant that the Zeru people had travelled to Toulouse, then north to Paris, and obtained copies of the Hautpoul papers from the Bibliothèque Serpente. Members of the Catholic Church and some non-clergy sympathetic to its aims were sometimes asked to keep a lookout for certain events or individuals, and Ferrara assumed that somebody who worked in the Sorbonne library had been asked to pass on details if somebody appeared there asking for access to those documents. A phone camera photograph passed up the chain to the offices of the *Congregatio pro Doctrina Fidei* would have been enough to identify the Zeru member or members involved.

That was not good news. Zeru was utterly fanatical in pursuing its destructive objective, and its ultimate aim would, in the eyes of many senior officials in the Church, potentially spell the end of both Christianity and Islam. What the group wanted to achieve was quite literally an Armageddon agenda. Whatever happened, they had to be stopped.

'Where are they now?' Ferrara asked.

'We don't know, but presumably they're already on the move. We haven't obtained the information we need' – that meant the cryptology experts at the CDF still hadn't cracked the sheet of encrypted text – 'so we don't know where they could be going. Make sure you initiate the changed priority as soon as possible.'

'Why the change of sequence?'

'We cannot risk the competition getting there first. David is the weak link.'

'Understood,' Ferrara said again, and ended the call. Caravaggio had obviously decided that Angela Lewis's ability to find hidden relics posed so much danger that she had to die immediately to prevent Zeru following her and seizing the Ark.

He shrugged, glanced at the third number on his sheet of paper and dialled it.

'About time,' a gravelly voice answered. 'We've been expecting you. Where are you now?'

'Still at least two or three hours away. The traffic's been heavy. What's the situation?'

'No change,' Luca Rossi replied. 'They're still in the hotel.'

'What do you mean, "they"? I thought it was just one person.'

'Nope. They're a couple. It looks like he brought his wife along for the ride. Is that a problem?'

'It might be, but you've got it the wrong way round,' Ferrara said. 'It's not the husband I need to meet, it's the wife. She's now my priority. Just make sure you know where they are, because I'd like to get this sorted out tonight.'

'Got it. Where do you want to meet? And at what time?'

Ferrara had researched Auch before he'd left Rome and already knew the area where his target was staying.

'By the steps that lead to the statue of the musketeer,' he said. 'Be there in two and a half hours, but you might have to wait for me for a few minutes.'

'No problem.'

He got back in his car, again checked the estimate the satnav was providing and pulled out onto the *autoroute*. He leaned back in his seat, relaxing his body as he steadily increased speed to exactly ten kilometres an hour below the maximum allowed. He definitely didn't want to get stopped by the *gendarmes* for speeding, because of the Glock pistol he was carrying. A traffic stop wouldn't normally result in either the driver or the car being searched, but there was no point in taking the chance.

Chapter 24

Auch, Gascony, France

Three minutes after she'd left, Angela stepped back into the hotel bedroom. Bronson noticed immediately that she wasn't carrying coffee or any other kind of refreshments.

'What is it?' he asked.

'That man you thought was following us back at Montségur? He's downstairs, sitting at a corner table in the bar. I saw him but I'm pretty sure he didn't see me.'

Bronson stood up. 'You're sure it was him?'

'Yes. I saw him clearly when we were walking down the path from the castle. He's even wearing the same clothes.'

'That's good enough for me. Okay, get your stuff packed up. We're out of here.'

Angela glanced at her watch. 'But it's almost seven o'clock. Shouldn't we—'

'No. We don't know who these people are or what they want, and I've no particular desire to hang around and find out. If he's mounting surveillance on us, which is pretty obviously what he *is* doing, there'll be a whole group of them involved, as I told you before. We're lucky we spotted him earlier, and doubly lucky you recognised him now. His job will be to tail us if we leave the hotel and alert the other people working with him that we're on the move. While we're holed up in here in a controlled location, they're probably out somewhere taking a break, getting a meal or whatever.'

'So how will we get out without him seeing us?'

'We won't. That's the point. Which corner of the bar was he sitting in?'

'The left, so he can see straight through to the lobby.'

'Right,' Bronson said, more or less thinking aloud. 'He knows we're in the hotel because he must have followed us when we came back after lunch. I didn't see him, but it was either him or another watcher we haven't identified yet. Nothing else makes sense. He can't watch our room, so he's doing the next best thing: covering the hotel entrance to see us if we leave, and to follow us if we do.'

'So how can we get out?'

'I think we turn what he's doing on its head. He'll sit there until we walk out of the building, but suppose we don't leave? Suppose he knows we're not safely tucked up in our room but somewhere else in the hotel, somewhere out of his sight. What's he going to do then?'

'That's obvious. He'll want to keep watching us.'

'Exactly. If I was doing his job, that's what I'd do. So we use that to take him out of the equation.'

'How?' Angela asked.

Bronson told her what they needed to do.

'It sounds a bit hit and miss,' she said when he'd finished.

'That's because it *is* a bit hit and miss, but right now I don't have any better ideas.'

'And you think that will work?' she asked, pointing at the external mobile phone battery Bronson was holding in his right hand.

'It's all I've got, so it'll have to.'

The battery was about five inches long and circular in cross-section, with a USB port and a charging socket at one end. Bronson slipped it into his jacket pocket and nodded to her.

'Ready?'

'What's the line from that road movie? "I was born ready" or something like that? Well, I'm not ready really, but I know we have to do this, so let's get on with it.'

They picked up their bags and carried them downstairs to the reception desk at the other end of the lobby, out of sight of the bar. Bronson asked the girl manning it if they could leave them there, which was no problem. He settled the bill at the same time, telling her they were having to leave unexpectedly for family reasons. He was fluent in Italian and spoke very good French.

They walked into the bar together, bought two coffees and sat at a table a few feet from their silent watcher. After a couple of minutes, they started discussing their evening meal, part of the off-the-cuff plan Bronson had put together in the bedroom. They made sure their conversation was audible to the watcher.

'Do you want to go back to the restaurant in the Place de la Libération?' he asked. 'It's a warm evening, we can sit outside, and the food's not bad at all.'

Angela shook her head. 'If you don't mind, I'd rather not. I'm really worn out tonight. Let's have a quick bite here in the hotel and then call it a night.'

'No problem. Finish your drink and we'll go and find a table.'

A couple of minutes later, they stood up and walked out of the bar.

The dining room was past the reception desk and down a short corridor with male and female lavatories on the right-hand side. As he reached the door of the male facility, Bronson pushed the door open and stepped inside, then waited with the door cracked open just enough for him to see along the corridor towards the lobby.

Angela continued walking towards the dining room and stopped outside, apparently to study the menu displayed there.

About half a minute later, Bronson heard footsteps along the corridor. Through the narrow gap he could see that the approaching man was the watcher from the bar. He took the mobile phone battery out of his pocket and waited for the precise moment to act.

As the footsteps reached the door, he stepped out behind the figure, wrapped his left hand around the man's mouth, rammed the end of the battery into his spine and dragged him backwards into the lavatory. The whole thing took only a couple of seconds, and the watcher was taken completely by surprise. He hadn't even begun to react when Bronson spoke to him quietly in French.

'What you can feel pressing into your back is the muzzle of a Colt Model 1908 pistol in twenty-five ACP calibre. It's not the biggest handgun in the world, nor is it the biggest calibre. If I pull the trigger, the bullet probably won't kill you, but I can guarantee that you'll never walk again, because it'll go right through your spine. At this range I can't possibly miss. Do not speak and do not make any sudden movements. Nod if you understand what I've said.'

The watcher had virtually frozen in place when Bronson started speaking. Now he nodded, just once.

'That's good,' Bronson said. 'I'm taking my hand away from your mouth. Do not shout or call out. Now place both your palms on the wall in front of you at head height and move your feet backwards so that your weight is on your hands.'

Moving slightly clumsily, the man did as he was told. In that position he wasn't helpless, but he wouldn't be able to react very quickly.

'Good. Don't move.'

Bronson slipped the battery back into his pocket and ran his hands down the man's torso. He found something he hadn't expected. The watcher was wearing a shoulder holster under his jacket. Bronson reached for the pistol with his left hand, and at that moment the man made his move. But because of his position he telegraphed it well in advance.

Stepping forward with his right foot, he swung his left arm, fist clenched, in a vicious scything arc towards Bronson's head. If the blow had connected, it would probably have been the end of the matter, but Bronson ducked under it.

The watcher's right fist followed his left, but he was still unbalanced because of the way Bronson had made him stand, and although the blow landed, it was lacking any real power.

It was at about that moment that the watcher realised the man who'd attacked him didn't have a gun in his hand, and rather than draw back his right fist for another blow, he obviously decided that the quickest way to end the fight would be to use his weapon. He swung his left fist at Bronson's face again, and at the same time slid his right hand inside his jacket.

Bronson grunted as the man's fist missed his jaw and ploughed into his left shoulder, then surged forward, wrapping both arms around the watcher's torso to prevent him pulling out his pistol. He drove him backwards and to one side, slamming the man's back into one of the wash basins. The basin acted as a fulcrum and the back of his head crashed into the mirror above the sink. Somewhat surprisingly, the glass didn't break.

Bronson twisted his body and drove the man over to one side of the sink, using all his strength to propel him backwards and straight into the tiled wall, releasing his grip on his torso the moment before impact. The back of the watcher's head cracked into the tiles, dazing him. Bronson took a half-step backwards and then rammed his right fist into the man's solar plexus. A short, hard jab, the way he'd been taught years earlier.

And that was the end of it. The watcher gasped as the air was driven out of his lungs and he slumped backwards against the wall of the lavatory. Bronson hooked his legs out from under him and he sat down with a thump.

Bronson reached into the man's jacket and removed the pistol, one of the ubiquitous Glock 17s popular with police forces and criminals everywhere. It had a full magazine but there wasn't a cartridge in the chamber, which he rectified immediately by pulling back the slide. He made sure that the watcher saw him do it as he got his breath back.

'Time we had a chat,' Bronson said, taking a couple of paces backwards out of the man's immediate reach and levelling the Glock at his stomach, 'but first take off your jacket and toss it over to me.'

The watcher had no choice and he obviously knew it. Sullenly he removed the garment and lobbed it in Bronson's direction.

'Now the shoulder holster.'

Again the man complied.

Bronson squatted down, stuffed the holster into his pocket and then, keeping the muzzle of the Glock aimed at the man, searched his jacket using his left hand. He found an almost full box of nine-millimetre Parabellum rounds in one pocket, which he transferred to his own jacket, and did the same with a cheap and basic Nokia mobile phone, a Samsung smartphone and the man's passport and wallet.

'How many of you are there? Watching us, I mean.'

'*Siamo in cinque*,' he replied.

The answer wasn't a surprise but the language the man used was.

'Five of you?' Bronson said, immediately switching to Italian. 'Not really enough for proper surveillance, though, is it? I saw you three times over at Montségur, and here you are again. Who are you working for?'

The man shook his head. 'You'll find out soon enough,' he said. 'I'm telling you nothing.'

In fact, Bronson wasn't particularly interested in who had decided to dog their footsteps, only in making sure they could slip away from them. And they needed to get moving.

'Okay,' he said. 'Stand up and strip.'

'*Cosa?*'

'Strip. You know, take your clothes off. Don't worry, I'm not interested in your body. Just get on with it.'

With a wary look at Bronson, the watcher clambered to his feet and obeyed, dropping his clothes in a pile in front of him. He paused when he got down to his socks and underpants.

'Yes, those as well,' Bronson ordered. 'Now go into the stall on the end and lock yourself in.'

He watched as the man walked to the end of the short row of stalls, opened the door and stepped inside.

There was a closet right behind the door to the lavatory. Bronson opened it and peered inside, then reached in and took out a wooden-shafted mop. He walked over to the now-occupied stall and slid the end of the mop shaft through the handle of the door, jamming it so that it couldn't be turned from the inside. It wasn't particularly secure, but it would keep the Italian busy for a while trying to break out, and then he'd have to decide whether or not to run out into the street naked. It would be some time before he would be able to raise the alarm and tell the rest of his team what had happened, and that was what Bronson was counting on.

He scooped up the Italian's clothes and shoes and wrapped them in the discarded jacket, slid the Glock into the waistband of his trousers and quietly stepped out into the corridor.

Angela was right outside the door, a worried expression on her face.

'Okay?' she asked, conjuring up a smile from somewhere.

'Okay,' Bronson confirmed. 'We've got a few minutes.'

'You didn't kill him, did you?'

Bronson shook his head. 'No, he's just very embarrassed because I got the drop on him, and also because he's now starkers and locked in a loo. We need to move. Grab the bags and let's get out of here.'

Bronson and Angela walked out of the hotel together and down the Rue d'Etigny to where he'd left the Peugeot hire car. He opened the boot and put their bags and the Italian's clothes in it, then he steered the car off down the street, intending to put some distance between themselves and the centre of Auch as quickly as possible.

'Where are we going?' Angela asked, fastening her seat belt.

'Buggered if I know. Let's just get out of here, lose ourselves in the French countryside and find somewhere else to stay. Then we can decide what to do about these Italian comedians following us around, and about the Ark as well.'

'Italians?' Angela asked. 'I didn't expect that.'

'Well, Mister Stark Naked and Locked in a Loo is definitely Italian, so it's a reasonable guess that the others are as well. If you put a team of watchers together, having a common language is pretty much essential.'

The Rue d'Etigny became the Rue de Metz after a couple of hundred yards. Bronson went straight on, following the street signs for the N21 and Tarbes.

'Tarbes is quite a big place,' Angela said, bringing up the town's information on her smartphone. 'We could lose ourselves there.'

'Sounds good,' Bronson replied. 'I just need to make a stop somewhere along the road before we get there.'

He found a lay-by a couple of miles outside Auch, stopped the car and got out. He pulled the shoulder holster out of his pocket, removed his jacket and donned the holster. Angela watched quizzically. He took the Glock from the waistband of his trousers, removed the magazine, racked the slide to eject the cartridge he'd chambered and replaced it in the magazine. Then he slid the magazine back into the butt of the pistol and holstered it.

'So he was armed?' Angela said, stating the obvious.

'He was, which does add an extra dimension to the degree of trouble we're in. You can bet that the others – he told me there were five of them – are carrying pistols too. But now I've got this Glock, we're not completely helpless.'

Bronson checked the man's wallet and removed about a hundred euros in cash, then took out the two mobile phones he'd found in his jacket. The Nokia looked like a burner, a cheap disposable phone with a pre-paid SIM card in it, but the Samsung was reasonably new.

'There's no way of telling if this has a tracking app installed,' he said, holding the smartphone up. 'If they're using something like Spyic or Cocospy, it's almost impossible to detect, because the tracking app is tiny, only about two megabytes, and it stays hidden unless you know the code to access it. So we'll have to dump it. In fact, we'll dump both of them.'

He pointed ahead.

'There's a rubbish bin over there. That'll do nicely.'

Chapter 25

Marco Ferrara followed the satnav's instructions and stopped his Alfa Romeo at the base of a monumental stone staircase on the Boulevard Sadi Carnot, part of French national route N21, which ran through Auch alongside the river. He pulled into a loading zone outside a small closed shop, got out and looked around him.

The evening was still quite light, and some distance away, up four flights of steps and in the centre of the huge staircase, he could see the dark shape of the statue of d'Artagnan. His real name was Charles de Batz de Castelmore, which didn't roll off the tongue quite as easily, and he had been born near Lupiac, some forty kilometres west of Auch, in about 1611. Seized on as hero by the French writer Alexandre Dumas, the fictional d'Artagnan's career and exploits bore only the most tenuous possible resemblance to what the man had actually done in real life.

A bulky figure detached itself from the left-hand wall of the staircase and walked towards him.

'Luca,' Ferrara said in greeting, and extended his right arm towards him.

'Marco,' Rossi replied, shaking his hand. 'Not seen you around for a while.'

The two men had worked together in the past but had never been friends.

'Right, where are they?'

'In the hotel. It looks like they've settled in for the night, though they might still nip out for dinner. If they do, we'll be right behind them.'

'Who's the man with the target?' Ferrara asked.

'No idea, unless he's her husband.'

'He's not. She isn't married.'

'I didn't know that. Well, we know he's English because we've heard them talking, and he acts like a husband or a long-term boyfriend. They look very comfortable with each other.'

'Describe him.'

Rossi did his best to provide a verbal sketch of the man he and the team he'd recruited had been following.

'He's quite big and looks capable,' he finished. 'Like he would be handy in a fight.'

'It doesn't matter how big he is. A nine-millimetre will take him down just the same.'

'I thought it was supposed to look like an accident.'

'It will. That was just a figure of speech,' Ferrara replied. 'Right, let's go up so I can see the hotel and maybe them as well. Where's your car?'

Rossi gestured behind him. 'I left it in the square. It was only a short walk down here.'

Ferrara nodded. 'You can direct me,' he said. 'Get in.'

He started the Alfa and pulled away from the kerb.

'Just go straight on. Auch is built on a hill, and there's a maze of narrow streets between the cathedral and the river. This might seem like a long way round, but it's a lot faster than trying to reach the square by any other route. When you get to a set of traffic lights, turn hard right to go back on yourself. It's a hairpin bend and there are no road signs at the junction from this direction. Typical of the bloody French.'

The lights were green when they reached the junction, and Ferrara hauled the MiTo round in a tight turn to head straight up towards the centre of Auch. He noticed a sign on the corner as he did so: the road he was on led to the Centre Historique and the Cathédrale.

'This is the Rue de Metz,' Rossi said. 'Keep going until you reach a Y-junction, and take the left fork to Mont de Marsan and the cathedral.'

Ferrara nodded, and a couple of minutes later made the turn.

'At the end of this stretch there's another set of traffic lights. Bear right into the Rue d'Etigny. When you approach the top, find a parking space.'

There were two spaces on the left near the end of the street. Ferrara waited until a car had driven past them on the other side of the road, and then pulled into one of them.

'Very convenient,' Rossi said, opening the passenger door and getting out. He gestured towards the stone building right behind Ferrara. 'That's the hotel where the targets are staying.'

They walked away from the car and into the Place de la Libération. Rossi swept his right arm out to indicate the open space.

'This is more or less it. The centre's quite small and the best way to get around it is to find somewhere to park your car and then walk.'

They were approaching a restaurant on their right when Rossi suddenly stopped and looked around him, then stared back towards the Rue d'Etigny.

'What is it?' Ferrara asked.

'The car. I didn't see the car.'

'What, your car?'

'No. The one the targets are using.'

Rossi pulled a mobile phone out of his pocket and rang a number. Then he looked at the screen.

'It's gone straight to voicemail,' he said. 'Where the fuck is he?'

'Where the fuck is who?' Ferrara demanded.

'Moretti. Stefano Moretti. He was supposed to be keeping watch in the hotel.'

Ferrara stared at him, anger showing in his face, though his voice was quiet and restrained.

'You can't see the targets' car and you can't raise the idiot who was supposed to be watching them? Let me hazard a guess here. They've spotted your man, this Moretti, somehow disabled him and then got into their car and driven away.'

Rossi didn't reply, just dialled another number on his mobile.

'Where are you?' he said when his call was answered.

Ferrara listened carefully to one side of the short conversation.

'Have you heard from Moretti? He's not answering his phone… Where are you now?… We need to meet… I don't care. Meet me outside the hotel right now. Bring the others.'

Rossi ended the call, glanced at his watch and looked at Ferrara.

'One of them was supposed to relieve Moretti in the hotel in half an hour,' he said. 'They weren't expecting to hear from him.'

'So your men have lost both targets they – and you – were supposed to be watching?'

Ferrara's rage was obvious, and made more so by his completely calm and controlled voice.

'We'll check the hotel,' Rossi said, and turned to walk back the way they'd come.

In the hotel lobby, Ferrara walked to the reception desk, where he was unsurprised to discover that his 'good friend' Angela Lewis had checked out less than half an hour earlier. He also managed to glance at the computer screen while he was talking to the receptionist, and learned that Lewis's companion was named Bronson, initial C.

Rossi walked into the bar to look around and emerged quickly, having found no trace of Moretti.

'So their car's gone, and according to the receptionist, they've gone as well,' Ferrara said as Rossi rejoined him. 'Your man?'

'No surprise, he's not in the bar. But he has to be somewhere here. I'll check the public rooms.'

As they walked down the corridor towards the restaurant, they both heard a dull banging sound coming from somewhere nearby. Ferrara pushed open the door to the male lavatory and immediately identified its source.

He held the door open for Rossi and pointed at the last stall, where somebody had obviously been locked inside. The occupant was trying to get out, banging or kicking the door, which had been secured by the shaft of a mop jamming the handle and preventing it from being opened.

'Your man, I think,' he said.

Rossi muttered a curse, walked over to the stall and removed the mop. When he opened the door, Stefano Moretti, stark naked, peered at him from inside.

'This had better be good,' Rossi said, 'or I'll fucking well leave you in here.'

-

Getting Moretti out of the hotel hadn't been as difficult as Ferrara had been expecting, because the watchers had various sets of clothing with them to ring the changes when they were following the targets.

Rossi had left Moretti in the stall and told him to lock the door from the inside, then he'd gone outside to where the other three members of the team were waiting. He'd taken a tracksuit and a pair of trainers from Moretti's bag in the boot of one of the cars, gone back into the hotel and handed them to him. A couple of minutes later, Ferrara, Rossi and Moretti assembled in the Place de la Libération to hear him explain what had happened.

'I was following them to the restaurant when he grabbed me from behind,' he said. 'He stuck a gun in my back and—'

'No he didn't,' Ferrara said.

'What? And who are you?' Moretti asked.

'I'm the person giving the orders around here. His name's Bronson and he didn't stick a gun in your back because he hasn't got one. We've been tracking these two since they left London. They flew to France, which means they couldn't have brought a weapon with them. What he did was stick something in your back that he told you was a gun. If you'd thought it through, you would have known he was unarmed.'

Moretti shook his head. 'No. He told me exactly what make it was. He—'

'Did you see it?' Ferrara asked.

'No, but—'

'Exactly. But now he *does* have a gun – your Glock – thanks to your stupidity. And I suppose you told him who you were working for.'

'No,' Moretti said. 'I would never do that.'

'He couldn't anyway,' Rossi chimed in, 'because he doesn't actually know who's paying for his services.'

'I hope you're not paying him much,' Ferrara said, 'because you're not getting much of a service here at all.'

'You have to work with what you can get,' Rossi said. 'This was what I got. Lose yourself, Moretti. You're no good to me now.'

'But he took my passport and credit cards, everything. I need to—'

'That's your problem, not mine. Get your stuff out of the car and then get lost, before I decide to retire you permanently.'

Ferrara watched as Moretti walked away across the square.

'Are you sure it's wise, leaving him alive?'

Rossi nodded. 'I can do without the complications of killing him here in France. He knows nothing about who we are. I told him this was an undercover deniable black operation on behalf of the AISE. I even had an ID card mocked up to show him.'

'And he believed you?' Ferrara's voice betrayed his disbelief. 'He really thought he was working for the Italian secret service?'

'Maybe. Or maybe not. I think he just wanted the money. I gave him the pistol to show that I was serious and to make the whole idea a bit more convincing. Anyway, he's not our problem any longer. He'll go to the *gendarmes* and tell them he was mugged and lost everything, and they'll arrange for him to have funds and an emergency passport. Or perhaps they won't. I really don't care.'

Ferrara nodded. 'The big problem is the targets. Thanks to Moretti's incompetence, they now know they're being watched, and Bronson – that's the name of the man with Lewis – has proved he's dangerous. He's also now got a gun. They've obviously left Auch and we're going to have to find them again. Have you any idea where they might be going?'

Rossi shook his head. 'No idea at all,' he said, 'but it doesn't matter.'

'What do you mean?'

'I mean I know something they don't. There's a tracker fitted on their car. And I know that because I put it there. I know my trade, and it was always possible that they might give us the slip somehow. So it doesn't matter where they go or how fast they drive, because I can always find them.'

Chapter 26

Tarbes, Hautes-Pyrénées, France

They stayed on the N21 and drove through Tarbes, Angela navigating using the app on her mobile. She'd already found a hotel that looked ideal, located a few yards off a roundabout to the west of the town. She'd used Google Maps to check it out, and it offered one important feature: a parking area behind the hotel and out of view of the road.

They checked in and took their bags up to their room. They'd missed dinner in the restaurant, so Bronson went down to the bar and ordered a large *baguette jambon* – basically a big ham sandwich – as an evening meal that they could share. They ate it sitting on the bed and flicking through the channels on the flat-panel set bolted to the opposite wall. Virtually the entire output, at least at that time of the evening, appeared to be either game shows or small numbers of French men and women talking earnestly into big hand-held microphones.

'The old joke about French television,' Bronson said, between mouthfuls, 'used to be that you could tell how important a speaker was by the size of the microphone they gave him. At least on French TV, size matters.'

'I might have known you'd reduce it to something smutty,' Angela replied, looking at the screen. 'But it does all look very amateurish,' she added. 'I mean, the only time you see a microphone on British television is if they're doing an outside broadcast somewhere, but here they've all got them held in front of their mouths all the time.'

'French television really isn't that good,' Bronson agreed, finishing the last bit of his *baguette*. 'They buy in a lot of stuff from America and then dub it, usually badly, into French, so you end up with troopers in Alaska moving their mouths in one way while entirely uncoordinated French comes out of the speakers.'

The room had a kettle and sachets of coffee and tea, so they made drinks and then settled down to continue decrypting the page of text they'd begun back in Auch.

'Before we start, I'll just check my emails.' Angela opened the lid of her laptop. She quickly scanned her inbox, muttering 'Dross, dross and more dross' as she deleted most of the messages. 'There's one from George Anderson,' she said. 'That alleged Israeli historian paid him another visit, and it wasn't a very pleasant experience. He told George that if he didn't get copies of the two missing documents, he would break both his arms right there on the street.'

'That's not entirely unexpected,' Bronson said. 'Whoever he is, he's no academic. I assume George handed them over?'

'Of course. And then spent a couple of unproductive hours at the library with a member of the *gendarmerie* explaining what had happened. Of course, there's nothing much anybody can do, because the only piece of identification George saw from the man was a business card that said his name was Israel Mahler, and we already knew he was using an alias. Anyway, George was quite shaken up by it.'

'Well, at least he wasn't hurt. Now we know there are two groups of people out there, one Italian and the other possibly Israeli, both looking for the same thing. We also know the Italians are armed – or at least the one I ran into was – and that the Israelis were quite prepared to cripple a man in broad daylight on a street in Paris. We are not dealing with nice people here.'

'Do think we should carry on?'

'Yes, I do. The best way to avoid contact with these two groups is for us to find the relic first. So let's get to it.'

Now that they'd worked out the encryption method used, it was just a matter of transcribing the plaintext based on the spacing created by the *scytale*. That produced a page of Occitan text that Angela then spent about an hour reworking into English. She separated the continuous text into individual words, then used a Catalan-to-English translator as well as a number of Occitan and Catalan dictionaries to translate each one.

The result wasn't elegant in a literary or indeed any other sense, and there were several sections that really needed a bit more work to be easily readable, but at least they understood what the text was telling them. Its meaning was clear enough and that was what mattered.

'This isn't exactly what I expected it to say,' Angela commented, looking again at the translation she'd produced.

'Nor me,' Bronson said.

They were reasonably sure that the text they'd translated was the document described as *velat* on the journal page, meaning 'veiled' or 'coded', so they weren't looking for any other piece of text. What they had in front of them was it.

They'd both expected the translation to explain where the Ark had been taken in the last days before the occupants of the castle of Montségur finally capitulated and left the fortress to descend the mountain, some walking to freedom but the majority heading for the flames. And it did do that, after a fashion.

The first few words of the text contained Old Testament references. Angela checked them on the Internet and found they described the construction of the Ark and how the Israelites had carried the object with them during their wanderings.

'I suppose that's just setting the scene,' she said, as Bronson started going through the text once again. 'It saves having to explain the background, though I guess almost everyone, certainly in medieval times, would already know the story of the

Ark of the Covenant. The next bit's more interesting, though it's not what you might call new or ground-breaking stuff.'

That part described how the Ark had vanished around the time of the siege of Jerusalem, though it didn't provide either the date of the event or any suggestions about where the relic had gone.

'They're probably talking about the second siege,' Angela suggested, 'which would make it 587 BC. The first siege was in 597 BC, a decade earlier, but the Temple was only destroyed at the end of the second one.'

After that, the narrative jumped over half a millennium to the time of the Crusades and the formation of the order of the Knights Templar, explicitly stating that the knights *had* recovered the Ark from a hiding place deep within the Temple Mount. It had taken them nine years to find it. Bronson had always assumed that the order had been formed specifically to recover the Ark. He also knew there were more than fifty tunnels under the Temple Mount that covered, along with numerous subterranean chambers, some thirty-five acres in all, plenty of space in which to construct a false wall to hide an existing chamber or do something of that sort, and the search would inevitably have been both long and difficult.

According to the deciphered document in front of them, the Templars had searched everywhere. Once they'd eventually found the relic, they'd summoned an envoy to travel from the Vatican to Jerusalem, and when he appeared they'd shown him the Ark and made a number of demands to be submitted to the Pope.

'That was obviously what sparked the issue of the *Omne datum optimum* papal bull by Innocent II, which exempted the Templars from all authority apart from that of the Pope himself,' Bronson said.

'That much we already knew,' Angela replied, 'or if we didn't know it for sure, we assumed that was what had happened. When the Templars eventually left Jerusalem, the order was the biggest institution in Europe after the Catholic Church itself, far more wealthy than most nations and much more powerful than the Pope, their nominal master. But what I didn't expect was that the Ark would then be taken to France, to what the author of this text calls the "Templar Cathedral", which is probably Chartres.'

'Because...?'

Angela looked at him. 'Lots of reasons. Do you know anything about Chartres?'

'I know where it is. Apart from that, no, not really.'

'Okay. The present cathedral wasn't the first one. We don't know how many previous churches had been built, but there were at least four and possibly seven, all of which came to some kind of calamitous end. When you look at a record like that, with buildings dedicated to God being regularly destroyed by acts of God, it does rather make you wonder why anybody's still a believer. Some bits of the present cathedral survived a major fire that engulfed the previous building in 1194. We don't know who paid for it, or the names of the master builders who constructed it, but there's a strong possibility that it was financed at least in part by the Knights Templar. The order was then at the height of its power in France, and as an extremely wealthy Christian organisation, it would have been strange if it hadn't contributed something towards it. Construction took about twenty-five years, and it was formally reconsecrated in 1260.

'It's a huge building, about four hundred and twenty-five feet long and a hundred and fifty feet wide. The tower rises to over three hundred and seventy feet, and there are more than a hundred and seventy stained-glass windows, which basically tell the story of the Bible in images. Inside, probably the most famous feature is the labyrinth, a circular structure marked out on the floor of the nave that's designed as a tool to assist worshippers in their devotions. It has a single entrance, which is also the exit, and there's only one path that can be followed to reach the centre. Although it's only just over forty feet in diameter, if somebody follows the path all the way in and then all the way out again, by the time they've completed it they will have walked about a third of a mile.'

'That should give them plenty of time to say their prayers,' Bronson said.

'Exactly. That is its purpose. Now, there's one very obvious connection between Chartres Cathedral and the Ark. On the pillars in the north portico on the outside of the cathedral are carvings that very clearly show the relic being transported. But it's the inscriptions underneath the carvings that are the really intriguing thing, because the Latin doesn't make sense. Let me just find some pictures of them.'

Angela opened up a search engine, and after a couple of minutes she showed Bronson a photograph of a curved stone pillar on which was carved a complex battle scene.

'That's supposed to show the Battle of Aphek, when the Philistines stole the Ark of the Covenant and carried it off to Ashdod. Remember I asked if you knew anything about a plague of haemorrhoids? Well, it was the Philistines who ended up suffering from that particular affliction.

'They had put the Ark in one of their temples, dedicated to a god named Dagon, but the following day they discovered their idol lying face-down on the ground, apparently praying to the Ark. They replaced the statue where it should have been, but the next day it was found lying on its face again and broken into pieces. According to the Bible, the Ark went on to cause the plague of haemorrhoids, followed by a plague of mice and then a plague of boils. Understandably, the Philistines decided they could do without all this, and after a few months they returned Ark to the Israelites.'

She found another picture.

'This shows the Ark being transported on a cart pulled by oxen with an angel guiding it. We know it's the Ark because in the carving just to the right there's an open box containing the items the Bible tells us were originally stored in it: the stone tablets, the rod of Aaron and the pot of manna. Some people believe this means the Ark was transported from Jerusalem to France by the Knights Templar and then hidden away inside, or perhaps underneath, Chartres Cathedral. And what we've discovered supports that suggestion.'

'You said the Latin was confusing,' Bronson said.

'Actually I didn't,' Angela replied. 'I said it didn't make sense, which is entirely different.'

She found another picture that showed the lower parts of the two curved cylinders on the pillar and pointed to the inscription on the left-hand side.

'This is what I mean,' she said. 'The Latin there spells out *ARCHA CEDERIS*, and on the right-hand cylinder we get the same two words as part of the longer phrase *HIC AMITITUR ARCHA CEDERIS*. The two words *ARCHA CEDERIS* are exactly the same in both inscriptions, and that's the first problem. When the cathedral was built, it's quite probable that some of the masons working on it would have been illiterate, but an illiterate mason would never have been allowed to carve an important inscription without supervision. So those phrases were carved because that's what somebody in authority wanted to be inscribed on that pillar.'

'What does it mean?' Bronson asked.

'That's the problem. People have assumed that *ARCHA CEDERIS* refers to the Ark of the Covenant, but it doesn't. In fact, at first glance the phrase is meaningless. In the Latin Vulgate Bible, the Ark of the Covenant is always referred to as the *arca foederis*. *Arca* is an ark or chest, and *foederis* means a contract or undertaking. Put them together and you have the ark of the contract or the Ark of the Covenant, the contract or understanding between God and the Israelites. But the Latin word *archa* normally translates as "archangel", as an abbreviation of *archangelus* – though its alternative translation as "box" works better in this case – and *cederis* isn't a noun.'

'So what is it?'

'Inscriptions were usually written in the simplest possible language so that they would be understood by the maximum number of people. "Here lies the body of John Brown", that kind of thing. The word *cederis* is Latin, but it's an obscure verb tense that most people – even people who spoke the language – would find difficult to understand. In fact, I've got to look it up myself.'

She opened another screen on her laptop and studied it.

'Right. *Cederis* is the second person singular present passive indicative of the verb *cedere*.'

'I see what you mean,' Bronson said. 'I don't know what that means in English, let alone in Latin. You'll have to talk me through it.'

'The verb *cedere* means to yield, to go away, or surrender. It's the root of the English verb "to cede". The tense refers to the subject of the verb, and there are three possibilities. If it was first person, the subject would be I or we. Third person means he, she or they, and second person means you.'

'So it means "you yield" or "you give up" in this case?'

'Yes,' Angela nodded, 'more or less, but we've not finished yet. Singular means the number of the subject, so it means you individually rather than you as a group of people. Present refers to the timing, and it means that the action of the verb is taking place now, at the present time. Passive refers to the voice. Verbs can be either active or passive. In this case, it means that you as the subject of the verb are having the action done to you, rather than you doing the action. And finally indicative refers to the mood of the verb, and again there are three possibilities – indicative, subjunctive and imperative. Subjunctive means something that might take place, imperative means that you're telling somebody to do something, and indicative means that something is really happening.'

The response to that was obvious, but Bronson asked the question anyway.

'So what does *cederis* actually mean in this context?'

'I was afraid you were going to ask me that. Okay, it translates as something like "you personally are right now having to yield in reality". When you add the noun, it becomes "the box that you personally are right now having to surrender in reality", more or less. I know that sounds incredibly clumsy, but it's what the expression means. If you wanted a really short version, which I guess you do, it would be something like "the box you are yielding". Some cathedral guidebooks translate this as "you are to work through the Ark", which is complete nonsense. The Latin means nothing like that.'

'Okay,' Bronson said. 'I more or less follow that. So that's what the first two words mean. What about the longer expression?'

'The guidebooks suggest that *HIC AMITITUR ARCHA CEDERIS* means "Here things take their course; you are to work through the Ark", and again they're completely wrong. The only word correctly translated is HIC, which does mean "here". First of all, the word *amititur* never existed in the Latin language, so that's an obvious problem. But *amittitur* spelt with a double T did exist. It was derived from the verb *amitto* which means to lose. *Amittitur* is another complex tense, this time the third person singular present passive indicative, and the short and snappy translation is something like "he or she is losing".

'The other thing to look at in the inscription is the shape of the fourth letter, because it doesn't actually look like a single letter T. Or a double T, come to that. It's more like a T combined with a C, a ligature of T and C, but that doesn't work because the word *amitcitur* also doesn't exist in Latin. It might have been a shorthand symbol to indicate a double T, but there's room to have carved two separate letters, so why didn't they? The other alternative is that it's just a stylized letter C, and that gives us another possible meaning. *Amicitur* is again the third person singular present passive indicative, this time of the verb *amicio*, which means to clothe or envelop or hide.'

'So it means something like "he or she is hiding",' Bronson suggested.

'Yes. So the most likely meaning of the longer expression, translating what the Latin words actually mean rather than what people think they should mean, is either "here he is hiding the box you are yielding", if we're going with *amicitur*, or "here he is losing the box you are yielding" if the verb is *amittitur*. The Latin certainly isn't clear, which may have been deliberate on the part of the person who prepared the inscription. With a relic as important as the Ark, maybe he decided that the inscriptions had to say something about it, but he didn't want to just come right out and say something like *ARCA HIC LATEANT*, which would mean "The Ark is hidden here". Anyway, to me, the first sentence makes far more sense than the second, and that does suggest that the box – by implication the Ark – was hidden at Chartres Cathedral when these inscriptions were carved.'

'That's interesting,' Bronson said, 'and thanks for the Latin lesson. I'm better informed but none the wiser. So it looks like the Ark was hidden somewhere in Chartres Cathedral, but according to this text it didn't stay there.'

'No. This says it was entrusted to the care of the Cathars a few years later, and that's certainly possible because it's thought that the Templars and the Cathars shared some common religious beliefs. Because the Ark was believed to be a way of talking to God, it would be the one religious relic that the Cathars would have venerated above all others; a confirmation of one of their most important core beliefs.'

'And the Ark being in the possession of the Cathars at Montségur also answers another couple of questions, like why King Louis IX seemed to tread very carefully around members of the Aniort family, who were closely involved with the Cathars. If they had the Ark, that would have been a tremendously powerful weapon, perhaps literally if the stories about it are true, but certainly metaphorically. And it would also explain what the king's men were looking for when they reduced the castle of Montségur to rubble when the siege was over.'

Angela nodded. 'There's also the suggestion that the Templars were in some ways an armed branch of the Cathar movement. The Cathars wouldn't carry arms – that's why they had to employ mercenary soldiers at Montségur to act as a garrison for the castle – but the Templars certainly did.'

'And then the four *perfecti* abseiled down from Montségur carrying the Ark, handed it over to Raymond d'Aniort and went their separate ways. If this is to be believed. And that could very well leave us some distance up shit creek without a paddle. Or a canoe, come to that,' Bronson said.

Chapter 27

Auch, Gascony, France

'That was good thinking,' Ferrara admitted, almost reluctantly. 'So where are they – or rather where is their car – right now?'

Rossi took out his smartphone and opened the tracking application. When it had loaded and collected the data, he showed the screen to Ferrara.

'Not far away,' he said. 'The tracker's stationary on the west side of Tarbes in a hotel car park, so I guess they've gone to ground. That's a biggish town about sixty kilometres south-west of here. You want to head down there now?'

'Yes, of course. I don't want the tracker to drop off or the battery to fail before we've reached them. But I don't think there's too much urgency. They're in a hotel and they'll think they've given us the slip and are safe. We'll find accommodation somewhere nearby. I'd like another tracker, or two if you have that many, put on their vehicle tonight to make sure we don't lose them, and then we'll see what they do tomorrow.'

'Do you want the other three men I recruited to go with us? They're not the best, as we know, but at least they'll do what they're told.'

'Might as well,' Ferrara said. 'They can act as bullet-catchers if there's any shooting, and we'll need them as extra bodies if we have to follow the targets on foot.'

Despite his explicit instructions from Cardinal Caravaggio, Ferrara was again disobeying his orders. The sight of the page of encrypted text had convinced him that he would not be able to decipher it; it was way outside his area of expertise. And as the Vatican obviously wanted the Ark either found or totally destroyed, it made sense to him to revert to the first plan the cardinal had suggested: keep following the Lewis woman and let her find the relic – because that was what she was good at – and then simply step in and take it from her. Then he could dispose of her and the man she was travelling with. Of course, if the experts employed by the *Congregatio pro Doctrina Fidei* finally managed to crack the encryption, that would radically change the situation. Then he would be able to kill them both before following the trail of the Ark.

Luca Rossi would do what he was told – the cardinal had made it clear that Ferrara was running the show – and the only other complication would be if the fanatical Jews from Zeru managed to work out what was happening and turned up somewhere.

But Ferrara thought he would be able to deal with that situation if it arose.

In the meantime, he would head off to Tarbes, fill his vehicle with fuel and find a hotel to get some sleep.

Tomorrow could be a very long day.

Chapter 28

Paris, France

Josef Gellerman had seen no point in leaving Paris until the Zeru team had identified a definite destination. The city was an international travel hub with excellent road, rail and air links, and from there they could easily and quickly get anywhere in the world.

The sighting of Luca Rossi near the Bibliothèque Serpente had been unexpected and unwelcome, because it meant that the *Congregatio pro Doctrina Fidei* had become involved. It also meant that the CDF had the same information as Zeru, so Gellerman knew they were in a race, a race that Zeru had to win. The clue was obviously the page of encrypted text. If they could decipher that, he was convinced they would know where to find the Ark of the Covenant.

Lemuel Dayan was both a computer expert and a talented programmer, and almost as soon as they'd identified Rossi from the video, Gellerman had told him to drop everything else and just crack the code. Neither of them had expected it would be that difficult to decipher a hand-written message encrypted during the medieval period, but it had taken far longer than they had anticipated.

Dayan's first efforts had involved mounting brute-force attacks to try all possible combinations of an Atbash cipher. That hadn't taken long but had produced no results apart from generating occasional random combinations of a few letters that happened to spell something recognisable, common enough in cryptology when working with ciphertexts.

Next he'd looked at Atbash variants, perhaps using two alphabets, but again this had produced no usable results, and this program had taken his computer a lot longer to run because of the greater number of variables. By the end of that, all he knew for certain was that the encryption hadn't used a substitution cipher. So he'd looked elsewhere, and the very next decryption method he tried had worked. Not the first time, but eventually.

All he had done was write a program that would start with the first letter of the encrypted text and then follow it with every third letter – he hadn't thought there was any point in trying it with the second letter – all the way through the encrypted passage, making repeated passes until every letter had been selected. Then the program would do the same with every fourth letter, and then every fifth letter and so on.

That generated a lot of pages of text that Dayan viewed on the screen of his laptop, feeding anything that looked like a genuine word into an online Occitan dictionary to check it. But when he looked at the output when the program had selected every thirty-first letter of the ciphertext, the first seven letters stopped him in his tracks.

'Josef,' he called urgently. 'I think we may have it. Look.' He pointed at the text on his screen. 'Those first two words are SANT DEU, and I've already picked up enough Occitan to know that that translates as "Holy God". That can't be a mistake or a random grouping.'

Gellerman stared at the screen, his gaze roaming over the other lines displayed there. Several other combinations of letters looked to him like real, albeit unfamiliar, words. He slapped Dayan on the back.

'Well done, my friend, well done. Print a copy of that so I can look at it and start working on the translation. We'll crack this today.'

Chapter 29

Tarbes, Hautes-Pyrénées, France

'This explains why the encrypted text was included within the Hautpoul papers, because the Aniort and Hautpoul families merged just under five hundred years later,' Angela said, looking at the plaintext they'd produced.

'Agreed,' Bronson replied, 'but I'm not sure it gets us much further. We'd established that the Ark was part of the Cathar treasure of Montségur and was what the four *perfecti* were carrying when they escaped from the fortress. This text just confirms that. And states that a man named Raymond d'Aniort took possession of the Ark. The end.'

'But we know other stuff, don't we?' Angela said encouragingly. 'Raymond d'Aniort wasn't just some man. He was deeply involved with the Cathars at Montségur and in negotiating the truce; he was the lord of Rennes-le-Château and Rennes-les-Bains and one of the most important nobles in the area. We also know he opposed the persecution of the Cathars and did what he could to help them. That implies he supported the Knights Templar, and you could argue that it was the Templars who actually owned the Ark. They'd found and recovered it from the tunnels deep inside the Temple Mount so they had a better claim of ownership than anyone else. It's called finders keepers because that's the way it works.'

'But they gave it to the Cathars,' Bronson pointed out. 'Or do you mean it was a loan? Something the Cathars borrowed from them?'

'Possibly. We know the Cathars and Templars had links in that part of France and maybe the Templars thought that the Ark would be as safe in Montségur at the top of that volcanic pog as it would be anywhere else. But they certainly wouldn't have wanted King Louis getting his hands on it, so smuggling it out made perfect sense. If the Cathars had the relic, they couldn't have carried it down from the castle when the siege ended because the Crusaders would have grabbed it. That was why they demolished the castle when it was all over. They weren't looking for any old treasure. They were looking for the Ark.'

'That all hangs together really well,' Bronson agreed. 'It explains the anomalies about the siege of Montségur, and really only leaves one question that we don't have an answer to.'

'Yes. What did Raymond d'Aniort do with the Ark of the Covenant?'

'Exactly. And I think that's a two-part question. What did he do with it immediately, because he would need to keep it somewhere safe, and where did it end up?'

'So where do we need to go next?' Angela asked. 'Bearing in mind that we now have a gang of armed men following us, should we go anywhere apart from back to Britain on the next available flight?'

'I don't think we have a problem with them. We got away from Auch without any sign that we were followed. That was why I stopped in the lay-by close to the city, to check if there were any other cars behind us, and there weren't. We dumped the two phones in case they were fitted with trackers, so I think we're safe enough. And I'm still taking precautions.'

Bronson pointed at the bedroom door, where he'd wedged a chair under the handle so that it couldn't be opened from the outside without making a hell of a lot of noise; then at his bedside table, where he'd placed the Glock, a dark, compact and utterly lethal final deterrent should anyone break into the room.

'Yes,' Angela said uncertainly, 'you are. But if we see any sign that these people' – she managed to make the word sound faintly obscene – 'are still following us, I reserve the right to cut and run. Like straight to the nearest airport. Agreed?'

'Agreed,' Bronson said. 'But I don't think it'll come to that.'

'So where do we go next, and why? Where did the Ark go after the *perfecti* carried it down from Montségur?'

'I think,' Bronson said, 'we can make another assumption here. I don't think Raymond d'Aniort was a Templar himself, but I think he was trusted by the order. If he hadn't been, they would have had some of their knights waiting for the four *perfecti* to appear with the Ark at the foot of the pog instead of him. So perhaps he was acting as a courier or agent for the order. As a local lord he and his retinue would have attracted less attention than a group of armoured Templar knights.'

Angela nodded. 'You're right about him being trusted,' she agreed, 'because the Aniort family and the Templars were very closely linked. Being the lord of Rennes-le-Château and Rennes-les-Bains in those days meant that Raymond d'Aniort didn't just rule those areas, but also owned them. The Aniorts supported the Cathars and were opposed to the Albigensian Crusade, meaning they were also opposed to the French crown, and they were so worried about having their properties confiscated that in 1209 they signed a treaty with the Templars, transferring their assets to the order for protection. Because the Templars owed allegiance only to the Pope, the French crown had no ability to seize or confiscate any property owned by them.'

'I didn't know that,' Bronson said. 'As for what Raymond did with the Ark, I think we can make another assumption, which is that he would have taken it to a place of safe-keeping, not wandered about the countryside with it strapped to the back of a donkey or something.'

'You have somewhere in mind?'

'I'm assuming that's what the last lines of the text are telling us, but I don't know what any of it really means,' he admitted.

'We've got a reference to Solomon and two sets of initials – CSA and COT – and I don't understand the last bit about the sanctuary for the stranger.'

'Let me put that into better English,' Angela said.

She busied herself with her laptop for a couple of minutes, then looked at him.

'That makes more sense,' she said. 'The first line claims that the "relic of Solomon" – another name for the Ark – was taken from Montségur to the "place of the castle of the Voisins" for safekeeping.'

'And that would be where?'

'The Voisin family was important in the medieval period in this area and they probably had lots of castles. But as you said, Raymond wouldn't have wanted to wander about the countryside carrying something as precious as the Ark, so it would be reasonable to assume that this castle, or the place where the Voisin castle was located, which isn't quite the same thing, was no more than a day's travel by horse and cart, and that means about twenty to twenty-five miles maximum. And there's one fairly obvious location that fits those criteria very well.'

'Which is where?'

'Rennes-le-Château, obviously,' Angela said. 'It's about twenty-five miles from Montségur. The Templars owned the village – in fact it was quite an important town in those days – because the Aniorts had transferred it to the order in 1209, and Raymond d'Aniort was the local lord. It's difficult to see where else they *could* have taken it. The only potential problem was the castle, which was owned by Pierre de Voisin, a supporter of the Albigensian Crusade. But there were plenty of other properties where Raymond and the Ark could have been safely accommodated.'

'So the Ark ended up in Rennes-le-Château, which makes sense now you've explained it. Obviously going there must be our next move. Is that the end of the search?'

'No, because of the last two lines of the text. The Occitan phrase *santuari a l'estranger* doesn't mean "sanctuary for the stranger", but "sanctuary abroad". Maybe the Templars decided to send the Ark back to the Holy Land, to Jerusalem. That sentence reads: "And the relic of Solomon rested in glory at CSA in the dungeon below the bell tower until the doom was upon them and then embarked at COT for sanctuary overseas." We have to assume that the writer was using initials to refer to places that would have been recognisable to people of that time, like UK or USA would be to anyone today. Or recognisable to people living in the Languedoc. Unfortunately, they mean sod all to us, so that's something we're going to have to work on.'

'Well, that's about as clear as mud,' Bronson said. 'Look, I'm knackered. Why don't we get some sleep and take a look at it with fresh eyes tomorrow morning? Maybe our subconscious minds will work overtime and give us the answer when we wake up.'

'Yes, and maybe they won't. But we do need some sleep, that's for sure.'

Chapter 30

Ferrara didn't want it to look as if they were travelling as a group, so he and Luca Rossi took rooms in a hotel near the centre of Tarbes, while the other three men booked into a budget hotel beside the railway station.

Rossi knocked on Ferrara's door just after seven the next morning, his mobile phone in his hand.

Ferrara was already up and dressed, in case they had to move quickly, and opened it immediately.

'Where are they?' he asked.

'Exactly where they were last night,' Rossi replied, showing Ferrara the screen of his smartphone.

'You put another tracker on their car?'

'Another two, and I removed the original so I can charge its battery. Wherever they go, we'll be able to follow them.'

'Okay,' Ferrara replied. 'There's nothing we can do until they move, so I'll go and have breakfast. Then I'll check out and wait downstairs in the lounge. Let me know as soon as the tracker starts moving. Make sure that you have a full tank of fuel in your car and that your other three men have as well. We can't afford to run out of petrol if the targets decide to take a long drive somewhere. How many cars have they got?'

'Two. Originally there were two of them in each. So we've got four vehicles available, which should be more than enough.'

'Good. Can you load your tracker app onto my mobile? In case we get separated.'

Rossi nodded. 'I'll do it now, if you like.'

Ferrara handed over his personal smartphone, not the burner he'd been given by Caravaggio, and watched as Rossi downloaded an app and fed in the information for the trackers.

'There you are,' he said, pointing at the screen. 'And there *they* are, loud and clear. Enjoy your breakfast. I'll see you later.'

–

Bronson and Angela had also got up early. They'd had breakfast in the hotel's dining room, then returned to their bedroom.

'Right,' Bronson said. 'I think you're right about Rennes-le-Château. They probably went there straight from Montségur with the Ark because it was a place that the Templars and Raymond d'Aniort controlled almost completely. But they didn't control the castle, so they probably only stayed for a few days – maybe a week or two – and then transported the Ark to a Templar fortress where it could be hidden. Let's look at that piece of text again.'

Angela read aloud her translation of the Occitan sentence.

'I don't think there's any doubt that CSA and COT are places,' she said, 'because if they aren't, it doesn't make sense. So we need to work out where they are, and we do have a couple of clues.'

'Yes. COT must be on the coast, if the Ark was taken on board a ship, and this CSA place has a bell tower and a dungeon, and was a place where the Ark could be kept safely, so that means it was somewhere fortified.'

Angela nodded. She was already studying a map of the Languedoc region on the screen of her laptop. She found Montségur and began looking at place names over to the east, between the castle and the Mediterranean coast.

'There's something I still don't understand,' Bronson said. 'That phrase about sanctuary overseas, and the idea that perhaps they decided to take the Ark back to where it had come from, to Jerusalem.'

'Outremer, Europe overseas, as it was called. So?'

'Montségur fell in March 1244,' Bronson said, 'so the earliest the Ark could have been shipped to Jerusalem would have been later that year. But unless I've got my dates screwed up, I thought Jerusalem was raided and sacked in July 1244 and abandoned by the Crusaders that same year. So the Templars couldn't have taken the Ark to Jerusalem because they didn't control the city any longer. And that expression about the Ark resting in glory doesn't suggest that it was only at this CSA place for a few days.'

'Now that,' Angela said, looking up from her laptop, 'is a very good point, which hadn't occurred to me. So they must have been heading for somewhere different. Maybe Cyprus? The Templars controlled the island from 1244 until the order was dissolved.'

'Maybe. But if that was what the author of the text meant, why didn't he write "Cyprus" instead? Or "the Island of Copper" – the name Cyprus is derived from a Greek word meaning "copper", I think – or something more specific? It's almost as if he knew the Ark was going to a place of safety, but he didn't know where because the Templars hadn't told him. But that makes a nonsense of encrypting the text in the first place. Why bother if it only tells part of the story? What would be the point?'

'Actually, I think we may be missing the point,' Angela said. 'I skimmed over it, but that phrase "until the doom was upon them" implies something important. The doom for the Templars must have been King Philip's men descending on their commanderies throughout France on 13 October 1307 and arresting everybody they could find on trumped-up charges of heresy. So maybe what the writer is telling us is that the Ark stayed at this CSA place until word of Philip's plan leaked out. And then the Templars moved it to a different place of safety.'

'So it wouldn't have embarked on a ship until 1307,' Bronson said. 'That means it couldn't have gone to Jerusalem or Cyprus because by then the Templar order had been suppressed and their properties seized in both those places. Perhaps that's why the text is so vague about what happened. Maybe the writer knew the Ark had been taken somewhere by sea but didn't know where because the Templars on the ship also didn't know where it was going to end up.'

'So if we're looking for the Ark in France, we're almost certainly looking in the wrong country.'

'That changes everything,' Bronson agreed, 'but we still need to identify these two places before we head off in a completely different direction.'

'Let's start with COT, then,' Angela suggested. 'That must be somewhere on the coast and it's a smaller area to search.'

They both studied the map on Angela's laptop. She altered the scale to zoom in and follow the coastline on the screen.

'I'm assuming CSA and COT are abbreviations for place names containing three words,' she said, 'because I don't think any French place name could realistically start with the letters CSA.'

They found nothing that seemed likely, so she tried a new tack.

'Let's forget the map for the moment,' she said. 'I'll do a search for Templar port towns or fortresses on that coast.'

The search was awkward, because she couldn't find a site that listed all the Templar properties in the region, only sites that discussed a single commandery or fortress. Again she found nothing obvious, but eventually she came up with one place that might fit the bill, though the name didn't.

'This might be it,' she said. 'There's a town called Collioure. It's right down near the Spanish border, south-east of Perpignan, but it's not actually that far from Montségur, only about seventy miles as the crow flies, so at medieval horse-and-cart speeds I suppose it would take about four or five days to do the journey. There's a Templar castle there, built in about 1207. It was later integrated into what's now called the Château Royal de Collioure, a huge building. It seems right, but the name doesn't... Oh, hang on a second.'

She accessed another website dealing with the town, and then grinned at Bronson.

'It does fit,' she said. 'The Occitan name of Collioure is Cotlliure, so there's the COT link. And there's something else about it that's relevant. Although it's in France today, it wasn't during the medieval period. Then it was a part of Roussillon and the property of the King of Aragon and Count of Barcelona. So when Philip the Fair blew the whistle on the Templars, the knights living in the castle at Collioure wouldn't have been affected. Which means they'd have had no trouble loading the relic onto a Templar ship in the harbour.'

'Well done,' Bronson said. 'That does work. So now let's find this town known as CSA.'

That search took longer simply because they had a much bigger area to cover, but eventually Angela pointed at a small settlement about twenty miles east of Montségur, north of Quillan and close to both Rennes-le-Château and Rennes-les-Bains.

'Campagne-sur-Aude,' she said. 'That fits CSA perfectly. And there was a Templar fortress there. The place was the property of the viscounts of Carcassonne, and in 1147 Roger de Béziers gave the village, and as a matter of fact the villagers as well, to the Templars. He had a big mortgage that the Templars cleared in return for his gift, and he wanted to take part in the Second Crusade, so he needed funds for the journey and to pay for his servants and equipment.'

'So that has to be our next stop after Rennes-le-Château,' Bronson said.

Chapter 31

En route Paris to Languedoc

While Josef Gellerman, Lemuel Dayan and Aaron Chason constituted part of the front-line operational side of the Zeru group, at their base in Jerusalem the second-line members tended to be of a more academic bent, and they could also call on the services of outside experts in various disciplines, including linguists and historians.

Although Gellerman had initially been confident he would be able to work out what the decoded text said, he'd quickly got bogged down in it and decided to get one of Zeru's experts involved instead. He had emailed a copy of it to Jerusalem. The people there, he knew, would turn it into a readable document that he hoped would lead them to their goal.

In the meantime, he doubted very much if the quest for the Ark of the Covenant would end up in Paris or anywhere nearby. If the Ark still existed, the consensus opinion at Zeru was that it had been hidden somewhere in the southern part of the country, most probably in the Languedoc, because they had detected hints that that was where it had last been seen. So as soon as they'd sent the email, the three men had climbed into their Renault hire car, Gellerman at the wheel, and driven onto the Boulevard Périphérique*, the Paris ring road. They headed anticlockwise towards the intersection at Gentilly, where they would pick up the A6a Autoroute du Soleil* to drive south out of the city.

While Gellerman and Dayan had been working on the decryption and translation of the ciphertext, Aaron Chason had not been idle. He'd made use of his contacts in the criminal underworld and the previous day had used the Paris Métro to take a trip up to Montmartre in the north of the city for a meeting in a cafe near the Cimetière de Montmartre.

There he had sat at a table with two men he had never met before. When all three of them had been satisfied that nobody could see what they were doing, and they had established their bona fides, Chason had lifted the lid of a briefcase the two men had brought with them and briefly inspected the contents. Once he was satisfied that the goods were as described, he had closed the briefcase, lifted it off the table and placed it by the side of his chair. In exchange, he'd passed over a folded copy of the French daily newspaper *Le Parisien* and directed the attention of the men to an article near the middle. The article had been obscured by a white envelope that bulged slightly. After another quick glance around to make sure that they were still unobserved, one of the men had picked up the envelope, lifted the flap and visually checked the contents. Then he'd slipped it into the inside pocket of his jacket.

Neither he nor Chason would have insulted each other by counting the money or removing any of the objects from the briefcase to inspect them closely. In the criminal underworld, reputation and trust were hard to earn and could be lost in an instant, so both parties knew what they were getting, and neither would have dreamed of trying to deceive the other.

A few minutes later, all three men had stood up and shaken hands. Chason had paid for the drinks and then they'd gone their separate ways.

The briefcase was now in the boot of the Renault, but the contents – three nine-millimetre semi-automatic pistols, two different models of Browning and a Czechoslovakian CZ 75, plus two full boxes of Parabellum ammunition – had been divided between the three Israelis. Because they'd seen Luca Rossi in Paris and knew the Inquisition was involved, Gellerman had decided that they wouldn't take any chances, and from now on they would all be armed, all the time.

They would head down to the Languedoc and find accommodation in Toulouse or Carcassonne or some other location, unless Zeru's experts in Jerusalem could give them a different destination before they got there.

Chapter 32

Hautes-Pyrénées, France

'They're on the move,' Luca Rossi said when Ferrara answered his mobile.

'I know. I saw it on my phone as well. I'm just leaving the hotel; I'll see you somewhere on the road.'

'Don't crowd them. On the way to Auch, none of us got closer than about one or two kilometres and that worked really well.'

'I know my business,' Ferrara said, somewhat sharply. 'I've done this kind of thing more times than I can remember.'

In the hotel car park, he put his overnight bag in the boot, then attached a mobile phone mount to the inside of the windscreen, clipped his smartphone into it and ran the charging lead from the phone to a socket on the dashboard. He checked that in his normal driving position he could see the screen clearly, which meant he would have no difficulty in following the target vehicle.

He studied the map display on his mobile. The tracker was moving down the link road that joined the N21 and the A64 autoroute, so the targets were going either west or east. It all depended on which way they turned when they got to the junction. If they went west, Ferrara knew he'd have to get out of the city centre pretty smartish to avoid being left too far behind, but until he knew whether to turn left or right, he couldn't leave the hotel car park.

Moments later, he had the answer. The steadily pulsing light on the display that represented the tracker had gone straight on at the intersection to the south side of the autoroute. That meant they were going east, because the road went nowhere else.

The N21 acted as a kind of a ring road around the east and south of Tarbes, and Ferrara checked his satnav again before deciding which route to take. There was a junction, a complex of two roundabouts and autoroute access, just south-east of the built-up area. That was about the only place where the targets could change direction to head north and seemed like the obvious place for him to go. If they did turn north, he could simply go round one of the roundabouts to follow them, and if they continued to the east, he would join the autoroute and slot in behind them.

Ten minutes later, he was driving south-east down the D817 towards the roundabout complex, keeping one eye on the screen of his smartphone, where the tracker symbol was approaching the same feature from the west.

Ferrara had always believed in getting eyes on his targets as soon as he could, and as he looked at the converging symbol, he realised that if he slowed up slightly, he would actually be able to see the target car. He eased the pressure on the accelerator, slowing down by perhaps ten kilometres an hour as he neared the autoroute. As he passed over the eastbound lane, he glanced right and saw a light grey Peugeot drive underneath the overpass. A quick look at his smartphone confirmed it was the target vehicle.

Rossi had told him the make and model of car the targets were driving, and his eyes-on check confirmed the description. It also showed that the targets hadn't found either of the trackers and stuck them on an entirely different car.

Ferrara turned the MiTo right at both the roundabouts and entered the slip road for the A64 autoroute, taking a ticket at the toll booth. According to his smartphone, he was three or four kilometres behind the Peugeot, and he knew he could quickly close that distance to about one kilometre, close enough to take any action necessary but far enough away that his car wouldn't be spotted.

–

Like all French autoroutes, the A64 was mainly straight and fast with a good surface, and was a very efficient way of covering long distances quickly. Unfortunately, what it didn't do was go where Bronson and Angela wanted, because it ended up in Toulouse.

Just beyond Lestelle-de-Saint-Martory, they turned off onto the D117, a narrower, twisting road that first took them south-west before turning south and then east to head through the Parc Naturel Régional des Pyrénées Ariégeoises, a very pretty area dotted with small villages. Bronson had been checking his mirrors ever since he'd left the autoroute but had seen no sign of any pursuing vehicles. He pulled off the road in Saint-Girons, where the road went around the village in a large loop to the south and over the river, and they stopped there for a few minutes. They ordered coffee in a cafe near the river, sitting outside in the sun at a round metal table shaded by an umbrella, watching village life, while Bronson tried to check that nobody was showing any particular interest in them.

One of the defining characteristics of the French is that they are very patriotic. In any group of French-owned cars, an observer can be reasonably certain that eight or nine out of every ten will be manufactured by Citroën, Peugeot or Renault, unlike the situation in Britain, where patriotism is often seen as a dirty word and the vehicles of choice for most people tend to be manufactured in Germany. Or Japan. Or Italy or France or any nation, basically, apart from Britain.

That simple fact, he hoped, gave him a slight edge. He knew two things about the people who were watching them. First, they were Italian, and second, they were armed. That more or less guaranteed they must have arrived in France by car, and so he could ignore the French-registered Euro-boxes.

From their vantage point he could see their parked hire car, but every car that passed or stopped had French plates. It looked to Bronson as if they had successfully shaken off the surveillance team, but he would keep one eye on his rear-view mirrors, just in case.

Just over quarter of an hour later, they got back on the road. At Foix they would turn south on the N20 towards Andorra and then head east, back on the D117 towards Lavelanet and Puivert. When they reached Couiza, they would turn south towards Rennes-le-Château.

-

In fact, one of the vehicles Bronson had seen had been occupied by two of Rossi's men. He had ordered them to drive through the village when the tracker had stopped moving to assess the situation. They'd spotted both the parked hire car and the two targets sitting outside the cafe, and the passenger had reported back to Rossi. The driver had then stopped out of sight in a quiet road at the other end of the village.

Rossi and Ferrara had both stopped their cars to the west of Saint-Girons when they'd seen the tracker come to a halt, and Rossi had ordered the last of his three men to do the same, keeping in touch with each other using their mobiles. They would simply stay where they were until the tracker started moving again, when the pursuit would continue.

Twenty minutes later, they were back on the road, Ferrara's Alfa Romeo leading the four vehicles shadowing the English couple, who still appeared completely unaware that they were the focus of so much covert attention.

Which was exactly the way Marco Ferrara wanted it.

Chapter 33

Aude, France

Ferrara had closed the gap between himself and the Peugeot every time the other vehicle entered a built-up area. The reason for that was simple. Although the tracker worked perfectly well, at junctions with multiple exits it was all too easy to pick the wrong road and find the target vehicle was no longer where you expected it to be.

So when the Peugeot reached the outskirts of Espéraza, Ferrara's MiTo was just three cars behind it and the Italian was only glancing intermittently at the screen of his smartphone. In traffic, he kept his eyes on the road, and especially on the rear of the grey Peugeot. Once he'd cleared the eastern end of the village, he relaxed slightly as the road opened up and he slowed down slightly.

A little under two kilometres later, they reached another village – Couiza – and again Ferrara tried to keep the Peugeot in view. But just as he entered the outskirts, the car in front stopped to allow an elderly couple to shuffle slowly across the road on a pedestrian crossing, and by the time Ferrara started moving again, the Peugeot was out of sight. He checked his smartphone and it appeared that the target car was continuing straight on.

He had to concentrate on driving as he was now in the middle of a short line of cars and there was heavy traffic in the opposite direction. He was almost in the centre of Couiza before he again checked his smartphone and saw that the tracker's position was no longer in front of him but behind him and some distance to the south.

He muttered an inventive Italian curse and started looking for somewhere to turn round. But the road wasn't very wide and was lined with houses on both sides behind unusually narrow pavements. And with the traffic moving in both directions, there was nowhere he could stop. He would have to make the turn at the next junction.

He passed a sharp and narrow left-hand turning and instead took the turning to the right, almost opposite. On the left-hand side of the road were several parking spaces outside a cafe. He swung the Alfa Romeo into one of them, then immediately backed out and turned left to head west, back along the road he had just driven down. That put the tracker symbol ahead of him and to his left, which was what he wanted.

There was only one road that the Peugeot could have taken: the D52 to Rennes-le-Château. Ferrara steered the MiTo onto it and saw that the tracker was now in front of him and about a mile away. He pulled into the side of the road for a moment and checked his satnav, because the last thing he wanted was to find himself in a dead end with the driver of the Peugeot looking straight at him. The map showed that there was a junction along the road, with Rennes-le-Château to the right. It also showed that this road was the only way into and out of the village, so he would take it slowly.

He indicated and pulled out. He knew about Rennes-le-Château. In fact, it was somewhat notorious within the Catholic Church because of the conduct of the local priest at the end of the nineteenth century, but to his knowledge it had nothing whatsoever to do with the Ark of the Covenant. Unless the Lewis woman knew something different, of course.

As he drove, he noted that the tracker turned right at the junction, following the narrow road up the side of the hill towards the village. That confirmed their destination. Now he had to decide whether to follow them or wait for them to come down the hill again. But he also needed to cover his bases, and although he'd seen a photograph of Angela Lewis, he had never seen her in the flesh. And all he knew about her companion was his name and a rough word picture supplied by Luca Rossi, whose principal skills lay in the application of violence rather than any kind of descriptive abilities.

His best option was probably to let Rossi go into the village and follow them while he remained in his car to resume his distant surveillance when they left.

He took the same turning as the Peugeot driver, and as he was approaching the village, he pulled into a free parking area on the left-hand side of the road, where he could leave his car in plain sight so that Rossi would see it as he drove up. He assumed that his fellow Italian would only be a short distance behind him, or perhaps even in front because of the delay when he had missed the turning.

He'd just parked and switched off the engine when his mobile rang.

Chapter 34

Rennes-le-Château, Aude, France

'This is a very strange place,' Bronson said, stopping in a car park on the side of the hill below the village centre. He'd already paid an admission fee near the top of the long, steep and winding approach road, which was a first. Most villages didn't charge tourists an entrance fee.

'You're right. There are a lot of peculiar stories told about this village,' Angela said, 'and a whole raft of unanswered questions. But none of them have anything to do with the Ark of the Covenant, otherwise there'd be other volumes of conspiracy theories doing the rounds. It's also,' she added, 'a very old place. Relics have been found here that date back over thirty thousand years to the Palaeolithic period, the Stone Age. In recorded history the first important occupiers were the Visigoths in the fourth and fifth centuries. They recognised the strategic importance of this site – it was quite a climb getting up to the top of this hill even in the car – and they built a fortress here. They also named the place, calling the area Rhedesium or Reddensis, which over time morphed into Razès. Rennes was derived from that. So as well as Rennes-le-Château, there's also Rennes-les-Bains, named after its natural hot springs, about three miles east of here.'

They climbed the wooden staircase that linked the parking area with the road into the village. At the top, they paused for a few seconds to catch their breath and admire the spectacular views out to the north and east.

'It is an impressive location,' Bronson said. 'There's no doubt about that. In the medieval period, if your forces occupied this hill you'd be able to control most of what you can see from here.'

Angela shaded her eyes and looked around, then turned towards the village.

'Nothing to do with Rennes-le-Château,' she said as they began walking, 'but there's a minor mystery associated with the castle of Bézu. That's about four miles south of here and now a complete ruin. Some people claim it was a major Templar commandery, but it wasn't, though the owners, the Sermon family, the lords of Albedun, had links to the order, and Bernard Sermon joined the Templars in 1151 as a *confrère*.'

'And a *confrère* was...?' Bronson asked. 'I know the French word translates as a fellow member, but what did that mean to the Templars?'

'A *confrère* was a married man who joined the order but who obviously couldn't take the same vow of chastity as the unmarried Templar knights and wasn't allowed to live in the same property as them. A *confrère* had to leave part of his estate to the order when he died, and Bernard donated huge sums of money to the Templars during his lifetime. The order did take over Bézu castle in 1292, but they had to leave it in 1307, so they only occupied it for fifteen years. The minor mystery starts in 1156, when Bertrand de Blanchefort became the Grand Master of the Templars.'

'You mentioned the Blancheforts before. Was he a local man?'

'Oddly enough, no. He came from Guyenne, near Bordeaux, in the south-west of France, and he had no connection to the local Blanchefort family. The same year that he was elected, the Templars organised a group of skilled workers to travel to the area around Bézu, and that's where the mystery comes in.

'First, they weren't French but German, and the suspicion is that they were recruited because they didn't speak Occitan and couldn't talk to the local residents. Second, this part of France is rich in metals. Ever since Roman times copper, lead, silver and gold have been dug out of the ground here, but most sites had been fully exploited well before the twelfth century. Third, these labourers were casters, people whose skill was working with metal, not miners who would have been employed to dig out the ore. So whatever they were doing in these hills it probably wasn't mining. It's much more likely that they were melting, reworking and casting precious metals like gold and silver that had already been extracted.

'Now, we don't know exactly what these men were doing here, but in 1307 the new owner of the castle at Bézu, a man named Othon d'Aure, was arrested and accused of counterfeiting money. Just to clarify, he wasn't producing fake coins made of lead with a thin coating of gold or anything like that. He was producing solid gold coins, but they weren't official coins of the realm. He was probably turning gold bullion that he had illegally acquired somewhere into gold coins that he could spend. And even more strangely, just a few years later, in 1344, several members of the Voisin family, who were then resident in Bézu castle, were accused of committing exactly the same crime.'

They passed a vertical stone slab on their right that bore the name Rennes-le-Château and the village crest or coat of arms, and on their left a bar restaurant and a large plan of the village, then continued into the settlement. It looked like a fairly typical French hill village, the lanes – they weren't big enough to be called streets – dotted with solid stone houses under reddish tiled roofs. Most of the windows had their shutters closed, and there was little sign of life, again typical of most villages in France, in Bronson's experience. At a sort of crossroads – two lanes, a very narrow street and what amounted to a track heading off to the right – they went straight on along the narrow street, which turned out to be the impressive-sounding Grand Rue, though it was neither grand nor really a road, being barely wide enough for a single vehicle.

They saw a glass-blower on the left, the kind of tourism-based activity that always seemed to spring up in places that got a lot of visitors, and almost opposite it, behind a low wall and a line of trees that gave it privacy and some seclusion, the stone towers and walls of the old Château Hautpoul, now a private residence.

They stopped for a few moments to look at the building. It wasn't a classic French chateau with turrets and spires; more like a medieval fortification with solid walls marked by few openings. In front of them was a square tower, the side facing the road pierced by a single vertical line of windows, two of them bricked up. To their left was a round tower, again with one of the windows blocked, the towers linked by a stone curtain wall to form one side of the castle.

'Not the most attractive chateau I've ever seen,' Bronson remarked, 'but it wasn't built to look pretty. It was built to keep people out.'

'How old is it?' Angela asked.

Bronson took out his smartphone, accessed the Internet and came up with the answer.

'According to Wikipedia, it's seventeenth century, but that's obviously wrong.' He tried another site. 'This looks more like it. There's a French site here that gives its history. Some of the cellars in the building date back to the time of the Visigoths, and the first above-ground stones were laid in the thirteenth century. It has to be at least as old as that, because it was standing at the end of the Albigensian Crusade in 1244. I read that it was captured by the Crusaders from the house of Trencavel, who had presumably built it on earlier ruins and given to the Voisin family because of their support for the campaign. It's been damaged and repaired over the centuries during the various conflicts down here and was renovated in the sixteenth and seventeenth centuries. It does look a bit battered and patched up.'

Angela took a couple of pictures and they moved on.

The Grand Rue curved around to the left by a souvenir shop, but they turned right instead, following the sign that pointed to the 'Eglise'.

'The core of the mystery,' Angela said, gesturing to the small building at the end of the path in front of them. 'The Church of St Mary Magdalene. The place where Bérenger Saunière was the priest from 1885 to 1917. He's the real puzzle.'

'I've read quite a lot about the man and the village,' Bronson said, 'and it's good to finally see the place. Let's do the tourist bit and have a look inside, then we can think about how the Ark fits into this. If at all.'

It was immediately clear that the Church of St Mary Magdalene was an unusual place of worship, if indeed it *was* a place of worship. Carved into the central stone above the porch was the Latin inscription *TERRIBILIS EST LOCUS ISTE*, with the longer inscription *DOMUS MEA DOMUS ORATIONIS VOCABITUR* on the horizontal stone behind it.

Bronson pointed at them. 'Help me out here,' he said. 'I know what the central one means, but what about the longer inscription?'

'That's more or less what you'd expect to read. It translates as "My house will be called a house of prayer", which is fairly conventional. The other isn't conventional in any way at all. It means "This place is terrible", which is not exactly what most people would expect to see as they enter a church.'

'There's another interesting inscription here,' Bronson said. 'Look right at the top, above the statue of Mary Magdalene. Can you see it?'

'Yes. *IN HOC SIGNO VINCES*. It means "By this sign you will conquer". That's quite an old Christian expression.'

'It is, but more interestingly, it has a Templar connection, though most people don't know it. There's a story that Don Afonso Henriques, who was the first King of Portugal – prior to 1139, Portugal was only a county, not a country – was praying one night before an important battle as part of the *Reconquista* against the Moors and claimed he saw those words emblazoned in the sky. The next day the Portuguese forces defeated a Moorish army at the Battle of Ourique. As a result, *In hoc signo vinces* has been the motto of Portugal since 1143, as well as a Templar motto, and it's also used by the Freemasons. The Templars were a major presence in Portugal – after 1307, they were renamed the Knights of Christ and carried on business as usual – and were a driving force behind a lot of the Portuguese voyages of discovery. You've only got to look at paintings of the ships they sent out with Templars like Vasco da Gama in command. Virtually every one of them had the red Templar cross pattée on the sails.'

As they walked into the church, the very first thing they saw was the font on the left-hand side. There was nothing unusual about finding such an object in a church, but a font being held aloft by a devil was at best unexpected.

Chapter 35

'Yes,' Marco Ferrara said, answering his mobile.

'It's me,' the unmistakable gravelly voice of Luca Rossi announced. 'I'm up in the village following the two targets. Where are you?'

'In the car park halfway down the hill. What are they doing?'

'Pretending to be tourists, as far as I can see. They looked at the castle from the outside, and they just walked into the church. I can't follow them in there because it's so small. What do you want me to do?'

'Just follow them when they come out and tell me if they do anything you think is important. If they pay attention to an inscription or anything like that. Anything that might suggest they've found some kind of clue.'

'Got it,' Rossi said and rang off.

Chapter 36

'The devil Asmodeus, I presume?' Bronson said. 'He's an ugly sod, isn't he?'

'You're not wrong there,' Angela replied.

The devil was depicted kneeling, his right leg bent, his left knee on the ground and the font resting on his shoulders. He was looking down, his gaze apparently locked on the black-and-white tiled floor of the church.

'Is he supposed to be holding something? With his right hand, I mean?'

'Yes,' Bronson replied. 'Apparently when the statue was commissioned the devil held a trident, though I don't know why. Asmodeus represents lust, so unless the idea was to pin down his victims, I don't know why he'd need a trident. Now, we have a devil, but we also have angels.'

He pointed above the font at a statue of four winged angels, each painted a different colour and each apparently making a part of the sign of the cross.

'They may help to balance out the devil,' he said, 'and the French inscription on the pedestal below the statue is almost a word-for-word translation of the Latin motto outside. *PAR CE SIGNE TU LE VAINCRAS* means "By this sign you will vanquish him". I suppose that's meant to refer to the sign of the cross. The old "spectacles, testicles, wallet and watch" mantra.'

Angela glared at him.

'That's the way I was taught it at school,' he said defensively, 'and it's one of those things that's always stuck, despite my lack of religion. The other things on that statue that are interesting are the bright red oval that contains Saunière's initials – BS – which seems a little showy for a priest who's supposed to be humble, and the basilisk on either side of the circle. As well as Asmodeus, you really do have to ask why carvings of a couple of legendary reptiles – serpent kings, in fact, and reputed to be capable of killing with a single glance – are found inside a supposedly Christian church.'

They walked further into the building, which threw up other obvious inconsistencies. The plaster statues of Mary and Joseph might be expected, but each of the figures was also carrying a child, which was unusual.

'That could be a reference to the Cathars,' Bronson suggested. 'Their beliefs supported the idea of a god of good and a god of evil, where Satan was the god of evil and Jesus was the god of good. More importantly, they believed that Jesus and Satan were both sons of God the Father, a divine being able to generate both good and evil. So maybe, if that statue of Mary is supposed to be holding Jesus, then Joseph is holding Satan. Have you noticed the slightly sinister aspect to this as well? Sinister in its old Latin sense, I mean.'

Angela nodded. 'Yes. You mean left, obviously. From where we're standing looking at the altar, Joseph is on the left, the sinister side, which is where you'd expect to find Mary. And unless I'm mistaken, because I'm not a churchgoer either, it looks to me like the way of the cross is in the reverse order to the way it's usually depicted. And then there's that statue of Mary Magdalene over there' – she pointed – 'holding a crucifix that's almost as tall as she is, and with an open book at her feet with a human skull on top of it. She's often shown in paintings with a skull, and that's usually a reference to John the Baptist, so that's Johannite and Templar, the belief that John could only baptise Jesus if he was his superior. There's a lot of symbolism here that certainly isn't Christian, but I have no idea what it all means.'

'And don't forget what's under your feet. The floor's made of alternating black and white tiles, and it's also thought that this same alternating pattern was used on the floor of the Temple of Solomon. Or it could represent a chessboard, and maybe even a game of chess between good and evil. The Templars were introduced to the game in the Middle East. Asmodeus over there by the door is definitely looking at the floor, or maybe at the board, as if he's planning his next move, and the kneeling angel of that group of four is pointing at it with her left hand, as if she's deciding which chess piece to move next. Then again, maybe it's just another hint towards the dualistic nature of the world that the Cathars accepted, which was good and evil, black and white, or perhaps a hidden reference to the Knights Templar and their black-and-white battle flag, the *Beauséant*.'

'Yes. Maybe all that's true, or perhaps none of it is. I think you could spend weeks here just looking at the inside of the church and trying to work out what each bit of it means or is supposed to represent, and I'm not sure it would be any clearer when you'd finished.'

'What do you mean?' Bronson asked.

'Look, everybody who's come here to investigate this, from treasure hunters to investigative journalist and conspiracy theorists, has assumed that all these odd things we're looking at actually mean something coherent, that they're all clues to something, some master plan, or maybe hints to locate a hidden treasure. That there's a purpose to it all. But just suppose that Saunière found something here in the church, or at least in the village, that completely destroyed his belief in the religion he served? Something that in his eyes utterly negated the core teachings of Christianity.'

'Like what?'

'I have no idea. Say he found a coffin in the graveyard containing the bones of a dead man and absolute proof that it was Jesus Christ, which would mean there'd been no resurrection and that Jesus had not been the son of God. For a priest, that would throw Christianity straight out of the window in an instant. Suppose something like that happened. What would Saunière have done?'

Bronson correctly assumed that was a rhetorical question and didn't answer.

'He couldn't leave Rennes-le-Château because this was his home and his job, and he was probably already halfway through renovating the church. He might have been so annoyed at having been sold a fiction from the start that he began what you might call a campaign of subtle professional vandalism, doing things in the church that look like proper Christian symbols – the statues of Mary and Joseph, for example – and then adding a twist like the two infants to show that they're not what they appear to be. He needed a font in the church so he picked a devil to hold it up rather than just a stone pillar. Things like that. Things with no purpose other than to confuse people, but not part of some overall plan. And we do know for sure that he ignored just about every order his superiors gave him for the rest of his life, which isn't what you would have expected from an alleged man of God.

'Okay, something like finding the body of Jesus would be a stretch, but – here's an idea – suppose he discovered not the Ark of the Covenant, because we know that went elsewhere, but the broken tablets that God had inscribed for Moses on Mount Sinai and that Moses had smashed when he found his people worshipping a golden calf. Along with absolute proof that that was what he was looking at. That might have been enough to completely disillusion him about the Catholic Church, because he would have realised that the Old Testament was true and that the Jews really were God's chosen people; that God had regularly spoken to the Jews through the Ark but had never spoken to any occupants of the throne of St Peter. Something like that could have been why the sign above the entrance to the church states that "this is a terrible place", because he would have known that every time he stepped into the pulpit to preach, he was promulgating a lie, compounding something he absolutely knew was a fiction. He would have known that both the Catholic Church and Christianity had no validity at all.'

'Actually,' Bronson said, 'that's a very interesting idea. As I said, I've read a lot about this place, and I don't think anyone has ever suggested something like that before. But there's still the money to explain, which is a separate question altogether. Saunière was living on a salary of nine hundred francs a year, barely above starvation level, and in 1892 the surviving records show that he had a debt of more than one hundred francs and just over eighty francs in his bank account. But over the next decade, he accumulated astonishing wealth. In some months he was reportedly spending sums equivalent to more than fifty times his *annual* income.

'His account books show that renovating the church, the cemetery and the presbytery took ten years, from 1887 to 1897, at a cost equivalent today to about four and a half million euros. But his far bigger expenses were building the Tour Magdala and the Villa Bethania and buying the land they stand on, which cost the equivalent of about ten million euros today, so that's almost fifteen million euros on just those projects alone. And we have no idea how much he spent in total on his extensive travels abroad, his living costs or his collections. He bought lots of rare and expensive books – one source says he even employed a full-time bookbinder at one time – and collections of stamps, and if he got through the equivalent of another five or ten million euros it wouldn't surprise me. So as a rough figure, this priest who was essentially bankrupt in 1892 managed to spend the equivalent of twenty or twenty-five million euros, possibly a lot more than that, over the next twenty-five years. That's an average of about a million euros a year.

'That money had to have come from somewhere, and the suggestion that he earned it all from simony, from mass trafficking, is complete nonsense, simply ridiculous. He kept detailed records, as he was required to do, and they show that he received about one hundred and ten thousand requests for specific masses during his thirty-two-year tenure here. He received a payment of between half a franc and one and a half francs for each one, so the maximum he could have earned from this practice – which pretty much every priest did as a matter of course at that time – was about one hundred and fifty thousand francs. That's only a microscopic fraction of the money that we know he spent.'

Angela shook her head. 'That's something else I have no idea about,' she said. 'Let's go back outside. There's something about this place that makes me feel uncomfortable.'

They left the church and Bronson pointed towards the gate that led into the cemetery. Above it, on the top of the arch, was a sculpture of a skull and crossbones, the skull looking rather unusual because it appeared to be smiling.

'There's a theory that the skull and crossbones symbol or flag dates back to the execution of the last Grand Master of the Knights Templar, Jacques de Molay, in Paris, when somebody stole parts of his skeleton after he'd been burnt alive, and that it became a symbol of the Templars after the dissolution of the order. So that may be another possible link.'

'Or it may be nothing of the sort,' Angela countered. 'It all depends on what you believe and what you accept. Look, I could do with a drink and a nibble. Let's find a cafe and forget Bérenger Saunière for the moment, because the one thing we definitely do know about him is that he had nothing to do with the Ark of the Covenant.'

Chapter 37

Campagne-sur-Aude, Aude, France

The three men from Zeru hadn't ended up in either Toulouse or Carcassonne, because one of the linguistic experts the organisation employed in Jerusalem had supplied a final copy of the decrypted and translated Occitan text.

Once that had been read and understood, it hadn't taken one of their historians in Israel very long to work out that CSA was almost certainly a reference to Campagne-sur-Aude and that COT meant Cotlliure, modern Collioure. Accordingly, Gellerman had been sent a text message and told to head directly to Campagne-sur-Aude.

The message hadn't included any orders or instructions or even any hints about what they should do once they reached the village. This was probably, he guessed, because nobody at Zeru had the slightest idea what they would find when they got there.

He had no intention of driving through the night to reach their destination. Because the Inquisition, in the person of Luca Rossi and whichever other enforcers he had working with him, was involved, they needed to be well rested and alert before they got to the village, in case the opposition was already there. So they'd found a hotel on the outskirts of Cahors, where they'd spent the night, and had driven on to Campagne-sur-Aude that morning.

It wasn't much of a village, just a collection of houses beside a bend in the river Aude, and they drove around it a couple of times trying to spot anything of significance. Most of the buildings seemed to be old but not medieval. The only one with any real appearance of age was the church, and when Gellerman and Dayan went inside to check it out, they discovered that even that was a combination of old and new. What they didn't find was anything that looked as if it might have been a Templar fortress, or any indication to show that the relic they sought had ever been there.

In the absence of any better ideas, Gellerman decided that they should park the car somewhere unobtrusive but with a decent view of the obvious approach road, which crossed the river on a narrow but picturesque bridge. If Rossi and the Inquisition were following the same clues as Zeru, sooner or later the Italian and his men would appear.

Then they opened the windows of the Renault hire car, chose sandwiches, snacks and drinks from a selection they'd bought at a garage en route, checked that their pistols were loaded, ready for use and immediately accessible, and settled down to wait.

Chapter 38

Rennes-le-Château, Aude, France

They found a cafe-cum-restaurant only a short walk away from the church and sat outside in a kind of sprawling garden dotted with tables and chairs. They ordered drinks and food, and while they were waiting sat in companionable silence enjoying the warmth of the sunlight filtering through the trees.

'This has been interesting,' Bronson said after the waiter had brought their drinks, 'and perhaps even instructive, but I don't think coming here has been particularly helpful to what we're doing right now. According to that document, we know the Ark was taken from Montségur to Campagne-sur-Aude via the "place of the castle of the Voisins", which we're assuming was Rennes-le-Château because this is the only place that seems to tick all the boxes. We also know that about the only building here where Raymond d'Aniort *wouldn't* have left the Ark was the castle itself, because the Voisins were opposed to the Cathars and by extension to the Templars as well.'

'Which is just as well,' Angela pointed out, 'because it's private property, so even if we had wanted to get inside to take a look around, we probably wouldn't have been able to.'

'Exactly. So the relic could have been stored in the church or almost any other building here, presumably under armed guard. We've no way of knowing where, and even if we could somehow deduce that it had been stored in that building over there, for example' – Bronson pointed at random across the garden at one of the adjoining properties – 'that still wouldn't help us. Let's hope we find something at Campagne-sur-Aude.'

Their food arrived shortly afterwards, a steak and salad for Angela and another cassoulet for Bronson – he'd definitely got a taste for that particular local dish.

'Going back to Bérenger Saunière,' he said between mouthfuls, 'there have been dozens of theories about where his money actually came from, most of them based on misinformation or by cherry-picking certain facts, something I've noticed both conspiracy theorists and conspiracy debunkers tend to do quite a lot.

'There was a story about him finding old manuscripts inside a hollow Visigothic pillar, manuscripts containing a secret that threatened the Catholic Church and allowed him to blackmail the Vatican. Bearing in mind the record of the Church when it comes to dealing with heretics or awkward criticism, I think if Saunière had found something like that he would have met with an unfortunate fatal accident quite soon afterwards rather than be given enough money by the Vatican to turn him into a multimillionaire. Anyway, that story seems to have been a complete invention.

'Then there was another tale about him finding half the money raised by Blanche of Castile to pay the ransom demanded by the Egyptians for the release of her son, Louis IX. There's some basis of truth in that, because Louis was captured and she did pay the ransom, but that's as far as it goes. Quite why Blanche would have raised a sum twice as large as the payment demanded, or why she would then have hidden the second half of it at Rennes-le-Château but didn't bother to recover it has never been explained.'

'So where do you think the money came from?' Angela asked, spearing another piece of steak.

'Good question. I think there are a few bits of information that would allow us to make an educated guess. Nothing definitive, but certainly suggestive. This settlement started life as a Visigoth fortress and the Visigoths were accomplished workers in gold. They sacked Rome and removed most of the wealth and treasure the city possessed, and that was almost certainly taken either to Carcassonne or to their fortress here, or perhaps split between the two. We know from history that Alaric II later had to abandon this fortress in a hurry and flee south when the Visigoths were threatened by the Frankish leader Clovis. It's at least possible that the Visigoths would have buried most of the treasure they'd amassed because they would have needed to move quickly. So finding buried Visigoth treasure in the vicinity of Rennes-le-Château is a definite possibility, and its probable existence is supported by the historical record.

'You talked about Bézu and the German casters who were imported to work in the area, and the fact that this region once had gold and silver mines. There's historical evidence that in the middle of the seventeenth century a cache of gold coins was discovered near here, and two large gold bars were found in the nineteenth century, one outside this village and the other near Bézu. Then there were the two instances of counterfeiting gold coins you told me about at the castle of Bézu. What I'm getting at is that historically, gold has figured quite a lot in this area.

'Then there's Saunière's often peculiar conduct, in which he was usually assisted by Marie Dénarnaud, his housekeeper. She was sixteen years his junior and most likely rather more than just his housekeeper. Witnesses stated that during the renovations to the church, Saunière lifted stone slabs from the floor to expose underground chambers, and there are references in wills and other documents to crypts and family burial vaults under the church. There's no doubt that a crypt and tombs exist beneath the building, and it seems likely that the entrance had been sealed up for over a century before Saunière took over.

'But it wasn't only the crypt that he explored. He and Marie Dénarnaud were seen at night digging up graves in the cemetery – so often that a complaint was lodged against him by the local council to make him stop. All this suggests to me that he quite literally dug up a treasure. Whether it was something hidden in a family vault under the church or a forgotten Visigoth grave lying deep down in the cemetery or a hidden cache of Visigoth gold is another matter. Don't forget that the church here probably dates from about the eighth century and it was the norm for Christian churches to be deliberately built on pagan places of worship to help stamp out the older religions. There could well have been much older tombs in the cemetery, and we know the Visigoths often included valuable grave goods with their burials.

'And then there was what happened after Saunière died in 1917. Marie Dénarnaud survived him by thirty-six years, and in July 1946 she sold her estate to a man named Noël Corbu because several of the properties needed repairing and she'd run out of money, despite the fortune Saunière had got through. He had deliberately placed everything in her name so that when he died he was quite literally penniless. The sale was an *en viager* transaction.'

'I've heard of that, but remind me.'

'It's a bit like equity release but without the massive fees and extortionate interest. Older people, usually widows or widowers and without dependents, sell their property to a third party in return for a lump sum that's usually about half what it's actually worth – that's called the occupied value, or *valeur occupée* – and a lifetime monthly payment from the buyer. They can stay in the house and the buyer only takes possession when they die. In Noël Corbu's case, it wasn't a bad deal for him, because Marie Dénarnaud died in 1953, only seven years after the sale. And there had been a sweetener. Dénarnaud had promised him that when she was on her deathbed she would reveal a secret that would provide him with untold riches, the clear implication being that this was whatever Saunière had exploited during his life. She allegedly said, "You shall have more money than you will be able to spend", which seems quite definitive, if it's true.

'Unfortunately for Corbu, Marie Dénarnaud suffered a fit or stroke a few weeks before she died, meaning she could no longer speak or write, so he was never given the information he had expected to receive and the secret died with her. But there are a couple of things she's reported to have said that I think are significant. Some of the villagers remember her saying that "the people of Rennes-le-Château walk on gold without knowing it", which certainly suggests Saunière's fortune had been based on something buried in the ground. She also said that "what was left was enough to feed the whole village for a hundred years and there'd still be some left", which implies that Saunière certainly hadn't spent it all. And that of course raises one very obvious question.'

'Yes. If there was still plenty of money or treasure left, why did Marie Dénarnaud have to sell her estate?'

'Noël Corbu asked her exactly that question, and her answer is interesting. She told him she "would never touch it", and I think we can read something into that. She was the housekeeper for a priest, which at least implies that she was a religious woman at a time when religion was a very important part of the lives of most people. If what Saunière had found was, for example, part of a hoard of relics that the Visigoths had looted from Rome, or perhaps a Visigothic tomb filled with gold jewellery and ornaments, she might well have regarded that as non-Christian and pagan, although the Visigoths were Christians. Or perhaps she simply saw it as stolen property or grave-robbing.

'That might have been why she refused to have any part of it. It might also have been the reason why she refused to tell Corbu the secret until she was near death. If she was ashamed of the source of Saunière's wealth, she wouldn't have wanted anyone else to know what it was until she had died.'

Angela nodded. 'There are lots of ifs and buts and maybes in all that, but it sounds more likely to me than some of the other crackpot theories that have been suggested. You know, sacred geometry, missing tombs, "Et in Arcadia ego" and cryptic clues hidden in old paintings, all that kind of stuff.

'Anyway, if you've finally finished stuffing your face with that cassoulet, why don't we have a coffee and then get back on the road?'

Chapter 39

'Now what are they doing?' Ferrara's question to Luca Rossi, fed through the tiny speaker in the earpiece of his mobile phone, still managed to convey his irritation. Rossi suppressed a smile as he answered.

'They're still sitting at the same table in the same restaurant as they were the last time you called. And they're still eating lunch and they're still talking. They're not looking for clues or digging holes in the ground or anything like that. They just look like a couple of tourists enjoying a day out.'

Rossi had finished the ham sandwich he'd ordered for his own lunch some minutes earlier and was now making his second cup of coffee last. He'd already paid so that he would be able to move as soon as the two targets left.

'And you still can't hear what they're saying?'

'No. As I told you before, they're sitting in the garden and the tables here are kind of scattered about. I'm about thirty feet away because when I got here that was the only table that was still vacant. If I wanted to hear what they were saying, I'd have to go and stand right beside their table, and unless I disguised myself as a waiter or possibly as a tree, that wouldn't work.'

'Okay. I was only asking.'

Rossi saw a waiter approaching Bronson's table.

'Some activity,' he reported. 'The waiter's just taken away their plates, but they're still sitting there. It's quite a hot day, so maybe they'll treat themselves to an ice cream before they order coffee.'

'Keep the line open,' Ferrara instructed. 'Let me know what happens. You're sure they haven't made you?'

'If they have,' Rossi replied, 'they're being really cool about it. I'm just a guy sitting by himself reading a book and occasionally talking on my mobile. I don't think either of them has given me a single glance since I sat down.'

A couple of minutes later, the waiter walked out of the restaurant carrying two coffees and a slip of paper that he placed on the table in front of the targets. Bronson handed him a couple of notes from his wallet.

'It won't be long now,' Rossi said quietly. 'They've skipped the ice cream and the waiter's brought them coffee. Bronson's just paid the bill, so I reckon they'll be on the move in five or ten minutes.'

'Good,' Ferrara replied. 'Follow them and call me when they get to their car, or if they do anything else I need to know about, like going into another building.'

'Understood,' Rossi replied, and ended the call.

Chapter 40

Campagne-sur-Aude, Aude, France

It was only a short distance from Rennes-le-Château to Campagne-sur-Aude. Bronson drove back down the narrow twisting road to Couiza, then turned west to skirt the village of Espéraza before heading south towards Quillan.

Campagne-sur-Aude was on the west side of the river, the approach to it being over a narrow bridge, the central part wide enough for only a single vehicle and with semicircular refuges for pedestrians and cyclists built into its sides. The stone walls were decorated with planters filled with flowers and the tall trees on either side made it look as if they were driving into somebody's garden.

'This is really pretty,' Angela said as Bronson pulled to one side to let a car pass before he continued.

'I can't argue with that,' he replied, glancing both ways as they drove over the river.

Ahead of them, beyond a white-painted house, they could see red tiles on what looked like the spire of a small church.

'It's obviously a small place,' Angela said, 'so just park anywhere once we're over the bridge. I think what we're looking for is near that spire.'

The road led them to an unusual sight. What had looked like a large roundabout on the map displayed by the Peugeot's satnav was actually nothing of the sort. A wide two-way road encircled a group of houses and the church, all built on a kind of circular development in the middle of the village.

Bronson parked to one side, backing the car into a space.

Angela opened her laptop, found a plan of the layout of the old Templar fortress, and then pointed through the windscreen.

'That's the fort, believe it or not,' she said. 'According to this, the original Templar fortification was surrounded by a more or less circular boundary wall with twelve faces, so it was a dodecahedron. In the middle of it was the chapel, aligned east–west. At the western end of that was the bell tower, and underneath it the dungeon. After 1307, the village became the property of the Hospitallers, and they changed almost everything, including removing most of the fortifications and defences that the Templars had created, keeping only a couple of the accommodation spaces and the chapel. In the next century they even changed that; what we're looking at right now is the new nave they built, which is almost the size of the original chapel and includes the door in front of us.'

Bronson nodded. 'So now it's a collection of village houses, built around the chapel presumably after the Hospitallers had left. I had hoped there'd be more of the original structure left than this.'

'Again according to this website, most of the houses were built after the French Revolution and the house of the commander of the fortress was turned into the town hall. But we can go and look inside the chapel. Some of that might be original.'

Bronson locked the car and they walked across the road to the chapel entrance and up the steps. The door was unlocked and they went inside.

–

'Who are those two?' Aaron Chason asked as the three men watched Bronson and Angela walk across to the church door.

'No idea,' Gellerman replied. 'They're probably just a couple of tourists.'

'They look English to me,' Dayan said.

'How can you tell?' Gellerman asked. 'I mean, you two look Jewish, but what about me? I look as if I was born in Oslo or Stockholm or somewhere, and I'm just as much a product of Israel as you.'

'True enough,' Dayan said, 'but I'll bet there are some interesting byways in your genetic make-up.'

They watched the two figures disappear from view and then resumed their scrutiny of the road across the bridge.

–

Marco Ferrara had been less than two hundred yards behind the Peugeot when Bronson turned off the main road to drive into the village over the narrow bridge. When he saw the other car manoeuvring into a parking space, he drove past it and slotted his Alfa Romeo into a vacant space a few yards further on. He doubted if the targets would even have noticed his car except as just another vehicle on the road.

He waited, watching the Peugeot in his rear-view mirror. When he saw the two targets emerge from it, he turned off his engine, got out of the car and started walking in the same direction they were taking. What he couldn't afford to do was to let them find some clue or piece of information that he wouldn't have. So although he wasn't comfortable with the idea, he knew he would have to get close enough to watch them carefully.

When they entered the church, he was only a few feet behind them, sunglasses obscuring much of his face and a guidebook in his hand. Just another tourist, or that was the impression he was doing his best to convey.

He took off the glasses as soon as he stepped inside the building and then hung well back, watching the two targets carefully while pretending to read from his guidebook and looking around at various features of the church.

–

Bronson's attention was immediately drawn to the semicircular end of the church facing them, above the altar.

'That's more impressive than I would have expected to find in a small church like this,' he said.

Stained-glass windows mounted in decorated alcoves contrasted with deep blue paint dotted with tiny silver stars, the roof apparently supported by gold-coloured tapering braces radiating from a central point. In fact, much of the interior was decorated in contrasting shades and colours marked by various small symbols painted in different colours. The decoration gave the place an almost sumptuous feel.

Angela took some general shots with her mobile and then walked towards the altar. Before she got there, she veered off to her right. In plan, the much-modified chapel resembled a crucifix with the altar at the top – the southern end of the structure, as she pointed out to Bronson.

'So the crosspiece of the crucifix, if you like, is the original Templar chapel and we're standing at the western end of it. The bell tower is above us and you can see the spiral staircase that leads up to it.' She pointed at the massive old stones that formed the staircase by the left-hand wall. 'According to that plan I found, the dungeon was on the opposite side to the staircase.'

'No dungeon here,' Bronson said, stating the obvious. 'You don't know if it was below ground or on this level?'

'That wasn't specified on the plan. But this was a chapel and I doubt the Templars would have wanted a place of imprisonment inside a place of worship, so most probably they would have dug into the bedrock under our feet. They were very accomplished tunnellers and engineers. But wherever the dungeon was, it's not here now.'

There were no indications in that corner of the original Templar chapel of a closed-off staircase or any other kind of structure.

'That's a pity,' Bronson said. 'I know we're looking for something that disappeared seven hundred years ago, so we're not going to find clues just lying about on the ground. We know that the Ark hasn't been here for all that time, but I would still have liked to see the place where it was kept. And I was hoping there would be something here that would tell us where it went.'

Angela nodded, her expression grim and almost resigned. 'I hate to say it, but I think this has all been a complete waste of time. I don't think there's any point in going on to Collioure. We know that all we'd find there would be the old Templar fortress, which is now part of that much bigger royal castle, and a modern version of the harbour where a ship from the Templar fleet turned up to collect the Ark. What we aren't going to find, either here or in Collioure, is any indication of where it went next or where it is now.'

'So you think this is it?' Bronson asked. 'You think this is the end of the trail?'

'You know me. When it comes to this kind of thing I'll forge right on to the bitter end, but realistically I don't think there's anywhere else we can go. The document we decoded sent us to Rennes-le-Château and from there to where we're standing now. The last place it referred to was Collioure, and all that happened there was that the Ark was loaded on board a ship, probably sometime in 1307 before the Knights Templars were arrested. That vessel could have gone anywhere.'

'Anywhere?'

'Well, not exactly anywhere. I suppose their choices were slightly limited. Most of the Mediterranean was out of their reach by that time. But they could have gone to Portugal, for example. The Templars already had a major presence there and they weren't persecuted in that country. So if the ship carrying the Ark sailed around the Iberian peninsula to Lisbon or Porto, the relic might well have ended up somewhere like the Convento de Cristo. And it could still be there, locked away in some forgotten chamber.'

'Or maybe it went to Scotland,' Bronson suggested. 'We know they had assets there, and in England as well. We also know that when the King's men entered the Templar commandery in Paris on the morning of 13 October 1307, they found the vaults were virtually empty. All the treasure that Philip himself had seen in the building just a few months earlier had disappeared, as had most of the knights, and we also know why.'

'La Rochelle and the eighteen galleys?' Angela suggested.

'Exactly. Gérard de Villiers was the Templar Master of France. He was one of eight provincial masters who handled Templar affairs in Europe – the others being the masters of Apulia in Italy, Aragon in Iberia, England, Hungary, Poitiers, Portugal and Scotland – all governed by the Grand Master of the order and his seneschal. Another thing we know is that the Templars had word of Philip's plan and took precautions. The order comprised isolated communities in their commanderies, literally surrounded by potential or actual enemies. They would have had friends at court and employed spies and informers as a matter of course. So in the weeks before Philip's men moved against the Templars, Gérard de Villiers and probably at least a dozen senior knights left the Paris commandery with horses and carts and made their way south-west to La Rochelle. And from that port a fleet of eighteen Templar galleys, loaded with most of the Templar assets, sailed into apparent oblivion and were never seen again. I think the most persuasive argument I've heard is that the fleet sailed north and made landfall on the Scottish coast just east of Edinburgh, probably at a place called Musselburgh near the mouth of the River Esk.

'One thing that's always puzzled me about this incident is how many historians claim there was no fleet because the Templars didn't own any ships. They apparently fail to recognise the fact that the order of the Knights Templar was both a terrestrial *and* a maritime force. At the height of their powers they had castles in the Holy Land, they owned the island of Cyprus and had establishments in Italy, Spain, England and Scotland. They were forever criss-crossing the Mediterranean and travelling up to the British Isles. Obviously they owned ships. That's self-evident. They couldn't have maintained the control they did unless they had a fleet.'

'So you think the Ark of the Covenant probably ended up in Scotland? Is that what you're saying?'

Bronson shook his head. 'Not exactly. I think it probably *went* to Scotland, either on a vessel travelling independently or perhaps as part of the treasure fleet that sailed from La Rochelle. We don't know when it was collected from Collioure, or what else the vessel was carrying, so the ship might have sailed around the Iberian peninsula to La Rochelle and then joined with the other ships. Sailing as part of a fleet would have provided an extra layer of security, and since the Ark was one of the most important assets the order possessed, protecting it would have been a very high priority. But what happened to it after the fleet arrived in Scotland is another question altogether.'

'Well it doesn't look like we're going to find the answer here, or any time soon, so we might as well find a hotel somewhere, maybe down in Quillan, and then book our flights back to London. I think we're done here.'

–

One of the characteristics that is true of most churches is that the acoustics are very good, and the former Templar chapel was no exception. While standing and looking at the altar and the wall and ceiling behind it, Ferrara was able to hear most of what the two targets were saying. Not every word, but enough to get the gist of their conversation.

And it was not good news, from his point of view.

It sounded as if they were definitely giving up the search, and as his orders from Cardinal Caravaggio were that he was to find and recover the Ark and kill the Lewis woman, or rather the other way round, that was not what he wanted to hear. At the very least he would need to contact Rome, explain what he had overheard – and why Lewis was still alive despite the cardinal's most explicit instructions – and find out what they wanted him to do next. If she was giving up the search because there were no further clues to be found, if the quest really had hit a dead end, what would be the point in killing her?

Committing murder was not something he ever undertook lightly, not for any moral or ethical considerations but simply because it was the one crime guaranteed to galvanise any police force into a flurry of activity and there was always the danger – small, perhaps, but always present – that he would make a mistake and be implicated in the crime. That was something he was extremely keen to avoid at all costs. He would far rather let Lewis walk, irrespective of what Caravaggio told him to do, than contemplate spending three or four decades locked up in a French prison.

He saw that Lewis and Bronson were about to leave. He closed his guidebook – which in fact didn't even mention the church he was standing in – and made his way unhurriedly back to the entrance. He wanted to exit the building before the two targets got outside so that there would be no suspicion that he was following or taking the slightest notice of them.

After that, he would obviously continue tracking their progress while he waited for a decision from Rome.

Chapter 41

About five minutes after Ferrara had driven his Alfa Romeo across the bridge and into the small village, another car made the same journey. Joseph Gellerman immediately recognised the driver.

'That's Rossi,' he said, and instinctively checked his pistol was to hand.

The three Israelis watched as the Italian parked his car about fifty metres in front of them.

'He's by himself,' Dayan said. 'We could walk up to him right now, stick a gun to his head and find out exactly what he knows.'

'We could,' Gellerman agreed, 'but it wouldn't work. Rossi almost never operates alone. He'll be waiting for somebody else to arrive. If we move on him we'll be in trouble until we know how many men he has with him. We could be outnumbered and outgunned. So we sit here and watch. And we listen.'

He turned to Aaron, sitting in the back seat.

'Pass me that camera bag, please.'

Chason reached down into the footwell, picked up a black fabric bag and passed it forward.

Gellerman opened it and took out a Sony digital camera and a long black tube with a cable attached. He switched on the camera and plugged in the lead of the shotgun microphone. He put the camera on the dashboard where all three men could see the screen on the back of it and turned it so that the lens was facing Rossi's car. Then he passed the shotgun mike to Dayan in the front passenger seat.

The Israeli took care to keep the end of the device at the bottom of the open window where it couldn't easily be seen, and aimed it straight at Rossi's car.

'We'll keep watching,' Gellerman said. 'He's here for a reason and we need to know what it is. I think the Inquisition knows a lot more about the location of the relic than we do. It can't be here – we already know that – and we also know that it can't be at Collioure, so maybe Rossi and his men know where we should be looking.'

'Rossi must know that the Ark left France from Collioure, so what's he doing here?' Chason asked.

'I don't know. We can't make any assumptions about what he knows or doesn't know. Our people in Jerusalem think the Ark probably stayed in this village for several years, maybe decades, so he might be expecting to find some clue in that church. Some of it looked old and it could have been part of the Templar fortress, so maybe there's an inscription or something in the building that we didn't see.'

A couple of minutes later, another two cars arrived, one driven by a single man and the other with two men in it. The new arrivals parked close to Rossi's vehicle, and one of the men got out and walked over to the driver's side of the Italian's car.

'I told you,' Gellerman said. 'He never works alone.'

He switched the camera to video and started to record the conversation going on in front of them.

'It's those tourists again,' Chason said, pointing through the window.

–

Angela and Bronson walked across the road from the church door to their hire car. They got in and for a few seconds just sat there, both of them staring through the windscreen at nothing in particular.

'This isn't how I expected it to end,' Angela said. 'Sitting here in a car in a microscopic French village knowing that we've reached the end of the trail.'

Bronson nodded and glanced at her, not sure how to respond, then looked around at the dusty street and the old, shabby buildings that surrounded them. Several things attracted his attention, and he looked back at Angela.

'I have a feeling,' he said after a minute or so, 'that not all the cars parked in this village belong to either locals or tourists. Or if they do belong to tourists, they seem to be following very similar itineraries to us.'

'What are you talking about?'

'Without making it blindingly obvious, if you glance to your right, you'll see a small white car parked in front of that house on the left-hand side of the road. I'm interested in cars, and I can tell you that's an Alfa Romeo MiTo and it's on Italian plates. Bearing in mind that the French always seem to buy their own domestic products, almost every other car here is a Citroën, Peugeot or Renault, so something like that tends to stand out.'

'So?'

'So when we were driving out of Rennes-le-Château, I noticed another white MiTo stationary in that car park about halfway down the hill. That was also on Italian plates and, just like the one over there, had a single occupant. I didn't note the plate number, but I'd be very surprised if there were two single Italian men exploring this bit of France in identical cars. So I think we're being followed.'

'Oh God. Really?'

'Really,' Bronson said. Keeping his hand as low as possible, he removed the Glock from his shoulder holster, racked the slide to chamber a round and then replaced the weapon.

'I hope the safety catch is on,' Angela said.

'Glocks don't have safety catches, or not in the sense you mean anyway. But don't worry. It won't fire until I wrap my hand around the butt and pull the trigger.'

'Are you sure you're not seeing something that isn't there? I mean, have you noticed anybody following us?'

'A couple of times I've seen a white car that could have been a MiTo in the traffic behind us, but apart from that, no. But there's one thing I forgot to check. When we were in the hotel in Auch, we know we were under surveillance because of what happened. Nobody followed us when we drove to Tarbes, yet here we are, looking at another Italian who's now popped up at least twice in our near vicinity. I think that when we were in Auch, as well as watching us, that group of Italians also watched our car. It wouldn't have been difficult to identify. I think that while it was parked, one of them attached a tracker to it, and that's why we're seeing that Italian again, if it is the same man. And there's something else,' he added.

'More bad news?'

'Yes. I've just noticed that over to our left-hand side there are three cars, one on Italian plates and the other two French, containing four men. They weren't parked there when we drove into the village, so they must have arrived while we were in the church. The Italian I questioned back in Auch told me there were five men in the surveillance team watching us. Now we have one Italian sitting in an Alfa Romeo, another man in an Italian-plated Lancia and three anonymous males sitting in what look to me like a couple of French hire cars. By my reckoning, one plus one plus three equals five, so I think there's a good chance that right now we're kind of in the middle of that same surveillance team.'

'Oh God,' Angela said again. 'What do you think they'll do?'

Bronson smiled slightly. 'I don't expect them to do anything except follow us,' he replied, 'because that's what surveillance teams do. Of course, if we'd walked out of that church carrying a box two and a half cubits long, one and a half cubits wide and one and a half cubits high, I'm quite sure we'd have been surrounded by men pointing pistols at us before we'd got halfway back to the car.'

'They're looking for the Ark, you mean?'

'Why else would they be following us?'

'So what should we do?'

'Go and have a cup of coffee,' Bronson replied.

'What?'

He pointed through the car's windscreen and over to the right, beyond where the Alfa Romeo was parked.

'There's a little *auberge* over there with tables and chairs outside. Let's go and have a coffee there and see what happens. My guess is that the staff at the bar will suddenly find they've got four new customers. That'll be the two of us and two of the men from the cars on our left. They'll send two men because two men having a beer or a coffee together looks less suspicious than a man drinking alone, and they can sit and talk to each other and at the same time listen to what we're saying.'

'And what will we be saying?'

'Pretty much the same as we said in the church. The surveillance team may be Italian, but they'll all definitely speak English; they wouldn't have been recruited for this job unless they did. So we talk about the trail we've followed so far and how we ended up here in this village, and why there's no point in driving all the way down to Collioure because there'll be nothing to find there, and how generally pissed off we both are. And then I think I'll put the icing on the cake by taking out my mobile and booking us a couple of tickets on a flight to London out of Toulouse tomorrow afternoon.'

Angela nodded. 'And are you really going to book the flight?'

'Unless you've got a better idea,' Bronson said. 'I think I might as well, because that's the reality of the situation. We've come to the end of the trail and there really is nowhere else we can go.'

'Right, then,' Angela said. 'Let's go and play out the rest of this charade.'

Three minutes later, they were sitting at one of the outside tables in front of the small *auberge* and Bronson was ordering a couple of *grand crèmes*, a *croissant* and a *pain au raisin* to fill any gaps left after their lunch in Rennes-le-Château.

A couple of minutes after the waiter had taken their order, two casually dressed men of average height and build with entirely unmemorable faces strolled down the street and took seats at the next table but one. They both nodded in a friendly fashion with a muttered '*Bonjour, monsieur-dame*' and then continued their quiet conversation in French.

Angela eyed them discreetly. 'You were right,' she murmured. 'I'll give you that.'

The waiter reappeared with a laden tray. Bronson handed him a ten-euro note, waved away the change and launched into his spiel.

'I know it's a real disappointment,' he said, 'and I'm just as pissed off about it as you are, but as far as I can see, there's nothing else we can do. We've tracked the relic from Montségur to Rennes-le-Château and then on to this village, and now we know that this is where the trail ends.'

Angela picked up the ball and ran with it, and for the next few minutes they batted a repeat of the conversation they'd already had in the church back and forth across the table.

Bronson noticed that the men at the other table had apparently finished their conversation and were now devoting all their attention to the coffees they'd ordered and to what he and Angela were saying. Their interest was far too obvious, which suggested they weren't the most experienced surveillance operatives. On the other hand, they were obviously getting the message he wanted to convey, which was really the point.

'So do you want to fly back to London tomorrow?' he asked. 'If you prefer, we can spend another day here, perhaps go and have a look around Carcassonne. It's up to you.'

At that moment Angela's mobile emitted a musical tone. She fished it out of her handbag, swiped her finger across the screen and looked at the message she'd just been sent. It took her a couple of minutes to read it. Then she shook her head and put the phone back in her handbag.

'Problem?' Bronson asked.

'No, just the bloody museum,' she replied. 'There's yet another staff meeting the day after tomorrow and it's one that I have to get back for. Carcassonne will have to wait for another time. But don't bother booking the flight now. We can do it from the hotel tonight. I'll need to make sure that George can pick us up from the airport.'

Bronson nodded. 'Okay, then. When you've finished your coffee, we'll get back on the road.'

Chapter 42

The three Israelis saw Luca Rossi issue verbal instructions to two of the men who had arrived in the village shortly after him, and watched as the pair walked away, further into the village and out of sight.

Josef Gellerman waited for three or four minutes as a precaution and then made a decision.

'This is our best chance,' he said. 'Lemuel, come with me. Aaron, get in the driving seat as soon as we've gone. Start the engine and be ready to pick us up when I raise my arm.'

The two Israelis checked that their weapons were loaded and cocked with the safety catches on. Then they stepped out of the Renault and walked casually towards the two cars, Gellerman telling Dayan what he wanted him to do when they reached them.

The vehicles had been reversed into their parking spaces, and Gellerman hoped that their approach from behind would be undetected. At least until the last moment. He could see immediately that Rossi's interest was focused on a building further along the street. It looked like a cafe bar or perhaps a small hotel, and he assumed that was where the two other men had gone.

As they reached the vehicles, Gellerman took the pistol out of his pocket, walked straight to the driver's door of Rossi's car and wrenched it open. Behind him, Lemuel Dayan exactly and simultaneously mirrored his actions with the second man in the other car.

'Don't do anything stupid, Rossi,' Gellerman snapped, aiming his pistol at the chest of the Italian, who had clearly been taken completely by surprise.

'Gellerman,' Rossi said, staring at the man behind the weapon. 'You're a hell of a long way from the Wailing Wall. Still looking for something your sad little country lost, are you? So you can use it to try and really fuck up the world?'

'You know what I'm here for because it's what you're here for as well. If you don't want me to squeeze this trigger you'll tell me what I want to know. Where is the Ark?'

Rossi started to laugh. He'd been involved in violence of one sort or another for most of his adult life, and one thing he didn't do was scare easily.

'Oh dear, oh dear. All this way to find a relic that vanished from history two and a half millennia ago. You must have been following the same trail we have. Sniffing along on the path of the Ark from Montségur to Rennes-le-Château and finally here to this shithole of a French village. Well here's the bad news, my radical Jewish friend. The trail ends right here and right now. The Ark isn't here, and I've no idea where it went. Nobody has. Not that I would tell you if I did know.'

'I don't believe you.'

Rossi shrugged. 'I don't give a shit whether you believe me or not. That's the truth, so you can take it or leave it. Now either pull that trigger or fuck off.'

Gellerman searched the Italian's face, looking for signs of deception, but found none. Against all the odds, it sounded as if he was telling the truth. And that suggested another obvious question.

'If you know the Ark isn't here, why you still waiting around?'

'Just tying up a few loose ends. What you might call final confirmation.'

Gellerman nodded. 'Are you carrying?'

'You know me. I'm always armed. Shoulder holster, left side.'

'Put your hands up. Palms flat against the roof of the car.'

Rossi complied. He had no choice.

'You know I'll shoot if you move?'

'Of course I know that. Just get on with it, will you.'

Gellerman reached inside the Italian's jacket and pulled out a Beretta nine-millimetre semi-automatic pistol, which he tucked into the waistband of his trousers. Then he took a step back, glanced behind him to ensure that Dayan was in control of the other man, and raised his left hand above his head.

Immediately he heard the chirp of tyres on tarmac and the revving of an engine as Chason accelerated the Renault towards them.

'I'd better not see you again, Gellerman,' Rossi said, his voice laced with menace.

'My own sentiments exactly,' the Israeli replied, backing away towards the car that had just stopped with a squeal of brakes directly in front of Rossi's vehicle.

Dayan opened the Renault's rear door and climbed in as Gellerman slid into the front passenger seat.

The moment the door closed, Rossi reacted. He got out of the car, his movements surprisingly fluid and economical for such a big man, bent down and reached under the driver's seat. As the vehicle containing the Israelis accelerated away, he stood up, a Glock 17 pistol in his right hand, and snapped off three quick shots. One of the bullets shattered the rear window of the fleeing car, but he had no idea where the other two had gone, or if he'd hit any of the men inside it.

Inside the Renault, Gellerman and Dayan aimed their own weapons and let loose a fusillade of shots. But they were firing inherently inaccurate weapons from an unstable platform as the car accelerated hard over the slightly uneven surface of the road, and neither man had much hope of hitting the target.

Seconds later, Chason drove the Renault out of range and around the corner.

–

Gunshots sound unlike anything else, and four people in the village reacted immediately and instinctively when they heard them.

Marco Ferrara scrambled out of his Alfa Romeo and looked back to where Rossi's car was parked, his right hand closing around the pistol in his jacket pocket. He saw the Renault accelerating towards him, heard the sound of its rear window shattering, and then the sound of other gunshots from within the car.

He had no idea who was in the vehicle, and the absolutely last thing he wanted to do was get involved in a gunfight on the streets of a French village, but right then he was out of options. The man in the rear seat of the Renault swung a pistol to point directly at him and squeezed the trigger.

Ferrara immediately dropped flat on the ground to create the smallest possible target, and at the same moment pulled out his own pistol and snapped off two quick shots at the car as it passed. Once it was out of sight, he jumped to his feet and ran along the street towards Rossi. He needed to find out what the hell was going on, and then they had to get out of the village before the *gendarmes* arrived.

–

At the *auberge*, the two men at the other table stood up as the speeding Renault headed in their direction, their right hands reaching for what Bronson was certain were concealed weapons.

He didn't think that was a very good idea, so he reacted faster, pulling the Glock from his shoulder holster and levelling it directly at them.

'I wouldn't do that if I were you,' he said in Italian. 'Both of you, stand still. Now take out your pistols with your left hands, one at a time. You first,' he added, pointing at one of the two men. 'Put it down on the table, then back away.'

Staring down the muzzle of an automatic pistol from a distance of about eight feet, the man knew he had absolutely no choice.

'Now you,' Bronson said when the first man had disarmed himself. 'Right. Now you can both get back to whatever rock you live under. Get lost.'

He replaced his weapon out of sight in the shoulder holster as the two men jogged away down the street.

The waiter stepped out of the bar at that moment, a dishcloth in his hand, and stared with fascination at the two automatic pistols lying side by side on the table. He took a couple of paces forward and stretched out his hand as if to pick up one of the weapons.

'I wouldn't do that if I were you,' Bronson said again, this time in French. 'Let me borrow that cloth for a moment.'

The waiter, looking slightly bemused, passed him the dishcloth.

Bronson used it to pick up the first of the pistols – they were both Glock 17s, which didn't come as too much of a surprise – then pressed the magazine release and worked the slide to clear the chamber, repeating exactly the same actions for the second weapon to make them both safe without leaving his fingerprints on them.

'Thanks,' he said, handing back the dishcloth. 'I'm sure the *gendarmes* will be along quite soon and they should take charge of these weapons.'

'But what happened?' the waiter asked. 'I heard shots.'

'It was the strangest thing,' Bronson said. 'We heard the shots as well, and so did the two men sitting at the other table. They just got up, left the pistols where they'd been sitting and ran away.'

'Really?' The disbelief in the waiter's voice was obvious. 'You must wait until the *gendarmes* arrive,' he added.

'Normally we would,' Bronson said, 'but we have an urgent appointment that we simply cannot miss.'

He glanced at Angela, who stood up, and they both walked away from the *auberge*.

-

'What the hell was all that about?' Ferrara demanded when he reached Luca Rossi, who was reloading the magazine of his Glock before putting it in his shoulder holster to replace the missing Beretta.

'That,' Rossi said, 'was Josef Gellerman and two of his henchmen from Zeru. I didn't know those bastards were involved in this.'

'I know his name,' Ferrara replied, 'but I've never seen him.'

Rossi stared at him for a moment. 'You don't sound surprised about running into Zeru,' he said. 'Did you know they might be around?'

Ferrara nodded. 'I heard from Caravaggio that they'd had access to the same information that we got from the library in Paris, but I didn't know they'd be likely to turn up here.'

'You should have expected it,' Rossi said flatly. 'Any hint about the location of the Ark and Zeru will be all over it like a rash. It would have been a big help if you'd let me in on that particular piece of information. I've had dealings with Gellerman in the past. He's tough and resourceful and doesn't give up easily.'

'I don't think shooting at them was a particularly sharp idea,' Ferrara said. 'We need to get out of here right now.' He turned around, again reaching for his weapon as he heard running feet behind him.

'Relax,' Rossi said. 'These are the two I sent down to that cafe to listen to what Bronson and Lewis were talking about. What happened?' he asked them.

The men glanced at each other in a nervous fashion, and it was a couple of seconds before one of them replied.

'They were talking about the Ark,' he said, 'just as you said they would. They're going to go back to Britain because they said this is the end of the trail.'

'Is that it?' Rossi asked.

'Not exactly. When we heard the shots, we both stood up to draw our weapons, in case we were being fired at. But that man Bronson was quicker, and before we could do anything he was pointing his pistol at us.'

'Oh for fuck's sake,' Ferrara muttered. 'Don't tell me he took your weapons.'

Both men nodded sheepishly.

Ferrara looked at Rossi. 'I have no idea where you get your men from these days, but they seem to be completely bloody useless. If I were you, I'd shoot the lot of them. I'd class it as nothing more than mercy killings. Now get on the road, all of you, right now, and scatter. This operation is terminated.'

As Ferrara turned and walked back towards his car, he heard the slamming of doors and the sound of engines behind him as Rossi and his men prepared to leave the village. He had almost reached his MiTo when Bronson and Angela Lewis walked past him heading in the opposite direction, Bronson holding the Glock in his right hand as a perfectly clear and obvious threat.

The Italian didn't even give them a second glance, just got into his car, started the engine and drove away.

-

Bronson's hearing was quite acute, and as he unlocked the Peugeot he could faintly hear the sound of an approaching siren somewhere to the south, getting steadily closer.

'The *gendarmes*, helpfully giving us notice of their arrival,' he said. 'I think Quillan is the closest town with a *gendarmerie*, and they're probably coming up the main road.'

'So what do we do?' Angela asked.

'Not use the main road, obviously,' Bronson replied. 'We'll take the scenic route and you can tell me exactly what that message was that you received while we were having our coffee, because it obviously wasn't from the museum. And you can also tell me who the hell George is, and why you think he's coming to pick us up from the airport.'

-

About five miles away from the village, just to the west of Couiza, Chason pulled the Renault into a parking area so they could assess the damage. The rear window had imploded from the impact of one of the nine-millimetre bullets Rossi had fired, covering the rear seat in glittering blue-white jewels of safety glass, but neither of his other two bullets, or the rounds fired at them by the other Italian, whom Dayan had recognised as Marco Ferrara, appeared to have struck the car. What they couldn't find was the bullet that had come through the rear window.

'The door windows were still open,' Dayan pointed out as they checked the interior of the vehicle, 'so maybe that's where it went.'

'Perhaps,' Gellerman agreed. 'Right, leave the glass on the back seat. When we return the car, we'll just say a stone flew up and hit it.'

'So where do we go now, if the Ark really has disappeared?'

'Just because we don't know where it is doesn't mean it can't be found. We'll go back to Jerusalem. There's no point in staying here, but this isn't over yet.'

Chapter 43

Toulouse, Haute-Garonne, France

Bronson couldn't be certain that somebody in Campagne-sur-Aude hadn't made a note of the registration number of his hired Peugeot after the shots had been fired, and so putting some distance between themselves and the village seemed like an extremely good idea. If he was on the spot when the *gendarmes* arrived, he was certain he would be questioned, either as a witness or perhaps even as a suspect in the absence of any other non-French people who could be blamed. But if he wasn't there and the *gendarmes* had to identify him through the car registration and then try to find him in the vastness of the country, that might well fall under the heading of 'too difficult' or simply 'can't be arsed', which would suit him very well.

So instead of crossing the bridge with the attendant risk of meeting a carload of *gendarmes* coming other way, Angela and Bronson headed west and picked up the mountain road, the D2, through Brenac. After about five miles, he was able to join the faster D117 through Puivert and Lavelanet. He stayed on the same road until he reached Saint-Antoine, just south of Montgaillard, where he joined the N20, the main road that ran from the border with Spain to the east of Andorra and all the way up to Vierzon, south of Orléans.

His plan was to reach Toulouse as quickly as he could while staying off the *autoroutes* where the car would be easier to spot and stop, and to surrender the vehicle as soon as he got there. Obviously he would still be traceable through the hire car company records if the *gendarmes* decided that he was a person of interest, but the reality was that he had actually done nothing illegal in the village apart from wave an unlicensed automatic pistol at two men who were carrying virtually identical weapons. And the only people who had seen him do that were the two Italian surveillance operatives themselves, whom he had no doubt had already swiftly made tracks into the middle distance.

But what he could not afford to do was be caught by the *gendarmes* still in possession of the Glock. So he'd reduced the pistol to its component parts and disposed of them, along with the shoulder holster and the bullets, in rubbish bins in various lay-bys and rest areas en route. By the time he joined the N20, all trace of the pistol had vanished from the car.

In Toulouse, he drove straight to the car hire company and handed over the Peugeot. Then he and Angela picked a hotel at random and took a taxi to their destination.

Angela had been noticeably quiet on the journey, and had refused to tell him anything about the email she had received or, for that matter, exactly who the mysterious George was and why he would be likely to pick them up at the airport.

'I'll tell you at the hotel,' was all she would say, and while Bronson concentrated on covering the distance as quickly as he reasonably could, she buried herself on various websites using her smartphone, occasionally muttering what sounded like muffled curses and just as often smiling with quiet satisfaction when something she was looking for apparently panned out.

'Okay,' Bronson said as he finally put down their bags on the floor of the hotel room not far from Toulouse's Blagnac airport and turned to face her. 'We're at the hotel now, so spill the beans. What's happened?'

'You've been very patient, not to mention very quiet, which I did appreciate. I've got a lot to tell you, so let's go down to the lounge. It looked quite a bit more comfortable than this bedroom.'

They went down to the ground floor, found seats at a corner table and ordered drinks. When they arrived, Angela took out her phone, navigated to the page she wanted and then looked at Bronson.

'Let me get the easy bit out of the way first,' she said. 'The only George I know is the same George that you know of. That's George Anderson, the academic from the British Museum who's working at the Bibliothèque Serpente in Paris.'

'The man who started this hare running.'

'Exactly. I needed to make sure that you didn't go ahead with booking a flight back to London, so I invented a mythical George to act as a taxi driver for us because that seemed like a good way of doing it. I was hinting that we would have to check that he was free to collect us before we booked a flight. And I had to do that because London isn't where we need to go. George was on my mind anyway because, as you obviously guessed, the email I received didn't come from the museum. It came from George himself. Let me read it to you.'

She leaned forward slightly to make sure that Bronson could hear.

'"Dearest Angelina" – sorry about that; he's always assumed that I spend most of my spare time robbing tombs like Lara Croft, and as she was played in the first movie by Angelina Jolie, that's what he always calls me – "no more fake academics or homicidal Israelis, thank God, and all is quiet in the street of the snake. But I have found something quite interesting. Nothing to do with the Hautpoul papers, or not directly anyway. I became curious about the other family names mentioned in that archive because of the unwelcome attention it generated, and I ran a few searches just to see if we held any other material that might be relevant. Nothing much turned up about the Blancheforts, the Voisins or the Aniorts, so that looked like a dead end. Then I had a bit of a brainwave. Two of those family names start with consonants, but the name Aniort begins with a vowel, so I did a search under D for d'Aniort or Daniort, just in case we had been sent anything else and it had been misfiled. I discovered that the library had received a small collection of papers under that name a couple of weeks before the Hautpoul material arrived."'

Angela looked up to make sure Bronson was paying attention, which he was. She stopped reading the email word for word and summarised the rest of the message.

'George confirmed that this folio came from the same notary in Limoux, and listed what most of the papers cover; they're the usual stuff you'd expect a noble family to accumulate, similar to what's in the main Aniort archive. But there was one document that didn't fit the pattern. It also wasn't recorded in the library's register, maybe because it was tucked inside another set of papers. It was a single sheet of parchment, written on both sides. George decided to call it the "Templar Codex" which he told me was—'

'Hang on a minute,' Bronson said, interrupting, 'I thought a codex was—'

'You're absolutely right,' Angela said, interrupting his interruption. 'The smallest possible codex is two sheets of paper attached together along the left-hand edge, so this isn't a codex. This is just George making a joke. He knows what a codex is as well as anyone. Anyway, the important thing is not what he's called it but what the document actually says.'

'Which is?' Bronson sounded impatient.

'First, it doesn't mention the Ark explicitly, though the Templars get a name-check. Second, it's not encrypted but plaintext. A plaintext written in Latin, in fact. Third, it's dated 1423, which is almost two centuries after the fall of Montségur and over a hundred years after the purging of the Templars. George sent me scans of the parchment and his translation of the Latin. I've translated it as well from scratch and my version is pretty much the same as his.'

'And it says...?'

'It refers to "the relic of Solomon" – which is a clear reference to the Ark of the Covenant – and states that it was collected by a "ship of the order" from Cotlliure in the autumn of 1307. The ship sailed out of the Mediterranean and up the Atlantic coast of Iberia. Bad weather forced it to take refuge in Lisbon harbour for a couple of weeks, and then it sailed on to La Rochelle. It remained in that harbour until several other vessels had been assembled and loaded with what the parchment describes as "goods from Paris" – and I think we know exactly what that is describing. The small fleet waited a few days for a break in the weather and then set sail early one morning.'

Angela stopped talking and looked at Bronson.

'Is that it?' he asked, 'because if it is, that doesn't tell us anything we didn't already know or hadn't worked out.'

'No, that's not it,' Angela replied. 'That's just the first part – the first third, in fact – of the story, and you're right: it confirms what we already knew. The next sentence describes the ships making landfall in a harbour on the southern side of the mouth of a wide river to the east of a castle on a rock. I don't know about you, but to me that sounds remarkably like a description of Edinburgh and the harbour of Musselburgh.'

'Yes, it does. My guess was that if the Templar fleet had reached Scotland it could easily have made landfall near Musselburgh. The present harbour is seventeenth-century, but there's been a harbour there since Roman times, and in almost the same location.'

'What the parchment says next removes any doubt about the location, because it describes transporting the unspecified "goods" south along a river to a town named after the order. You know about this kind of thing. Where are they talking about?'

'Temple,' Bronson replied immediately. 'It can't be anywhere else. That means the river they used was the Esk. Temple was originally known as Balantrodach, from a Gaelic phrase that meant "town of the warriors", which was a direct reference to the Templars, but obviously "Temple" rolls off the tongue rather more easily. The Templars were granted the land by

David I back in 1128, when the first Grand Master of the order was Hugues de Payens, and it became their most important base and main preceptory in Scotland. And although the Knights Templar order was officially abolished in 1312 in England and Scotland because of the papal directive in the *Ad providam* bull, they weren't persecuted to anything like the same extent in Britain as they were in France. In fact, most of them were assimilated by the Hospitallers and very few were found guilty of anything.

'So a landing at Musselburgh makes sense. The other interesting thing about Temple, and about Midlothian, is that it's been a major producer of coal pretty much since the second century and the Roman occupation, which means there are plenty of abandoned mines in the area where the Ark and whatever else the Templars took out of the Paris commandery could have been secreted away as an alternative to storing them in their preceptory.'

'Bravo. So that's the second part of what this misnamed Templar Codex is telling us, but it's the third part, the biggest section of the document, that's the most interesting. That states specifically that at the end of the fourteenth century, in 1398, a small fleet of ships set out from Scotland and sailed west across the Atlantic carrying the relic of Solomon and a considerable quantity of other goods from Paris, all guarded by a group of Templar knights. The Templars were looking for somewhere safe to hide the items they were carrying to avoid any possibility of them being seized by either the Hospitallers or the still hostile Catholic Church. The final part of the text describes the return of only two ships from that expedition after having found safe places to store the cargo in the country where they'd landed.'

'Are you serious?' Bronson asked. 'This was, what, about a century before Columbus set sail to find a westerly route to the East Indies and found a new world instead?'

Angela nodded. 'I'm perfectly serious, and so, I believe, is whoever wrote this piece of text. You mentioned Columbus.

There are two things you need to know about him. First, and despite what virtually every American believes, Columbus didn't discover America. What he actually discovered were some of the islands of the Caribbean and a few bits of Central and South America, but he never saw or landed on any part of North America and had no idea that that vast continent lay just over the horizon. So when Americans talk about pre-Columbian times or celebrate Columbus Day, they're just perpetuating a fundamental error about the discovery of their nation. They're honouring a man for something he didn't actually do.'

'Okay, so if it wasn't Columbus, who was it?'

'It was a Venetian explorer named Giovanni Cabotto, more commonly known to us as John Cabot. He set sail from Bristol in England on board a small ship called the *Matthew*, and made landfall on the coast of Newfoundland in June 1497 – and I really don't need to point out the obvious significance of that name in this context. Despite being a Venetian, Cabot's voyage had been funded and sponsored by King Henry VII of England, and so the flag he planted was British and he claimed the new continent in the name of the king. Of course, even he wasn't the first, though he was the first one to get there during the period when Columbus was exploring the world.

'Apart from the native Americans who probably reached the continent over a northern land bridge during some interglacial period several millennia earlier, the honour of being the first people to reach America belongs to Leif Eriksson and his crew of Vikings who landed, again in Newfoundland, about half a millennium before Columbus even set sail. There's a place called L'Anse aux Meadows – which is named after a kind of jellyfish, oddly enough – in northern Newfoundland. This site has been fully excavated and partially reconstructed. The remains there are clearly Viking and date from around 1000 AD. And there are plenty of relics in that part of the continent to prove that explorers who used a runic language – meaning Norsemen – were regular visitors.

'Finally, if Columbus really had discovered America, the continent would probably have been called Columbia or something like that, but it was actually named after a Florentine explorer and navigator named Amerigo Vespucci. He sailed across the Atlantic at least twice between 1497 and 1504, once for the Spanish crown and the second time for the Portuguese ruling family, and then wrote a couple of very popular booklets about what he claimed to have seen and done. He established that Brazil was part of a new continent and not an unexplored part of the East Indies, as Columbus always believed, and he named the continent he'd visited "the New World", a name that stuck. Then a cartographer called Martin Waldseemüller, who had studied Vespucci's publications, applied a variant of the man's first name – America rather than Amerigo – to a 1507 map he was preparing that included the new continent, and that name also stuck. That's why America is called America. It's named after a bloke from Florence who had nothing to do with its discovery.'

'I think I knew some of that already,' Bronson said. 'So what was the second thing?'

'What?'

'You said there were two things I needed to know about Columbus. The first was that he didn't discover America. What was the second?'

'Oh yes. As well as being an explorer, Columbus was also the world's first true socialist.'

'What? What do you mean?'

Angela grinned at him. 'Think about it, about what Columbus did. When he set out, he didn't know where he was going. When he got there, he didn't know where he was. When he got back, he didn't know where he'd been. And he did it all on borrowed money. Isn't that more or less a definition of true socialism?'

Bronson laughed. 'Got me there,' he said.

'It's an old joke, but it's also true. Right up to the end of his life Columbus believed he really had found another route to the East Indies and had landed on bits of that region that hadn't been discovered before. Allegedly, if any of his ship's company disagreed with this contention, he had them flogged or even executed. He was, by most accounts, a spectacularly unpleasant man to deal with.'

'Okay,' Bronson said. 'Let's get back to this claim about an expedition across the Atlantic. Is there any independent evidence that that could have happened?'

'Oddly enough, yes, though some of it is more circumstantial than concrete, and it suggests that the expedition of 1398 was just one of a series of voyages by the Templars that had probably started as early as the twelfth century. When the first of the Spanish conquistadors reached Yucatán, the arrival of white men apparently didn't surprise the natives because they'd already encountered similar men who had visited years earlier and had taught them many things. According to the monks who were a part of Columbus's voyages, the natives were also already familiar with red crosses on white tunics, which was the standard garment worn by the Templars over their armour. And there's one other piece of anecdotal evidence that's interesting. Have you ever heard the name Kukulkan?'

Bronson thought for a moment, then nodded cautiously. 'Yes. I think he was an Aztec god, or maybe Mayan.'

'Mayan, actually, and in carvings and sculptures he was normally depicted as a feathered snake. But strangely, after about 1200 AD, Kukulkan, who was also known as Quetzalcoatl to the Aztecs, was usually described as a human being rather than a serpent, a white man who wore a robe or cloth and who had blue eyes, blonde hair and a beard. Don't forget that neither the Maya nor the Aztecs had beards. Just imagine how a Templar Knight, with his battle sword and armour, his white tunic and Caucasian features and beard – because the Templars didn't shave – would have appeared to the natives, arriving in a huge vessel powered by the wind. It's easy to imagine them seeing him as a divine being, as their god come to life. And apparently Kukulkan taught the Maya exactly the kind of things that a Templar Knight would have knowledge of, subjects like agriculture, astronomy, mathematics and medicine. It's a long way from being conclusive, but it's certainly indicative.'

'Yes, but that's the wrong place,' Bronson said. 'You said the parchment states that the Templars crossed the Atlantic from Scotland, which means they would have landed somewhere in the north of the continent, or maybe even in Canada, rather than in the Caribbean or South America.'

'I know. Those legends about the Maya are just a bit of unconfirmed circumstantial evidence that suggests the New World wasn't really that new even before Columbus set out. There are plenty of other stories about different groups of people making the journey across the pond, including Basque and English fishermen working the Grand Banks and even a bunch of Irish monks. But there is one piece of unambiguous evidence that definitely places travellers from Europe in Canada during the medieval period. I can't find the date, but when roadworks were being carried out in the town of Chester in Nova Scotia, two coins turned up that were later identified as being Italian, from the republic of Genoa, and minted between 1139 and 1339. They were apparently a very common type of coin at the time, hence the wide date range, but the point is that nobody travelling to the area in the seventeenth century when colonisation started would have had those coins in their pocket. That would be like you today carrying around a couple of seventeenth-century groats. They had to have been taken to Nova Scotia at some time in the medieval period. And there's one other indicator of the Templars having been in the area. Have you ever heard of the Overton Stone?'

'Heard of it, yes, but I can't remember what or where it is.'

'Okay, Overton's a town on the western coast of Nova Scotia, and there's a granite boulder there that has some interesting and very clear carvings on it. There's a fairly typical cross pattée inscribed within a circle and with four dots outside the circle next to the ends of the arms. The Templars often used to mark their crosses with dots, though usually between the arms. It looks very similar in style to other known Templar carvings. And next to it are three native symbols, presumably carved by somebody from one of the local Mi'kmaq tribes.

'The Mi'kmaq have an established oral tradition about men wearing white robes emblazoned with red crosses landing on their shores centuries ago, which is another pointer towards the Templars. The carvings show a crescent moon off to one side and a central carving of a feather overlying what look like tobacco leaves. The carvings haven't been properly dated, but most estimates suggest they've been there for at least half a millennium. They're certainly very old.

'Now, what I haven't told you about this piece of text is what it says the Templars did when they reached their destination. Or what their actual destination was.'

'Okay. I'm all ears.'

'The small fleet set out in 1398 under the leadership of Prince Henry Sinclair – I'm sure you've heard something about him before.'

'I have, yes. He was the Earl of Orkney and the Lord of Roslin, and the grandfather of William Sinclair, the man responsible for constructing Rosslyn Chapel, which is something of a mystery carved in stone. But I didn't think he was a member of the Knights Templar.'

'I don't think he was either, bearing in mind that the order had been suppressed nearly a century earlier. What I think happened was that when the Templars were merged with the Hospitallers in Scotland, there was a hard core of Templars within the combined order whose prime and secret responsibility was the safe keeping of the Templar treasure and the Ark itself. I think this inner circle of knights had sworn to guard the Ark but realised that the beliefs and standards of the old order were changing, and that the Knights Templar were never going to exist in the future as a separate body, which left them in something of a quandary about what to do with the Ark and their treasure. They probably thought that if they remained part of the Hospitaller movement, eventually the treasure would be discovered and the Ark, as an ancient and obsolete relic, would be broken up and the gold melted down. I know that's just conjecture, but I think it kind of hangs together as a theory.

'So when the opportunity to travel to a new land presented itself, they probably saw that as the ideal solution to the problem. They could travel on board the ships as passengers, taking the Ark and the treasure with them, and then find somewhere at the end of the voyage where they could hide it away for all eternity. Paying for their passage wouldn't have been a problem, and I would imagine that Prince Henry Sinclair, contemplating setting out across an uncharted sea to a largely unknown destination, would have been pleased to have a group of Templar knights on board as a fighting force to combat any danger they might encounter.'

'You're right,' Bronson said. 'It does hang together and it does make sense. So does that piece of parchment tell us where they hid the loot?'

Angela smiled slightly at him, and then nodded. 'Yes, it does. But I don't think you're going to like the answer.'

'Try me.'

'Right. The fleet ended up in Nova Scotia – New Scotland – after the Atlantic crossing, which might seem an appropriate place to land, but in fact it only acquired this name in 1621, well over two hundred years after the expedition. The place the Templars chose to hide their treasure was a small island located in a bay full of other islands on the south coast of the unusually shaped peninsula they had reached at the end of their voyage. The original name of the bay was chosen years later by the French, who were early settlers in the area, and they called it La Baye de Toutes Iles.

'That's as far as the parchment goes, and I only got that far with the location because the writer included a small but fairly accurate map on the reverse side of the sheet. The island itself is roughly marked, but there are so many islands in the area that it's difficult to be certain which one is being indicated. However, because of other information, which will become obvious to you in a minute, I think I know exactly which one it is.

'In about 1760, it was called Smith's Island by the English settlers who had largely supplanted the French, then it was renamed Gloucester Isle, but that name didn't last very long either. By about 1780, it had acquired its present name, based upon the kind of trees growing on it, and the bay in which it sits had also been renamed by the English. Today it's known as Mahone Bay, and as you might have guessed, the island the Templars chose is now called Oak Island.'

Bronson didn't respond for a moment, and then he said just two words.

'Oh shit.'

'I couldn't have put it better myself.'

Chapter 44

Paris, France

George Anderson's interest in the misfiled Aniort documents, and in particular the parchment, had been noticed by one of the permanent staff members at the Bibliothèque Serpente. He was a man who occasionally found ways to supplement his income by performing additional tasks that involved little more than observing what people were doing and occasionally taking surreptitious pictures of either individuals or documents and passing them on to a French mobile number.

Over the last couple of weeks he'd photographed two academics, one Italian and the other Israeli, who had been particularly interested in an archive of papers relating to an obscure French noble family. Those images had eventually been viewed by a senior cardinal in Rome and had been the catalyst that had led to Caravaggio issuing his changed orders to Marco Ferrara about the elimination of Angela Lewis.

When Anderson had left the library for lunch the previous day, the staff member had taken pictures of the Latin text on the sheet of parchment and forwarded that to his usual contact number as well.

And that was why, the day after Ferrara had been forced to abandon his quest to locate the Ark of the Covenant, and to drive away from the village of Campagne-sur-Aude before the *gendarmes* arrived, Caravaggio issued him with exactly the same instructions once again, but told him to proceed to a very different destination.

Chapter 45

Toulouse, Haute-Garonne, France

'Right,' Bronson said, sounding terminally irritated. 'If this bunch of Templars buried the order's treasure at the bottom of that pit on Oak Island, we might as well pack up and go home right now. It's a private island, people have been searching for treasure in the Money Pit for the last three centuries, and as far as I know, they've so far recovered the square root of sod all.'

Angela nodded. 'You're absolutely right. There's a major company with lots of resources trying to reach the so-called treasure vault at the bottom of the Money Pit right now, and if they can't get it, there's no possible way we could do anything. Mind you, at least this information does clear up one matter. Assuming this document is accurate, we now know that the Oak Island Money Pit was built by the Templars.'

'Funnily enough,' Bronson said, 'I've always thought it was. I know there were theories about it being the treasure of Captain Kidd or some other pirate, but none of that ever really made sense to me because of what we know about it. It's just too well thought out, and too complicated and sophisticated. There's obviously some kind of vault, presumably full of treasure, buried over a hundred feet down under the surface of the island. That in itself is a fairly major piece of engineering and certainly a lot deeper than any pirate would be prepared to dig to hide something. There's the shaft above it with oak platforms every ten feet or so, which was presumably how they dug down to create the treasure vault in the first place. Then there could well be another way of getting down to the vault, some hidden tunnel on the island that no one's found yet. And finally there's the booby-trap, the system of flood tunnels designed to make absolutely certain that if anybody did manage to dig down the shaft and get anywhere close to the vault, seawater would flood in and stop them.

'That's where radiocarbon dating has proved useful. The team doing the exploration at the moment recovered some of the coconut fibre that had been used to prevent the water collection system on the beach on the island from clogging up, and the dating analysis came up with a date in the thirteen hundreds, if I recall. That would fit well with the Templars building the Money Pit.

'That defence system isn't something dreamt up by an illiterate pirate captain and cobbled together by his crew of seamen. It's a major piece of really clever engineering, designed by somebody who knew exactly what they were doing and constructed by people who were dedicated, knowledgeable and highly skilled. We absolutely know for certain that the only people living in the Nova Scotia area at that time were the Native Americans, and they definitely didn't possess either the skill or the knowledge to attempt something like that. The project could only have been undertaken by one of two entities. It could have been a government, but that makes no sense, because if a government had something big to hide they could simply create a secure vault in their own country and put it in that. The only other option is that it was done by a military unit employing military engineering skills and military discipline, and the only possible candidate to fit that bill at that time would have been the Knights Templar, doing their best, as the order faced enemies on all sides, to preserve their most valuable assets. So,' he finished, 'I suppose we just forget it?'

'Yes, and at the same time no, because there are a couple of things that I gleaned from this document that I haven't told you yet. First of all, the fleet that Prince Henry Sinclair sailed across the Atlantic was quite small, probably no more than six or seven ships, but the treasure fleet that sailed out of La Rochelle consisted of eighteen vessels that were probably of a similar size to Sinclair's. You can't load the cargo from eighteen ships onto six similar vessels, obviously. According to this parchment, the Templars picked out only the most valuable pieces of treasure to take with them on the voyage and left the remainder, which must've been about two thirds of their total treasury, hidden somewhere in Midlothian. It doesn't say where, but because the Templar properties were all by then in the hands of the Hospitallers, they certainly wouldn't have felt safe leaving it in one of their buildings. So my guess is that somewhere in that area there's a disused and abandoned coal mine that now contains something a lot more valuable than the coal that was originally dug out of it.'

'Okay, that all makes sense, but there's still the awkward fact that we can't get onto Oak Island unless we go as tourists in an organised group, and if we did visit we wouldn't be able to do anything to recover the treasure.'

'I know, but we're not interested in recovering the treasure. We're looking for one very specific item, the Ark of the Covenant, and I didn't say that that was hidden anywhere on Oak Island. In fact, I didn't say it was hidden anywhere in Nova Scotia or even anywhere in Canada.'

Bronson looked interested. 'No, you didn't,' he agreed. 'So where is it?'

'According to this parchment, the Templars realised that the Ark was fragile. It was only a wooden box covered in gold plating with a gold lid, and if it got wet it would simply rot away and disintegrate. And getting wet would have been inevitable if the flood tunnel booby-trap had been triggered. The gold and silver bullion or whatever the rest of their treasure consisted of would be completely unaffected if the vault flooded. But the

Ark was precious to them, and so they hid it somewhere else. What I don't know is exactly where.'

'Ah,' Bronson said. 'Any clues?'

'Yes, but they really won't make any sense until we actually get over there and start searching.'

'Right. I'll look for flights.'

'You don't have to,' Angela said. 'We're booked on a flight out of Blagnac at five past two tomorrow afternoon, which is quite a civilised time. That will take us north to Amsterdam, home of canals and hookers, where we'll arrive at about four. We'll have to wait around there for an hour, just long enough to get a drink and a snack, and then it'll take us just over seven and a half hours to fly across the pond. We arrive in Boston at—'

'Boston? Last time I looked, that was in America, not Canada.'

'Well spotted. If you recall, I didn't say where the Templars had hidden the Ark, only that they'd buried their treasure on Oak Island. Anyway, we'll get to Boston at twenty to seven in the evening, if the flight's on schedule, and that's local time, obviously. The return flight will be a week later, because I reckon if we haven't found it by then, we're probably not going to find it at all.'

'What about visas?' Bronson asked.

'We don't need them. We're both citizens of the United Kingdom, so we're eligible to travel to the States under the Visa Waiver Program. I've already been online to sort out the ESTAs – the Electronic System for Travel Authorisation approvals – that we'll need.'

'You *were* busy on the way back this afternoon, weren't you? So what's the plan when we get to Boston?'

'We'll be knackered when we arrive because of the time changes and stuff, so I've booked one night in an airport hotel. Then we get up bright and early the next day, hire a car and get on with it.'

'I've always said there's nothing more dangerous than a man with a plan,' Bronson said, 'but with you they quite often seem to work. So once we're awake and we've got wheels, where do we start?'

Chapter 46

The team of three Israelis from Zeru had unwittingly been following Angela and Bronson, albeit taking a different route, and had also reached Toulouse and booked into a hotel. They'd returned the hire car and apologised for the shattered rear window, claiming that a stone thrown up by a truck heading in the opposite direction had been the cause. Unfortunately, they hadn't, they claimed, got the registration number of the vehicle, and the truck driver, apparently unaware of what had happened, had simply continued on his way. The car hire firm hadn't been pleased because the vehicle would now be off the road for a couple of days while the glass was removed and a new rear window installed, but accidents happened and that was the end of it. The insurance company would cover the costs.

Before they used their return airline tickets to go back to Jerusalem, Gellerman and Dayan played the video recording they had made in Campagne-sur-Aude of Luca Rossi talking to the other man. Neither had any particular expectation that they would glean any useful information, but they still thought it was worth watching it, or more accurately, listening to it.

And unexpectedly, they did find out something they hadn't known before.

Gellerman had assumed that Rossi and his men had been following the trail indicated by the encrypted text, but the recording they'd obtained using the shotgun microphone made it clear that this hadn't been the case. Rossi had been following two people, two English people, who very obviously *had* managed to decipher the text. It was also clear that the couple involved – who might very well have been the two 'tourists' that Aaron Chason had noticed and pointed out – had been in the village at that moment, because Rossi had been briefing the man to take one of the other new arrivals and go and eavesdrop on their conversation in a local bar. All of which was interesting, but not particularly helpful.

What *was* helpful was that Rossi had also provided their names. The woman was called Angela Lewis and the man's surname was Bronson. With the trail in France effectively cold, the fact that the English couple had been involved in the search gave them a measure of importance, particularly as they had apparently decrypted the text, something the Inquisition, with all its resources back in Rome, had so far not managed to do – which was why Rossi had been following them.

If the Ark still existed, maybe the English couple would stumble upon another clue that would allow the search to resume.

Gellerman made copious notes about exactly what had happened when they'd been in Campagne-sur-Aude, including the names Angela Lewis and Bronson, which he suggested should be checked and the two people identified as a matter of some urgency, and included everything in an encrypted email that he sent to his superiors at Zeru in Jerusalem. He concluded by saying that he, Dayan and Chason would remain in Toulouse awaiting further orders rather than fly back to Israel.

Even a decade or so ago, finding a particular person was a highly skilled and extraordinarily tedious task, involving physically checking parish registers, local councils and national archives for documents like birth and marriage certificates and then travelling to various locations to talk to people who might conceivably know or have known the target. Today, with the plethora of online directories and databases and other sources of accurate information, the job is a lot easier, and most of it can be done sitting in a comfortable chair, looking at a computer screen and using a mouse and keyboard. Law-enforcement organisations in any country – and people with non-official access to the same systems – can track almost anybody's movements electronically, because in today's totally connected world, every airline ticket, hotel booking and car hire requires the use of a credit card.

And because of Zeru's sympathisers within the Mossad and Shin Bet, Gellerman knew that identifying the English man and woman, and more importantly finding out where they were and what they were doing, probably wouldn't take very long.

The search for the Ark wasn't over yet, not by a long way.

Chapter 47

Boston, Massachusetts, United States of America

'God, I feel about as sharp as a sponge,' Bronson said, rolling over in the wide double bed and peering at the unfamiliar surroundings of the bedroom at the Hilton, chosen by Angela because it was the only hotel that was actually *at* Boston's Logan International Airport.

'And good morning to you too,' Angela replied, sitting up in bed and looking at him brightly. 'I'm going to take a shower. Maybe you can think about getting up while I'm in the bathroom. It would be good if you were at least sitting up when I come out rather than just lying there farting and grunting and complaining.'

'I need coffee. Preferably intravenously.'

'We'll get some downstairs. And some breakfast as well. Now stop lying about moaning and move it.'

Once he was shaved, showered and dressed and had put himself outside the American equivalent of a full English and two large cups of coffee, Bronson both looked and sounded rather more like a human being than a bad-tempered ape.

'Jet lag always screws me up,' he said apologetically. 'What's the time difference here?'

'That depends where you're talking about. If you mean from the UK, it's five hours, but we flew out of France so it's six.'

Bronson looked at his watch, which he'd reset to local time the previous evening on the aircraft when the pilot had given his short 'Welcome to Boston and the United States of America' speech.

'It's now just before ten in the morning,' he said, 'so that means in Paris it'll be four o'clock in the morning.'

'Wrong,' Angela replied. 'Luckily for us, this planet always spins in the same direction, and that means that wherever you are in the world, places to the east of you are always earlier, ahead of you in time, I mean, and places to the west are always behind you. So right now in Paris it's four o'clock in the afternoon.'

'Got it, I think.'

'That's good, because we need to get moving.'

–

One of the less obvious advantages of working for any part of the higher echelons of the Catholic Church, and especially for a department of the Vatican itself, was that the very mention of Rome could open doors that would otherwise remain firmly closed. So after Cardinal Caravaggio had issued his new orders to Marco Ferrara and Luca Rossi, he had also approached a middle-ranking Catholic official in Massachusetts.

Christianity is by far the biggest single religion followed by American citizens, and can be found in two different flavours. Roughly half of all Americans espouse the Protestant faith, while about a quarter of the population – just over seventy million people – are Catholics. So in fact Caravaggio had been somewhat spoilt for choice, despite the rather unusual request he was making. He needed somebody with contacts in a sector of society with which a man of the cloth would not normally be familiar. A man who would know and be able to recruit the kind of people for whom the law was more of a challenge than a code of practice. The kind of people, in short, who would undertake the task Caravaggio had in mind without asking too many awkward questions, and who would also be prepared to carry out one very specific action should the circumstances demand it.

And that was why two men sitting at a table on the far side of the hotel dining room finished their coffee almost simultaneously and stood up a few seconds after Bronson and Lewis had left the room. They had had no trouble identifying their targets, thanks to a photograph of the Lewis woman, and had known exactly where to look for her because of information culled from the bank that had issued Bronson's credit card, information that had made its electronic way through the American banking system and then on to London, Paris and Rome before ending up on Caravaggio's desk at the *Congregatio pro Doctrina Fidei* in the Palace of the Holy Office just outside the walls of the Vatican. That data had then made the return journey by email across the Atlantic to the cardinal's contact in Massachusetts.

Wherever the English couple went, Caravaggio's thinly disguised orders would ensure that he would be informed about their movements and actions within minutes. And that meant he would be able to resolve the situation if Lewis stumbled upon the location of the Ark before Ferrara and Rossi managed to get there.

–

The car Bronson ended up with was a Buick Encore, described by the attractive young woman at the car hire desk in the airport – they chose the company not because of its name or reputation but simply because it had the shortest queue – as a 'great subcompact SUV', whatever that was supposed to mean. In fact, it was nothing like as bad as he had feared, not being a fan of American cars, and felt and handled more like a normal European saloon car than any American vehicle he'd driven before.

'That's probably,' Angela pointed out after doing a brief bit of research on her smartphone, 'because it's not built by Americans. The badge might say Buick, but this was put together by a bunch of South Koreans, and these days they build good cars over there, even if they do put the steering wheel on the wrong side.'

Bronson had programmed the Encore's built-in satnav to take them the fairly short distance, about fifteen miles, north-west to Westford.

'You've been a bit quiet about where we're actually going,' he said, 'apart from Westford, I mean. I presume that's where we'll be starting the search? And I suppose this is just as important, but what proof have you got – apart from the parchment, obviously – that the Templars were ever in Massachusetts or this part of America?'

Angela nodded. 'Good question. Let me tell you about one rock-solid clue that we won't be able to see.'

'That sounds helpful. Or do I mean unhelpful?'

'Just listen and then you can decide. In April 2010, Rhode Island was hit by a particularly violent storm. Once it had passed, a local resident down in Newport on the south coast was strolling along the beach at low tide not far from a place called Fort Adams when she discovered a large boulder on a pebbly beach. There's some doubt about whether what she found was just a large rock or if was a part of the island's bedrock. But there was no doubting the inscription that she read along one side of the stone. There are clear pictures of this on the Internet, and although the carving is a bit faded and damaged because of the action of the waves, the words are perfectly readable. It's in Latin, which is interesting in itself. But what's more interesting is the inscription, *IN HOC SIGNO VINCIS*, which takes us all the way back to the church at Rennes-le-Château and the Templars.'

'Absolutely,' Bronson said. 'That's the inscription at the very top of the portico, above the statue of Mary Magdalene. It was one of the mottos of the Knights Templar.'

'And you told me,' Angela reminded him, 'that it was also the motto of Portugal.'

Bronson nodded and glanced at her before returning his gaze to the road. 'Exactly. So who carved it? Was it the Templars, or some Portuguese explorer on a voyage that never made it into the history books?'

'Good question. On the other side of the stone there are more markings. One of those reportedly looks like a cross pattée, but that doesn't help because the Portuguese ships often used that symbol on their sails. But as far as we know, most of the Portuguese voyages went south and then east around Africa, heading for the East Indies, or west across the middle of the Atlantic after Columbus's expeditions. And because of what George found in Paris, we do know that a group of Templars travelled to this part of America. My guess – and that's really all it is, just a guess – is that this stone is part of the bedrock and that the inscription was carved by the Templars when they got here, perhaps as a kind of thanks that they had survived the voyage from Scotland.'

'And we can't see it?'

'No, because the action of the waves has reburied it, though its location is known. And realistically, even if we did go to the beach and dig away the sand and pebbles, we wouldn't find out any more than I've told you.'

'Okay, so scratch that. It's interesting and it sounds fairly conclusive, because it does demonstrate that there must've been either a Templar or a Portuguese presence in this area in the medieval period. Assuming that it's genuine, of course.'

'Actually,' Angela said, 'there are quite a lot of ancient relics that have been found on this side of the Atlantic, everything from what look like megalithic tombs to inscribed stones covered in runic symbols, but America has a large fraternity of archaeologists whose main purpose in life appears to be debunking any piece of evidence that doesn't fit with the accepted timeline and history of the continent. It's funny how every megalithic tomb seems to be identified by them as a root cellar built by some unknown colonist, and every runic inscription as an obvious hoax. Basically, they've already decided that at some point in prehistory the Native Americans arrived and the next important thing that happened was the arrival of Columbus, which of course we know for certain never took place. Anything that doesn't fit into that history they simply dismiss as fake without, of course, bothering to actually investigate it. Because they know they're right they don't have to even look at anything that contradicts their cosy version of the history of America.'

'An attitude that's unfortunately incredibly common among members of the scientific community everywhere,' Bronson said. 'Mention almost any fringe subject to most scientists – UFOs, Bigfoot, paranormal phenomena, anything like that – and they dismiss it out of hand without so much as a second thought or even looking at the evidence. And in fact there's compelling evidence to support most of those subjects. I think the majority of scientists – present company excepted, of course – have their minds hermetically sealed as part of whatever course they study at university. Okay, the inscribed stone is obviously out, so what's next?'

'The parchment doesn't say anything explicit, which I suppose is not surprising. It just gives hints that would have meant more to a Templar in the fourteenth century than they do to us in the twenty-first.'

'Like what?'

'Well, one oddity is the Latin phrase *quod est superius est sicut quod est inferius*, which more or less translates as "as it is above so it is below". It comes from a hermetic or alchemical text written on a thing called the Emerald Tablet, or the Tabula Smaragdina, which is supposed to date from a couple of thousand years ago, though the earliest known source for the expression is a book in Arabic that dates to between the sixth and eighth centuries.'

'Didn't the ancient Egyptians use an expression similar to that?'

'They did. I think it's to do with the afterlife of the pharaohs, how they were supposed to ascend to the Milky Way and travel along it in the same way that their boats travelled along the

Nile. Something like that. I think it's a very old expression, probably dating back to prehistoric times, when early man saw things in the heavens and tried to associate them with things happening on earth just to try to make sense of the world. But in this particular context I think it may be more specific than that because of the phrase that follows it: *in insula et in monte*, meaning "on the island and on the hill". To me, that could suggest some structure or other on high ground, on a hill, that mirrors or is similar to a structure on an island. So maybe we should be looking for another vault that's the same sort of design as the one on Oak Island.'

'I hope you're wrong about that,' Bronson said, 'because that could mean we never get into it. Look, we're coming into Westford now. Where do you want me to go?'

'We need to find Depot Street. Just follow the satnav.'

Depot Street turned out to be quite a busy road with no obvious places to stop apart from the driveways of one of the large and elegant houses that lined it, which Bronson didn't think would go down terribly well. So he turned into a much quieter side street called Beaver Dam Drive and left the car on the road well clear of the junction.

'And this,' Angela said a few minutes later, pointing at a flat slab surrounded by concrete posts linked by a chain, 'is the memorial to the Westford Knight. Allegedly,' she added.

A noticeboard on the left-hand side provided information, and behind the chain and concrete posts was a vertical stone marker, somewhat like a gravestone, making a bold and unequivocal claim. Bronson read it out loud. '"Prince Henry First Sinclair of Orkney born in Scotland made a voyage of discovery to North America in 1398. After wintering in Nova Scotia he sailed to Massachusetts and on an inland expedition in 1399 to Prospect Hill to view the surrounding countryside, one of the party died. The punch hole armorial effigy which adorns this ledge is a memorial to this knight."'

Within the chained-off area was a flat stone slab on which lay a bronze-coloured effigy of a medieval knight in full armour, which very clearly had been put there a lot more recently than 1399. And on the left of that was an expanse of flat black stone, apparently a part of the bedrock of the island, on which faint markings could just about be discerned. The rock was protected by a sheet of glass mounted in a metal frame.

'Whoever had that stone carved didn't mince their words,' Bronson said. 'I presume this wasn't erected by a national museum or group of mainstream historians?'

'To be honest, I have no idea who erected it, when or why, but it is interesting. The punch-hole markings on that flat slab are supposed to depict a medieval knight with his sword on top of his body and with the blade broken to show that he was dead. On his left side is a shield that supposedly displays the coat of arms of the Gunn family.'

Bronson peered closely at the slab in front of him 'I can't make out anything on it,' he said.

'Nor can anybody else, and that's one of the problems. There's some suspicion that the markings may occasionally have been improved, shall we say, by locals trying to keep the story alive, at least before that sheet of protective glass was installed. The counter-argument is that the only way the markings can be properly seen and studied is by doing a cloth rubbing, the same way you'd do a brass rubbing in an English church, and that has been done.

'If the device on the shield has been correctly identified as that of the Gunn family, the most likely individual this could relate to is Sir John Gunn, a kinsman of Prince Sinclair. He was born in 1320, which fits with the dates of the Sinclair expedition, and the date and place of his death are unknown, which also fits, though in a negative manner. If he died out here in Massachusetts in 1399, his family back in Scotland might never have known how, when or where he died and the family or clan records would never have been updated.'

'Okay,' Bronson said. 'I presume this doesn't get a name-check on the parchment?'

'No, but it's interesting and possibly relevant. Now, we've got one more stop to make in this area and then we can head down to Newport.'

They could almost have walked to their next destination, but Bronson wasn't happy leaving the car on the street, so he followed Angela's directions, turning right out of Beaver Dam Drive, down Depot Street past the Westford Knight and then right onto Main Street.

'It's that yellowish building on the right,' Angela said. 'The J. V. Fletcher Library. There should be a car park at the rear of the building.'

Inside, behind the staircase on the ground floor, they found the second probable Templar artefact.

'This is known as the Boat Stone or Ship Stone, and you can easily see why.'

Bronson looked down at the clear carving of what was very obviously a medieval ship on the side of the stone and nodded.

'There's no mistake about that,' he agreed. 'What's the history of it?'

'The rock was found when some roadworks were being done in this area in 1930. It was dug out of the ground under the road, and that fact alone means that we're not looking at a modern fake concocted by somebody trying to promote the idea of the Sinclair expedition. Nobody would go to the trouble of doing this carving, then digging up a road to bury it below the hardcore and repairing the road just on the off-chance that a bunch of workmen would dig it up again a few years later.

'It's also worth pointing out that the rock and the carving have been analysed using a geological weathering technique, which came up with an age of about six hundred years for the carving. So that also eliminates any possibility that it's a fake. The carving was made using the same hammer-and-punch technique that was believed to have been used on the Westford Knight carving.'

'What sort of a ship is it?'

'Some people claim it's a knorr or knarr, a Viking cargo vessel, clinker-built and powered by a square sail – you can see the sail very clearly in the carving. They were about fifty feet long, could carry around twenty-five tons and are known to have routinely crossed the Atlantic to supply Viking bases in Newfoundland and elsewhere. But bearing in mind the date of the Sinclair expedition, I think it's more likely to be a cog. These were also clinker-built with a square sail, and by the thirteenth century they'd pretty much supplanted the knarr in northern waters because they could carry more cargo and had high sides and a flat bottom, both of which are clearly shown in this carving.'

'What does the arrow mean?' Bronson said, pointing at the stone. 'And is that a number there?'

'No one knows for sure,' Angela replied. 'One suggestion is that the arrow might have pointed towards whatever structure the Templars had erected to live in, and the number – it's 184 – could have been the distance to reach it, in paces or strides or some other unit of measurement.'

'They're Arabic numerals, though,' Bronson pointed out. 'If this stone is that old, shouldn't they be Roman numerals?'

'Strictly speaking, they're Indian numerals, though they were known as Arabic because they were used by Arab traders in Europe from the tenth century. They were in common use in Britain and Europe by the fourteenth and fifteenth centuries, so that does fit. Once the printing press had been invented in the mid fifteenth century, Roman numerals were abandoned except for some specialised uses like clock faces, because the Arabic numerals were so much easier to read, and a lot shorter as well. It's easier to write and read 789, for example, than DCCLXXXIX, which you need to interpret. In this case, 184 would be CLXXXIV, still a cumbersome seven characters instead of only three.'

'Okay. So where did the arrow point?' Bronson asked.

'The original location of the stone was known because of the roadworks, but nobody bothered to take a note of its orientation before they moved it. But no traces of any Templar building have been found in this area, so the orientation wouldn't have helped in any case.'

Before they left, they looked at other items in the Westford Knight display, including a photograph of the cloth rubbing of the stone, which clearly showed the sword with the broken blade, the shadowy figure of a knight, and a shield, though Bronson couldn't make out any details of the heraldic device on it. Some of the older pictures of the stone, taken in the 1940s, showed the features of the carving in much more detail.

'Okay, so now where do we go?' he asked, starting the car.

'Straight down to Newport,' Angela said, reprogramming the satnav with a new destination, 'because there we'll find a building that very probably does date from the time of the Templars, no matter what American historians choose to believe.'

-

As Bronson steered the Buick away from the J. V. Fletcher Library, a man sitting in a greyish Honda Accord parked on Main Street about a hundred yards away started his car's engine and pulled out to follow. Fifty yards behind him, a man in a Toyota sedan replicated his actions. They had watched the targets collect their hire car and had been behind them all the way from Logan International Airport. They would follow them wherever they went, alternating position so that the driver of the Buick wouldn't see the same car behind him all the time.

As he drove away, the man in the Toyota used his hands-free kit and dialled an Italian mobile telephone number. He had no idea of the identity of the man who answered, but he did know that he was the person pulling his strings.

'What are they doing now?' Cardinal Caravaggio demanded.

'Driving around and doing the tourist bit. They've looked at the Westford Knight – that's a kind of local attraction – and visited a local library. Right now they're back on the road.'

'Call me whenever they stop. And don't let them see you.'

Chapter 48

Jerusalem, Israel, and Toulouse, France

While Zeru was not an officially sanctioned Jewish organisation, its unstated but clear objective was something that almost every citizen of the country fundamentally agreed with to a greater or lesser extent, so it was able to rely on semi-official help in a number of fields. Information that the organisation requested or needed was never officially acknowledged, though official resources were often used to obtain it, and this level of under-the-counter cooperation even extended into parts of the security services and the military.

So when one of the principals at Zeru flagged up the names Lewis, Angela, and Bronson, no first name, as an 'anything known' request, it didn't take long for positive results to be obtained. Passport control records showed that both Angela Lewis and Christopher Bronson, believed to be her former husband, had visited Israel more than once. Further information on both was somewhat scanty, but Lewis was an academic and Bronson was a British police officer. Scans of their passports accompanied the response.

That prompted a different enquiry from Zeru directed towards a sympathetic officer in the Mossad. They knew that Bronson and Lewis had been in Campagne-sur-Aude, so now that they had their passport details, they asked if either target had crossed any border, although that was impossible to check in Schengen countries. Again the response was quick, and again it was positive. The day after the incident in the French village, they'd both flown to Boston in Massachusetts.

'Boston?' Dayan asked, when he read the encrypted email. 'What the hell are they doing over in America?'

'They must have found a clue or been given some more information,' Gellerman said. He thought about the situation for a few minutes, then nodded. 'We should follow them. Find out what supporters we have over there and get their contact details. I'll talk to Jerusalem and tell them where we'll be, then I'll book flights and a hotel. You have both got valid American visas?'

Both Dayan and Chason nodded. Because members of Zeru might have to travel almost anywhere at short notice, they had visas for most countries where the validity period was over a year. The American B1/B2 visa was valid for ten years from the date of issue and allowed them to spend up to a hundred and eighty days in the States at a time, so they held them as a matter of course.

'We'll leave the pistols in a storage locker somewhere here in Toulouse, maybe at the airport. Aaron, make sure you identify somebody in Massachusetts who can supply us with weapons. We don't know what we'll be facing over there.'

'Of course,' Chason replied. 'In America, finding pistols is never difficult, not even in Massachusetts.'

Chapter 49

Rhode Island, United States of America

'Newport is where you said that inscribed stone was found on the beach,' Bronson said as they drove over the Sakonnet River Bridge from the mainland to Rhode Island, the open water to their left scattered with private yachts riding on buoys or at anchor, and a couple of marinas to their right.

'Yes, right down at the southern tip, not that far from where we're going. I hope the clues in this parchment will make more sense once we're actually on the spot, because some of them relate to the terrain, like that one about the island and the hill. And we need to see the place, to be there, to recognise and identify landmarks.'

'What other clues are there?'

'There are really two others that might help to pinpoint where we should be looking, but the one I'm most interested in is the Latin phrase *medium inter finibus ubi flumen currit ad meridiem*. It translates as "halfway between the coasts where the river runs south". That seems quite specific, but it's also a bit vague. The only thing it conveys for sure is that we need to find a river that flows towards the south. What we can do nothing about are the man-made changes that will have altered the landscape in the centuries between the Templars walking this ground and now. That's the other reason I want to explore at least some of Rhode Island, to get a feel for the way the environment might have changed.'

Like most American roads, the highway was good and largely straight without too much traffic, and for some time they drove through pleasant open countryside. Soon they started seeing scattered houses and the occasional industrial unit, and they ran into a lot more traffic as they passed the airport, but even so it continued to flow freely. The suburbs of Newport were quite built up but still felt spacious, because most of the houses were individually designed rather than built as identical units, and were well separated on large lots, not crammed together in the rows that were a feature of most British towns. As they neared their objective, the roads and streets narrowed, but many of them were one-way to avoid congestion.

'This seems like a very pleasant place to live,' Angela said. 'Lots of open spaces, attractive houses and all the rest.' She checked something on her smartphone. 'They aren't even expensive, most of them. According to this website, you can get a perfectly reasonable three-bedroomed detached house for around two to three hundred thousand, and that's dollars, not pounds. Obviously it depends on the area, but that's less than I would have thought.'

'Or for about the same money,' Bronson pointed out, 'you could buy a two-up, two-down terraced cottage in one of the cheaper bits of Kent. But I think I'd still rather live in England.'

The satnav took them into Bellevue Avenue, and then right into Pelham Street. About halfway along, Angela pointed to the right.

'That's it,' she said. 'That's the Newport Tower. Just park anywhere along here.'

Bronson locked the Buick and they walked over towards one of the strangest-looking buildings he had ever seen. It was almost circular – actually it was octagonal, but because of its size this was barely noticeable – with eight pillars forming eight arches. Above them the walls continued upwards, but there was no roof or any kind of covering; it was obvious that it was just a circular shell. What it looked like to Bronson could be summed up in a single word: old.

'What is it?' he asked. 'I mean, I can see that it's a tower, but what was it for? And who built it?'

'Two predictable questions, both entirely valid. And the short answer to both is the same: nobody knows. The prevailing theory is that it was a grist mill – a mill that grinds cereal into flour – built in colonial times, and presumably powered by wind.'

'It doesn't look like a windmill to me. Or even like the remains of a windmill.'

'Nor to me, and that's the first problem. It's the wrong shape and the design doesn't make sense. Windmills almost always taper from the base upwards and they're usually built of wood because they have to be able to turn to take advantage of the prevailing wind. If you can't turn the entire windmill then you have to be able to turn the bit that the sails are attached to. The conventional theory is that the colonists built a wooden windmill here but it blew down in a storm in about 1675, and so they replaced it with this stone structure. There are a few stone windmills still standing, but the one characteristic they all share, with one exception, is that the base is a solid stone tower. The exception is a thing called the Chesterton Windmill in Warwickshire, which does look a bit like this but only stands on six pillars rather than eight.'

'But if they built a stone windmill because the wooden one was blown down in a storm, why did they build a tower that would be inherently weaker and much more difficult to construct than a solid tower? Logically, a solid tower would make much better sense.'

Angela nodded. 'Exactly. The related problem is that despite the claim that a wooden windmill was blown down here in a storm, there's no record whatsoever of this one being built. There are various extant documents that refer to a mill in this area, but that's all, and it's possible that they called it a mill because they had to call it something.'

'So you think it pre-dates the arrival of the colonists?'

'I do,' Angela said. 'Let me ask you a question. When you saw it for the first time, what was your initial impression?'

'I thought it looked old. Certainly older than seventeenth-century. We're used to seeing very old buildings in Britain and to me this looks more medieval than anything.'

'And probably one reason why you thought that was because of the way it's been built.' Angela pointed at the tower in front of them. 'As far as I'm aware, every surviving colonial building in America – and some of those were erected over a century before the colonists began building anything here – is either some form of timber-framed property or it's been built using shaped stones. So why, if the colonists here really did want to build a windmill of this peculiar shape, would they have abandoned the established building techniques that they were familiar with and were using on every other building they constructed, and instead decided to revert to a construction method that is unequivocally medieval and much, much more difficult?

'That would be like a builder in Britain today deciding that he wouldn't bother with bricks and breeze blocks and plaster-board and all that kind of stuff and instead use mud bricks, rough timbers and wattle-and-daub to build a house. It simply makes no sense. This tower, whatever its purpose, was built using rough and unworked field stones of all shapes and sizes, a medieval building technique that would have been obsolete for centuries by the time this part of America was colonised in the early seventeenth century. The only possible reason for that was if the builders themselves were medieval and didn't have either the skills or the tools to shape the stones they were using. And if you think about it, when Prince Henry Sinclair set out from Scotland to cross the Atlantic in 1398, his crew would have included sailors, navigators, carpenters, sailmakers and men with all the other skills needed to sail and maintain a wooden ship, but the one craftsman he almost certainly wouldn't have needed or wanted on board would have been a stonemason.'

'As usual,' Bronson said, 'what you say makes perfect sense. So if this was built by Sinclair and his men, or even an earlier

Templar expedition, what was it for? Presumably not a windmill.'

'No. In 1939, somebody took an aerial shot of this part of Newport from almost directly above the tower. One thing about aerial photography is that it often reveals underground structures that are completely invisible to anybody standing on the ground. The picture wasn't particularly clear, but there is just the faintest hint of a buried or vanished rectangular structure right next to the tower on its eastern side. And again this is pure conjecture, but if there actually was a rectangular building next to the Tower, the ground plan would look the same as the Temple Church in London, with a circular nave and a rectangular chancel. So maybe what we have here is the ruins of a medieval chapel.'

'Really?'

'Well, it's not been proved, obviously. But there's something else. In fact, there are several other things. The tower may look round, but it's not perfectly circular and has slightly different dimensions depending on whether you measure it from east to west or north to south, which suggests it wasn't designed by an architect or constructed by experienced builders. If it had been built in the seventeenth century, it would have been symmetrical. And at one time the interior was covered with a layer of smooth white plaster, the remains of which can still be seen on the inside of some of the columns. Nobody has yet come up with any sensible idea as to why that would have been done if it was in fact a windmill, but it would make very good sense if the structure had been the circular nave of a chapel.

'As far as I know, the Knights Templar were the only people who built churches to that plan, with a round nave and a rectangular chancel; the reason for that design is because that's the plan of the Holy Sepulchre in Jerusalem, so the Templars were replicating that shape in their chapels. It's also worth remembering that Prince Henry Sinclair came from Orkney, and on the Orkney mainland you can still see the remains of the Round

Kirk of Orphir, built in the 1120s. That's the only surviving medieval round church in Scotland and was also modelled on the Holy Sepulchre, so he would have been familiar with the design.

'And there's another bit of evidence that is suggestive but not compelling. In 1948, an archaeological dig carried out inside and outside the tower found that some of the ground outside the structure contained layers of stones that could have been intended as foundations. Records from colonial times show that no other structure was built next to the tower after 1639, when the town was founded, so if there had been anything there, it must have pre-dated the arrival of the colonists.'

For a couple of minutes they both stood and looked at the old stones that formed the structure in front of them.

'Whatever it is,' Bronson said, 'and whatever the reason for constructing it was, it is a weird building. Has any dating been done on it?'

'Yes, I meant to mention that. In 1993, radiocarbon dating was carried out on the organic components of samples of the mortar. The results suggested a date range of between 1635 and 1698, and a mean of about 1680 was proposed. But all that proves is the date of the mortar, not the date of the structure itself. If this was built and then abandoned in the last couple of years of the fourteenth century, by the time the colonists arrived over two hundred years later, it probably would have needed a lot more work than just repointing. To keep it standing they would very probably have had to remove virtually all the old mortar and replace it with new. That's the easiest and most obvious explanation for the dating.'

'Interesting,' Bronson said as they walked back to the car, 'if slightly weird. So has seeing it in the flesh helped?'

'Not really. I don't know what I was expecting to find here, but Newport is so built up and developed that I think we're wasting our time. The island is also very flat, which means the clue about the island and the hill doesn't really make sense unless there's a hill on the mainland that would fit. And there isn't a river flowing south, as far as I can see. There's a thing called Bailey Brook, but that's certainly not a river – it's barely even a stream. But the biggest problem is the amount of development. If the Templars had constructed a hidden vault anywhere on this island, I'm quite sure somebody would have found it by now. And if somebody had found it, and it did contain the Ark of the Covenant, then the whole world would know about it.'

Bronson started the Buick and eased it away from the kerb. 'So where to now?' he asked.

'Let's retrace our steps and get out of Rhode Island and back into Massachusetts. Head back towards Boston and we'll find somewhere to stay on the road, a motel or something. I don't want to drive too far in case what we're looking for *is* here after all. There's a nearby town called Taunton. I know it's only early afternoon, but let's stop somewhere there for the night and I'll do some more research.'

'And what are you looking for now? Presumably somewhere that fits the clues so far, the hill and the island and the south-flowing river, I mean.'

'Exactly. Nothing anywhere here seems to match up with any of that, so I'm beginning to think we're definitely in the wrong place, but I need to check before we do anything else. And then there's the last clue. We've got to find the well that isn't.'

Bronson glanced at her. 'The well that isn't what?' he asked.

'The well that isn't a well, obviously. Do try and keep up, Chris.'

Chapter 50

Boston, Massachusetts, United States of America

The rules relating to gun ownership in Massachusetts are among the most stringent and restrictive in America, but as with every rule ever made or every law ever passed, there are ways around them. The man that Aaron Chason had been put in touch with through another of his contacts explained the deal in very clear and unambiguous terms.

'The three pistols in this briefcase are part of my personal collection,' he said.

The two men were meeting in a small and fairly noisy bar in the Back Bay area of central Boston, not far from the hotel the three Israelis had booked. They were sitting at a table in one corner and talking quietly so that neither of them could be overheard. The man opposite Chason had introduced himself only as 'John' and looked like a successful businessman, clean-shaven, well dressed and slightly overweight.

'There's a Glock, a Browning and a Colt, each with one spare magazine,' he went on, 'all nine millimetre, and there are two boxes of fifty rounds as well. I would like them back when you've finished whatever you're doing here, in the same state that they are now.'

He glanced around before continuing, and then passed Chason a slip of paper with a mobile number written on it.

'But remember this. I only want the weapons back if you don't use them. That number' – he pointed at the slip of paper in front of the Israeli – 'is a prepaid mobile, a burner, and you or one of your men must call me on it every afternoon between five and six and talk about anything. During that conversation, you must say the word "Israel". That will tell me that you have not used the weapons. If I don't receive a call or you don't say that word, I will assume that you have fired them. I will then stage a break-in at my house and tell the police they've been stolen. Do you understand?'

'Perfectly,' Chason replied. 'And thank you for your help. My masters back in Jerusalem will be very appreciative.'

In Chason's hotel room, Josef Gellerman and Lemuel Dayan were looking at the latest information supplied in an encrypted email from Zeru, the data obviously having been obtained from a contact in the Mossad. Gellerman guessed that a low-priority watch order had been placed on Bronson and Lewis. They now knew the arrival time of the flight the two targets had been on, the hotel where they'd spent the night, and details of the car that Bronson had hired the following morning.

'The trouble is, we're playing catch-up,' Dayan said. 'This isn't like Britain, with a traffic camera on every corner so you can track somebody. Over here, the traffic cameras just cover junctions or stretches of freeway and are only useful for seeing how the traffic is flowing, not for following an individual car. We'll have to wait until they book a hotel for the night and follow them from there.'

When Chason returned carrying a brown leather briefcase, they each took one of the pistols and checked it. They were all in excellent condition, virtually as new, and the man who had supplied them had refused to accept any form of payment, being happy to help people who were doing something for the homeland of his grandparents and parents. They loaded the weapons and the spare magazines, and then settled down to wait for the information from Israel that would allow them to continue the chase.

Chapter 51

Taunton, Massachusetts, United States of America

'So what's with this well that isn't a well?' Bronson asked. 'And why did you pick Taunton? Just because it has a nice friendly English name, or was there another reason?'

They'd pulled off the main road back to Boston and found a smallish but quite comfortable hotel on the outskirts of Taunton. Angela had logged her laptop into the building's Wi-Fi and was beginning to trawl the Internet, doing more research.

She glanced over at him. 'You're right about English names,' she replied. 'We're just outside Taunton, and within a fairly short driving distance there's a Bridgewater, a Halifax, a Kingston and a Plymouth, so the names are familiar even if the landscape isn't. I picked Taunton because it wasn't that long a drive, but also because it's one of the very few locations I've found where there's a river that flows almost due south. That fits neatly with the Latin phrase *ubi flumen currit ad meridiem*, but Taunton is only "halfway between the coasts", the *medium inter finibus* bit, if you use quite a lot of poetic licence and assume that the north coast is part of the bay where Boston stands. The whole expression suggests to me that the two coasts are supposed to be either side of a landmass, and that means we should be looking for an island or a peninsula. That's why I wanted to explore Rhode Island.'

'Which didn't help. And you still haven't told me about this blasted well.'

'That's the last clue from the parchment,' Angela said. 'The Latin phrase reads *sub puteus quod no habet aqua. Sub* means below or underneath and a *puteus* is a hole dug to find water, so the whole expression translates as "beneath the well that has no water", and I don't really know what that means. It could be referring to a well located on high ground and telling us to look on the low-lying terrain nearby. Or, because a *puteus* can just be an exploratory hole dug to try to find water, rather than a functioning well, perhaps we should be looking for some kind of abandoned working. Or is it a dry well, a well that once produced water but the supply has now dried up? Strictly speaking, the Latin for a well is *puteum fodere*, which is not what this says, and the other translation for *puteus* is a pit, the sort of place you'd use to store grain.

'The short, snappy answer is I don't really know what this means, so I'm trying to think of all the possible permutations on maps and documents on the Internet that might help clarify it.'

'So you need to find a place that's on an island or a promontory, more or less in the middle of it coast to coast, where there might be a hill and definitely a river that flows south from that position. And where there might also be a well or something that looks like a well. Is that a fair summary?'

Angela nodded. 'That's pretty much nailed it, yes.'

'Right. You've got the Latin and the background historical information, so you dig away at that. As befits a simple soul like me, I'll just look at the pretty pictures of maps and stuff on my phone and see if I can find anything that fits the bill.'

About twenty minutes later, Bronson looked across at Angela with a slight smile on his face.

'I don't know if this is the right location,' he said, 'but it does seem to tick most of the boxes you told me about.'

'Let me see.'

He passed her his smartphone, and she used her fingertips to manoeuvre the image around the screen and increase and decrease its size as she studied it.

'You're right,' she said. 'That does fit with everything we've got from the parchment. I just didn't expect it to be there. I was sure we'd find it somewhere here, in Massachusetts or maybe Rhode Island, because the Newport Tower more or less proves Sinclair's party must have spent quite some time in the area.'

'True, but if the information on that plaque by the Westford Knight is accurate, Sinclair and his men would have wintered in Nova Scotia, and that would have given them time to create this vault or whatever it is.'

'Well it's worth a look, no matter what. It doesn't look that far. Can we drive there?'

Bronson shook his head. 'It's further than you think,' he said, calculating distances quickly. 'I reckon it's nearly seven hundred miles by road, so we'd be looking at ten or twelve hours' driving at least. It'd be a lot quicker, and a whole lot easier, to fly. I'll just check how often flights head that way out of Boston.'

Five minutes later, he looked up.

'If we'd worked this out earlier, we could have hopped a flight today,' he said. 'The flight time's only an hour and three quarters, and there's an evening flight leaving at about half past six. But we've got to drive back to Boston and hand over the hire car and still get to the airport in time to hang around for two completely bloody pointless hours waiting to go through security. We don't have enough time. Simple as that.'

'And there's another delay,' Angela said. 'We can't catch a flight today because we haven't yet got our Canadian eTAs.'

'Our what?'

'Electronic Travel Authorisations. I did the application process while you were fiddling about looking at flights, but I haven't yet had confirmation they've been approved. We can't get on board an aircraft until we have them. I presume the next flight will be tomorrow. What time does it leave?'

Bronson checked his phone again.

'Inconveniently early,' he said. 'The scheduled departure time is ten past nine, and it arrives at about ten minutes to twelve. I know that sounds like a two-and-three-quarter-hour flight, but it's not. The time in Halifax is one hour different to Boston. At least this time I shouldn't get jet lag.'

'Is that the only flight?'

'It's the only one I'd want to take. There are two others around midday, but one goes via Toronto and the other via Toronto and Washington, so they take all day to get there. But it does mean we can't stay here in Taunton. I'll book us a room at the Hilton for tonight so we're on the spot, but we'll still have to be up by six tomorrow morning.'

Angela's phone emitted a faintly irritating beeping noise, and she opened the message.

'That's good,' she said. 'Both our eTAs have been approved, so you can book two seats on that aircraft tomorrow morning while you're at it. And then find us somewhere to stay in Halifax.'

Twenty minutes later, they were back on the road, heading for Boston's Logan International Airport and the on-site Hilton.

-

Tucked invisibly into the line of a dozen or so cars behind them were the Honda and Toyota that had been shadowing them all day. The man in the Toyota was again talking to Cardinal Caravaggio in the centre of Rome, but even as he provided the non-productive update on the activities of the targets, Caravaggio interrupted him. Other information had reached him from an entirely different source.

'They're heading back to the Hilton at Logan airport and they've booked a flight to Halifax tomorrow morning,' he said.

'Do you want us to follow them to Nova Scotia?'

'No thank you. I'm making other arrangements for that. Just follow them back to the hotel and report to me immediately if they stop anywhere en route. Once they've handed back their hire car, you can stand down. And thank you.'

The man in the Toyota nodded to himself as he ended the call. That day's work – if that was the right noun to apply to driving about Massachusetts and Rhode Island keeping the back end of a small Buick in sight – had been the easiest two thousand bucks he and the man driving the Honda had ever earned.

It was just a shame that neither of them would get to claim the fifty grand promised by the anonymous man in Italy if he'd ordered them to take out the targets.

Chapter 52

Massachusetts, United States of America

'We've got them,' Lemuel Dayan said, looking at a priority email that had just appeared in his inbox. 'They've booked into a hotel in a place called Taunton.'

'Where the hell's that?' Gellerman asked, looking over Dayan's shoulder at the screen of the laptop.

Dayan used Google Maps to display Massachusetts and then pointed.

'There,' he replied. 'Down towards Rhode Island. Probably about thirty-five or forty miles from here.'

All three men had been prepared to leave the hotel at very short notice, and the only thing they had unpacked was Dayan's laptop. In less than ten minutes they'd vacated their rooms, checked out of the hotel and were sitting in their hire car and navigating their way through Boston's busy streets, Gellerman at the wheel.

Getting to Taunton and finding the hotel took them just under an hour. It wasn't a large establishment, and the first thing they did was look around the car park to try to spot the Buick Encore that they knew Bronson had hired at the airport. There were only about a dozen cars there, but that definitely wasn't one of them.

'They've probably gone off somewhere,' Chason suggested, which didn't help.

'Exactly,' Gellerman said, pulling their car into a parking space. 'We can follow their electronic trail easily enough, but we need to see them to be able to follow where they go and watch what they do. Wait here. I'll go inside and see if they're in the public rooms anywhere.'

There was no sign of the targets in the restaurant or lounge, which was not unexpected. If the car wasn't at the hotel, there wasn't much chance that the targets would be either. He decided to take a direct approach as a final check. He walked over to the reception desk and smiled pleasantly at the girl sitting behind it.

'I was hoping to meet some friends of mine here,' he said. 'Chris Bronson and Angela Lewis. Do you know if they've checked in yet?'

'Just a moment, sir.' She tapped away briskly on the computer keyboard and then fiddled with the mouse. 'Yes, they checked in earlier today, but they checked out again a couple of hours later. I think Mr Bronson said something about a family emergency.'

Gellerman nodded, made what he hoped were appropriately sympathetic noises and walked briskly out of the hotel.

'They've gone,' he said as he opened the car door and sat down. 'They checked in and then checked out again.'

'Where did they go?' Chason asked, then shook his head, realising it was a stupid question.

Gellerman didn't even bother responding, just looked at Dayan.

'Make sure your mobile is switched on and the battery has plenty of charge. They've checked out of here but they certainly aren't going to be sleeping in the car. They'll have booked another hotel somewhere, and as soon as we know where it is, we'll get back on the road.'

Dayan looked at the screen of his smartphone to check his inbox, then shook his head.

'Nothing yet.'

He put the phone on the dashboard and connected the charging lead to the car's USB power output. Then they settled down to wait, because there was nothing else they could do.

Chapter 53

Gatwick Airport, London, England

Marco Ferrara had no idea whether the group of zealots from Zeru knew where the trail was now leading, or whether he and Rossi would meet any opposition when they finally reached their destination. But as they made themselves as comfortable as they could in the alleged executive lounge at London's Gatwick airport, he was preparing for any contingency.

'I'll tell the cardinal we need weapons,' he said quietly to Rossi, preparing a text message to send to Rome. 'I'll ask for a couple of pistols and a rifle as well, just in case. I'm sure the Inquisition will have some contacts over in Canada who can help.'

'Good idea. I feel undressed without a pistol under my left arm. You want another drink?'

Ferrara shook his head. 'No. Once I've sent this, I'm going to try and get some sleep. You should too. Whatever happens, tomorrow is going to be a very long day.'

The instructions from Cardinal Caravaggio had been clear enough: Ferrara and Rossi were to proceed at once to Nova Scotia in Canada, which was where the historians in Rome had decided the Latin text on the Aniort parchment referred to, and be prepared to travel onwards from there if necessary.

There'd been a slight delay while they sorted out their Canadian eTAs, and American ESTAs for good measure just in case the search shifted to the south, but the delay hadn't affected the availability of flights: the only one that hadn't already been fully booked was the one they had taken. And at least that flight would get them to Halifax at midday, whereas the others all arrived mid evening.

That was the good news. The bad news was that the aircraft flew direct from Toulouse to Gatwick and then disgorged its passengers there for an eleven-hour stopover before the hop to Halifax.

The two men had used the time as best they could, pre-booking a hotel in Halifax, organising a hire car they could pick up at the airport, and looking at the scan of the parchment that had prompted the renewed search, and the first translation of it. They soon had a reasonable idea what they were likely to be looking for. What they didn't know was exactly *where* they should be looking, but hopefully they'd get more information from Rome.

And if all else failed, they could follow Bronson and Lewis, wait until they had found the Ark, then kill them both and grab the relic. That would work just as well and would probably be easier.

Chapter 54

Massachusetts, United States of America

As it turned out, the three-man team from Zeru didn't have that long to wait in the corner of the car park of the hotel in Taunton. About ninety minutes after they'd discovered that the birds had flown, Dayan received an email message, followed by two more over the next half an hour. The first confirmed that Bronson's credit card had been used to book a room at the Hilton hotel at Boston's international airport. That was enough for them to get moving and head back towards Boston, because now they knew exactly where the targets were going.

The second message informed them that the same card had been used to book two seats on the following morning's flight out of Boston to Halifax in Nova Scotia, and the third gave details of the hotel Bronson had booked in Halifax, and his hire car. That told the Israelis roughly where the search for the ancient relic would resume, but also created a problem.

They now had three pistols and ammunition, and what they couldn't do was get them on board an aircraft, not even in the hold luggage. The two choices they had were either to hand the weapons back to the man who'd supplied them and then fly to Halifax unarmed, or to keep them and drive up through New Hampshire and Maine, then cross the border into New Brunswick in Canada and carry on to Nova Scotia. If they handed them back, they didn't know how long they would have to wait before they could find an alternative source of weapons, and all three of them believed the endgame was near. So in the end it was a simple decision: they would keep the pistols and drive to Nova Scotia.

What they would have to do well before they got anywhere near the border was to conceal the weapons and ammunition. They knew that if the car were to be subjected to a thorough examination, no hiding place would work and they would then be arrested. That was not a particularly daunting prospect, because Gellerman knew enough people in the government of Israel to ensure that they would be released, probably long before the case could come to trial. But it would mean the end of the operation, and that was not acceptable. So the pistols had to be concealed somewhere that wasn't obvious.

They stopped at a hardware store on the outskirts of Boston. Gellerman went inside and bought a craft knife, a roll of heavy-duty black duct tape, a set of thin nylon overalls, a small tub of hand cleanser and a roll of paper towels.

They would find a secluded location ten miles or so from the border crossing point, somewhere well off the main road. Then Chason, who was the smallest and nimblest of the three of them, would don the overalls and crawl under the front end of the Buick, one side of it jacked up so he'd have a bit more room to manoeuvre. Gellerman thought the three loaded spare magazines could probably be taped onto the lower part of the steering column, and the pistols themselves could be attached to suspension components, or perhaps to the chassis subframe. It all depended on what Chason found when he got under the car. Duct tape was ideal because it was strong and very flexible, so it wouldn't rip or tear while the car was moving. Obviously they'd drive slowly to minimise any strain on the tape, so it should hold.

That was what they hoped, anyway.

The other factor was the timing.

Gellerman entered the border crossing point at St Stephen in New Brunswick into the satnav and it came up with an arrival time late in the evening. He had no idea if that crossing point was open twenty-four hours a day, but even if it was, they certainly weren't going to arrive at that sort of hour. Three adult males in one car, all carrying Israeli passports, claiming to be holidaymakers and trying to get into Canada at eleven o'clock at night would set alarm bells ringing for even the doziest customs or border protection officer. At the very least the car would receive a thorough search.

'Right,' he said. 'That timing won't work. We'll revert to Plan B. Lemuel, book us rooms in the same hotel in Halifax as Bronson, and then find us a hotel for tonight somewhere near the border. We'll aim to get to the crossing point tomorrow morning at around ten, just another carload of tourists in the queue, eager to see what Canada has to offer.'

'There are plenty of towns in that area,' Dayan said, looking at the screen of his smartphone. 'The closest and probably the best is Bangor, because that's right on the main road. I'll find something there.'

A few minutes later, he put his phone back on the dashboard.

'It's done?' Gellerman asked.

'It's all done. There's a Marriott just west of the city centre that looks all right. It's got free Wi-Fi and a free breakfast, so that's where I've booked.'

He leaned forward again and picked up his phone, then accessed the satnav and entered the address of the hotel.

'We'll get there about nine thirty this evening according to the satnav, and I told them on the booking site we'd be arriving late. We should stop for a quick meal somewhere along the road. Then we can just check in and go to bed.'

Chapter 55

Halifax, Nova Scotia, Canada

The aircraft landed a few minutes early, and the hire car was ready and waiting for them when Bronson went to the desk in the terminal.

'Hotel first, I guess,' he said as he drove away. 'Then we'll start digging around for clues. Have you got any fresh ideas?'

Angela shook her head. 'Not really, but I still think Oak Island is part of the clue leading to the location of the Ark of the Covenant. We need to buy a detailed topographical map of Nova Scotia, because if we don't have that, we're not going to get anywhere.'

The hotel had a gift shop on the ground floor, near the reception desk, and to Angela's surprise, it had a good selection of maps on sale, including the pure tourist type, the maps decorated with pictures of the various attractions and with bold arrows pointing to the location where those particular delights could be sampled. But it also had more detailed maps, similar to the Ordnance Survey series produced in Britain and with a comparable level of detail. They bought one that showed almost the whole of Nova Scotia, and another that just covered the central area of the peninsula, the part they were interested in.

In their room, they spread out the more detailed map on the bed, and both of them stood and studied it.

'Let's start from the beginning of the Latin clues,' Angela suggested. 'The first two phrases are *quod est superius est sicut quod est inferius* and *in insula et in monte*, which translate as "as it is above so it is below" and "on the island and on the hill". They're probably meant to be read together and tell us that there are similar structures on the island – Oak Island, in fact – and on this hill, wherever it is.

'Then we have *medium inter finibus ubi flumen currit ad meridiem* or "halfway between the coasts where the river runs south". As you spotted, there is one place on the peninsula that really does seem to match that. There's a major river, the Gold River, that runs almost due south across the country and drains into Mahone Bay. And the midpoint between the north and south coasts of the peninsula is this place here, beside the river.' She jabbed her right forefinger at the map. 'New Ross. So that's where we need to go.'

'And what about this peculiar well?' Bronson asked.

'I have no idea. I'm hoping that we can find something when we get there that will help identify it. The Latin was *sub puteus quod no habet aqua*, "beneath the well that has no water", and I still don't know exactly what that means. Right, let's get going.'

Chapter 56

Nova Scotia, Canada

The border crossing had been slightly easier than Gellerman had expected. Their car had been stopped, as had every car in the queue ahead of them, and their passports and eTAs had been scrutinised, as well as the rental agreement for the car and the vehicle's insurance documents. They had explained that they were tourists taking their first look at Canada, and Dayan had produced their hotel reservation confirmations in Halifax for that night, and their return air tickets to Toulouse, all of which seemed to satisfy the officer. He'd opened the boot of the car and glanced inside, but hadn't even touched any of their carry-on bags. They could actually have left the weapons in the briefcase, but Gellerman was pleased they'd hidden them. You could never predict how any crossing of a manned border was going to go.

He steered the hire car off the main road in an area called Benson Corner half a dozen miles beyond the border and stopped in a pull-off that was shielded from the road by trees and bushes.

While Gellerman stood beside the car keeping a lookout, Dayan jacked up the vehicle. Chason pulled on the nylon overalls and slid lithely under the front of the Buick, the craft knife in his hand. Ten minutes later, the car was back on the road, each man now with a pistol and a spare magazine concealed in his clothing.

Dayan glanced at his watch and then at the satnav, now programmed with the address of the hotel in Halifax.

'It looks like we'll get there an hour or so after the targets,' he said.

Gellerman nodded agreement. 'That shouldn't be a problem. Wherever they're looking, they're not going to find the relic this afternoon. If its hiding place was that obvious, it would have been discovered years ago. We'll check in, sort ourselves out and wait for the targets to leave the hotel, or to come back if they're already out, and then we'll follow them. One of us will have to keep watch in the lobby until we spot them. And don't forget this might not be the end of the quest. It could be just another clue they're looking for, so make sure we can all leave the hotel at short notice. Keep your bags packed and just take out what you need when you need it.'

'I think I'll give Jerusalem a prod,' Dayan said, picking up his mobile phone. 'Maybe Luca Rossi and the Inquisition are still in the hunt somewhere. If so, they should have some idea of his movements.'

Chapter 57

New Ross, Nova Scotia, Canada

'There's not much here,' Bronson remarked as he drove the hire car through New Ross and over the crossroads by the white-painted church, heading north. It looked like a small, pleasant village marked by the occasional store and other commercial enterprise, the houses well spread out. It appeared prosperous, the buildings all seeming to be in good condition. The Canadian version of small-town America, in short.

'Can't argue with that,' Angela replied. 'I was expecting a bit more development here. It's really just a scattered village.'

They stopped a mile or so further on, pulling off onto the right-hand side of the road where dozens of cut logs were stacked, presumably ready for transport to a lumber mill somewhere. While Bronson again studied the detailed topographical map they'd bought, Angela went back to her smartphone. She'd noted a handful of sites that looked interesting – at least from their point of view – and had bookmarked them to check again once they were on the spot.

'According to this site,' she said, 'there's supposed to be a castle back there in New Ross.'

'A castle? The biggest thing I saw was that church in the middle of the village.'

'Well, perhaps not *exactly* a castle,' Angela conceded. 'Maybe I should have said the remains of a castle.'

'Bits of the walls, you mean? Or just the foundations?'

'Sort of. Okay, to be completely accurate, a few stones that might at one time have been part of a castle. Or part of a house.

Or a wall. Or maybe they're just a bunch of interesting-looking rocks. It all depends on your point of view.'

'But who would build a castle out here, and why?'

'Exactly. Building a castle would have been a massive undertaking. There would have to be a good reason for doing it and it would need to be erected in the right place. I don't think New Ross would work. It's not at the top of a hill – in fact, we've been climbing slowly ever since we drove out of the village – and that was where castles and fortresses were usually erected, for obvious reasons. And in any case, there really wouldn't have been any need for a structure like that. In the accounts I've been looking at, the local Mi'kmaq people were quite friendly, but even if they hadn't been, Sinclair's force included the Templars, armed and armoured knights with their full battle regalia, and no doubt bowmen as well. The Templars were the special forces troops of the time and would have been perfectly capable of defending themselves against any Indian attack, so they certainly wouldn't have needed a castle to hide away inside.

'And there are the simple logistics. They'd have needed stonemasons and dozens of labourers to construct even a small stone fortification, and it's doubtful that they had enough people to do anything like that. If they had needed a defensive structure, they could have erected a simple wooden stockade in a couple of days.'

'So no castle, then?'

'Unless I'm missing something crucial and far from obvious, no.'

'Shame,' Bronson said. 'I quite like castles. But you're right. It doesn't make sense on any level.'

While Angela continued scanning various websites, Bronson turned his attention back to the map.

'This is interesting,' he said after a while, folding the map sheet to present a much smaller section.

'What?'

'We're looking for a well, right? There's one marked right there. See that small circle?'

Angela nodded.

'The problem,' Bronson said, opening up the map again and pointing, 'is that there are hundreds of them. I've just done a search using my phone on a Nova Scotia government website, and there are more than a hundred and seventy wells in and around New Ross. But I also checked the settlement date, which was 1816, so most of them will have been dug after that year, because there would have been no reason to find a water source until the first houses were built.'

'We need to find a map of the area before it was settled.'

'I've already looked,' Bronson replied. 'There aren't many, and those that are available don't show that kind of detail. I think we'll have to just look around the area ourselves and see what we can find.'

'Anyway, well spotted, pun intended. So we have achieved something. We've seen New Ross and identified a couple of hundred wells. I need to check these websites again and see if there's any other information available.'

'And I need to buy a few bits and pieces if we're going to go exploring. Torches, a shovel, that kind of thing,' Bronson said. 'I'm getting hungry, so let's head back to the hotel now and we'll come out here again in the morning.'

Chapter 58

Halifax, Nova Scotia, Canada

The Nova Scotia resident Francesco had told Marco Ferrara to contact was calling himself John Smith, a very obvious alias, and Ferrara's sole means of contacting him was via a burner mobile. He didn't seem surprised by the Italian's request when the two men met in a cafe in the centre of Halifax.

'Two pistols and a rifle?' he asked. 'And ammunition, obviously.'

'Obviously,' Ferrara replied. 'Fifty rounds for the pistols and twenty for the rifle, if you can do that.'

'Of course,' replied Smith. 'None of that's a problem. I'll need payment in cash,' he added.

'How much?'

'In Canadian dollars, one thousand for each weapon and ammunition, so three thousand in total. If you don't fire any of them, I'll buy them back off you for half that.'

That was more or less the kind of price Ferrara had expected, and it wasn't as if he'd be paying out of his own pocket, so he nodded agreement.

'When and where?' he asked.

'Call me in one hour and I'll tell you. You have got wheels?'

Ninety minutes later, Ferrara handed over a wad of brown Canadian hundred-dollar bills, checked the weapons he'd been given and then put them back in the sports bag Smith had used to transport them to the quiet road to the south-east of Halifax, near Cow Bay, that he'd selected for the handover. He put the bag in the boot of his own hire car and shook hands with the Canadian.

Half an hour after that, he positioned himself with a newspaper and a cup of coffee in the lobby of the hotel Bronson and Lewis had booked into and began his surveillance, a Colt nine-millimetre semi-automatic pistol tucked into a belt holster – also supplied by Smith – on his left-hand side.

He had no idea if the two targets were in their room at the hotel, in the dining room or out somewhere, but it was obviously a good idea to begin keeping watch. And he needed to keep his eyes open in case the men from Zeru were also mounting surveillance.

About an hour after he'd sat down, the targets walked into the hotel and went straight through to the dining room. He recognised them from the brief sighting he'd had of them at Campagne-sur-Aude.

He called Rossi's mobile, told him that Bronson and Lewis were back and then went into the coffee shop to get something to eat.

Tomorrow he would make sure he got up early and followed the targets, dogging their footsteps wherever they went.

And the moment it looked as if they'd found what they were looking for, he would step in to seize the prize and kill the English couple at the same time. It was just a shame, he thought, that he wouldn't have time to really savour ending Angela Lewis's career. And her life.

Chapter 59

Nova Scotia, Canada

Before they returned to New Ross, Bronson knew they needed to buy some tools. What he didn't know was exactly what they would need, but some items were obvious, like a couple of decent torches with plenty of spare batteries, a trenching tool – a kind of combined shovel and pickaxe – a crowbar, a length of climbing rope, safety helmets, gloves, hiking boots, stout poles, overalls, an axe, a sheath knife, compact binoculars and so on. The sort of stuff they would need if they did find their way into a cave or tunnel.

A hardware store in the western outskirts of Halifax supplied what they wanted, and with the boot of the hire car loaded, they set off along the Fishermen's Memorial Highway, which ran more or less along the southern coast of Nova Scotia. When they reached the junction just north of Chester Basin, they turned right for New Ross.

And it was at about that stage in their journey that Bronson became certain they were being followed.

'This is getting a bit like France all over again,' he said.

'In what way?' Angela sounded puzzled as she glanced out of the window, because the one thing that was perfectly obvious to her was that the terrain of Nova Scotia bore almost no resemblance to that of southern France.

'Not the landscape. The car behind us.'

She turned to glance behind her. 'That blue Ford, I think it is?'

'It is a Ford, and it is blue, and it's also been a prominent feature in my rear-view mirror since we left the hotel this morning. When we stopped at the hardware store, that car pulled into a parking bay about fifty yards down the road. When we drove away, it took up position behind us again. I was altering speed on the freeway back there, and the Ford's driver did the same, just matched whatever speed I was travelling at. I don't know about you, but I'm getting a bit tired of being followed.'

Angela didn't tend to panic, but she looked decidedly nervous as she glanced at Bronson.

'Do you think it's those Italians, the same ones who were watching us in Auch?' she asked. 'And will they be armed?'

'That's two questions, and the answer to both of them is that I don't know. I've been trying to get a look at the driver, but the car's always been too far away. But if it is the Italians, they're a long way from home and I don't know how easy it would be for them to find weapons over here. If they flew from France, obviously they couldn't have brought pistols with them.'

'Are we safe? Are they just watching us, or what?'

'I think we'll be perfectly safe until we find something, because the only reason for them being behind us is to grab the Ark.'

'So what can we do?'

'What's the geology of Nova Scotia?' Bronson asked, a complete non sequitur.

'What? Oh, well, I think there's quite a lot of granite, but I don't know too much about it. Ah – you mean are there any caves? Is that what you're asking?'

'Yes.'

'There certainly are on the north coast, by the Bay of Fundy, but around here I don't know. Hang on – I'll check the topo map.'

A few minutes later, she shook her head.

'Nothing that I can see,' she said, 'and if there were caves, they should be marked.'

'Okay. Look beyond New Ross, out in the country, and see if you can find a quiet-looking road with a secluded pull-off marked. Not a lay-by but somewhere we can drive off the road and be out of sight of any passing traffic.'

'Like the start of a lane, something like that?'

'Exactly like that. Without a house at the end of it, obviously.'

'There are several,' Angela replied a minute or so later. 'The one that looks least developed is Forties Road. That's the turning opposite the white church in New Ross. There's not much along that road once you get clear of the village. It looks like there are quite a few places along there.' She looked at Bronson. 'What are you planning?' she demanded.

'One way or another we need to lose the two people in that car behind us. I'm making this up as I go along, but we definitely need to find somewhere quiet. When I've worked out how to do it, I'll let you know.'

'Well be careful. They might be armed – we just don't know.'

'I'm assuming that they are. Basic rule of combat: always assume that your opponent is better armed than you are, and more competent than you expect. Then you don't get surprised.'

The road, a ribbon of tarmac running through the forested landscape, was smooth and more or less straight, and with little traffic in either direction. On the outskirts of New Ross, they drove past the Ross Farm Museum and continued towards the village centre. When he saw the white church ahead of him, Bronson indicated and turned off the road, but not at the junction. Instead, he parked outside a cafe on the left-hand side of the road.

Angela looked at him enquiringly.

'We'll grab a coffee and something to eat,' he said, 'but that's not why I've stopped. We're not dressed for tramping about the woods, so we'll get changed before we leave here.'

Exactly as he had expected, the Ford pulled into the same parking area about half a minute later. The road was so straight that whatever they did would be obvious to anybody in the following car.

Bronson and Angela ignored the Ford, walked into the cafe and chose a table by the window, both of them watching the other vehicle. In fact, there was nothing to see; it simply sat there at the far end of the car park, with no movement from the occupants.

Outside again, Bronson took off his jacket, which he placed on the back seat of the car, then opened the boot, took out the two pairs of overalls and handed the smaller set to Angela.

'Dark green, I notice,' she said. 'Is that deliberate, so that we can hide in the woods?'

Bronson nodded. 'If they'd had any in camouflage pattern, I'd have bought them instead.'

They put on the boots as well, and Bronson sorted out some of the other equipment he'd bought so that it was readily to hand. Then they got back in the car and pulled away. Passing close to the Ford would have been a little obvious, so he kept well over to the right as he left the parking area. The sun was glinting off the other car's windscreen, so all he could see were two vague shapes inside.

Almost as soon as he rejoined the main road, he followed Angela's directions and indicated left to turn into Forties Road.

'I'll take a look at Google Maps and try and find you a good spot to stop. And while I'm doing that, you can tell me what your plan is. Assuming you've got one, obviously.'

'Not as such,' Bronson admitted. 'It all depends what we find when we get to wherever we're going. I was thinking that I go to ground somewhere while you walk off the road and deep into the woods, making a lot of noise and talking to me all the time – "Hey, look at this, Chris", that kind of thing – so that the men in the Ford will think we're heading into the woods together and will follow. Then I'll pop up behind them and sort them out.'

Angela was quiet for a long moment, the silence almost hostile. When she replied, her voice was cold.

'So I'm a stalking-horse, am I? Is that really the best you can come up with?'

Bronson shrugged. 'I'd love to hear some better ideas,' he said, 'but we need a diversion. We need to focus their attention in one direction while I come at them from a different direction. You stamping about in the woods and holding an imaginary conversation with me is the only option I can think of. And that will also keep you out of danger.'

'I just know I'm going to regret this,' Angela muttered.

She turned her attention back to her mobile.

'Right,' she said. 'Keep going. The best place is called Barrs Corner, which seems to be just the name of an area. There's a big pond or a small lake marked on the map, and next to it is an opening that goes nowhere except to another small lake. Maybe it's used by fishermen to park their cars. I don't know. It's on the left, and I'll give you plenty of warning when we're getting close.'

'Thanks. Look, when we get there, you keep well out of the way, just in case it all goes wrong. And take the car keys as well.'

About ten minutes later, as they approached a gentle right-hand bend, Angela pointed ahead.

'It's just around this bend. You can see part of the lake on the right. And that's the pull-off on the left.'

Bronson checked the mirrors. The Ford was about a quarter of a mile behind them. He indicated left, crossed the road and drove into a short but fairly wide entrance, the way ahead blocked by trees and undergrowth about fifty yards in.

'Perfect,' he said, stopping the car on one side of the open area and getting out. 'We need to be quick. They'll have slowed right down when they saw me indicate, but I guess they'll be here in a minute or two, and we need to be out of sight by the time they stop.'

He opened the boot, took out the trenching tool, which he gave to Angela, and took the axe and knife for himself.

'What do I do with this?' Angela asked.

'If either of them gets past me, hit them over the head with it,' Bronson suggested.

Moments later, they'd both disappeared into the trees that surrounded the flat ground where the car was parked.

Angela made her way along the rough path that followed the western edge of the water, moving noisily but saying nothing because their shadowers had not yet arrived. She'd covered about fifty metres when she glanced behind her. The Ford was just pulling into the entrance, so she immediately moved into the treeline on her right and started talking as if Bronson was walking right beside her.

Bronson had ducked into the edge of the wood and then turned back towards the road, which he hoped was the direction they wouldn't expect him to have gone. Most of the trees were pines or firs – he'd never have made a botanist, that was for sure – and he was able to move quickly and quietly on the carpet of pine needles underfoot.

The human eye is particularly well adapted to detect movement, a hangover from the days when our distant ancestors were prey animals as much as they were predators, and the instant he saw the nose of the Ford turning towards the pull-off, he froze in place beside a tree, watching and waiting.

–

Ferrara drove the Ford hire car off the road and looked ahead at the vehicle parked there.

'I can't block them in,' he said as he stepped out of the car. 'The opening is too wide for that.'

'Hopefully we won't have to bother,' Rossi replied. 'Judging by all the gear they bought back in Halifax, I reckon they must have already located the Ark in a cave or something. Once they've dragged it out, we'll put it in the back of our car and get it shipped from here direct to Rome. Bronson and Lewis can stay right here. There are foxes and wild cats and even a few bears here in Nova Scotia and their bodies wouldn't last long.

You or I can drive their car back to Halifax and just dump it somewhere there. Nobody will miss them, and that will be a nice tidy ending to the story.'

Rossi took a pistol from his pocket and worked the action to load the first round.

Ferrara chuckled and cocked his own pistol.

'Right,' he said, 'let's do it.'

Chapter 60

Lemuel Dayan's prod at Jerusalem had produced positive results, but not exactly what they had been expecting. One of Zeru's contacts in the Mossad had produced two pieces of important information.

First, they were told that Marco Ferrara and Luca Rossi had flown to Nova Scotia and booked rooms in a hotel in Halifax, which wasn't good news. But far more importantly – the Vatican wasn't the only organisation that employed informers – photographs of a piece of parchment bearing a Latin text had been found at the Bibliothèque Serpente in Paris and sent to Jerusalem. The text was unencrypted and related directly to the quest. The original Latin text and a translation had been sent to Dayan's email address, and the three-man team had spent the next couple of hours studying the clues in conjunction with maps of Nova Scotia, trying to work out what they meant.

'The one thing we do know,' Josef Gellerman said, 'is that we're in the right place. Or the right country, anyway, because Ferrara and Rossi are here as well as the English couple. And our reading of the clues is probably similar to theirs.'

'Which means what?' Aaron Chason asked.

'That the river running south is probably the Gold River, and the place halfway between the coasts is most likely either New Ross or somewhere very near it,' Dayan replied. 'What we don't know about is the well, and the best way to find that is probably to go over there.'

'Yes,' Gellerman agreed, 'and make sure we find the relic before those two bastards from the Inquisition get their hands on it.'

Chapter 61

In the world of firearms, there are two sounds that are quite unmistakable. The first is the noise made by cocking a pump-action shotgun, and the other is the distinctive click-clack sound of the slide of an automatic pistol being pulled back and released. Bronson clearly heard both men preparing their weapons.

They were speaking Italian, but he understood every word. If he'd needed any justification for what he was intending to do, that was it. He'd also recognised the driver as the man he'd seen in Campagne-sur-Aude, the man with the white Alfa Romeo MiTo.

He remained exactly where he was for a few seconds, watching the two Italians. As he expected, they separated and began walking along each side of the rough track, following the route he knew Angela had taken a few minutes earlier.

He calculated distances and angles, and then set off after them, walking quickly but silently on the pine needles that covered the ground between the trees. As he followed them, he began edging towards the left-hand side of the treeline, moving closer to the rough track but always keeping behind the closer of the two men. He daren't risk being seen in either man's peripheral vision.

Ahead, he could see a section of the track that was much narrower due to a large growth of bushes and young trees encroaching on it from the right. That was as good a place as any to make his move.

As he had expected, the Italian on the right-hand side of the track, who was slightly behind his companion, paused briefly as the other man moved through the gap, separating the two of them. The moment he came to a stop, Bronson stepped out of the trees right behind him. There was going to be no finesse with this, and he knew he only had the one chance.

Holding the axe by its head rather than the handle, he smashed the tool onto the back of the Italian's head. Instantly the man tumbled forward, the pistol dropping from his hand, falling to the soft earth with barely a sound.

Bronson grabbed the weapon and stuck it in the waistband of his trousers, then bent down and picked up the unconscious Italian. The man was quite slim, and Bronson was strong, and he had no difficulty in lifting him bodily over his shoulder.

As silently as he could, he stepped back among the trees and undergrowth, dumped the Italian behind a thick growth of timber, then returned to the edge of the track, the pistol now in his hand.

The other armed man had stopped, turning his head from side to side, his pistol raised and ready, obviously looking for his companion.

Bronson could easily have shot him where he stood, but he wasn't in the business of killing people unless it was unavoidable, so he just watched and waited, guessing that the man would turn back and search the area behind him, and then he could take him. But as the Italian started to retrace his steps, something entirely unexpected happened.

Bronson saw a square black object appear above and behind the man's head, and for the briefest of instants he had no idea what it was. Then realisation dawned as the shovel blade of the trenching tool crashed into the back of the Italian's head and he fell forward.

Angela had obviously taken him at his word. And very efficiently, too.

'So what do we do with them?' she asked, stepping over the now unconscious man and walking over to Bronson.

'Nicely done,' he said, giving her a brief hug. 'I expected you to be a lot further down the track.'

'I was, but I started to get worried about you and doubled back. Where's the other one?'

'In the woods, having a kip.'

'Good. So what's the plan?'

'I think we call in the thin blue line. That'll get these two out of our hair for a while.'

Bronson picked up the pistol the second Italian had dropped and handed it to Angela.

'Watch him for a few minutes while I sort out contestant number one,' he said.

Both men were still deeply unconscious, and by the time they'd even started to come round, Bronson had dragged them to a couple of trees near their hire car. He'd wrapped their arms around the tree trunks and tied each man's wrists together using some of the climbing rope he'd purchased earlier. Then he'd taken their car keys, opened the boot and found the spare ammunition for their pistols, plus a Winchester hunting rifle and a box of twenty rounds of 30.06 ammunition, which he'd transferred to the boot of his own hire car on the reasonable grounds that having a weapon that couldn't be traced to him would probably be quite a good idea.

While the two men were still unconscious, he'd wiped both the pistols and pressed their right hands around them to make sure their prints were on them, then removed the magazines and jammed the weapons into their waistbands.

He'd made a call to the Royal Canadian Mounted Police, the local variant of the thin blue line, using one of the Italians' phones, to say that he'd seen two men waving pistols around, and given the approximate location. He'd also given the make, model and registration number of their car and left the phone switched on so that its position could be triangulated. Finally he'd used the sheath knife to puncture two of the tyres on the Ford so that even if the Italians did manage to get free, which he doubted, they still wouldn't be able to drive away.

As he drove the hire car out of the pull-off, he waved to the two Italians, who were now both fully conscious and clearly seething.

'You didn't question them,' Angela said as he started driving back towards New Ross. 'I wonder who they were working for.'

'I probably wouldn't have got much sense out of them,' he replied, 'but they were both Italian and my guess is that their ultimate employer might be the Vatican, through a few cut-outs, of course. But I doubt they'd ever have admitted that to me. And we know what they were looking for because of what they said to each other when they got out of the car. Their idea was to take the Ark and leave us to rot in the woods.'

'Nice. So is that the last we'll see of them?'

'I hope so. I've done some checking. The Canadians are stricter than the Americans when it comes to firearms. Most hunting rifles, like the one we now have in the boot, don't even need to be registered, though I should have a permit to own a weapon. But there are strict rules about pistols. I doubt those two men will be released for at least a few days.'

'But they have both got quite nasty wounds on the backs of their heads. Won't that raise a few questions? Like maybe they're entirely innocent and have been set up?'

'Possibly,' Bronson agreed, 'but in my experience, the corporate police brain is a fairly simple structure. No matter what the details are, the fact is that the Mounties will find two non-residents of Canada each in possession of an unregistered or stolen pistol. That's an offence, and that'll be what appears on the charge sheets. They probably won't be too bothered about how they got hold of the weapons, or who tied them up, or who made the call to summon the cavalry.'

'So now we can start looking properly,' Angela said, and once again she took out the folded topographical map and her smartphone.

Chapter 62

New Ross, Nova Scotia, Canada

It felt to Josef Gellerman as if he'd been tramping around and about New Ross for the entire day, though they'd actually been there for only about four hours. They'd started near the church, looking for an old well or any other structure where a band of wandering medieval knights could have hidden the most precious religious relic of all time.

They'd found nothing within the village – which hadn't been a surprise – and had then started widening the search area, moving around the outskirts of New Ross in an expanding concentric circle, skirting private property where they had to and walking through woods and fields and along the banks of the Gold River.

And they'd seen absolutely nothing.

What they didn't know was that they had been seen, and not just by the handful of people they'd passed as they walked around the village.

Trail cameras are usually motion-activated and battery-powered and record images and videos on an SD card, but a new generation of solar-powered cameras is becoming available. These employ a modified 3G or 4G Android smartphone, encased in a waterproof housing, to transmit data to a specific wireless network.

When the three Israelis had walked through one particular area of rough ground, two of these cameras, each painted in camouflage colours and almost invisible among the trees, had recorded their progress and transmitted short video sequences to the recipient network. That had raised an immediate alarm.

Chapter 63

'Where do you want me to go?' Bronson asked after a few minutes, as they neared New Ross.

'Just park anywhere that looks convenient, preferably somewhere near the church. We'll need to have a bit of a hike around the place to get our bearings. But I have found out something about *a* well, and that something does fit the clue in the parchment.'

'Oh yes?'

'The source is a little flaky. It's a website that makes all kinds of extravagant claims about what people have found in and near New Ross, but it's short on actual evidence. Or even photographs of what it believes is there. Anyway, what it claims to have discovered about one particular well does make sense, or at least it's a possible explanation of the text on the parchment. It says that this well technically isn't a well at all, but a cistern. It says the water supply for it comes from some unspecified mountain via an underground tunnel because the groundwater in the New Ross area is contaminated by uranium. What it doesn't explain is how the Templars could have known that if they built the well, which is what the site seems to be implying.'

'And is it contaminated? Does a glass of water here glow in the dark?'

'There *is* uranium in Nova Scotia, yes, just like there is in most of the rest of the world, and the area around New Ross does have slightly higher concentrations of the element than some other parts of the province. But as far as I know, the water doesn't glow.'

'So where's the well?'

'Ah. That's something else this website isn't very good at: producing facts. Things like the location of these various hidden rooms and possible tunnels and probable Templar treasure vaults – those are just some of the claims – and of course the mysterious well. It claims to have used ground-penetrating radar to locate some of these structures. If I was being charitable, I'd assume this vagueness was to keep the important discoveries secret to avoid looters, but I have a feeling that the more likely reason is because whoever is behind the website doesn't want people looking around and finding absolutely nothing to support their claims.'

'Are these the same people who think a pile of rocks mean a castle was built here?'

'I can't remember, but it wouldn't surprise me.'

'So what are we going to be looking for? A six-hundred-year-old well, presumably?'

Angela shook her head. 'Even if we could locate it, I don't think looking at it would help us very much. I have the feeling it's somewhere near the centre of the present village, but that's about the only indication I picked up. If I'm interpreting the clues on that parchment correctly, the well is nothing more than a marker. The vault or whatever you want to call it is deep underground, just like the Money Pit on Oak Island, and was probably built the same way. They dug the hole, built the vault and an access tunnel to it, then filled in the hole and created the well on top of it as a marker and a defence mechanism. Finally they filled the well with water, so that if anyone dug down near it, the shaft would flood. That's the way I read it, anyway.'

'So?' Bronson asked, parking the hire car well off the road about fifty yards from the church.

'So what we need to find is the entrance to the tunnel that the Templars dug.'

'That's something else that sounds easy if you say it quickly. How do we find it? In fact, where do we even start looking?'

'First we look around. Get the hiking poles out of the boot and follow me.'

Bronson had hidden the Winchester rifle under everything else so it was invisible when he opened the boot. He reached in, grabbed the two poles and the binoculars and locked the car.

They walked away from the church and down the road towards the cafe they'd stopped at earlier that day.

'If we assume the well is somewhere near the village centre, then the first thing we need to look at is the terrain, the way the land slopes away.'

'Why?' Bronson asked.

'Basic geometry. The Templars would have wanted the tunnel to be level, obviously, so that would be the base of a triangle. The depth of the vault below the ground would form the short side and the hypotenuse would be the slope of the ground between the entrance to the tunnel and the top of the well. The well would have to be at least fifty feet deep, probably double that, so that means we can forget about anywhere on higher ground than the village centre and on all the surrounding land that's less than fifty feet below the centre. I know that all sounds a bit arbitrary, because it is, but we have to start somewhere.'

They walked down the road until they found a rough path, more like a game trail than something used by people, which took them away from the road and into the undeveloped area around the village.

For a little over two hours they wandered around the edges of the settlement, trying to find any sign of a tunnel entrance or anything similar, then Angela grumpily told Bronson that she needed a drink and food and a dose of inspiration. They climbed back up to the road to the cafe and found a vacant table.

'I think we're looking in the wrong place,' she said, stirring a cup of coffee far more vigorously than necessary. 'Most of the land around here is farmed, as far as I can see, and that means it's been occupied for the better part of half a millennium. If there ever had been a tunnel entrance, somebody would have found it centuries ago. I was hoping to find a few cliff faces where the Templars could have piled up rocks to conceal an opening, something like that, but this area is all fields and grassy slopes.'

'On the other hand, it would have been easy ground for them to construct a tunnel,' Bronson pointed out. 'Not like hacking their way through rock.'

Angela nodded. 'Yes, but that also means the entrance would have been obvious and visible. They could have planted trees and bushes around it, I suppose, but trees die and fall down, and sooner or later somebody would have seen the opening.'

'So what do you want to do?'

'I don't know. The reality is that the clues from the parchment fit this place better than anywhere else in Nova Scotia, as far as I can tell, so although we haven't found it, I still think it must be here, just a hell of a lot better hidden than I expected.'

'That,' Bronson sad after a moment, 'might be the operative word.'

'What?'

'Hidden. I've just remembered something I saw but didn't notice, if you see what I mean.'

'What?' Angela repeated.

'Finish your coffee and I'll show you.'

Chapter 64

'Tell me what you see,' Bronson said, handing Angela the binoculars and pointing across an open field.

She brought the binoculars up to her eyes and scanned the ground in front of them.

'A field,' she said, stating the obvious, 'a hillside opposite, and an old barn backing onto the hill. Is that it?'

'Not quite. Now tell me what you don't see.'

'No idea.'

'You see the barn, right? What does a farmer use a barn for?'

'I don't know,' Angela said grumpily. 'Somewhere to store hay or keep his tractors or ploughs or something.'

'Exactly. So what's missing? What should be there but isn't? In front of the barn?'

'I don't… Oh. I see what you mean. The ground's quite soft, but the area in front of the barn looks more like a lawn than a field. No tyre tracks. And if the barn was in use – as a barn, I mean – the ground should be churned up.'

'Exactly. I think we should take a look over there.'

'Hang on. If you're right and that isn't a barn but a building concealing the entrance to the tunnel and made to look like a barn, that must mean that somebody already knows about the Ark. You wouldn't find a tunnel entrance and not explore it, would you? So why don't we already know that the relic has been found?'

'That's a very good question.'

They both turned at the sound of the unfamiliar voice.

Facing them in a loose semicircle were three men, the one who had spoken tall and almost Scandinavian-looking, while the other two were shorter and much darker in complexion. But their appearance wasn't what grabbed and held Bronson's attention: it was the automatic pistol that each man was holding and pointing at him.

'Who are you?' he asked.

The tall man shook his head. 'I'm holding the weapon,' he said. 'That means I ask the questions and you answer them, Bronson. And that goes for you too, Lewis.'

Bronson had been surprised by the appearance of the three men, but the fact that they knew their names was a much bigger shock.

'Who—' he began again.

'You don't need to know who we are,' the man said. 'What you need to do is shut up, listen to me and do what you're told. If you don't, the woman standing next to you will suffer. Please believe me when I say that I don't make idle threats.'

There was something about the man's voice, a kind of cold and detached determination, that told Bronson he was entirely serious. He glanced around the field and the surrounding area, but there was no sign of anybody else within view, or even within shouting distance. Against one man armed with a pistol he might have a chance. Against three men carrying weapons it would just be an unusual way of committing suicide. Or, worse, getting Angela shot. He had no option but to do exactly what he was told and wait for an opportunity to try to turn the tables.

'Let me give you a reality check,' the man said. 'We know who you are because we've been following your trail all the way from the south of France. We know what you're looking for, and we know that it's probably only a few dozen yards away from where we're standing right now. We also know that we're going to take it away from here and back to where it should be.'

'Let me guess,' Angela said, sounding more irritated than frightened, and having obviously made a deduction about the nationality of the men and their probable motive. 'You've got some crackpot scheme to use the Ark to justify the building of the Third Temple in Jerusalem.'

Bronson noticed that the aim of all three pistols held by the men had shifted to Angela.

'There's nothing crackpot about fulfilling our destiny,' the tall man said sharply, a statement that confirmed Angela's suspicions.

'Even though that would probably spark a conflict between Christianity and Islam that could engulf the entire world? It would be like the Crusades all over again, but with jet fighters and tactical nukes instead of horses and battle swords.'

'If that's what it takes, yes. We're prepared to die for our beliefs and for Israel.'

'Spoken like a true fanatic,' Bronson said, 'and if you want to die, I'd be very happy to give you a hand.'

The three pistols, moving as if coordinated, shifted back to point at him.

'Enough,' the man snapped. 'You think the Ark is somewhere inside the building in front of us, and so do we, so let's go and find out. You two lead the way, just in case there are any nasty surprises waiting for us. And you can lose the poles as well.'

They had no choice and they knew it. Bronson and Angela laid their hiking poles on the ground and walked off across the field towards the barn that probably wasn't a barn at all.

Although the building had looked somewhat ramshackle from a distance, when they got close to it they could see that it had a strong steel frame and that the boards secured to it were about an inch thick and held in place by multiple bolts. The front was dominated by two wide doors, again with steel frames, and the lock that secured them in the centre was clearly a high-quality product.

Bronson tried turning the handle, but it didn't budge even a fraction of an inch.

'I think we're all going to be disappointed,' he said, 'unless you brought a tame locksmith along with you.'

'As a matter of fact,' the tall man said, 'we did. You two, move over there. Aaron, do your stuff.'

One of the other men tucked his pistol into the waistband of his trousers and stepped forward, taking a soft leather tool roll from one of his jacket pockets. He released the drawstring to open it up and stared at the lock for a few seconds. Then he nodded, selected a torsion wrench and what Bronson recognised immediately as a set of skeleton keys for a warded lock and set to work, applying pressure with the wrench while he probed the interior of the keyway with the skeleton keys.

It took him a little over five minutes before they all heard a distinct click. He turned the substantial steel handle of the door and pushed it open about six inches before packing away his tools and taking a few steps backwards.

'Inside,' the first man said, gesturing with the muzzle of his pistol towards Bronson. 'You stay here,' he told Angela, 'just in case your boyfriend decides to do something stupid. Aaron, watch her.'

Bronson pushed the door open a couple of feet so that he could step inside, and immediately looked round, searching for anything that he could use as a weapon. But he found himself standing in a largely empty space. From the inside, it looked just as much like a barn as it had from the outside, though bereft of the type of machinery and vehicles that most people would expect to find on a farm. There were no windows, but he could see perfectly clearly thanks to a row of fluorescent lights mounted above the centre of the space, which he assumed had switched on when the door had been opened. Along the right-hand wall was a workbench with a selection of tools clipped to a pegboard above it, but the presence of the tall man right behind him told him that he would never make it if he tried to grab a hammer or something.

At the rear of the building, where he knew the hillside began to slope upwards, was what looked like a solid wooden wall. If they were in the right place and their deductions had been correct, he knew that the entrance to the tunnel must be somewhere behind it.

He looked behind him just as the man who'd picked the lock prodded Angela into the open space.

'Don't just stand there,' the tall man snapped. 'Find the tunnel entrance.'

Bronson and Angela both walked over to the rear wall.

'Are you okay?' Bronson asked quietly.

'I'd feel a hell of a lot better if I was sitting in a car or an aircraft and heading away from this place,' she said, 'but they haven't hurt me yet and I would quite like it if that situation continued. So is there a bloody door here or not?' she added, looking at the wooden boards in front of them.

'There's nothing obvious. Because of the framing and the way the boards have been bolted to it, we can't be looking at a door that slides or opens conventionally inwards or outwards, which covers most possibilities.'

'Maybe we've got it wrong. But if we have, then those Israeli bastards might decide to shoot us and start looking somewhere else, and I'd rather they didn't do that.'

Bronson was still looking at the boards, staring at one particular place on the wall.

'This could be it,' he said. 'See that horizontal gap between those two boards? If you look closely, you can see something silvery glinting in there. I think that's a hinge for a horizontal cantilever door, which means that somewhere here there must be a switch for a motor, because I don't see any way of opening it manually.'

He walked the length of the wall, checking every board but saw no sign of a switch. Then he retraced his steps and stopped just to one side of where he thought he had seen the hinge.

'I need a long screwdriver,' he told the tall man.

'What for?'

He pointed at a hole in one of the planks. 'I think there's a switch on the other side of this.'

'A lot of the planks have got holes in them,' the man pointed out. 'What's special about that one?'

'The other holes that I've looked at are natural, where knots have fallen out of the wood. This one has been made with a drill.'

'Aaron, get him a screwdriver with a long blade and take it to him.'

A few moments later, Bronson slid the end of the screw-driver blade into the hole he had detected and applied gentle pressure. Nothing happened, so he pressed a little more firmly and detected a faint click from behind the wooden board.

Immediately he heard the sound of an electric motor, and with a creak the central section of the rear wall began moving, the lower section tilting upwards and outwards into the open space while a part of the upper section also moved outwards, the two parts connected by the long horizontal hinge he had seen.

A waft of cold and slightly musty air made its presence felt as all five of them stared at the entrance to the tunnel that had just been revealed.

Chapter 65

There was a distinct click from somewhere in the tunnel and a sudden flare of light as the first of a line of fluorescent tube lights flickered into life, quickly followed by the others, until they were looking down an arrow-straight illuminated tunnel, roughly eight feet high and eight feet wide and perhaps seventy or eighty yards long, carved out of the earth.

The tunnel was supported about every ten or twelve feet by an inverted U-shaped timber frame, the wood at least six inches square. Solid wooden planks linked the frames to form a roof and two walls. Each frame had an obviously old metal sconce bolted to it, probably to take an oil lamp, the timber above the sconces blackened with soot.

Angela shivered slightly. 'God, this looks old,' she said.

'Of course it's old, you stupid woman,' the tall man said. 'It's been here for over six hundred years. You two, walk in front of us, just in case the Templars included any nasty surprises for unexpected visitors.'

With a brief glance behind him, Bronson started walking slowly along the beaten-earth floor of the tunnel, Angela at his side and the three Israelis about ten feet behind them.

'Do you think there are any booby-traps?' Angela asked, her voice little more than a whisper.

'Definitely not. This tunnel may be six hundred years old, but the door we've come through and the wiring and lighting are twenty-first-century. If there were any booby-traps, whoever found this tunnel would have shifted them, probably centuries ago.'

'You think somebody knew about this that long ago?'

'It stands to reason,' Bronson said quietly. 'I don't believe that the entrance to the tunnel wouldn't have been discovered soon after New Ross was settled. And I'll bet you that whoever found it built a barn or something to hide it, and that the building there now is one of a long line of replacement structures. And you obviously know what that means.'

'Yes. Somebody has been keeping this place a secret since the late-medieval period, because it's not recorded in any of the archaeological records of Nova Scotia. And that does make me wonder about who they are and what their purpose is.'

'Well, we may be about to find out.' Bronson gestured in front of them, where the last half-dozen fluorescent lights illuminated the end of the tunnel and revealed a dark opening over to their right.

'Keep going,' the tall man ordered from behind them.

As Bronson led the way towards the opening, another lighting circuit clicked into life. Not fluorescent tube lights this time, but wall lights mounted in sconces that appeared identical to those in the tunnel.

'They must've been triggered by a PIR sensor,' he said. 'And that's definitely twenty-first-century technology.'

The space they entered was another tunnel, slightly wider and taller than the one they'd just walked down but only about twenty yards long, with a pool of darkness ahead of them. As they approached, another set of lights slowly started brightening to reveal a circular chamber, a dark shape to one side of it. And then a spotlight, obviously mounted somewhere on the roof of the chamber, snapped on, the beam bathing the shape in brilliant light.

Bronson and Angela stopped at the entrance, transfixed.

There, directly in front of them, gleaming golden as if newly polished, was the fabulous Ark of the Covenant, resting on a shallow plinth. It seemed almost to glow in the spotlight, and Bronson thought he could detect a faint humming sound coming from it.

The tall Israeli emitted a sound somewhere between a moan and a yell and rushed forward, brushing Angela aside as he did so. He stopped about a yard from the Ark, put his pistol on the ground and knelt before the relic, lowering his head in prayer.

Then he stood up, took a couple of paces forward and tentatively reached out to touch the lid of the Ark. The instant he did so, there was a sharp crack and he tumbled backwards and fell to the ground. But he was up and on his feet in a moment.

He picked up his pistol and turned back to face the other two Israelis, who had also entered the chamber, moving in front of Bronson and Angela.

'This is the true Ark, the casket of God,' he said. 'And I have felt its power.'

The walls of the chamber were covered with hanging drapes, and as the Israeli spoke, one of them fluttered and drew back to reveal the classic figure of a medieval Knight Templar in full armour with a battle sword in his hand.

To Bronson, it was surreal, bizarre and unbelievable: three armed Israelis facing a medieval knight standing on one side of a subterranean chamber lit by electricity, with the Ark of the Covenant on the other side.

'Who dares enter this sacred place?' the knight demanded, his voice seeming to be magnified by the chamber. As he spoke, he lifted his sword in a threatening manner.

The tall Israeli didn't hesitate, just raised his pistol and squeezed the trigger. The chamber rang with the sound of the shot. At that range there was no possibility he could miss, but the medieval figure didn't even flinch, just swung the battle sword in a lethal arc towards the intruder.

Bronson could hear the hissing sound as the blade cut through the air.

The Israeli stumbled backwards, pulling the trigger twice more at point-blank range.

And as quickly and as inexplicably as the knight had appeared, the figure simply vanished.

Bronson took a couple of steps forward, intending to grab one of the pistols held by the other two Israelis, whose attention was entirely on the Ark and the events unfolding in front of them.

But before he got close enough to seize a weapon, a heavily built black-clad figure materialised behind him and pushed him and Angela through the drapes on the left-hand side of the chamber and into a small room illuminated by a dim bulb in the centre of the ceiling. Almost before they could react, the figure closed a steel door and turned the key on the inside. Then he – it was obviously a man – turned to them, pointed at a flat-screen television mounted on the wall and said, 'Keep quiet and watch.'

The screen was divided into quadrants, each displaying the feed from a surveillance camera positioned inside the chamber of the Ark. And what it showed was the three Israelis in a state of confusion.

-

As soon as the apparition had vanished, Gellerman strode across to the hanging drape from behind which the knight had appeared. He pulled back the curtain and found himself facing a featureless steel panel, with no sign of the body of the man he had just shot. He grabbed at the other drapes to reveal similar steel plates.

He whirled around, scanning the chamber, then looked back at the panel and rapped on it with the butt of his pistol. It sounded completely solid.

'I don't know what's going on here,' he said, 'but it doesn't matter. We came for the Ark and we've found it, so let's get out of here. Get Bronson and Lewis to carry it.'

Dayan turned round to carry out Gellerman's order.

'They've gone,' he said.

'They must have run down the corridor. Get after them. There's nowhere out there they can hide.'

Dayan rushed out of the chamber but returned in a matter of seconds.

'They aren't there,' he said. 'I can see all the way to the far end of the corridor. They didn't go that way.'

The three Israelis stared around them. Very obviously something was going on that they didn't understand.

'It doesn't matter,' Gellerman said. 'You two, grab those.' He pointed behind the plinth on which the Ark sat to where two stout wooden poles leaned against the wall. 'We'll take it right now.'

Dayan and Chason strode across to the relic, threaded the poles through the rings on either side of it and picked it up – not without difficulty, as it was clearly heavy.

As they lifted it, the spotlight illuminating the Ark snapped off and the lamps in the sconces began to dim. From somewhere in the chamber a noise that sounded like a distant multitude of people shouting and screaming became audible, its volume rapidly increasing until it was a deafening roar. At almost the same instant the shadowy figures of another half a dozen fully armed Templar knights suddenly appeared around the perimeter of the space, each chanting the medieval Latin battle cry of the order – *In hoc signo vinces* – and raising his battle sword. They closed in on the three men, whose wide eyes and horrified expressions clearly showed their abject terror.

'Get going!' Gellerman shouted, spinning round and snapping off a fast volley of shots at the threatening figures as the other two men stumbled out of the chamber carrying the Ark between them. None of his bullets had any obvious effect, and the muzzle flashes and echoing bangs simply added to the surreal and bizarre scene that was unfolding.

As the three Israelis ran from the chamber, the figures of the knights followed, but only as far as the entrance. There, unseen by the three fleeing men, who were running as if their very lives depended on it, the six knights flickered out of existence and the lamps in the wall-mounted sconces slowly began to brighten.

-

Inside the hidden room, the man in black picked up a remote control, aimed it at the television screen and pressed a button. The view changed to cameras located at intervals along the long corridor, and in silence the three of them watched the Israelis carrying their prize towards the open door at the end. Once they had disappeared through it, the unidentified man pressed a button on a small control panel beside the television, and the door closed. He pressed another button, and the camera feed showed two large electrically controlled bolts snapping into place.

'We're now secure,' he said. 'I think that went quite well, don't you?'

Angela stared at him. 'Would you please tell me what the hell is going on here?' she said. 'Starting with who you are and then moving on to what just happened.'

'Gladly. My name is Michael Rogers, and I'm a Templar knight.'

That didn't help very much, and Angela's expression suggested that she was, if anything, even more confused than she'd been a few minutes earlier.

'Let me introduce you to the others,' Rogers said, 'and then we'll explain what's going on.'

He unlocked the steel door and stepped outside, Bronson and Angela following closely behind him.

In the Ark chamber, where the now-empty low plinth sat like an accusing witness, the first person they saw was the Templar knight in full regalia, who was clearly unharmed despite what they'd seen happen just a few minutes earlier.

'That went well, Brother Michael,' the Knight said. 'A very successful operation.' He switched his glance to Bronson and Angela. 'I imagine you have a few questions.'

'You have no idea,' Angela said. 'Let's start with why, who, what, when, where and a side order of how. First of all, who are you and why aren't you dead? I saw that Israeli shoot you at point-blank range.'

'My name's Roger Pemberton, and like Brother Michael, I'm also a Templar knight. As for why I'm alive, the Templars in the medieval period had armour made of steel. Ours is made of layers of Kevlar, and there's lots of padding under this tunic. But I was in no danger at all, because that wasn't me in the chamber. Or to be exact, what you saw out there *was* me, but at the same time it wasn't.'

'What?' Angela demanded, her voice clouded with frustrated confusion. Or perhaps confused frustration.

'I think he means we've been watching a performance,' Bronson suggested. 'A projection, or maybe using mirrors, something like that.'

Pemberton nodded. 'Actually, we're a little more sophisticated than that. My part in that scene was played out a lot earlier and recorded. What you saw was a hologram. Just like the six knights who appeared when the Ark was lifted.'

'What did you mean when you said it was a very successful operation?' Bronson asked. 'As far as I can see, you've been doing some kind of play-acting, and as a result of that, those three Israelis have got away with the Ark of the Covenant.'

'Well, yes and no, really. Let me begin at the beginning. I find that's usually quite a convenient place to start.'

Chapter 66

Pemberton pulled aside another of the drapes lining the chamber and led the way into what looked like the kind of comfortable sitting room normally found in a gentleman's club. It had wood-panelled walls and half a dozen leather easy chairs, the space illuminated by concealed lighting. One of the chairs was occupied by a slim man with dark hair and eyes, his features dominated by a nose that looked as if it had been designed for a slightly larger face. He was casually dressed in jeans and an open-necked shirt.

He stood up as they approached, gave a wide smile and extended his hand.

'You must be Angela Lewis and Chris Bronson,' he said. 'You're very welcome here. My name is David Gillon.'

Bronson's feeling of confusion at the bizarre turn of events only deepened as he shook hands with another stranger who knew exactly who he and Angela were.

'David works for an institute in Jerusalem,' Pemberton said. 'Michael and I are just local boys.'

A faint glimmer of light illuminated in Bronson's brain.

'*An* institute or *the* Institute?' he asked.

Gillon nodded. 'Very perspicacious, Chris,' he replied.

'What are you talking about?' Angela sounded about ready to explode with frustration.

'We appear to have stumbled into the middle of an operation run by the Mossad, the Israeli intelligence organisation,' Bronson said. 'But I still have no idea what's going on.'

'Sit down, both of you,' Pemberton said, 'and we'll try to explain.' He took a seat himself on one side of the room, his armour clanking. 'Now, as we told you, Michael and I are both Templar knights. And unlike various assorted groups of nutters and fantasists around the world who claim to have Templar roots, we're the real deal. We can both trace our lineage back as far as a man named Gérard de Villiers.'

'The last Templar Master and Preceptor of France,' Bronson said. 'The man who commanded the galleys that sailed from La Rochelle in 1307.'

'You know your Templar history, Chris. The short version of our story is that the surviving knights who reached Scotland maintained their beliefs and traditions after the order was purged, but abandoned their oath of celibacy. They were the guardians of much of the assets of the order, and of course of the Ark of the Covenant, and remained a separate group within the Hospitaller order. I'm sure you already know that a number of Templars accompanied Prince Henry Sinclair to Nova Scotia in 1398 to create a secure repository on this side of the ocean. They brought some of the treasures of the order with them, as well as the Ark.'

'The Ark,' Angela pointed out, her voice registering a mixture of irritation and confusion, 'that you've just let three Israeli thugs walk away with.'

'Not exactly,' Gillon said, 'but we'll get to that in a minute, I promise.'

'Our ancestors constructed what is now called the Money Pit on Oak Island,' Pemberton continued. 'The booby-trap system they built is still working today, though I suspect the treasure concealed there will ultimately be recovered. They also built this complex to house the Ark for all eternity. You've possibly heard of the title baronet of Nova Scotia?'

Angela nodded. 'It was a settlement scheme created in the seventeenth century to get people to buy land in Nova Scotia. If they bought a big enough plot, they also became a baronet. I presume your ancestors bought what is now New Ross?'

'Bits of it, yes,' Pemberton replied, 'including this bit, obviously, and we still hold the titles. Then there was the argy-bargy with the French when they claimed the colony back from the English, so it wasn't until early in the nineteenth century that our ancestors were able to permanently settle here. Our families have guarded the Ark ever since. The tunnel and this complex are original, built by Prince Henry Sinclair's men. We just added the present barn – it's about the tenth building that's concealed the entrance – these rooms around the chamber, the cameras and lighting and the electronics.'

'Who knew the Ark was hidden here?' Bronson asked.

'Our families,' Roger said, 'but something of this magnitude is difficult to keep entirely secret, obviously, and because of the origin of the relic we felt obliged to tell certain very senior Israeli intelligence officers that we had it. Not politicians, obviously. Then about a year ago we were approached by a colleague of David here because the government of Israel believed it was facing a problem. Not an immediate problem, but one that had the potential to destabilise relations in the Middle East on a permanent basis. Have you ever heard of a man named Zerubbabel?'

Bronson and Angela both shook their heads.

'I'm not surprised,' Rogers said. 'I'll let David tell you the rest.'

'He was a character in the Hebrew Bible and the Old Testament,' Gillon said, 'and he gets an occasional name-check in the New Testament as well. He allegedly led the Jews back to Judah after the Babylonian captivity, and more importantly, he was the man who initiated the building of the Second Temple in Jerusalem in about 520 BC. Those three Israelis are members of a group of radical activists who took his name for their own organisation, though it's normally shortened to just Zeru. They chose that name because their entire aim is to build the Third Temple in Jerusalem, and they believe that the trigger for this to start, the sign from God, if you like, would be the recovery of the original Ark of the Covenant.

'Zeru has been a thorn in the side of the Israeli government for the last three decades, and the consequences of them initiating their plan would be utterly catastrophic, and not just for Israel. Jerusalem is now, and has been for most of recorded history, a divided city, where Christians, Jews and Muslims live in close proximity and uneasy harmony. Almost anything could destabilise the city and the region, and something like the Ark of the Covenant being discovered could inflame passions to the extent that open warfare would break out between the three religions, especially if radical Jews attempted to seize the Temple Mount to try to build the Third Temple. So my organisation decided it was time to do something about it. We needed to effectively destroy Zeru as a political force.'

'By giving them the Ark?' Angela almost shouted.

'By giving them the Ark,' Gillon repeated in a much quieter voice. 'Because that Ark is not quite all that it seems to be.'

'But we saw that Israeli get knocked over when he touched it,' Bronson pointed out. 'I thought that was the kind of power the Ark was supposed to possess.'

'Allegedly, yes. What you actually saw was a man being knocked off his feet by a discharge of static electricity. We built up a decent charge in the box before you arrived.'

'I thought I heard a humming sound,' Bronson admitted.

'Exactly. We wanted to put on a good show for them and we guessed that the leader – his name is Josef Gellerman – would want to touch it. We thought that literally giving him a shock, doing the business with the holograms and making the two of you apparently vanish into thin air would make the three of them grab the Ark and run with it. Which is exactly what they did.'

'We didn't want to give them time to stop and think about what was happening,' Pemberton clarified. 'We wanted them to think they were involved in a real paranormal experience created by the Ark to try to stop them taking it away. If they'd stayed in the chamber and looked around, they might have found the projectors and realised it was all a set-up. A piece of theatre.'

'So that wasn't the real Ark? Is that what you mean?' Angela asked.

'Obviously,' Gillon replied. 'The last thing we'd do is let those Israelis anywhere near the genuine article. You followed a trail of clues, yes? An encrypted text that led you from Montségur to Rennes-le-Château to Campagne-sur-Aude and then on to Collioure. And then the trail went cold. That text was entirely genuine, and we've known about it for a while through a contact in Limoux.

'But the parchment with the Latin plaintext was created by us in Tel Aviv, based on information provided to us by Roger and Michael here, and was as accurate as we could make it. Then it was inserted in the apparently misfiled Aniort papers in the Paris library. If you do a radiocarbon dating of the parchment, you'll find it's virtually new, and the ink won't stand up to analysis either. All that was designed to get Zeru into this place to grab the Ark, and we even prompted them a few times with tips and hints from apparent sympathisers in the Mossad. We didn't expect you two to be here as well, frankly, though we've also been keeping an eye on you, so we modified our plan slightly when we saw Gellerman capture you outside the barn. Actually, it all worked out really well.'

'But the Ark?' Angela said, returning to her theme.

'We had it made in America,' Rogers said, 'and the Mossad picked up the tab. It's a good replica of the real thing, but there are one or two differences. First of all, it's not solid gold, not even the lid, just plated with a thick layer of the metal; much of the weight comes from a lead sheet in the lid of the box. There's nothing on it to immediately suggest that it's anything other than the real thing, which was essential if the men from Zeru were to accept it as genuine.'

'They aren't entirely stupid,' Pemberton pointed out. 'They will obviously run non-destructive tests on it, including XRF testing – X-ray fluorescence – and the plating is thick enough that it will show as high-carat gold. We needed to make it as convincing as possible. The gold plating is actually worth quite a few thousand dollars. We doubt Zeru will do much more than physically examine the Ark and test the metal before proclaiming it the genuine article, mainly because of what Gellerman will tell them about how and where it was discovered and what happened here.

'That's the thing about fanatics. They see what they want to see, not what's really there. They're probably on their way right now to a shipping company to have it crated and sent to Jerusalem, but once they've made the announcement, the Israeli government will make sure that the relic is thoroughly examined and the results of that examination published as widely as possible.'

'And that will prove the Ark is a fake?' Angela asked.

'Much more than that,' Gillon said. 'We decided that the best way to effectively destroy Zeru and end their crackpot scheme was to make them a laughing stock. So etched very clearly into the lead sheet that provides most of the weight of the lid are a few words that will show up with crystal clarity on an X-ray. The words are "Made in America" and "Property of Lucasfilm Ltd props department".'

Angela burst out laughing.

'Once that's happened, I don't think we'll hear any more from that particular source about building a Third Temple. So,' Gillon continued, 'I'm sorry that you've had an entirely wasted journey following the trail of the Ark, but I think your presence here in search of the relic probably helped convince Gellerman and the other two that they really had found the genuine thing, and for that we thank you.'

'A good job all round,' Rogers said, standing up. 'So now you know the truth about all this, we suggest you enjoy yourselves here in Nova Scotia for a few days until you fly home.'

The meeting, such as it was, was clearly over.

'Is there anything else we can tell you?' Pemberton asked, also standing up and starting to remove his armour, obviously preparing to leave.

'Well, yes, obviously,' Angela said. 'Now we know that the Ark we saw was a fake, where's the real one? In one of these other hidden rooms here?'

Pemberton and Rogers looked slightly shocked.

'Certainly not,' Pemberton replied. 'It's much too valuable – and for that matter much too dangerous – to be kept here. This is a secure site, but it's nothing like secure enough to contain the genuine Ark of the Covenant.'

'So where is it?' Bronson asked.

'Where it's been for the last fifty years,' Rogers said. 'Crated to conceal what it is and locked away in the best and most secure bank vault we've been able to identify.'

'You mean just like at the end of *Raiders of the Lost Ark*,' Angela said. 'Where the Ark is taken to some kind of secret government warehouse.'

'Exactly like that,' Rogers agreed. 'I mean, where do you think they got the idea from?'

Author's Note

Ethiopia and the Ark of the Covenant

The descriptions of the churches of Lalibela, the cathedrals at Axum and the building where the Ark of the Covenant is supposed to be kept are accurate. There is no proof that the relic actually is in Ethiopia, and as is explored in this novel there are compelling reasons for believing it isn't there.

The truth of this particular matter will only be revealed if the Ethiopian authorities allow their alleged Ark to be properly examined, and there's no indication this is ever likely to happen. And obviously, the Ethiopians potentially have far more to lose if they do this than they have to gain.

Eachine E10W mini quadcopter

This nano-drone exists and is exactly as described in this novel. It's designed mainly for indoor use, because it's so small and light that it's at the mercy of even quite light winds, but it can operate outside on still days. It's much more than just a toy.

Montségur and the Cathars

The events described in this novel relating to the end of the siege of Montségur are as historically accurate as it is possible to be so long after the event. The precise reasons why more than two hundred Cathars were prepared to die in the flames of the execution pyre rather than renounce their heretical beliefs and simply walk away have never been established. And it is also true, according to contemporary accounts, that they walked into the pre-prepared stockade led by their bishop and singing hymns, as if they were entering a church rather than facing prolonged and agonising execution.

Aniort, Blanchefort, Hautpoul and Voisin families

The relevant parts of the histories of these noble French families are as stated in this novel, including the involvement of the Aniorts in the events leading to the end of the siege of Montségur. The actions taken by Pierre-Roger de Mirepoix, Raymond de Perella and Escot de Belcaire in this context are accurately described. It is also historical fact that King Louis IX treated the Aniort family with notable deference despite their obviously heretical views and actions.

Perhaps surprisingly, it is also true that a French notary refused to surrender the Hautpoul family papers when requested to do so by the then head of the family, Pierre d'Hautpoul, in 1870, and that Élisabeth d'Hautpoul did state it would be dangerous to hand over the papers. She also suggested that they should be decoded and examined, though she did not say why. As far as is known, the Hautpoul family archive has never been examined and is still being held in safe keeping by a notary somewhere in the Languedoc region of France.

The treasure of the Cathars

Something was smuggled out of the castle of Montségur just before the end of the siege, but nobody knows what it was. The descriptions of the transportation of the Ark from Montségur to Rennes-le-Château and on to Campagne-sur-Aude, and its subsequent journey to Nova Scotia, are fiction. The old

Templar fortress at Campagne-sur-Aude is as described in this book.

Cathedral of Sainte-Marie, Auch

The bas-relief carving showing four monks carrying the Ark of the Covenant is accurately described. The face of the monk on the right bears more than a passing resemblance to that of Elvis Presley, and his hairstyle appears to be astonishingly modern.

The Vigenère cipher

The Vigenère cipher wasn't invented by Blaise de Vigenère, which is what most people think, but by Giovan Battista Bellaso and published by him in 1553 in his book *La cifra del Sig. Giovan Battista Bellaso*. The cipher used a *tabula recta* or Vigenère square, the alphabet written out as a block, twenty-six lines deep and twenty-six lines across, each new horizontal line containing the alphabet shifted one character to the left. So the top line started A B C and ended with Z, the second line started B C D and ended with A, the third line started with C D E and ended with B, and so on. The shifting of the start of the alphabet meant that each line was an individual Caesar cipher.

It was called a polyalphabetic substitution cipher because it provided up to twenty-six different alphabets to use based on a repeating keyword, the horizontal rows being selected by the letters of the keyword (key: row) and the vertical column by the letters of the plaintext (text: column). For example, if the keyword was DENBY (DENBYDENBYDENBY and so on) and the first word of the plaintext message was SOUND, the encoder would read down to the fourth horizontal line (D from DENBY), then along that row to the vertical column headed by the letter S (from SOUND), and note the letter where those two lines intersected. That would be the ciphertext for S. Then he would read down to the fifth line, the E row, and across to the O column, and note the ciphertext letter at the intersection. And so on.

If the keyword was short, like DENBY, then cracking the cipher would be possible because it would only use five alphabets, and each plaintext letter could only be represented by five different ciphertext letters. Not easy, but possible. But if the encryption was done with a keyword that was a phrase of twenty-six letters, it would be almost impossible to decipher, as each plaintext letter would have twenty-six possible ciphertext equivalents. Deducing the keyword was crucial.

Vigenère himself produced a variant called the autokey cipher, which used a table of ten alphabets and a previously agreed key letter followed by the first twenty-five letters of the plaintext message itself as the keyword; this was significantly more difficult to crack.

The French called the Vigenère cipher *le chiffre indéchiffrable*, meaning 'the unbreakable cipher', and it *was* unbreakable for about three hundred years, until in 1863 a man named Friedrich Kasiski developed a method to decrypt it.

But he wasn't the first. In 1854, Charles Babbage, the astonishingly gifted nineteenth-century English polymath, and inventor of the Analytical Engine – a mechanical computer that contained all the basic concepts and ideas embodied in today's electronic computers – devised a way of cracking the more complex autokey cipher, but he never published his solution.

Agenzia Informazioni e Sicurezza Esterna (AISE)

The AISE is Italy's secret intelligence service, responsible for the country's external security. It was formerly known as the Servizio per le Informazioni e la Sicurezza Militaire, or SISMI, acquiring its new name in 2007 after yet another reorganisation of the Italian intelligence community. It is analogous in its functions and operations to America's Central Intelligence

Agency (CIA) and Britain's Secret Intelligence Service (SIS, or MI6), and is only allowed to operate outside Italian territory. It makes heavy use of HUMINT (human intelligence) in its operations.

Chartres Cathedral

This is an astonishing building for all sorts of reasons, irrespective of anybody's religious beliefs or lack of them. It is enormous, with stunning acoustics, wonderfully impressive architecture, including huge flying buttresses to cope with the massive weight of the walls, beautiful stained-glass windows and of course the famous labyrinth. Because the nave is used to seat worshippers, quite often the labyrinth is hidden beneath rows of folding chairs, but it's usually possible to see enough of it to get a good impression of its size.

One of the most impressive features of the cathedral is the wealth of beautiful stone carvings that adorn it, inside and out, most of them in remarkably good condition. They often tell a story of some kind, or depict a significant event or an important character from history, and truly represent the pinnacle of the stonemason's art. The carvings depicting the Ark of the Covenant and the inscriptions below them are exactly as described in this novel. They can be seen in the north portico, outside the building.

Rennes-le-Château and Bérenger Saunière

The descriptions in this novel of the village of Rennes-le-Château, the church there and the life and extravagances of the village priest are as accurate as it is possible to be. The source of Saunière's colossal wealth has never been explained. In fact, it's easier to be definitive about what it *wasn't* derived from. He certainly didn't make his money from mass trafficking, as has been repeatedly claimed by people who haven't done their research, and nor did he find strange parchments in the church that allowed him to blackmail the Vatican and/or the pope.

We do know roughly how much he spent, and we know more or less what he spent it on. It also seems clear, based upon the way he renovated the church, that his faith in God and his belief in Christianity probably took a serious hit while he was in the village. The most likely explanation for his conduct is that he found something on his various digging expeditions that was of such value that it turned him into a multimillionaire almost overnight and destroyed his faith at the same time.

But we'll probably never know exactly what it was.

The Money Pit

In the last decade of the eighteenth century, a young man named Daniel McGinnis allegedly found a depression in the ground on Oak Island. He believed that it might be a spot where pirate treasure, possibly that of Captain Kidd, had been buried, and started digging. Records from this period are sparse, unreliable and contradictory, but according to most accounts, the digging – first by McGinnis and a few friends, and later by groups of treasure hunters, some having formed companies to carry out the work – exposed a vertical shaft. The earliest accounts mention a layer of flagstones, and then some kind of marks every ten feet or so as the excavation progressed, while later accounts state that they found platforms made of oak logs every ten feet. Other accounts claim that as well as the log platforms, the shaft also contained layers of charcoal, a kind of putty or clay, and a flat stone bearing strange and indecipherable markings.

The one thing that is consistent in every story is that when the excavations reached a depth of about eighty or ninety feet, the shaft flooded with seawater, which could not be pumped out because it was fed into the shaft by a tunnel system. Every expedition met the same fate, with parallel shafts flooding at about the same depth.

Subsequent investigations showed that far from it being a simple, if very deep, shaft, at the bottom of which lay a wooden vault of some kind, the island possessed a highly sophisticated defence mechanism, clearly designed to frustrate any would-be treasure hunters, which it has done very successfully for well over two hundred years. Briefly, a system of stone box drains constructed on the beach in Smith's Cove fed into an underground flood tunnel, which terminated in the area above the buried vault. All attempts to bypass, block or even locate the flood tunnel failed, but there was no doubt about its existence. Or its effect.

It is clear that the Oak Island vault had been constructed by people possessing a very high degree of engineering ability and building skills, and it is also certain that they had come from overseas, from Europe, in fact. The local native American people, the Mi'kmaq, had neither the skills nor the need to construct something of this type. And there were unambiguous clues: several of the timbers used to construct some of the structures in Smith's Cove – the purpose of most of which is still not understood – show European building techniques such as wooden dowels, pegs and notches and the like, and bear clear and distinct Latin numerals. Radiocarbon dating and dendrochronology produce dates for samples of this wood of around 1650, a century and a half before Daniel McGinnis started digging.

If one radiocarbon date is accepted as being accurate, other radiocarbon dates must be accorded the same status, and this is important for what comes next.

As stated in this novel, the original work done on Oak Island is so clever, complex and sophisticated that very few people could have carried it out. A pirate captain with a crew of seamen wouldn't have had the knowledge or the patience to do so: it had to have been a team of skilled and dedicated men with engineering abilities of a very high order. And at that time – we're talking about the thirteenth or fourteenth centuries, for reasons that will become clear – about the only organisation that possessed these qualities, and had any need to create such a structure in such a location, was the order of the Knights Templar.

It is also a highly relevant fact that none of the treasures or assets of the Knights Templar, apart from a mere handful of relics, have ever been found. Exactly where the combined wealth of the order – which at the time of its dissolution was richer than most European countries – was concealed has never been established. Of all the possible hiding places, Oak Island is certainly one of the most likely.

The counter-argument is that if the dating of the timbers found there is accurate – and it is – then by the time the work was done, the Templars had already been extinct for over three centuries. But this assumes that the timbers found either in Smith's Cove or in the excavations around the Money Pit date back to the time of the original construction, which is almost certainly not the case.

The stone box drains constructed on the beach had obviously been designed to operate for centuries, and layers of coconut fibre had been used to prevent silt and sand from blocking them. Coconuts are not native to Nova Scotia. In fact, the closest source of this material is probably Bermuda, some one thousand miles distant. This fact argues that the Oak Island structure must have been carefully planned well in advance, with a ship or ships first collecting the coconut fibre from Bermuda or perhaps from the islands of the Caribbean and then sailing north to Nova Scotia to carry out the work.

The other indisputable fact is that the box drains and the flood tunnel must have been part of the original construction: it had to have been built as a piece. Therefore, the coconut fibre also had to have been part of the original construction. And that leads to an obvious and unarguable anomaly.

In 1993, samples of the coconut fibre were subjected to radiocarbon-dating analysis by Beta Analytic Incorporated, and the results were unequivocal. Far from matching the analysis of the wood samples, which dated to the mid seventeenth century, the coconut fibre dates were centuries earlier.

Two samples were sent. The first one produced a date range of 1168 to 1282, and the second a range of 1036 to 1298, giving a mean date of about 1229. Further analysis and expert opinion by the company produced a hand-written conclusion that, with ninety-five per cent certainty, the fibres dated to between 1168 and 1374. Radiocarbon dating can provide quite wide variations for several reasons, but the general or average figure is sufficiently accurate to allow certain conclusions to be drawn, and the most obvious is that, based on the radiocarbon dating of the coconut fibre, and hence the Money Pit's original construction, it was probably built in the thirteenth or fourteenth century. The earlier dates for the fibres most likely mean that an expedition was sent to collect this material before the Money Pit was constructed.

That means that many of the wilder theories about what may have been buried in the vault – such as Marie Antoinette's jewellery, pirate treasure, valuables looted from the British invasion of Cuba, or the treasure of the Fortress of Louisbourg – can be immediately dismissed because the dates don't work. Whatever was or is in the vault had to have been put there when the structure was built, and the most obvious contender is the missing treasure and assets of the Knights Templar, because those dates certainly work. The Templar treasure vanished in 1307, which fits almost perfectly with the radiocarbon dating.

All of which of course begs the question: what about the wood found in Smith's Cove, the mysterious U-shaped structure and the slipway, and the wood hauled up from the depths under Oak Island by the hammer grab on almost every episode of the *Curse of Oak Island* television show? The short answer is that long after the Money Pit vault was constructed, a different group of people must have spent time on the island, more or less in the second half of the seventeenth century, again based on the radiocarbon dating of wood samples. They clearly did work of some sort underground and in Smith's Cove, and then disappeared, leaving behind an enigma.

They also probably left behind two bodies buried deep underground. Two fragments of human bone were recovered from about a hundred and sixty feet and subjected to both DNA and radiocarbon analysis. One came from the Middle East and was dated to between 1682 and 1736, while the other was of European origin and was dated to between 1678 and 1764.

Whoever these people were, they certainly did some kind of deep excavations, because of the depth from which wood dating to around 1650 has been recovered.

Without going too far into the realms of pure speculation, perhaps the most probable explanation is that the people who appeared on the island in the seventeenth century knew exactly where and how something had been buried in the underground vault, and had visited the island to recover it. They may have known about the flood tunnel because they were the descendants of the people who had constructed it. In which case, when the present team of explorers finally locate and gain access to the buried vault – which they have the technological ability to do, without question – they might find that the cupboard is bare. Which would be unfortunate on several levels.

The one conclusion that can be drawn about the Money Pit is that it is certainly well named. Ever since Daniel McGinnis stuck his spade in the ground in the last decade of the eighteenth century, it has not only consumed enormous amounts of money spent by explorers trying to reach the hidden vault, but has also taken the lives of at least six men, or eight if you include the two bodies that probably lie deep below the surface.

And to date, as far as is known, none of them has managed to recover anything of any value from their labours. A money pit indeed.

Although there is no completely unambiguous proof to confirm that Prince Henry Sinclair visited this part of North America with a coterie of Knights Templar at the end of the fourteenth century, the circumstantial evidence is nevertheless compelling. The anomalous relics mentioned in this novel – the inscribed stone on the beach, the coins from Genoa found at Chester in Nova Scotia, the Westford Knight memorial, the Boat Stone and the Newport Tower – are all real and are exactly as described.

They are dismissed by mainstream American archaeologists because they refute the accepted timeline and history of the North American continent, and are regarded as coincidences, misidentifications or straight fakes. These statements – and I use that word advisedly, because they are only statements, not arguments backed up by anything bearing even the most distant relationship to a fact – are difficult to sustain if the relics are given even the most cursory possible examination.

The Boat Stone, for example, displays a clear and unambiguous drawing of a medieval ship, and geological weathering analysis – a proper scientific technique – gives an approximate age of the carving on the rock of six hundred years. It can't be a misidentification because the carving is too clear and precise for that. So if the Boat Stone is a fake, detractors have to explain why the fake was prepared in the fourteenth or fifteenth century. Instead they just ignore it, and pretend it doesn't exist. That's so much easier.

The reality is that some six hundred years ago, somebody spent some considerable time preparing that carving for a reason that today we can only guess at, and the simplest possible and most obvious explanation is that that individual knew exactly what a medieval ship looked like because he had arrived on the American eastern seaboard in one as either a passenger or a member of the crew. Nothing else makes sense.

The Hebrew title of the Mossad is המוסד למודיעין ולתפקידים מיוחדים, or *Mossad Merkazi le-Modin ule-Tafkidim Meyuḥadim*, meaning 'the Central Institute for Intelligence and Special Operations'. It's the principal Israeli intelligence agency, responsible for collecting intelligence, and for counter-terrorism and covert operations of all types. It answers directly to the prime minister of Israel and to nobody else, and is not bound by the laws of the country. Or by the laws of any other country, come to that. In terms of personnel, it's the largest intelligence organisation in the West apart from the American Central Intelligence Agency, and, uniquely among the Western agencies, it has an undeclared but clear policy of assassination of people perceived to be enemies of the Israeli state, employing a unit known as the Kidon. This is a part of the Caesarea department, and since the end of the Second World War it has been reliably estimated to have carried out at least 2,700 assassinations.

The agency's headquarters are in Tel Aviv, but like everything else the Mossad does, the location is not advertised or widely known. In fact, the Mossad works from a group of nondescript buildings that look as if they might belong to an insurance company, located between a shopping centre and a cinema complex near the Glilot highway intersection.

The attitude of Israel in general and the Mossad in particular to what might be loosely termed 'foreign relations' is essentially biblical. Basically, it's 'an eye for an eye and a tooth for a tooth', and terrorists and other undesirables know perfectly well that if they kill an Israeli or do anything to harm or threaten the country, the Israelis will kill them. It's a very simple and probably quite effective policy, which is one reason why Israel and its assets have always been seen as hard targets, unlike much softer nations like Britain, where the worst that can happen to most terrorists, assuming they don't get killed in the act, is a fairly comfortable life in prison, paid for by the very people they tried to attack and kill. Unless, of course, they can prove in court that they had a deprived childhood or some other extenuating circumstance and manage to walk free with just a slap on the wrist to have another go.

Zerubbabel and Zeru

Zerubbabel, as is stated in this novel, was an Old Testament figure who initiated the building of the Second Temple in Jerusalem. The Zeru organisation is a product of my imagination, but the idea of a Third Temple being constructed on the Temple Mount in this troubled city is an ever-present shadow over the future of Jerusalem. As the entire purpose of such a temple would be to house the Ark of the Covenant, the implications for Jerusalem would be extremely serious if the relic were ever to be discovered.

It would probably be better for the future of humanity if the lost Ark – assuming it still exists – remained lost for all time.